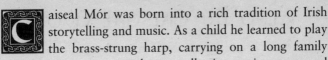 aiseal Mór was born into a rich tradition of Irish storytelling and music. As a child he learned to play the brass-strung harp, carrying on a long family tradition. He spent several years collecting stories, songs and music of the Celtic lands during many visits to Ireland, Scotland and Brittany. He has a degree in performing arts from the University of Western Sydney and has worked as an actor, a teacher and a musician.

Also By Caiseal Mór

The Watchers series:
The Meeting of the Waters
The King of Sleep

The Wanderers series:
The Circle and the Cross
The Song of the Earth
The Water of Life

The Tilecutter's Penny
Scratches in the Margin
The Moon on the Lake
Carolan's Concerto

For children:
The Harp at Midnight

THE
RAVEN
GAME

BOOK THREE OF THE WATCHERS TRILOGY

CAISEAL MÓR

POCKET
BOOKS

LONDON • SYDNEY • NEW YORK • TORONTO

If you would like to write to Caiseal Mór, he can be contacted at the following e-mail address: harp@caiseal.net

More information about Caiseal and his work can be found on his website: www.caiseal.net

... by Earthlight, an imprint of
... Limited, 2002
... Pocket Books, 2004
... uster UK Ltd
... my

... Mór, 2002
... al Mór

The right of Caiseal Mór to be identified as author of this work has been asserted by him in accordance with sections 77 and 78 of the Copyright, Designs and Patents Act, 1988.

1 3 5 7 9 10 8 6 4 2

Simon & Schuster UK Ltd
Africa House
64–78 Kingsway
London WC2B 6AH

www.simonsays.co.uk

Simon & Schuster Australia
Sydney

A CIP catalogue record for this book is available from the British Library

ISBN 0 7434 6855 4

This book is a work of fiction. Names, characters, places and incidents are either a product of the author's imagination or are used fictitiously. Any resemblance to actual people living or dead, events or locales is entirely coincidental.

Printed and bound in Great Britain by
Bookmarque Ltd, Croydon, Surrey

Acknowledgements

There are many people involved in the production
of a novel besides the author. I am very grateful
to all those folk who contributed their expertise,
time, advice and wisdom to this project.

For the past eight years I have been fortunate
enough to be under the wing of Selwa Anthony, my
literary agent. Selwa is one of those remarkable
people who is gifted with patience, wisdom and a
healthy dose of good karma all rolled into one.
My thanks, as always, go to her first and foremost.

Another companion on this journey is my editor,
Julia Stiles, who has worked on every manuscript since
'The Circle and The Cross'. Thanks again Julia.

Thanks also to Jodi Lee whose support at Simon and
Schuster Australia I will sorely miss.

Finally thanks to all the readers who share this
journey with me and to those who visit my website or
write to me wiith their kind comments.
At your suggestion I have placed a pronounciation guide
on my website. The URL is; www.caiseal.net.

Enjoy.

Sydney, July 2002

PROLOGUE

ou must hold a very high opinion of yourself. I suppose you think you're the pig's whisker. There you sit, all smug and conceited, while you listen to me pour my heart out. I'll wager I remind you of some quaint romantic hero from one of those ridiculous fables the troubadours tell.

Well I'm not some silly songbird sporting a bunch of dainty feathers round my pretty little arse. I'm a Raven. A bird of death. A creature of the carrion kind. So I'll thank you to have some bloody respect and keep your mouth shut while I'm sharing my recollections.

Though I must admit it's beyond me why I bother with your lot. You're all tree-killers and bough-splitters. Ever since your people came to this country you've done nothing but fritter away the forests in your breathtaking rush to build ships, houses and boxes to be buried in.

And where will it finish up? I'll bloody tell you. One day there won't be a stick of timber left standing in this land. And then you'll have to answer to my folk. Where are we going to settle our nests when the oak is no more? Have you ever thought of that? Where are we going to perch to preen our feathers if there isn't a rowan, an elm or a yew to be found?

You're a blight on this Earth, you Gaedhals. I don't know

1

why we suffer to let you live. And don't give me any of your empty-headed prattle about the unavoidable consequences of civilisation encroaching upon the last few vestiges of unspoilt woodland.

That's all just a bloody excuse to cut down more trees.

I'll let you in on a little secret, shall I? I've been watching you folk for a long while. I warn you, you're sowing the seeds of your own downfall. May I live to see it. As sure as I'm sitting here spinning you this yarn, the day of reckoning will arrive.

Now put another log on the fire while I get on with my tale.

I've heard others repeat different parts of this legend but I certainly didn't pick it up from some wandering halfwit who claimed to be a storyteller. I knew all these folk. I lived during these times. I know what I'm talking about. So take heed. You might learn something about where and when the fate of your people was sealed.

The intriguing thing about fate is that we all have the power to steer it for ourselves. So why do so many of your folk make such a mess of it? I'll tell you. You're all self-centred for a start. None of you know how to listen. You're all too busy pressing your opinions on others.

Talk, talk, talk, that's all I ever hear from you people. Gossipy talk. Insulting talk. Drunken talk. Conniving talk. Cheating talk. Persuasive talk. Treacherous talk. Covetous talk. Tree-cutting talk. What a boatload of bastards you all are!

Whatever happened to honour and compassion? Are the ideals of integrity and purity no longer worthy of veneration? Have you all forgotten there are higher rewards to be had from life than fine bed linen, fashionable boots and a belly full of beer?

I don't really expect any of your lot to understand what I'm talking about. I'm a Raven. My folk approach life from an entirely different standpoint. We consider our fate to be bound up with our destiny. Sometimes fate can help us reach for destiny. But fate may be our downfall too. It all depends on how we live our lives. In the end our destiny is to return, life after life, until we learn to be better Ravens.

Of course I am an exceptional case. It's a long while since death pulled up a chair at my hearth to chat about the weather. I'm under a geis. That is to say, I've had a ban placed upon me. And a very powerful one too. Some would call it an enchantment, a kind of magical imprisonment.

I'm stuck in this body, all feathers, claws and parasites, until the day I earn my death. I'm paying for a crime I should have known better than to commit. If I'd used my head I'd have never got myself entangled in my brother's fate in the first place. And now you can see for yourself the mess I'm in.

All for a geis.

In the days of my youth, when I still walked in human form, even the Gaedhals trembled at the merest mention of the word. The mystical influence of the geis steered the destiny of many an ambitious king or greedy champion.

Perhaps I'd better keep it simple so you'll understand. I'll explain it this way.

Let's say I place a geis on you. For the sake of an example, from this day on you're forbidden to cross the path of an angry badger. It's now more or less a certainty that eventually one of two situations will arise.

Either you'll flout the prohibition because you're a big-headed buffoon who has no respect whatsoever for a geis. And we all know what happens to flouters.

Or quite by accident you'll trip over an otherwise agreeable badger who'll bite you on the back of the leg because he's been having a bad day. Before he scuttles off into the woods, or what's left of them, you'll notice him frothing at the mouth.

In either case the magical force of the geis will lead ultimately and inevitably to your sad and probably agonising demise. There's no question of it. In truth a geis is part prophecy and part prohibition, though the distinction between the two is blurred at the best of times.

And for obvious reasons a geis is a very personal matter. You don't want to go round the village letting everybody know what your private prohibitions might entail. The next thing you'd know, your former lover, the wild-eyed one with the wounded pride, would be spotted wandering off into the night with a small cage and a bag full of badger bait.

So don't expect me to reveal the secret of my geis to you. Because I won't let you in on it. I'm content to let everything sort itself out in its own sweet time. I don't want to hurry fate along. And I'm not all that eager to face my destiny.

I've spoken before to you of destiny. What more can I tell you?

The Queen of the Ravens, the Morrigán, explains destiny this way. She considers, and I hardly dare dispute her, that this world and everything in it is simply a vast game. By her reckoning it is so immense that few are able to grasp the reality of it.

Each one of us is but a small piece in that game. And most of us are too busy playing out our parts to sit back and recognise it for what it really is.

The Dark One, the Morrigán, sovereign of our folk, points to the Brandubh to illustrate her point. Are you keeping up with me? I'm doing my best to make this easy for you to grasp. Try to keep your mind off daydreaming about axe-blades and splinters or I'll jump on your back and tear away some tasty flesh and save my breath for breathing.

The Brandubh is an ancient game played upon a board seven squares by seven. And within the confines of its simple design the whole of creation is represented. Five white pieces; they're the Gaedhals, or Fir-Bolg, or whatever you will. Twelve dark pieces; they're the Ravens.

The high-king of the white spends all his time trying to reach the sanctuaries at the corners. The Ravens harass his pieces and try to block him in. And when they've caught him on all four sides he is their prisoner and must surrender the board.

Are you listening? It's hard to tell. You all wear such daft expressions on your faces.

There are many more subtle motifs woven into the fabric of the game which I won't attempt to explain to you now. I'm sure you're struggling with what little I've told you.

The Druids used the game in divining the future, for they understood that all which seems real is but illusion. And some of them learned the patterns of play so well they found they could manipulate the world to their will.

The origins of the Brandubh are hotly disputed. Some say the Fir-Bolg had it first; others claim the Danaans contrived it. But the name means 'the Raven Game'. And it is just as likely it was the Raven kind who first devised it.

I've lapsed into the esoteric with all my prattling about geis and Brandubh. You may heed my foolish talk or not. It won't make the story any shorter. In truth I barely understand all the concepts myself. If you don't follow me now, perhaps my tale will help you see my meaning.

'Twas the Raven Game that snatched me away from my kin and set me on the path of my geis. And I'll tell you how I came to be this way if you'll listen.

At least if you're sat here with me for a few hours, you can't be out cutting a swathe through the forests in your never-ending pursuit of neatly split timber.

Chapter One

Two dozen pairs of feet flew silently over the dry packed earth near the open gate to the outpost. These warriors were well versed in the ways of clandestine warfare. Blades drawn, points held high, they took up their positions and waited for a word from their leader.

But Goll Mac Morna was in no hurry to begin the fight. He leaned against the unguarded gatepost and smiled a secret smile, savouring the scent of victory on the breeze.

Within the enemy's wooden enclosure no one stirred. All were sleeping soundly, even the sentries whose honour would surely be questioned if they managed to live through this night. In the distance a dog barked but the howling was far away. Too far away to wake anyone or betray the presence of the raiders.

As they waited, each of the intruders inwardly prepared for the conflict. Sweaty hands fumbled sword hilts. Nervous bowmen whispered love poems to their bows. One or two shared a private joke, laughing under their breath to relieve the nervous tension.

Suddenly clouds above the little outpost parted and the scene was drenched in the gorgeous silver glow of the full moon. The war-leader sighed, watching the changing hues of the night.

Deep blue-black turned to shining grey as the bright orb of evening cast her eye upon the scene. Goll glanced across at one woman who waited with the other warriors.

She was neither tall nor particularly striking. Her dark hair was matted and filthy from months living rough in the open. But she never failed to rouse intense emotions in him. And that was a miracle considering what a cold-hearted, ruthless, uncompromising blackguard he was generally considered to be.

While the war-leader indulged his lustful thoughts there was a sound from one of the timber houses. A figure emerged into the night, stumbling as she sang a bawdy verse under her breath.

The old woman was withered by the seasons. She was no longer capable of bearing a blade in anger, but Goll decided this old hag should be the first to fall. He cupped his hands to his mouth and produced a call that perfectly mimicked the cry of an owl.

His warriors gripped their blades a little tighter or kissed an arrow as they made ready to leap out into the attack. But a strange thing happened just at that instant. The old woman was no more than halfway across the broad courtyard when she stopped abruptly and sniffed at the wind.

The effects of whatever she'd been drinking suddenly lifted from her head and she stood up straight. She scanned the shadows carefully with squinted eyes that widened with each intake of breath as she tried to steady herself.

Again Goll smiled. He could almost hear her heart racing. So he made the owl call again, withdrawing the order to strike. He'd always reckoned there was a certain enjoyment to be had in observing fear take hold of an enemy.

Instances like these were pure gold to him. They had become the most satisfying moments in his life. And he was the sort of man who never let an opportunity for satisfaction slip by.

The female warrior stared across at Goll. She silently begged him with her eyes to give the command, but the war-leader held up his hand, signalling he preferred to tarry a little longer. He took careful note of her eagerness. And he reminded himself that Mughain was sometimes a little too keen for blood. She would have to be taught patience.

When Goll did not give assent to her plea, the warrior woman drew her bow anyway, the arrow point aimed at her target's heart. In a flash she was ready to loose the deadly missile. The war-leader noticed her readiness but he still held back.

Then the old stranger sniffed the breeze again, perhaps sensing Goll's malice in the air. The hag faltered for a second. Her chilled feet tripped on the uneven ground. Then her eyes rolled wildly.

She was in the grip of panic. So Goll chose that moment to step out of the shadows. The old woman saw him immediately and drew in a deep breath to cry out.

But whether it was shock or the effects of all the mead she'd consumed, the call never passed her lips. With both hands clasped tightly to her chest she wheezed loudly and turned pale grey. And then, exhaling a muffled groan, the hag fell forward on her face, as cold as death and just as still.

Mac Morna could hardly restrain himself from laughing. The first of his enemies to fall in this fight had died of fear. He thought to himself that if only he could harness the power of fright he could conquer the kingdom of the north with no more than the twenty or so warriors he had along with him now.

With that thought still sitting sweetly in his mind he spoke the first words he'd uttered since they'd left their encampment at dusk.

'Show no mercy.'

He didn't need to raise his voice in the confined courtyard.

He spoke with no more force than if he were having a casual conversation, but his words cut through the band of warriors like an icy wind. Immediately the raiders were skirting around the inner walls of the fort to take up new positions at the door to each house.

Goll yawned as he strode openly across the courtyard, daring the defenders to come out and strike him down. But no one stirred. All was silent. The brisk autumn air was chill but not unpleasant. All seemed at peace in the tranquil moonlit night.

No more than ten paces from the door of the main building an instinct struck the war-leader. Whatever it was that came to his mind it made him spin around on his heel to face the seemingly lifeless body of the old woman.

The hag was gone. Before he knew what was happening a cry rose up and a ghostly shadow flitted across his vision to the left.

'Arise!' the old woman screamed. 'The enemy is upon us!'

Goll pointed his sword in the direction of the voice but the woman had melted into the shadows again. As he grunted in frustration the moon was being swallowed up behind a cloud. The war-leader glanced up at the sky just long enough to be momentarily blinded as the whole scene plunged into impenetrable darkness.

He heard a shuffle nearby then the answered calls of the old woman's comrades. Goll swung his blade wildly at the sound of rushing footsteps, but the sword found no mark. In the next instant a torch was thrust out through the door of the main building and three men emerged.

Goll sensed danger behind him and stabbed his sword out with a low growled challenge. A brief orange flash of steel reflected brightly in the torchlight was all the answer he received. But he'd chanced his arm and the old woman had slipped under his guard.

Sharp stinging pain stabbed at his forearm and his blade dropped with a dull thud to the ground. Just for an instant Goll thought all his ambitions would surely end here in this little outpost at the hands of a goat-keeper's grandmother.

In determination he focused his eyesight as he spun round once more on his heel. Then a familiar sound met his ears. It was the whispered hush of an arrow shaft cutting through the air. The war-leader drew a sharp breath, waiting for the painful point to bury itself deep in his chest.

But it never came.

Beside him a body slumped down with a groan and a knife fell to the earth. Goll shuddered as he always did when he witnessed a death. It was not a shudder of fright. It was an expression of exhilaration. In the next breath the warrior-woman called Mughain was at her war-leader's side.

'Are you hurt?'

'No,' Goll grunted indignantly, gingerly touching his arm where he'd been cut.

'Didn't you see her?'

'No!' he bellowed. Then the war-leader softened a little, realising he owed this woman a debt of gratitude. 'Thank you, Mughain,' he stated coldly as he put a firm hand on her shoulder.

She smiled with admiration and touched his fingers lightly. Then she drew another arrow from her quiver, put it to the bowstring and went to help her comrades.

Goll Mac Morna retrieved his sword and held it for a few moments before his face. To his surprise he noticed his hand was shaking. So he quickly passed the blade into his left. But the shivering was just as noticeable.

'Fool!' he berated himself under his breath. 'You're becoming too arrogant. You very nearly lost your life to an old woman.'

The courtyard echoed now with the exultant shouts of

warriors going about their bloody work. A few of the enemy emerged from their houses but were quickly cut down before they had a chance to offer any resistance. By the time Goll recovered his breath, the first of the buildings was already ablaze. He turned to the body of the old woman lying on the cobbles nearby and gave the lifeless form a heavy, well-aimed kick.

He knew the gesture was futile but it was also very satisfying and strangely seemed to ease the pain in his arm a little. That done the war-leader raised his voice above the din.

'Death to the Gaedhals of the North!' he bellowed. 'Death to the followers of Éremon!'

Dark shapes flitted between the burning houses, echoing his call. The nightmare scene was lit brightly now by orange flames and glowing red smoke. Black forms sprawled all about where they had fallen in defence of their homes. The fight was already finished, with only a few drops of southern blood spilled in the struggle.

Goll's blood.

Though victory had been swift, the war-leader curled his lip in contempt. This was not warfare. This was raiding. It was a cowardly and dishonourable way to face the enemy. And he'd had enough of it.

'I am Goll, Champion of King Eber Finn of the South!' he shrieked, as if this simple declaration might somehow restore his honour.

Then he swore to himself. 'A curse on my king for sending me off to do this dirty work. Eber is not fit to rule. But bide your time, war-leader. The day will dawn when you will rule this land both north and south.'

The words had no sooner left his mouth when Mughain dragged a captive before him. She threw the boy on the ground and he lay there grovelling at the champion's feet.

'Will this one suit your purpose?' she asked.

Goll nodded. 'He seems harmless enough.'

'My lord,' the lad begged, 'have mercy. I'm not a warrior. I'm a farmer's son. I was sent here by my family to help tend the livestock for this outpost. I'm not a fighter.'

'Have no fear,' the war-leader replied in an uncharacteristically soothing tone. 'You'll not be harmed. I have other plans for you.'

'You don't really mean to let him go, do you?' Mughain gasped in disbelief. 'He'll run straight to Éremon with the news of this raid. Then we'll have all the Fian of the North on our backs.'

'And about time we brought this war out into the open,' Goll answered sharply. 'I'm tired of sneaking around in the shadows, striking here and there like a ghostly visitor. I'm a warrior. I seek a fair fight.'

'But can we hope to defeat all the assembled warriors of the north alone?'

'We can.'

Goll turned to the boy. 'Remember all you see here tonight. I want you to report every detail to your king. Do you know my name?'

'Goll Mac Morna,' the lad stuttered.

'That's right,' the war-leader smiled. 'In days to come you'll look back and recall how I spared your life so that you could bear news of my deeds to every settlement in the north. I'll be High-King of the Gaedhals one day. Do you understand?'

The boy nodded, frightened now by the determined light in the warrior's eyes.

'We'll be outnumbered,' Mughain pressed. 'Éremon will hunt us down and slay us one by one.'

'We'll not be beaten,' Goll assured her without taking his eyes from the boy.

The war-leader sheathed his sword and faced the woman. 'Are we finished here?'

Mughain nodded.

Goll turned back to the boy. 'Do you know the woods at the far end of this valley? Where the stream is broached by a roughly built ford?'

'There is a round hill there that was once a Danaan fort,' the frightened youth replied meekly.

'Tell King Éremon I'll wait for him there. I wish to speak with the King of the North. Make sure he understands that he is to bring only two dozen warriors. We'll meet on the top of that hill above the ford in three days time.'

The lad gave a hesitant nod and the war-leader put a hand on his head. 'May the gods who bless you bless your task and guide you safely to King Éremon.'

Goll lifted his head, dropped his hand to his side and spoke one last command to his warriors. 'Take him to the river and see that he is safely on his way.'

Chapter Two

alan the Brehon judge sat cross-legged in the stone hut. He stared across the low fire in front of him. There was no other light within the tiny building and for all he knew it could have been day or night in the world outside.

His fingers gently stroked the bloody cowhide that had been draped over his naked form. His legs were beginning to feel weak. His shoulders ached. And his eyes were stinging from the smoke which hung in the air.

Opposite him sat the wise-woman known as Sorcha. Her eyes were still bright and calm. Her clothes were clean, her tunic neatly brushed as always. But her hair was a filthy tangled mess of matted strands framing her soft features. Across her forehead from ear to ear the hair had been shaved in the Druid fashion. The resulting dark stubble marked her as belonging to the holy orders.

In the firelight Dalan occasionally thought he glimpsed a golden glow around the crown of her head. This, he told himself, was the onset of the Frith. It was an experience he'd never known before, but under the expert guidance of this woman he had set out on the path of the disciplined seer.

Since the passing of King Brocan of the Fir-Bolg and Fineen the Healer, Sorcha had become his closest companion and confidante. He was glad of her presence here in the stone house. With her here to guide him he knew all would be well.

The Druid woman stared directly at him, observing every gesture with a vigilance that was almost threatening. He met her eyes and frowned at what seemed to be her uncharacteristic lack of tenderness. A sudden desire came over the Brehon to speak a few words to her, to tell her how much he appreciated her honesty and her dedication to their quest. But he managed to control the urge. He knew his own thoughts were meaningless and trivial now he had embarked upon this ritual journey of the Frith, the art of seeing beyond time and place into the future or the past.

The air was not stale within the little hut but it was still. Dalan swallowed hard as Sorcha squinted. She wanted to be sure he was comfortable. The Brehon smiled but the woman allowed no emotion whatsoever to show on her face. Indeed, he felt as if she were silently rebuking him for this familiarity.

Dalan closed his eyes, striving to concentrate on the task at hand. His responsibility was a great one. King Brocan of the Fir-Bolg had disappeared within the depths of the Aillwee caves and had named his son Lom as successor to the kingship. But the chieftains of the Fir-Bolg were not happy with this choice. Lom; his twin brother, Sárán; and their sister, Aoife, each had a well-earned reputation for rash, ill-considered actions. Brocan's grant of sovereignty to his son had proved unpopular even though tradition sanctioned the handover of kingship to the firstborn as a temporary measure.

Since the chieftains had disputed the appointment and there was no other suitable candidate for kingship, Dalan the Brehon had been called on to act. It was his duty as a judge to arrange the ritual of the Tarbh-Feis, the Bull Feast. This act of seership was practised only by a Druid who could be trusted to tell the truth. The seer had to be someone who had nothing to gain by promoting one candidate over another.

Dalan had offered himself for this duty and the chieftains had accepted him gladly. They all knew he had no special love for Lom. And no other Fir-Bolg Druid could have been so acutely aware of the consequences of this ritual.

This is how the Tarbh-Feis was carried out.

A white bull without any mark or blemish was slaughtered then roasted over a huge fire pit while Dalan sat silently watching. He'd already ceased to speak and would not utter another sound until his vision was declared.

As the flesh seared over the flames, the juices of the roasting were gathered and mixed with a quantity of the bull's blood to make a broth. When the carcass was well cooked, Dalan drank the broth and devoured the flesh until he could not eat another morsel. Then he was bathed in the remaining blood of the bull and wrapped in its hide. In the stone hut he and his guardian, Sorcha, were shut off from all light for three days and nights.

It was the Druid woman's duty to ensure he didn't drop off to sleep during the time of confinement. As Dalan rarely ate meat, the effect of the feast had been almost immediate. His head swam with a giddy nausea. His guts grumbled full of gas and he sweated foul odours.

And outside, all the chieftains, elders and many lesser folk of the Fir-Bolg waited for the news of his vision. By the second night a dozen fires dotted the field and the faces gathered around were anxious. Such an act of augury had not been needed in four generations. Everyone was apprehensive for the outcome.

To Dalan the feast now seemed as if it had been a lifetime ago. He had no way of knowing how much time had passed but he was beginning to despair that the visions would not come to him at all. The Brehon lowered his chin onto his chest and sighed.

In the next instant his head turned sharply under the blow

of an open hand slapped hard against his face. The Brehon opened his eyes wide and saw Sorcha staring sternly down at him. She didn't say a word, only raised a warning finger to him and frowned.

Dalan shook himself and sat up straight again as the Druid woman resumed her seat at the opposite side of the little fire. Sleep was beginning to taunt him. He tried to reckon time and decided two days must nearly have passed. The visions would come soon enough, he told himself.

With determination he began a steady rhythmic breathing. He had learned this technique when he was a lad as a method of keeping his mind alert but his body relaxed. The Brehon put all his concentration into this simple act, focusing his attention on the little flickering flames of the fire.

A long while passed like that as the Druid's vision began to blur and his head spiralled with a thousand thoughts that threatened to intrude on his sacred duty. Time and again he frowned in frustration at his ill-disciplined mind. But still his rational self wandered down a hundred paths without finding the one he was searching for.

Then at last he realised he was struggling against himself, wasting his energy and serving no good purpose by fighting with his conscious thoughts. As Sorcha placed a small slab of turf on the fire he let the breath come to him naturally again and abandoned the strict regime of steady breathing.

The Druid woman still stared at him with no emotion on her face. And Dalan found something else to admire about her. The discipline and focus she exhibited were beyond his understanding. Then he recalled that she had dwelled alone in the forest among the Raven kind for most of her life. She was accustomed to long periods of silence. She had come to know herself. This made her a stronger, more resilient person, or so her old teacher would have told her. She was not concerned with what others thought of her. As a result the weight of her responsibilities was not so great and she was better able to perform the duties of her calling.

And Sorcha had been trained as a Fritheoir, a seer who could wilfully induce the trance state in order to visit the world between the worlds. Dalan had no experience at this craft. He was gifted with the Faidh, the spontaneous revelation of visions over which he had no control.

He was glad this Druid woman was watching over him now. Her experienced eye would surely know if he lapsed into a dangerous state of exhaustion. For even though he'd taken the Quicken Brew, no one among the wise knew whether its effects carried over to the dream world.

Dalan felt a dryness in his throat and glanced down beside him for his wooden water cup. Slowly he moved his hand to pick the vessel up and found to his astonishment that he had no feeling at all in his fingers. In the next breath he abandoned the idea of drinking. He was deeply dismayed at the lack of sensation in his hands. He looked up to meet Sorcha's eyes, hoping somehow to silently convey his concern.

But what he saw made him forget his fingers immediately. It was not Sorcha who sat opposite him in this little darkened stone room. It was another woman. A shining woman. And Dalan's thoughts were full of awe for the beautiful creature who smiled back at him.

Her hair was fiery red like hearth embers and her eyes were deep pools of green that contrasted sharply with the deathly pallor of her complexion. The Brehon frowned, certain he recognised her from somewhere. But it wasn't until the scent of lavender caught in his nostrils that he knew for certain who she was.

'My name is Isleen,' he heard her whisper. 'I'm Isleen the Watcher. Lochie would have come to visit you also but he's busy observing the trouble in the north.'

18

Dalan tried to speak but his jaw was slack and wouldn't move.

'I'll wager you didn't expect me to turn up just as you were slipping into your trance,' the Watcher went on. 'I prefer this world between the worlds. Here beliefs drop away into the void of possibilities. There's no code to slavishly enforce. I get so bored with rules. I don't know how you do it without losing your mind. Then again, you've not been around as long as Lochie and I. We're old hands at immortality.'

She laughed sweetly and Dalan thought the sound of her voice was like the tinkling of tiny golden bells. Then a thick sweat broke out upon his brow as his instincts screamed to him of danger.

'Don't fret, my darling,' she cooed. 'I'm not going to hurt you. And I won't lie to you. I'm going to show you exactly what the future holds. Believe me, it's far more frightening than anything I could conjure from the depths of my evil imagination.'

She winked at him in such a familiar manner that he trembled to his toes with discomfort. Then abruptly the room filled with a blinding light. The Brehon had to squint and turn his head away from the bright source.

'I'm sorry about that,' Isleen told him with a hint of mockery in her voice. 'I just wanted to make sure I had your full attention. When you've done this as many times as I have, you realise some folk can be so frightened they lose consciousness. A few searing sparks of light works wonders at waking the terrified mind.'

Then the light faded and Dalan was alone in the room. The Watcher was nowhere to be seen. The fire had flared up and was burning with a deep blue flame such as the Brehon had never encountered before. The blue was flecked with bright orange dots of light that constantly shimmered and died.

These colours were so beautiful that Dalan found himself desiring to possess the secret of the making of this fire. Something in the hue of it was soothing. It was familiar and reassuring. As each orange speck was being born, another was burning out, seeming thus to pass the same spark down the generations.

It was then the Brehon realised he was looking on the sacred soul-fire. His teacher had often spoken about this marvel, but until this moment Dalan had never understood what was meant by the term. His heart and spirit bathed in the wonder.

'It's astounding, isn't it?' Isleen agreed and Dalan knew she was still nearby and could hear his every thought.

Then he felt a gentle hand on his shoulder. Dreamily he turned his head to see the Watcher standing close behind him. She leaned closer and he could feel the warmth of her belly through her cloak. It made his skin tingle with delight and sensual desire.

'Careful, Brehon,' Isleen warned him, understanding the effect her proximity was having on him. 'You're no match for me. I'd eat you up without a second thought. Leave such fantasies for the warrior kind. They at least have passions enough to quench. You Druids can't compete with them for that.'

She sat down beside him and waved her hand before his eyes. A Brandubh board miraculously appeared between them.

'Shall we play?' she offered.

Silently the Brehon agreed. Without a thought he moved the first white piece to begin the game. Isleen smiled to acknowledge the wisdom of his opening gambit. She moved her piece. Then Dalan made another hasty move which Isleen matched as quickly.

In moments he was so engrossed in the match he lost all sense of his surroundings. But he was no equal to the Watcher at this pastime. In a space of twenty turns her Raven-black pieces had surrounded his high-king. The Brehon looked up and shrugged to concede defeat.

What he saw took him by surprise. They were seated now in a large well-lit cavern. Nearby, on beds draped with white shimmering silks and fine honey-golden furs, lay Brocan, Fineen and King Cecht of the Tuatha-De-Danaan. On other beds placed deeper into the cave he recognised many of the Danaan folk who had retreated into the Otherworld when the Gaedhals had first come to Innisfail.

None so much as stirred from slumber. All was tranquil in this cavern of a hundred torches burning with unquenchable light.

'They are at peace,' Isleen assured him. 'They have chosen the long sleep over a life which would surely have become monotonous and mundane. Sleep is best for them. They may awake one day to find a hundred generations have passed in the world outside. I can't say what their fate may be. Perhaps you will join them soon enough?'

Dalan turned away from the scene sharply. The horror on his face showed just how much he was repulsed by the idea.

'As you wish,' the Watcher sang mockingly. 'One day you may think differently. I offer this to you as a little mercy in exchange for helping my companion and myself. Take the sleep.'

'No.' The Brehon frowned and glanced back towards the Brandubh board.

'You're black this time, I think,' the Watcher told him.

The pieces had changed remarkably while he'd been observing the cavern of sleep. The roughly carved wooden figures had been transformed into intricately worked sculptures of fine bone. The dark pieces known as the Ravens were now beautifully formed caricatures of the black birds of death. All were individuals, each with a smirk or scowl that

21

defined its personality. But the Druid was drawn to the white pieces and didn't pay the Ravens too much heed.

The white high-king was seated on an ornate throne. He wore a circlet on his head and his face was Eber Finn's. At his right hand was a figure that closely resembled Lom dressed in his war-gear. To his left sat a character with the same face but dressed in Druid robes. This was obviously meant to represent Sárán.

But it was the piece placed directly behind the high-king that disturbed Dalan most. This figure was clad in a cloak of feathers. There was a harp at his feet and he had features which made the Brehon shudder.

Dalan picked the piece up with trembling fingers and examined it more closely. It was his own face that stared blankly back at him from the carved whalebone. He immediately handed the figure to Isleen and she placed it down on the board in a new position to open play.

'See if you can notice the pattern in this game,' she suggested.

They played through and the match was over quickly, much to the Brehon's frustration. It was rare for him to be so easily defeated. He looked up from the board to express his congratulations to Isleen and the surroundings had changed once more.

They were back within the stone hut. Dalan's gaze was dragged down into the blue flames. And flitting between the orange flecks he clearly saw the forms of many birds. Black birds with long beaks and powerful wings.

Ravens.

The birds circled the sky as if waiting for the opportunity to land. Suddenly Dalan understood what they were waiting for. Below the birds was a green hilltop surmounted by a ruined fort.

The wide rampart in front of the hill was strewn with the

22

mangled aftermath of a bloody battle. Corpses cut with hideous wounds were spread out all around and laid one upon the other in great heaps. A heavy fall of snow was dusting them in frosty powder.

Warriors wandered between the carnage, picking out spoils or turning over the dead in search of missing comrades. A wailing went up from many women and smoke pervaded the scene. A tattered blood-red standard fluttered in the breeze. It was embroidered with a design the Brehon did not recognise.

Among the piles of the slain strode a young man issuing commands in a severe but respectful tone. Dalan smiled. The youth reminded him of old King Brocan, though this young man had long black hair and a wiry body.

'Lom,' the Brehon whispered.

'Indeed it is,' Isleen agreed. 'Lom, King of the Fir-Bolg of the Burren. A proven warrior and a just ruler. Though his reign may well be ruinous and he is fated to suffer punishment, he'll be well remembered.'

Just then another figure, adorned in the blue robes of a Druid, stepped up from behind. There was no mistaking Lom's twin, Sárán.

'Will he be Lom's adviser?' the Brehon asked in dismay.

'They'll work well together while the last kingship of the Fir-Bolg endures.'

'The last?'

'There will be no more kings among the folk of the Burren after Lom,' she confirmed. 'The Fir-Bolg will retain their chieftains who will be absorbed into the Council of the Gaedhals.'

The fire flickered as a breeze tickled the fingers of flame. And as Dalan watched intently the two young men began to change form before his eyes. Both began to sprout black feathers from every part of their bodies. In a few short breaths they were clothed in wings and beaks exactly like those of the Raven kind. Their clothes and armour dropped away and the two brothers called out in one mournful caw that turned the Brehon's blood to ice.

As they spread their wings to join their new kindred in the skies the snow fell heavier. The warriors on the battlefield pulled their cloaks around their shoulders and retreated to their firesides. Then they all simply melted away as the snow blanketed the scene in white.

The corpses rotted before Dalan's eyes as if the days were strung together and each lasted no more than a minute. In a breath the snow lay thick, shrouding the dead in a cold communal winding sheet.

And then the frozen whiteness withdrew, melting quickly away. All that was left was a field of bones bleaching in the spring sunshine, picked at by an occasional wolf or crow. Upon this very hilltop where the battle had been fought Eber Finn now stood under another banner. The flowing green flag was unadorned by any device. The Brehon understood in his heart there was some deep symbolism behind this banner, though he knew not what it might be.

Eber Finn knelt down on the grass and a Druid stepped forward bearing a cup and a torc of gold. He placed the torc about the king's neck and handed him the cup. As Eber took a sip from the vessel a great cheer went up. And Dalan knew, without being told, that this was the rite of king-making being enacted according to the custom of the Gaedhals.

Then the king spoke and the Brehon heard every word as clearly as if Eber had been seated right next to him in the stone hut.

'Now and forever our two peoples north and south will be one,' he declared. 'And the Fir-Bolg will be as our brothers. They will sit at the Council of Chieftains and retain the western part of this land forever under the kingship of the

Gaedhals. And I will take another wife of the blood of my own people and she will rule as my queen and equal.'

A warrior-woman with battle scars upon her forearms stepped forward. Her name was raised up on the voices of the assembly. But Dalan didn't recognise her at all.

The fire died down suddenly then flared up once more. Then all Dalan saw was Aoife, daughter of King Brocan, sleeping soundly beside her father, her mother and many of the Danaan kind.

He frowned at this and turned to face Isleen.

'Will everyone sleep?' he asked her.

'Not everyone.'

She pointed back towards the flames. The Brehon followed her gaze. In the midst of the fire he could discern the shape of a man picking his way over the roots of a mighty oak tree growing in a beautiful moss-green forest. There was no mistaking him. By his golden hair and powerful warrior physique it could be no other than Mahon, son of the King of the Danaans of the West. As he wandered he called out in despair over and over again, 'Aoife! Aoife!'

'Perhaps one day he'll find her,' Isleen shrugged. 'Who knows what the future holds for certain. Only those who have the sight can say with surety. Even these visions you see before you are just a glimpse of what might be. It is within the power of even the lowliest of mortals to change their fate.'

'I don't believe you,' the Brehon replied coldly. 'I believe there is no escaping one's fate once it has been revealed.'

The Watcher laughed again. 'I didn't say it was easy. But it is possible. Don't confuse fate with destiny. And never give up hope. Take heed of me. After all, I have a lot more experience of the world than you do. It would be wise of you to concede that you don't know everything. Then you will have a chance to discover the full range of possibilities with which you are being presented.'

Abruptly the fire died away and the Watcher pointed to the Brandubh board once more.

'Let's break with custom,' she hummed mischievously. 'I'll play nine games with you before you go. And you'll play the Ravens each time instead of swapping the white with me. Look for the hidden message in the game. This is a great mystery I'm revealing to you. It will change your life. And one day when you're as old as I am, the knowledge of it may bring some comfort.'

Dalan nodded and they commenced their tournament, though at first he could discern no pattern or hidden message in the progress of their games. But after the eighth round he glimpsed something about the Brandubh he'd never noticed before.

There were times when his instincts told him to follow a certain path yet he often let his mind take precedence. Whenever his thoughts interfered in the process of making a move he left a gap in his defences which Isleen would exploit. Her high-king slipped past him time and again to find sanctuary in the corners of the board.

During the ninth game he decided to play out a pattern he'd chanced upon and he stuck to it unerringly until he began to see some change in his fortunes. To the Brehon's utter amazement he soon had the advantage. Within two dozen moves he had the white high-king surrounded on four sides and Isleen was bowing to him in admiration.

'You've learned much this night,' the Watcher sighed. 'I've never been defeated by one so young. Perhaps we might have made a fine love-match, you and I. What do you think?'

As she spoke he was staring into her fiery green eyes. There was a light about her face that took his breath away. And though his gut cried out for him to be wary, every fibre of his being wanted to taste her lips on his.

'Be careful, Brehon,' she warned. 'I must admit the idea

is enticing even to me, but you have work to do. You must find the song that will free Lochie and myself from our prison.'

'Sorcha believes she has found the Draoi song,' he replied, dreamy-eyed.

And suddenly he regained his senses. Isleen's face had changed from an enticing maiden into that of stern-faced mother.

'Sorcha?' the Watcher snapped. 'Who's she?'

'She is the Druid woman who is helping me. She is a master of the Draoi craft.'

'That young thing? I hope I'm not trusting my liberty to one such as her.'

'She has great knowledge of these matters. She's been trained in the art of the Frith. She uses her skill at the Draoi to summon her visions.'

Isleen narrowed her eyes. 'This young woman has found the song which will free us?'

'She has.'

'Then we shall see.'

'What do you mean?'

'I'll bring her here and appraise her song.'

In an instant Sorcha was seated beside Dalan with her arm linked over his. There was no fear in her expression as she looked into Isleen's eyes but there was concern when she glanced at the Brehon.

'Sing me your song, Druid woman,' the Watcher commanded.

'I can't be sure if it will have any effect,' Sorcha answered nervously. 'I've pieced it together from my own memories and those of some of my colleagues. No one among our folk considered these Draoi songs important.'

'Sing,' Isleen insisted. 'I'll be the judge of whether this Draoi chant is effective or not.'

'And what of Lochie?' Dalan inquired. 'Won't you share this gift with him?'

'When Lochie realises what has happened he'll be nagging at you like a month-old calf crying for the teat. Don't worry about him.'

'Are you ready to face the gates of death?' the Brehon asked. 'Are you prepared to meet your ancestors in the Halls of Waiting?'

'I've been ready for this moment since before your grandmother was a child,' Isleen snapped. 'I want to hear the song. I want to be free of this burden on my spirit.'

'I can't even say if the song is complete,' Sorcha hesitated. 'I can't make any promises.'

'Sing!'

With that the Druid woman moved position so she was sitting cross-legged with her back straight. She placed her hands on her knees, palms uppermost, and took a dozen deep breaths as she conjured the melody to her mind.

Then, when she was ready to commence the Draoi song, she began a low hum. The interior of the stone hut began to vibrate so gently that it was almost indiscernible. Dalan sensed the floor trembling gently in harmony with the low droning note. Then he felt a tingling in his fingers and understood that this would be the most powerful song he'd ever heard.

The Watcher sat forward and closed her eyes to listen. Once in a while she mumbled something under her breath but for the most part she merely rocked back and forth in time with the pulsing drone.

There was no doubt in the Brehon's mind. Sorcha had found the song that could release the Watchers from their long enchantment. The Druid woman began to mouth the words of the song, a slow steady poem in a language Dalan could not understand.

Isleen sat back perfectly still and her eyes rolled to the back of her head. 'You've found it,' the Watcher gasped in delight. 'I'm free.'

Sorcha raised the pitch of her song so that the Brehon had to cover his ears with the palms of his hands. Her voice had reached an unnatural level he'd never heard before from any living creature and his eardrums were aching from the sound.

The stone chamber was beginning to glow with a gentle blue light which seemed to emanate from the mossy rocks of its walls. As Sorcha sang, the glow turned a vibrant purple then red. The Watcher's face reflected the colour of this strange illumination as balls of bright scarlet light formed in a great circle around the room. Isleen's hair was shining as if it were fashioned from fine strands of the purest gold.

Isleen sat up, her arms raised to the ceiling, and began to hum along with the gorgeous melody as if her spirit was being lifted to new heights by this Otherworldly tune. As her fingers stretched towards the roof the colour of the light began to change again. Now Dalan had to cover his eyes at the stark intensity of the yellow brightness which threatened to blind him.

Just then he heard Isleen cry out in the ecstasy of transformation, and though his eyes were stinging from the light he dared to glance towards her. For a brief moment he could hardly believe his eyes. The Watcher had begun to split into two distinct entities. Above her, floating like seaweed on the tide, there was a semitransparent double of herself glowing with a deep viridian brightness. The fingers of this ghostly apparition were still touching the form which sat below, as if they could not quite let go of it yet.

Then the balls of bright light started a slow steady journey towards the centre of the room, gradually closing in about the Watcher. As they travelled, the lights changed their hue once more to take on a sickening green glow from which Dalan was forced to look away.

His fingers found the edges of the bloody bull hide and he grasped it tightly. Then, with a mighty effort, he pulled it hastily up over his head to shield his face from the unbearable brilliance, breathing a sigh of relief when his eyes were free of the stinging pain. But the light was so powerful that even the thick hide was no shield against it. And Dalan marvelled at how it seeped into his little sanctuary, exposing every membrane of the cattle skin. He couldn't even banish the intensity of it behind his closed eyelids.

Suddenly the Brehon realised that Sorcha's voice had dropped away again and she'd returned to the low-pitch humming which had started the song. The light had also returned to the original blue and he was tempted to throw off his cloak and take a look around him.

Abruptly the Druid woman ceased all sound and in that split second a terrifying scream filled the tiny stone chamber. The Brehon was almost on his feet before he realised his legs were paralysed. He stumbled forward and fell face first, narrowly missing the fire. When he rolled over onto his back, the Watcher was still seated on the floor, her eyes blazing green with anger.

'Why didn't you finish the song?' Isleen demanded furiously.

'That's all I can recite,' Sorcha protested. 'There must be more to it. I just haven't been able to find anyone who knows the missing part.'

'Then you must find them!' the Watcher shrieked. 'I came so close to freedom. I won't be denied it now.'

'I promise I will search this island high and low until I've found the fragment which frees you,' the Druid woman vowed.

But in a flash Sorcha was gone and the Brehon was left alone with Isleen.

'There will be more trouble than you can imagine in this

land if you don't find the missing part to the song,' she promised ominously. Then her expression changed to one of deep suspicion. 'Are you deliberately withholding the song of release from me?' she spat. 'Are you playing some sort of game with me?'

'I am not,' Dalan assured her. 'Sorcha has done her best. You must be patient until we've located someone who can recall the missing verse.'

'I give you fair warning, Druid. If you haven't tracked the remainder of the song down by Samhain Eve, Lochie and I will visit a terrible retribution upon you.'

'What would you possibly gain from that? If you punish Sorcha and myself, then who will be left to help you? You rely on us for your freedom.'

'There are other Druids.'

'None who knows as much about you or the song you seek as Sorcha and myself. You'd have to be a fool to discard us so easily.'

'Sorcha is a slip of a girl with no knowledge at all,' Isleen hissed. 'It would not damage our cause if she were locked inside a standing stone for the rest of eternity with my seven brothers and sisters.'

'If you punish anyone, it should be me,' Dalan cut in.

Then the Watcher knew she had discovered his weakness. 'So you think very highly of this Sorcha. Is she very important to you?'

'She is wiser than any woman I've ever known and more trustworthy than the sunrise. I would give my life into her hands without a moment of hesitation. She is purity of spirit and the light of love. She's my guide and my companion and I want nothing but to walk with her down the generations of our long lives together.'

'That will certainly be your destiny if you serve us well,' Isleen promised him. 'But if you have not made some progress soon, Lochie and I will be forced to deal you a sharper lesson. Do you understand?'

Dalan nodded and closed his eyes, suddenly weary beyond all reckoning. When he opened them again the Watcher was gone and the fire had returned to its familiar reddish glow. And Sorcha sat opposite him again, bathing him with a warm smile and loving eyes.

Chapter Three

Are you listening to me? Wake up! If you let your eyes glaze over in the presence of a Raven you could well find them gone before you know it. There's nothing so tasty as the glazed eyeballs of Gaedhal. Do you have any recollection of the tales I told you about the Watchers and the coming of your ancestors to this country?

I didn't think so. Put ten Gaedhals in a room and you'd have less collected intelligence than twenty sheep. Your folk are short on memory and shorter on conscience. Well I'll be brief because I've better things to do than repeat myself again and again. But if I don't remind you of a few matters that passed earlier, you'll likely go round spreading lies and hearsay. Bloody typical.

Long ago, before your people blighted these green shores with the pestilence of your bark-stripping ways, Innisfail was plagued by another race of warring bastards. Their king called himself Balor and his people added an epithet to his name which referred to the nasty enchanted eye he kept in a tower on Tory Isle.

This eye was a fiendish thing of fire that burned all it looked upon to ashes and all it glanced at to cinders and all it blinked at into shrivelled scalded lumps of steaming mush. Not surprising he was known as Balor of the Evil Eye. Of course no one would have called him that to his face for fear of being turned to mush, ash or cinders.

But even this weapon wasn't enough to turn the tide of war against the Danaans and the Fir-Bolg who had joined forces to rid the land of him and his folk, the Fomor. So he devised a terrible plan to ensure that even if his people were defeated, his enemies would continue to suffer for generations to come.

He chose nine trusted Druids and cast an enchantment upon them so they were no longer mortal, no longer beings of flesh and blood but akin to demons who could change shape at will. And it was their task to harass the Danaans and the Fir-Bolg forever more.

Now it so happened that Balor was eventually defeated. But that is another story. As time passed the Watchers grew weary of their work and one by one they retreated into the form of standing stones to find the only rest they could expect. Until at last only two remained.

And it was these two who filled the Gaedhals, your strange-smelling ancestors, with the inspiration to set out from their own country to find Innisfail, subdue the country and claim it for their own. And there was never a darker cloud yet over this island than the morning Éremon's ships anchored off the eastern strand of this fair land.

The last two Watchers were not resigned to their fate as their companions had been. These two, who sometimes called themselves Lochie and Isleen, had heard there was a way to break their enchantment and claim the respite of death.

They set Dalan the task of tracking down a song they believed would cure their unusual malady, and to make sure he did his best to find this song as quickly as possible they spread havoc wherever they went.

They certainly knew how to manipulate others to their own ends. If only Ravens had learned that skill there might yet be some forests worth nesting in. If I'd had half their knowledge I'd have brought down a plague of crawling gnats upon the Gaedhals long ago.

Meanwhile the Fir-Bolg and the Danaan were busy fighting among themselves and it was only at the behest of Dalan the Brehon that they ceased their tribal stoushes long enough to put up a creditable defence to the Gaedhals.

Now, only the Goddess Danu herself knows how your dull-witted forefathers managed to learn the art of working iron and steel weapons while the Danaans were making do with brittle bronze. Some things can never be fully explained.

Iron gave your folk the edge, if you'll excuse my turn of phrase. The Danaan Druids did their best to bring storm and tempest against the invaders but to no avail. Finally, in desperation, they came up with the ultimate defence.

Immortality.

No need to quiver at the thought of steel-tipped arrow heads if you know they can't kill you. No reason to flinch at a sharp silver sword if you're certain the blade will never be more than an inconvenience.

The Quicken Brew was an ancient recipe for a draught that would heal all ills, banish death and grant eternal youth. With this weapon the Danaans hoped to cheat the Gaedhals of victory. And they had another trick up their sleeves, for the old ones were wily buggers.

They caused a doorway to open between this place and the Otherworld. I can't begin to explain to you what the Otherworld is exactly. I'm sure you're struggling to keep up with me as it is. Let us just say it is a place like this yet completely different.

Never mind.

At this time the King of the Fir-Bolg had twin sons and a daughter. And they were more trouble than a bagful of farting ferrets. Arrogant, self-centred and wilful was Aoife, and her brother Sárán was all that and cunning as well. As for the other twin, the less said about him the better.

Sárán fell under the spell of the Watchers, stole the Cauldron of Plenty from his father and delivered it into the hands of Eber Finn. What a ruckus that caused! The cauldron had been bestowed on King Brocan as a token of peace but it brought only war in the end.

Aoife fell in love with Mahon, a son of the Danaan king, and against her father's wishes she secretly planned to run off with him. But Mahon never responded to her little games of attention-seeking and petty manipulations, so when Eber offered her his hand she jumped at the chance. Mostly out of spite, I imagine.

Eber for his part was as foolish a Gaedhal as any who ever lived and that's saying something. He took Aoife's bait. Hook, line and small lead weight. But to give her credit a change had come over her. For a while. Who could tell if it would last?

And Sárán reformed himself too. He was fully repentant for his foolish actions and resolved to change his life. But you and I both know what resolutions are like. Best not to bother if you're promising the impossible. There's nothing worse than letting yourself down.

Now, if you think you have a grasp on the events leading up to this part of the tale I'll go on.

While Dalan was journeying in the land between the worlds, Sárán was waiting outside by a fire. Lom came by at sunset and shared a cup of warm mead, but he was off to his own bed by midnight, leaving his twin to keep the vigil through the dark hours.

Sárán reflected on all that had happened since the coming of the Gaedhals to Innisfail. He bitterly recalled the last battle his father had fought against the Danaans and blushed when he remembered his own foolishness at trying to provoke further conflict.

With genuine fondness he thought back to Fineen, the Danaan healer he had wounded that day. And he remembered the forgiveness he'd been offered by that wise gentle soul. He'd learned much from Fineen and he felt sure the healer's wisdom would serve him throughout his long life.

Then his mind wandered to the Quicken Brew, the properties of which were still largely a mystery to him. He understood that the concoction had healing power; he'd witnessed that at first-hand. But he couldn't grasp how such a brew could prolong life indefinitely.

Now that his father had gone through the door to the Otherworld which the Danaans had opened, Sárán's life had certainly taken a new direction. His sister, Aoife, would soon be wed to the King of the Gaedhals. And if all went well, his twin would be elected King of the Fir-Bolg by the following evening.

As a result, Sárán could be expected to be elevated to the position of Druid adviser to Lom. And he could probably count on being a close confidant of Aoife. Between them he would have the ear of the two most powerful Fir-Bolg in the southern kingdoms.

If he had ever dared to dream that any of these things might one day come to pass he would have laughed at himself for being overly ambitious. And yet by some miracle the world had changed beyond his recognition. It was a transformation that might have been plucked out of the ancient tales, an exercise in Draoi craft of the highest order.

'I am a shape-shifter,' he whispered to himself. 'This is what it means to change form completely.'

He was still congratulating himself as the sun rose on the eastern horizon, kissing the top of a distant standing stone and spilling its light upon the land.

Sárán realised, then, that he'd spent the whole night seated too close to the fire. He coughed the smoke out of his lungs and picked up an iron cooking pot that had been a gift from Eber Finn. Then he went down to the well to wash it out and fill it in preparation for boiling up some oats for his breakfast.

He wasn't gone long so he was a little surprised to find someone seated at his fire when he returned. The cloaked figure was faced away from him but he guessed by the ornate style of the garment that his visitor was a Gaedhal.

Sárán decided it would be best to behave as politely as possible to this stranger. He still considered the Gaedhals an unpredictable and somewhat barbaric people.

'Will you share some porridge with me?' he asked.

The figure stood up immediately and turned around. The hood of the cloak concealed the stranger's features but, when Sárán caught a glimpse of a wisp of long red hair he nearly dropped the cooking pot there and then.

'Do you have butter and honey?' the woman inquired and there was a scent of lavender about her.

'I have butter,' the young man replied in shock, certain now of the identity of the stranger. 'But I don't have any honey,' he added, his throat dry.

'Then allow me to supply you with some,' the woman offered sweetly.

From under her cloak she produced an earthenware jar. She immediately removed the cork and the air was flooded with a sweet aroma such as Sárán had never known before. So intoxicating was the scent that the young Druid almost forgot his fright.

She took a step towards him and every movement of her

body under the cloak spoke of a sensual paradise awaiting him if he would but surrender to her completely. He caught himself breathing in sharp shallow bursts and then he blurted her name into the night as if hearing the sound of it could somehow banish her from him.

'Isleen!'

The woman laughed girlishly and threw off her cloak to reveal the men's travelling clothes she usually wore.

'Sárán!' she giggled. 'It's good to find you still have that air of innocence about you. I find it very alluring, you know.'

'You're one of the Watchers,' he stuttered.

'There's no use in lying to you,' she replied with a hint of sarcasm. 'I suppose I'll just have to tell you all about myself over a bowl of porridge.'

'I don't trust you.'

'That's very wise considering what I put you through the last time we travelled together,' she agreed. 'If I were you I'd be quite angry.'

Then she pouted her lips and half shrugged her shoulders. 'Are you still angry with me?'

Sárán frowned. This was the same Isleen who'd led him to believe she was a Druid and tricked him into stealing the Cauldron of Plenty from his father. This had triggered a chain of events that had led to war. But there was an air of vulnerability about her he hadn't noticed before.

'I've just had the most terrible experience and I think I need to sit down for a while and recover,' she told him.

He held out his hand, offering her a seat on a log. But she did not sit down.

'I've come to make amends for all the trouble I caused you,' she went on, taking a tentative step towards him. 'Why don't you put the water on to boil and I'll tell you all about my plan.'

Sárán brushed past her and she touched his hair with her

fingers as he went. But the young Druid showed no sign of weakening his resolve. He placed the pot among the coals and stirred up the fire around it.

'I could have been banished for what I did,' he spat without turning away from the cauldron. 'I was just a tool for you to use. And when you were finished with me you left me to my fate. I know you are a sworn enemy to my people and I know you have gifts beyond my imagination, but I don't fear you, I despise you.'

'If you really understood the extent of my talents you wouldn't dare to speak to me in that manner,' she flashed and a hint of malice glinted in her eyes. 'But I'll forgive your youthful foolishness for the moment while you hear my side of the tale.'

'Dalan and Fineen told me all about you.'

'But what would they know?' she countered. 'Only half-truths passed down the generations from one bard to another. They don't know the truth. There is a saying. If you want to hear bleating, listen to a goat talking about the ocean. If you want to hear the music of the crashing waves you must go to the seashore.'

'In the name of Danu, leave me alone,' Sárán begged. 'My life has changed for the better. I've no wish to become involved in matters for which I have no understanding.'

'I have come to help you.'

'I don't want your help.'

'I've just been with Dalan inside the stone hut,' she pressed. 'I revealed to him the future. I let him see your brother as a great war-leader with you standing in glory by his side. But what I didn't tell the gentle Brehon is that none of those things are possible unless you accept my counsel and my help.'

The young Druid stood up and turned to face her. 'You were born an enemy of my people,' he reminded her. 'How can I ever trust you?'

'You are wrong,' she smiled. 'I was born of the Fir-Bolg. I am one of your people. But our folk were allied with the Fomorians in those days. And when the allegiance of our kings shifted to the Danaans I was trapped on the wrong side of the battle lines. Lochie and I had already committed ourselves to this terrible fate because the Danaans had always been enemies of our tribespeople. We saw this form as being an effective way of fighting them.'

'Then why do you continue to spread havoc among the Fir-Bolg, if you're born of our blood?'

'We gave our word to Balor that we would do everything in our power to harass the enemies of the Fomor,' she admitted. 'I was a Druid. To break my word, no matter what the reason, would have been contrary to my sacred oaths upon initiation. The kings of our people condemned us as outlaws when they made a new alliance with the Danaans. What choice did we have?'

'You speak of your sacred oaths to truth,' Sárán countered, 'yet you spread deception and lies throughout the land.'

'You have no idea what bitterness is, do you?' she scoffed. 'I wish I could have retained some of your childish innocence. You must trust me when I tell you that after you've lived an unnaturally prolonged life you will come to redefine what you call truth. My truth is that I am a Watcher. Without help I can't change that state of being.'

'So you have some gifts but not enough power to heal your own malady?'

Isleen laughed. 'At last I believe you begin to understand me.'

'And why are you so interested in me?'

'You are just starting out upon the road of immortality,' she explained. 'I see in you a little of myself as I once was. It's true that it would serve my purpose well to protect and promote you. But you will gain something of great value in return.'

'What exactly do you propose?' he asked, beginning to become interested.

'You haven't been initiated into the Druid Circle as yet, have you?'

Sárán shook his head.

'Dalan has been putting off the day and Fineen has withdrawn into the Otherworld.'

'Then let me be your guide. I'll teach you three arts of seeing: the Imbas Forosnai, the Tenm Laegda and the Dichedul do Cennaib. These three crafts are known to only a few in these days. Dalan certainly knows nothing of them.'

'And you'll lead me through my initiation?'

'I will teach you the secret signs of the trees known to the Danaan and the Fir-Bolg of old but forgotten in the passing of the generations. You alone of all your people will have the gift of the Ogham signs which Ogma first created and which only the Sen Erainn remember. And yes, I will take you through your initiation and anoint you to your vocation.'

'But who will recognise your authority to do so?'

'At the door to a house it matters not whether the dog, the cat or the master of the residence greets you. It is enough that you are welcomed in. No Druid will question that you have attained the Holy Circle.'

Sárán placed two handfuls of oats in the boiling water then sat for a long while as he considered all Isleen had said to him. His own arrogant, vain nature worked with Isleen's powerful charm to override his judgement. He briefly resisted, proud of all he had achieved since his teacher had passed away. But a fox will always chase the chickens, as they say. At last he voiced one last concern.

'Can you give your word that I will never again be placed in a compromising position, nor asked to do anything that would be a disservice to my people?'

'Unless you are responsible for the deed yourself, I can't

imagine such a circumstance arising.'

'Do you swear to be truthful to me in every detail?'

'As much as it is my ability to do so,' she promised. 'I may be a Watcher and I may possess some remarkable gifts, but I can't know everything.'

Then she squatted down beside him, stirred the bubbling oats with a spoon and offered him the pot of honey.

'Take it. There's plenty more where that came from.'

Aoife. How can I tell you about that girl? She preferred to get her own way. But if that wasn't possible she'd make the best of things and turn events to her advantage. She snared Mahon, a Danaan prince, and captivated the poor wretch entirely.

And after a while, like a toy that has lost its initial allure, she soon bored with him and left him in the toy chest more often than not. This vain young thing convinced herself she was meant for better things. So when her father, King Brocan of the Fir-Bolg of the Burren, offered her in marriage to Eber Finn, she nearly wet herself with excitement.

And like her brother Sárán she made a private vow to herself that she would do everything in her power to be a good queen to her new husband. As long as she wasn't regularly confronted with the sad, pathetic, lovable, boyish, helpless, enticing, handsome countenance of young Mahon, she was certain she could keep her vow without too much trouble.

After all, she had taken the Quicken Brew. She would live forever. Her husband, a mere Gaedhal, would age soon enough and be dead in no time at all. Then she'd be free to track down the poor Danaan prince and have her wicked way with him once again. Plenty of time. No sense in getting too sentimental about it all.

While Dalan was seeking inspiration among the standing stones in the ancient house of divination near Dun Gur, Eber Finn was pacing up and down his hall in frustration. It had been two weeks since Aoife and her brothers had arrived at his fortress and still she had not been given permission to marry him.

The chieftains of the Fir-Bolg had withheld their blessing on the match. They insisted on waiting until Lom was officially declared king. And though Aoife was just as keen as he was to seal their promise formally, she had acquiesced to their demand.

Eber's frustration had begun to turn into suspicion that the Fir-Bolg chieftains might have some other motive in putting off the wedding. Perhaps they were still unsure of the alliance with the Gaedhals. The king began to worry that his future was not as secure as he had imagined.

He was acutely aware that his brother, Éremon, was amassing a huge force ready to march south and impose his rule on Eber's territory. The days were slipping by and still Eber's hands were tied. If he had enough warriors at his disposal his brother would not dare launch an invasion of the southern territories.

It seemed certain now that Eber would only keep his kingdom by a show of force. Only if Éremon saw that the Fir-Bolg folk were ready to defend the south would he be likely to withdraw.

'I'm tired of fighting,' the king groaned to himself, resentful of his brother's threat.

Before he'd gone into the Aillwee caves at the challenge of King Brocan, Eber had been keen for conquest of the north.

But his experiences in the depths had changed him profoundly. He'd discovered that life was a precious gift and that battle was a senseless waste of that gift. And he'd realised that his soul was weary beyond words with waging war. The warrior path he'd been so dedicated to all his life had become empty for him.

After Aillwee he'd searched desperately for ways in which he could avoid a conflict. But in the end he'd had to accept there was no alternative but to engage in at least one battle, even if it was just a short skirmish that shook the confidence of the northerners. So he'd reluctantly ordered the preparations for war.

His craftsmen had been forging weapons continuously for weeks. His bondsmen were bringing in their harvest to help feed the gathered warriors. But the Fir-Bolg could not march with his folk until the treaty was formally ratified. And each day they tarried at Dun Gur partaking of his hospitality they consumed as much as all the warriors of his people.

The chamberlain was warning that, if this continued, there would not be enough food to see the settlement through the winter. If the combined army waited here much longer, the reserve supplies of Dun Gur would simply dry up as the lough had done. Eber had countered that there would be food enough for all once they'd conquered the north. But he had hardly convinced himself, so it wasn't surprising that the chamberlain had not been impressed either.

There was a shortage of milk, butter and cheese. The last of the best mead had been sent as a gift to the new Fir-Bolg king, so there was hardly a decent drop to be had in the fortress. Eggs were scarce because so many of the king's poultry had been slaughtered to feed his guests.

The latrines were overflowing because they were simply not designed to cater for so many people. New trenches had had to be created further away from the fortress. And worst of all, the lough had reached its lowest level yet. The once clear blue waters had become a stinking mass of sodden muddy ground impassable to man and beast alike. The fish that had dwelt there flapped about and suffocated and their rotting corpses tainted the air. Only geese still visited the shores. Every other bird had gone. Fresh drinking water had to be carried in barrels from a wellspring which continued to trickle in the midst of the mud.

The words of his old Druid counsellor, Máel Máedóc, rang in his ears. There was hardly a day went by that he didn't recall the geis the old man had laid on him before his death in the depths of the Aillwee caves. He closed his eyes and could hear Máel Máedóc's voice again.

'If your brother should come with the blade of battle lust you will not draw a weapon against him. If your brother should denounce you to your kinfolk you will make a gift of two portions of your land to him. No black pig shall perish within the borders of the country which you rule. No bird will feast within your hall. No woman shall have cause to call you miserly. No rival will ever suffer hunger while he dwells on your land. You will devise the Code of the Fianna, so that folk in future will remember you for your wisdom.'

The king had a terrible instinct that soon this geis would come to its completion and all his hopes for peace would be shattered.

And that was just one of Eber's many troubles. The day Aoife had arrived Isleen had disappeared. He told himself he needed her now more than ever, but the truth was he missed having her in his bed. He longed for her companionship and her quick laughter.

And though he never thought he'd admit it to himself, he also missed Máel Máedóc. The old man had perished in the depths of the Aillwee caves and now Eber had no one to advise him. The king was beginning to wonder whether it wouldn't be easier to simply hand over the kingdom to his brother without a fight. At least he would spare the lives of his warriors, and possibly save his own neck if it came to that.

When he was tired of pacing the hall Eber Finn sat down beside the central hearth, put his head in his hands and stared into the softly glowing embers. The air was chilly so he called for more turf.

A servant appeared at the door and sheepishly bowed, explaining that there was none to be had until the carts returned from Dun Aillil. Lom had graciously offered to supply the fortress with fuel as long as his people were lodged there but the wagons weren't expected until the morning.

Eber received the news with quiet acceptance then turned his attention back to the fire which had died down to a low glow. And there he sat, turning the embers over with an iron poker and silently bemoaning his situation, until well after dark. So engrossed was he in all his troubles, he didn't notice his servants lighting the oil lamps or bringing a great bowl of water to wash his hands in before the evening meal. He stayed there when all that was done and a mood of defeat began to descend upon him.

If Isleen were here, he told himself, she'd know what to say. She'd have a solution for him. Isleen would find a way to win over the Fir-Bolg chieftains. She would soothe his aching head, hold him to her breast and everything would be all right again. He no longer liked what the Druids said of her. She might be a Watcher, whatever that might be, but he missed her sorely.

For the first time he found himself questioning his infatuation with the young red-headed Fir-Bolg princess called Aoife. He'd heard folk say that she was no more than a stubborn spoiled girl. And she had a reputation for a very short temper and a wilful way.

Her only asset might have been the knowledge she had

gained at her study of the Druid path. But she hadn't even excelled in that. All in all, Eber told himself, Aoife might not prove to be the great queen he'd hoped for. But he needed a marriage with her to reinforce his alliance with the Fir-Bolg.

The king was sinking lower into his chair, stretching his feet as close as possible to the fire to draw the last warmth from the dying embers, when Aoife entered the hall. She immediately set about ordering the servants as if this were already her home.

'Bring that timber to the fire and build it up,' she commanded, as if she'd been running the household all her life. 'This chamber is icy cold. How could you allow your king to suffer so?'

Eber looked up with a frown of confusion. 'Where did all that firewood come from?' he asked, watching with unbelieving eyes as more and more split timber was stacked against the wall.

'I sent out servants this afternoon with three carts to collect what they could of fallen timber in the forest,' she replied. 'I hope you don't mind. I just couldn't bear the idea of you sitting here in the cold without any fuel.'

'I don't mind,' Eber answered, still surprised but now pleasantly so. He wondered whether he'd been too hasty in his assessment of her.

'I'll send them out again tomorrow, with your approval. I'd like to make certain this hall is warm. You can't be receiving the chieftains of your people or the king of my folk into a cold, unwelcoming chamber. Someone might take offence.'

Eber sat forward. 'You're right,' he nodded. 'Thank you for your thoughtfulness.'

'I just hope I haven't offended you by ordering your servants about as if they were my own.'

'They'll be yours to order as you wish when we're wed,'

Eber replied. 'I give you full authority to do as you see fit in this household from now on.'

His opinion of her was restored. Once more he noticed the brightness in her green eyes, and her lightness of spirit.

'If you'll excuse me then,' she bowed politely, 'I'll go and see to your evening meal. If you are to administer these folk through these troubled times, you must stay strong.'

'Thank you,' Eber mumbled.

He was genuinely unused to having someone consider his personal needs. All his effort, his every thought, was on the security of his people and the future of their settlement in this land. It seemed as if, just by taking command of a small area of his life, Aoife had relieved him of a great burden.

She turned to leave for the stone kitchens at the summit of the hill fort, but before she'd reached the door Eber stood up. 'You will join me, won't you?' Eber asked. 'I mean, you will share the evening meal with me.'

'I would be honoured to sit at table with you, my lord,' she replied politely.

'And bring your brother, King Lom of the Fir-Bolg, to dine with us,' he added.

'Lom hasn't been confirmed in his position yet,' Aoife told him. 'And this night he'll be staying close to the sacred circle near where the divination is taking place. It is our custom to proclaim the king immediately after his confirmation has been received through the auspices of the Bull Feast.'

'So we'll be alone?' Eber inquired.

The young woman nodded her reply.

'I'm afraid I have no mead to offer you,' he admitted. 'I sent the last as a gift for your brother.'

'No mead!' she exclaimed, her voice suddenly full of indignant outrage.

Eber shrank back. He hadn't meant to offer her any insult. It was just that all his stocks of liquor had been depleted.

'Why didn't you tell me?' she asked him, shaking her head with a smile. 'I'm sure I can find some honey liquor for us to share. In a fortress as large as this one there's bound to be someone keeping a secret hoard of the stuff for a special occasion. And I have a nose for it.'

She winked, bowed her head slightly and was gone, leaving Eber standing before a large roaring fire with servants bustling all about him. Some were sweeping and others were busily brushing down the great oak table which lay folded against the wall when it wasn't in use.

After a few moments the king sat down again in his chair, sighed deeply with satisfaction and turned his mind back to the dangerous intentions of his brother in the north. Suddenly all his problems didn't seem to worry him quite so much.

Chapter Four

ahon, son of King Cecht of the Danaans, crouched low in the bushes where the sentries would not see him. He peered across the space where the lough had once lapped peacefully against the shore and could not believe his eyes.

The waters of Lough Gur had almost completely receded. The moonlight on the muddy field made him frown in contempt of the Gaedhals. When his father had been King of Dun Gur the lough was full of fish and dancing reeds.

In Mahon's mind this was a punishment brought upon the Gaedhals for their mismanagement of the land and disrespect for the ways of the Danaan folk.

'They've broken the treaty with my people,' he whispered. 'Eber promised to care for this lake and the lands all about. If my father had thought the Gaedhals would ruin this place he would never have given it over to them in return for sealing the peace.'

'Your father had no idea Eber was a treacherous bastard,' a voice replied from the bushes beside him.

Mahon nodded. 'I suppose you're right. Our people were in awe of your folk with your iron weapons and your longships.'

'I don't belong to the Gaedhals any more, remember?' the

other man cut in. 'My king betrayed me. I've been banished from my people. I'm an outlaw. As you well know.'

'We've both been banished,' Mahon agreed. 'My father's people have retreated into the Otherworld. My foster father has forbidden me to return to his home. You're my only kinfolk now, Iobhar. You're my true brother.'

'You can still say that even though you know I am in love with Aoife?' the other man asked.

'You may be in love with her but you have no idea of her true nature. She's flighty and dominating. I'm not sure she cares at all for you or me. I'm beginning to believe all Aoife is concerned about is Aoife. I know for a fact she scorns any man who fawns over her and doesn't treat her as an equal. If you can accept her for that then you may earn her affection.'

'I don't understand you,' Iobhar declared. 'You speak so ill of her. I can't recall the last time I heard you say something complimentary about the girl. Yet here we are sitting at the edge of the lough like two nesting geese. Do you really intend to steal into Dun Gur and rescue her?'

'Would you have her wed to that double-crossing king of yours?'

'No,' Iobhar snapped. 'Indeed, if I get the chance I'll introduce Eber Finn to the fine edge of my sword and see what he thinks of that.'

'Then enough talk,' Mahon hissed. 'Let's carry out our plan just as we decided. But remember to keep your head down. If we're set upon I want you to make good your escape. Their blades can't harm me. I've taken the Quicken Brew. So I'll hold off the sentries if we're discovered. Do you understand?'

'I do,' Iobhar answered sharply. 'I'm not an idiot! It's better to be a retreating outlaw than a dead one.'

Mahon pointed across the mudflat towards the fortress on the other side. 'That's the place where the boats used to land.

But there's no chance of making it over to the wharf. The mud would surely suck us down or we'd be discovered before we got halfway to the island.'

'The only entrance to the fortress is by that bridge,' Iobhar confirmed. 'And it's heavily guarded. How are we going to get across? And even if we make it inside the walls, how are we going to escape with Aoife?'

'I told you, I have a plan,' Mahon asserted.

'A plan!' the Gaedhal spat contemptuously. 'It's all well and good for you to talk of standing to my defence while I get away. If we're captured there's not much they can do to harm you.' Iobhar grunted before he went on. 'There's only one way in or out and that's through the main gate. If we're cornered inside Dun Gur I'll have no chance of escape. And I'll surely be killed if Eber Finn gets hold of me.'

'I wish you'd stop worrying,' the Danaan snapped. 'We'll be safe as long as we stay together.'

'We haven't got any weapons,' the Gaedhal pointed out. 'How are we going to defend ourselves if we're set upon by the guards?'

'I told you to stop worrying. We'll find a way.'

'You're right,' Iobhar decided. 'Perhaps Aoife is just too troublesome to warrant all this. Maybe she isn't worth so much bother. On reflection I probably should just go north to King Éremon and offer my services. I'm sure he'd welcome anyone banished from his brother's kingdom.'

The Gaedhal grumbled under his breath when Mahon offered no reply. 'What if we do manage to make our way past the guards, the sentries and all the common folk without being recognised?' he went on. 'Imagine we're able to find our way into the royal hall without raising any suspicion, find Aoife's chamber and convince her it's safe to come with us. How will we escape the fortress?'

Mahon looked across at his companion with a frown of

frustration. 'At the other side of the island there's a narrow causeway which leads across the lough. It's only wide enough for one person to walk at a time but it leads to safety.'

'Then why don't we enter the fortress across that causeway?'

'Because it lies at the bottom of a steep descent and there's no path to the summit from the foot of the hill. There was a subsidence many winters ago which rendered the path almost useless. It would take us a full day to climb to the top and we'd be exhausted afterwards.'

'How are we going to get to the path from the summit?'

'I know a way,' Mahon assured his friend. 'You must trust me.'

'That's what Aoife told me,' Iobhar moaned. 'If I hadn't listened to her I would never have been banished from my people. I could be seated by the fire in one of those halls up there if it wasn't for her.'

'I've had enough of your sour words!' Mahon snapped. 'If you don't wish to help me, you can stay here and wait until I return. Perhaps I'd be better off without you if you're going to be continually picking holes in my plans.'

'I'm sorry,' Iobhar offered. 'I don't mean to criticise you. I just have a gut feeling that this isn't a wise course of action.'

'Going to Eber and asking his leave to steal away his betrothed and take her to the Northern Kingdom wasn't a wise idea either,' the Danaan noted dryly. 'But that didn't stop you trying. I've forgiven your betrayal of our friendship but I can't forget your stupidity.'

Iobhar fell silent as he swallowed the rebuke. It was true he had been foolish. He'd known full well that Mahon was in love with Aoife but he'd been taken in by her desperate plea for freedom from the constraints of the Fir-Bolg court and the duties of her Druid training.

'I wouldn't have acted the way I did if Aoife hadn't

convinced me she was in love with me. She talked so much that a cloud of infatuation came over me. I was certain it was my destiny to rescue her and escort her to the court of Éremon where she'd be free of her obligations to the Druid orders and out of reach of her father's wrath.'

Mahon didn't offer any reply.

'She cast a Draoi-spell on me,' Iobhar added bitterly. 'It was as if I had no mind of my own.'

'Then perhaps you've learned a valuable lesson,' the Danaan cut in. 'You are not of our kind. Aoife might entertain the notion of wedding you or one of your people, but the fact is we are different from any of the Gaedhals. We will not perish and go to the Halls of Waiting as you surely must. Our people have, for the most part, gone to dwell in the Otherworld.'

'I've heard that some have taken the form of seals or stags and live in the forest under the cover of those guises,' Iobhar added.

'Then you know more than I do,' Mahon told him. 'My folk are scattered. I'm alone. And so is Aoife. She might be foolish enough to think that a marriage to Eber will offer her some degree of happiness for now. But she knows in her heart that the day must come when her husband will be an old man while she is yet young.'

'I can't imagine her being content with that situation,' the Gaedhal scoffed.

'Neither can I.' Then Mahon sank back down into the bushes again and fell silent. All his concentration was focused on the large causeway which had been built as a bridge over the mud and led to the main gate.

'We'll watch and wait,' he said finally. 'There must be a way into the fortress. Perhaps an answer will present itself.'

'You keep the first watch,' Iobhar suggested. 'I need some rest. You can wake me when you've solved the riddle.'

'You'll come with me then?'

'How could I let you go off alone into the midst of your enemies without my sword hand by your side? We've been through too much together to part company now over a slip of a girl who cares nothing for either of us. And life has been a bit slow lately. I could do with some excitement.'

With that the Gaedhal pulled his cloak over his head, rolled onto his side and let sleep take him.

Mahon lay flat on his stomach, peering at the bridge. He thought of Aoife and whether she was worth the risk to his friend's life. But despite his reservations and the chill night air, he was warmed by Iobhar's words.

While Mahon lay in the bushes trying to devise a way of sneaking past the sentries at Dun Gur, Dalan was being led from the house of divination.

The stone circle and ancient ritual ground were not far removed from King Eber's fortress, so there was a great gathering of the hosts of the Fir-Bolg and Gaedhal waiting to hear the results of his vision. Around the holy circle of stones which had been built by the ancient ancestors of the Fir-Bolg, a throng had gathered. At the front of the crowd stood the chieftains and elders of the people.

Prominent among these neatly groomed figures was the young warrior who'd been nominated to the kingship of the Fir-Bolg. Lom stood with a solemn expression on his face, his long jet-black hair held back from his face by a slender rustic-looking circlet of tarnished silver. His cloak was an old travelling garment his father had often worn. It was sun-bleached, weather-stained and its edges were tattered. He wrapped it tightly round his upper body to conceal a bright, newly dyed saffron shirt. The final touch to his modest attire was an ancient silver torc such as any of the royal bloodline might wear.

In contrast the chieftains were dressed extravagantly. Some wore green cloaks; many wore purple, and a few boasted rare yellow garments with a woven design of check patterns in varying colours. Some of the older chieftains had caked clay into their hair to make it stand in strange sculpted shapes upon their heads. The younger leaders were less inclined to do this because it was rumoured the Gaedhals saw this time-honoured fashion as barbaric.

Lom glanced around the assembly and noticed that outwardly his people were already changing. Many had adopted the clothing styles of the foreigners. Their cloaks were longer; their trousers tied close to their calf muscles with leather strips, and their hair held back away from their faces. No one was trying to look as though they belonged among the Gaedhals. There was still a strong flavour of the Fir-Bolg in the bright colours and ornate bronze trinkets they all wore. But the changes were easily spotted.

The young warrior was certain his father, Brocan, would have been furious at such a flaunting of the ways of the Gaedhals. But he realised that with the passing of the old king the Fir-Bolg had been freed from some of the constraints of tradition.

In being exposed to the vibrant culture of the foreigners, his kinfolk were finding new expressions of their old ways. Cloak pins were being worn high on the left shoulder by craftsman and warrior alike. Once this would have been exclusive to the fighting class who had to have their sword arm free of encumbrance.

And among the chieftains small gold ornaments had begun appearing. These items had been acquired from the Gaedhals through trade. In Brocan's day gold was worn only by a king or used as an offering to the Goddess Danu.

Lom noted that a few of the younger chiefs had dispensed with their torcs of silver and were daring to wear highly polished brass. It wasn't gold but it gave the impression of the royal metal. Among the Gaedhals, anyone of chieftain rank was permitted to wear it.

The young man understood he would be overseeing many changes during his reign, some of which he would not entirely agree with. But he reasoned to himself that on the balance it was better to enter into a closer relationship with the foreigners. Indeed he was certain there was no other way in which his kinfolk would retain some degree of independence. The Gaedhals possessed weaponry and skill at arms ensuring any conflict would be devastating and futile. The only way to protect his people and their traditions was through cooperation with the newcomers.

In the light of a hundred torches the sacred circle seemed a much merrier place than usual. The sombre stones were transformed from grey bleak stumps of ancient rock into glowing orange shapes that seemed to pulsate with the energy of all the gathered people.

No one spoke as they waited for Dalan to approach the circle. They had all made their way here as soon as it had been announced the Brehon was being led from the house of divination. Lom had no idea how long he would have to wait but he was not at all nervous about the result.

In the three days since Dalan had disappeared into the stone hut to seek his vision, Lom had found peace with himself. He'd decided that if the Brehon were to divine him as unsuitable for the kingship, he would serve dutifully the man or woman chosen to the position.

And secretly Lom would not be broken-hearted if some other were selected to take the reins of the leadership. A king's life was not his own. The common folk were relatively unconstrained by tradition, but the royal household had rules imposed upon them which regulated the most insignificant aspects of their lives. There were strict customs governing the manner in which a king could address guests of differing social standing, or the colours the ruler was permitted to wear on various occasions. All these rules had their beginnings in ancient times. Some made perfect sense but a great many had lost their meaning and seemed to Lom to be pointless.

He decided that if he were to be confirmed to the kingship he would work with his Druid counsellor to review these customs and regulations to make life a little easier at court. He expected to face resistance from the older chieftains but he was determined to press ahead. A wind of change was blowing in with the Gaedhals and he wanted to fill his sails in its breeze.

As he scanned the assembly Lom asked himself whether his brother Sárán would be allowed to take up the appointment as king's counsellor. His twin had few friends among the chieftains. He was outspoken and abrasive when dealing with the council of leaders and he had a reputation for making rash decisions.

But no one could deny his courage. When he had decided to accompany Aoife into the Aillwee caves Sárán had proved he was brave enough to back his convictions with action, even if the action had been foolhardy in the extreme.

He trusted his brother as only a twin can. They shared more than a similarity of appearance. There was a deep bond between them which had grown stronger in the last few weeks since their father had withdrawn into the Otherworld and their sister had become betrothed to the King of the Gaedhals. Nevertheless Lom was uneasy about allowing Sárán to take on the role of royal adviser. When he was honest with himself, as he was much more these days, he would have preferred a counsellor with more experience of the world.

He looked around for Sárán, but his brother was nowhere to be seen. Lom shrugged his shoulders recognising it was typical of his twin to disregard his obligations. The young warrior decided he would not stand for such behaviour if he took on the kingship.

Unfortunately most of the Danaan Druid class had withdrawn into the Otherworld. Very few learned members of the holy orders were of Fir-Bolg blood. Only Dalan and Sorcha remained among the Fir-Bolg of the South. And Dalan had already promised to guide King Eber of the Gaedhals. Lom resolved to approach Sorcha, the Druid woman of the woods, to request her advice. He knew he risked his brother's wrath but Lom had to follow his instincts. And they told him his twin would not be a particularly good choice for counsellor.

As all these thoughts were cascading through his mind, each spawning a new tangent or another challenge, four foreign warriors entered the stone circle bearing a huge cauldron on their shoulders. The vessel was obviously full of liquid. Supervised by two of their chieftains they lowered the cauldron with great care onto the soft grass and then, without a word, they departed. Lom couldn't guess what the significance of the vessel might be. He'd never seen such a thing before in the centre of the sacred ring.

Another Gaedhal who stood outside the circle raised his voice. 'I am Naithí,' the stranger declared. 'I am a chief among the Gaedhals. I am the messenger of my king and the representative of my people.'

Lom regarded the man with awe. He was taller than any Fir-Bolg chieftain and he seemed as broad about the shoulders as a horse. His arms were bare even though the night was chilly, and his golden blond hair was neatly braided with silver trinkets that sparkled in the firelight.

But it was his face that unsettled Lom. The skin was painted entirely red so that the whites of his eyes stood out.

Many among the Fir-Bolg recalled that the warriors of the Gaedhal had painted their bodies with red ochre before the Battle of Sliabh Mis, and more than a few of them shuddered at the sight of this foreigner.

'King Eber of the Southern Gaedhals sends his greetings to the new king and the kinfolk of the Fir-Bolg.'

Lom squinted trying to make out this warrior-chieftain's features under the paint. He decided it was a wise ploy in both war and diplomacy to cover the face in red ochre. In battle it added a fierceness to a warrior's features. In diplomacy it concealed the chieftain's nuances of expression which might otherwise have been closely scrutinised.

'This cauldron is full of fine sweet mead,' Naithí went on. 'The last of the Iberian brew we brought with us from our homeland. It is only fitting that this gift should seal the friendship between our two peoples and secure our lasting alliance.'

The chieftain raised his arms high in the air and looked to the moon. His hands were huge and every Fir-Bolg beheld him with the same feeling of wonderment.

'I am the giant called Naithí,' he declared. 'May the gods who bless you bestow their blessings upon your assembly this night and also upon your new king.'

Then the chieftain stepped to the back of the crowd so no one could say he'd tried to interfere with the Fir-Bolg ritual in any way. Lom watched him depart and wondered how many of the Northern Gaedhals were giants like this man.

Just then three great bronze trumpets sounded from the far side of the ritual grounds. Their hum was low and rumbling and it brought absolute silence to the assembly.

Lom strained his neck to catch a first glimpse of the processional torches that would lead Dalan to the centre of the stone circle. For a long while he couldn't see anything at all and he found himself getting impatient. Sweat was gathering at the back of his neck where his father's rough old cloak rubbed against his skin.

The trumpets sounded again and this time they were humming at a higher pitch. Then the first torchlight appeared on the path which led down from the house of divination. The assembly was utterly quiet but the air was buzzing with tension, excitement and apprehension.

The future of the Fir-Bolg folk of the Burren was at stake. This was the Druid who had stepped into the vision world to ensure that their future would be a secure one. He was already an esteemed Brehon judge, a keeper of the Law and the Lore; but with this act of seership he had confirmed his place among the wisest and most valued of those of the holy orders.

When Lom caught sight of Dalan he knew what the Brehon had seen in his vision. The Druid was walking with the aid of his staff, shrouded in his distinctive cloak of Raven feathers. His eyes were not those of a man who had spent three days confined within a small stone hut. They were clear, sparkling and attentive to all that was taking place about him. There was a solemnity and a hint of resignation in Dalan's expression. Lom prepared himself to be anointed as King of the Fir-Bolg. There was now no question in his mind that the Brehon would confirm him.

The young man's heart began to race. He felt his face flush red and his breathing became suddenly shallow and strained. He turned his head slowly to survey the gathering. Everyone else had seen the Brehon's expression but they were still looking on expectantly as Dalan was helped over the lowest stone and into the circle. Perhaps, he told himself, they had no idea of the outcome.

As soon as Dalan was standing on the soft grass within the sacred ring he raised his staff to the heavens. When he'd found the moon he faced her for a long time in silent contemplation. The crowd was growing impatient but no one denied him this simple gesture. After all, he'd performed a valuable and difficult task for the good of his kinfolk.

Lom's knees felt weak. He coughed then tried to minimise the noise by covering his face with his cloak. When he looked up again Dalan was making his slow way towards the centre of the grassy circle where the Gaedhals had lain their cauldron.

The Brehon paused to taste the liquid on the tip of his finger. Then he turned around to scan each of the stones which bordered the sacred ring. When he'd made a complete circuit in a sunwise motion, he made another. This time he made eye contact with as many of the gathered Fir-Bolg as dared meet his gaze. Some offered him a smile of friendship. Others were as expressionless as the stones. But no one turned away from him once his eyes caught theirs.

When the Brehon came to where Lom stood at the front of the crowd, directly under the moon, he paused. The two of them stared at each other for a long while. Then Lom felt a gentle nudge at his back. Sárán stepped out from behind his twin. He was dressed in a beautiful blue robe that shone with the same lustre as the night sky.

Dalan's lips curled a little in what could have been a smile or a mild grimace. Sárán squinted and frowned, taking the gesture to be a grimace.

The Brehon raised his staff and pointed directly at Lom.

'The two Ravens will rule,' he began. 'The one will be king and the other his counsellor.'

The gathered people gasped in surprise at the directness of his speech. It was rare for a seer to express his vision so bluntly without any poetic artifice.

'Lom will be the last king of the Fir-Bolg of the Burren,' Dalan went on.

The assembly was muttering now in outrage and confusion. Many simply couldn't believe what the Brehon was telling them.

'His reign will be short, bloody and futile. Yet he will be remembered as an honourable king and his name will live on long after he has left us.'

Now there was even more confusion. It was well known that Lom had taken the Quicken Brew and had surely gained the gift of immortality. Yet Dalan was speaking as if King Lom would perish.

'Come into the circle, Lom,' Dalan commanded, 'and take on the mantle of kingship.'

As he spoke the chieftains stepped forward also, bearing gifts and signs of the high office to which Lom was to be inaugurated.

'And what if I refuse?' the young man countered.

Now the mumbling became a low roar as some folk agreed that he should not accept the kingship if his reign would bring ruin on them all.

'You cannot reject your duty to your people,' Dalan explained. 'You were born to this destiny. It is not yours to steer at will. You must answer the call you've been waiting for all your life.'

'I won't be responsible for the ruination of my people,' the young man shot back.

'I haven't spoken of any such circumstance. I have said you will be the last of our kings. The Fir-Bolg will prosper as far as I can tell.'

There was silence as everyone contemplated the Brehon's words. Then Dalan spoke again.

'I have seen the two young Ravens, the sons of Brocan. They will rule the Fir-Bolg and lead our people well. That's an end to it. No one else has been nominated to the kingship. There was no hint in my vision of any other contender. Lom will be king of our people.'

The chieftains waited until the Brehon had finished speaking then gathered around him bearing the symbols of office.

'Step forward, King Lom,' Dalan commanded. 'I have come to confer upon you the authority to rule.'

The young warrior felt his twin's elbow nudge at him again and he turned around sharply.

'Go on,' his brother whispered.

Lom bit his tongue, not wishing to cause a disturbance at this most solemn of occasions. He felt a sudden revulsion for his brother and an urge to put as much distance between them as possible. He stepped towards the circle. In moments he'd been helped up over the barrier of low standing stones. He stood at the perimeter for a few breaths then raised his arms to the sky in silent blessing just as the giant Naithí of the Gaedhals had done.

When he'd calmed himself Lom realised there was no point in trying to avoid this destiny. He made a commitment to himself then. He promised he would be a just king, that he would oversee many changes. And with all his heart he prayed to Danu he would have the strength and wisdom to follow his instincts and steer a path of his own making. If Sárán was to be his adviser, he told himself, then he would have to be careful what, if any, of his brother's advice he took seriously.

With these decisions made, Lom felt ready to step forward. He did so with a strong confident gait that betrayed no anxiety or hesitancy. Dalan could see the determination in the young man's eyes and he was relieved.

And though many questioned whether he was fit to rule, none doubted the courage it took for him to accept his fate. Already many in the crowd were making private promises to honour him. For the augury of the Bull Feast was not to be taken lightly.

Dalan waited by the cauldron of honey wine until Lom was a few paces away. Then he spoke up. 'I name you king,' the Brehon decried.

Then two chieftains moved forward to remove Lom's old

cloak. It was tossed aside as if it were an old rag. The roughly fashioned circlet of silver was likewise discarded, as were all the young warrior's clothes.

For a few unsettling minutes Lom found himself standing naked before his people while Dalan stared him straight in the eyes. There was a challenge in that stare which dared the young man to act, to prove his worth in some way.

Lom knew what he had to do. He turned around to face his people, lifted his arms to the sky and his face to the moon once again, emulating the giant Gaedhal.

'May the ones who bless us bestow their blessings on us,' he said softly.

To his everlasting surprise and delight the voice of every Fir-Bolg at that assembly repeated his words.

And that was how Lom, son of Brocan, was acknowledged as King of the Fir-Bolg.

Chapter Five

ahon roused Iobhar from sleep around midnight. The Gaedhal peered back at his friend with bleary eyes that would have rather remained closed.

'Give me a drink,' he demanded.

'We haven't any.'

'I can't take much more of this,' Iobhar declared in a rebellious tone. 'If I don't get a drink soon I'm going to leave you to your schemes and head north.'

'There's mead by the barrel in Dun Gur,' Mahon hummed enticingly.

'But we're outside the fortress,' Iobhar reminded him.

'I've found a way in. But we have to act quickly.'

The Gaedhal opened his eyes again and sat up. 'I'm not risking my life on this,' he stated. 'If your plan isn't foolproof I'll have no part of it.'

'It's relatively safe,' the Danaan muttered as he pointed across to the causeway.

Iobhar focused on the stone bridge and saw the shapes of two warriors pacing towards the gatehouse which stood not far away from where they were hiding in the bushes.

'I've been watching them,' Mahon enthused. 'Every once in a while they saunter over to this side of the lough, sit down by the fire in the gatehouse and then wander back to the fortress.'

'You woke me up to tell me that?'

'If we catch them while they're in the gatehouse we'll have weapons, armour and a way into the fortress.'

Iobhar looked his friend in the eye. 'You're determined to go through with this, aren't you?'

Mahon nodded. The Gaedhal sighed heavily, giving in to the inevitable.

'Very well,' he conceded. 'I'll come with you. But only because you haven't a hope of rescuing Aoife by yourself.'

'The barrels of mead didn't influence your decision?' Mahon quipped.

'That issue was at the back of my mind. I admit it.'

'If we go now we'll reach the gatehouse before the guards,' the Danaan advised. 'The door is shrouded in shadows so we should be able to make our way in without being observed.'

'And how do we convince these two warriors to surrender their weapons and armour?'

'There's bound to be some furniture lying about,' Mahon snapped back, beginning to lose his patience. 'We'll find a way.'

'Are you suggesting we threaten them with stools?'

'Let's go!'

'Very well,' Iobhar shrugged as he withdrew from the cover of the bushes to follow his comrade down to the gatehouse. 'I suppose a splinter can be very painful if it's administered properly.'

They spoke no further words to each other as they approached the small stone house that served to guard the causeway. Without being observed they slipped through the doorway and into the warm shelter. In the centre of the floor the fire was dying down to low embers. And in the meagre light it was evident the gatehouse wasn't even equipped with a chair.

'I'm relieved,' Iobhar whispered. 'I wouldn't be comfortable if the odds were weighted too heavily in our favour. I see there's a small lump of turf in the corner. Do you mind if I arm myself with that?'

'Be quiet!' Mahon hissed. 'We don't want them to suspect anything.'

The Gaedhal shook his head in disbelief as he stepped back deeper into the shadows. Mahon stayed close to the door, waiting for the approach of the two sentries.

It wasn't long before they heard footsteps approaching the house. Then they heard the sound of two men talking. They were complaining about the lack of chairs in the gatehouse.

'King Eber has a grand hall on top of the hill,' said one. 'I'll wager he has plenty of seats for his guests and a large fire to warm them.'

'We don't count for nothing,' the other agreed. 'All I want is a sit-down now and then. Where's the harm in that?'

They were still grumbling about their miserable lack of furniture when they pushed aside the leather flap which served for a door and entered the room. Almost immediately one of them stamped his foot and swore.

'That's it!' he shouted. 'I've had enough! I'll swear there was half a lump of turf in the corner when we were over here last. Where's it gone then?'

Iobhar could restrain himself no longer. He knew if he didn't act immediately he would find himself breaking out into a very undignified fit of laughter. So he stepped out of the shadows holding the lump of turf.

The two warriors didn't have time to draw their swords before Mahon rendered one unconscious with a savage blow from a rock. Iobhar applied his turf to the other and to his relief the second warrior was soon also senseless on the floor.

'I'm beginning to wonder how my people managed to defeat the Danaans in battle,' the Gaedhal admitted.

'Because we allowed it,' Mahon told him. 'But that's a long

story. I promise I'll tell it to you after we get Aoife out of Dun Gur.'

With that they stripped the two warriors of their armour and tied their hands and feet with strips of leather.

'This should keep them secure long enough for us to penetrate the fortress, find Aoife and make our escape,' Mahon told his companion.

In a short while they were walking over the causeway towards the fortress and the large sentry fire which guarded the approach to the hill fort. Their spirits were high after so easily dealing with the two warriors but it wasn't long before Iobhar came to a frightening realisation.

'What if the warriors at the fire realise we're impostors?' he hissed urgently at his friend.

Mahon's jaw dropped — clearly he hadn't considered that possibility either. He gave a shrug of acceptance; it was too late to turn back without arousing suspicion. Instead he pulled his warrior's cloak over his head and wrapped it tightly against his face.

Iobhar followed his friend's lead, though he was truly frightened now and convinced they'd be caught. He was still clutching the lump of turf. He didn't want to drop it either. It had become something of a talisman. He could feel the dried fuel crumble in his fingers whenever his fear began to get the better of him and strangely he found that soothing.

Too soon it seemed they came to the watch-fire where the other sentries gathered to keep out the chill. They had almost passed by when one of the older veterans called out.

'You didn't stay over there long!'

Iobhar stopped walking, frozen to the spot by fear. Then, without removing his cloak from about his face, he turned towards the veteran.

'What are you doing?' Mahon whispered, pulling at his friend's arm. 'Keep moving. Ignore him.'

But the Gaedhal didn't hear him.

'You should have been over at the gatehouse a while longer,' the veteran added. 'Why have you come back so soon?'

Iobhar broke free of Mahon's grip and took a few steps forward. Then he raised his hand and tossed the little lump of turf to the veteran. The old man caught it.

'It's wet!' he exclaimed, though he couldn't have known it was Iobhar's sweat that had caused the dampness.

'Bloody cold!' Iobhar managed to say in his gruffest and deepest tones.

Then he coughed and added. 'We're going for some mead.'

The sentries all broke out in fits of laughter which brought a frown to Mahon's face and a look of concern from Iobhar.

'Go on then,' the veteran told them. 'You've done your share for the night. The watch changes in a short while, we'll do without you.'

Mahon and his friend quickly turned to go, but just as they were leaving the veteran called out to them again.

'If you find any mead, keep it for us,' he laughed.

Then he turned back to the fire. 'Those two!' he gasped in delight. 'If they're not complaining about having no stools to sit on or the dampness of the turf, then it's the lack of mead in the fortress that gets their goat. They never stop.'

'A lack of mead in the fortress?' Iobhar hissed under his breath. 'What can he mean by that?'

But Mahon had no wish to stand around discussing the matter with his friend. He led the way up to the walls of the hill fort and they passed through the open gates without anyone offering them a challenge.

Sorcha waited until Dalan had been led away towards the stone circle before she started back to their camp on the banks of the lough. The two Druids had been offered the finest houses in Dun Gur but they preferred to be away from the crowds of people. Eber Finn respected their request and had assured them privacy.

The Druid woman was exhausted. Her matted hair was tied up into a ball at the back of her head as it had been throughout the ordeal of the Bull Feast. Her clothes were stained with sweat and although she couldn't sense it she knew she must surely stink like a rotting carcass at mid-summer.

How she wished the lough were full of water. Sorcha would have given anything for a cooling midnight swim to wash the ordeal of the house of divination out of her system.

Before she was halfway to her lean-to on the banks of the lough she had forgotten all such thoughts. She had moved beyond the point of exhaustion. Now she was simply placing one foot in front of the other without thinking.

Indeed her mind became quieter than it had been since that first day Dalan had arrived at her stream to tempt her into the outside world again. To be fair, she hadn't needed too much coaxing. From the moment their eyes had first met she had yearned to know more about this travelling Brehon and his strange quest.

She had been delighted and honoured when he asked her to join him on his road. But as was her way, she had let little of her feelings show. Dalan certainly hadn't guessed that, from the very start, she had been just as attracted to him as he had been to her.

The stillness that swept over her now was so familiar and so alluring. It reminded her of the countless days she had spent alone in the depths of the forest. The only words she ever spoke in that time were the supplications of the fire ritual and the occasional thought shared with her constant companion, a great black She-Raven.

As the memory of her winged friend came clearly to mind Sorcha stopped to lean against a stone that had been placed by the side of the road to mark the boundary of the territory of Dun Gur. Her hand rested against the spindly lines of Ogham script that adorned the edges of the lone sentinel.

Sorcha breathed deep and slow, hanging her head until her chin rested against her chest. Her eyes focused on her bare feet. Her toes were black with soot and they ached terribly. The Druid woman laughed at herself.

She'd been so eager to get away from the house of divination she'd neglected to put on her boots. And she'd been so numbed with tiredness she hadn't even noticed the sting of nettles around her ankles.

But she noticed it now. As she rubbed her itching skin Sorcha realised her whole body was black from the smoke of the little fire which it had been her duty to tend inside the stone hut.

She let herself slide down the stone until she rested on her knees in the grass at its foot. And there the Druid woman folded her hands in her lap and struggled not to lose consciousness completely. It was a brief battle, during which her head began to spin and her vision became blurred and distorted.

But the onset of slumber was banished abruptly with a sharp shock.

'You can't sleep here!' someone snapped aggressively.

Sorcha looked up, fighting to regain her senses as she sometimes did when woken from the depths of a dream. Her head lolled as she attempted to focus on a dark shape which sat on the grass before her. But her limbs were heavy and she had no power over them at all.

'Get up!' the stranger insisted in a rasping tone that grated at her. 'This is no place to be resting. Go home with you, you silly girl.'

Now if there was one thing that was going to rouse Sorcha from her drowsiness it was being called a silly girl. The Druid woman gathered all her strength and managed to sit up straight on her knees.

'I'm a grown woman,' she retorted. 'And I'm a Druid.'

All of a sudden her eyesight cleared and Sorcha squinted at the figure standing in front of her on the grass. And though she had a great deal of experience in these matters she jumped a little when she realised what manner of creature had been addressing her.

The Raven shuddered its wings and stepped back at her reaction.

'I'm not that ugly, am I?' the bird cawed.

'No indeed,' the Druid woman replied. She knew how touchy Ravens could be about their personal appearance. 'You're quite beautiful,' she added.

The bird cocked its head to one side to regard her more carefully. There's no creature quite so sensitive as a Raven that suspects insincerity.

'Don't use those honey words with me. I'm too smart to be fooled by empty-headed compliments.'

'Of course you are.'

'I know you, don't I?' the bird cackled.

'Do you?'

'Don't confound me! Do I know you or don't I?'

'My name is Sorcha.'

'So it is,' the Raven replied cautiously. 'And how do I know you?'

The Druid woman didn't have any idea but she was afraid to say so in case she offended the creature.

'I live in the forest,' she ventured. 'I tend the holy spring and the ritual fire.'

74

'You're a Druid.'

'I am.'

'You've already told me that!' The Raven hopped closer, becoming more confident by the moment. 'I'm not stupid, you know! I'm considered very wise among my own kind.'

'I'm sure you are,' Sorcha nodded.

But before the conversation could go any further the pair were interrupted by the flurry of wings and the arrival of another black bird.

'What's all the fuss?' the second Raven demanded to know. 'It's the middle of the night. Decent folk are perched in their trees asleep with their feathers over their faces.'

'I caught her loitering by our rock,' the first bird squawked.

'She's exhausted, you fool. She's just taking a rest on her way home. Let her be. Must you stick your beak into everyone's business?'

'How dare you speak to me like that, Crínóc?' the first bird screeched. 'I'm your mate. I deserve a little respect now and then, especially when we have visitors.'

'I don't have much respect for you when we're alone, Crínán. Why should I offer any when there are strangers about?'

'You're a bitter old bird,' Crínán hissed. 'I don't know why I stay with you.'

'Because I'm the only woman who'll put up with your complaining, your mindless cawing and your endless fascination with the doings of folk whose business isn't any of yours.'

'I don't trust the Gaedhals. They've been cutting down the forests all about. And I'll be cooked alive on a slow turning spit before I let them take my home away to be fashioned into a longboat.'

'She's not a Gaedhal.'

Crínán hopped a little closer and cocked his head to the other side to inspect Sorcha more closely. 'How do you know she's not?' he drawled, his tone full of suspicion.

'How many Gaedhals understand our speech?' his mate asked.

Crínán grunted or as close to the sound as any Raven can approximate. 'She looks like a Gaedhal to me.'

'Are you a Gaedhal?' Crínóc inquired, her tone full of exasperation.

Sorcha shook her head.

'There you are. She's a Fir-Bolg or a Danaan or some such. They're not enemies to the Raven kind.'

'I'm born of the Fir-Bolg of the Burren,' the Druid woman confirmed.

But Crínán was not convinced.

'Where did you learn the speech of the Raven kind?' he said slowly as if he believed she could only have a slim grasp of what he was saying.

'I shared my dwelling with one of your folk before she went off to answer her calling.'

'What was the name of this Raven?'

'I don't know. She never told me.'

Crínán jumped forward until his claw was resting menacingly on Sorcha's leg.

'I don't believe you!' he stated, squeezing his claws slightly in threat.

'But I know where to find her,' the Druid woman added quickly, fearing the situation was about to turn very nasty indeed.

'Where would that be?' Crínán pressed.

'At the court of the Morrigán.'

'What?' Crínóc stuttered, pushing her mate aside.

He stumbled backwards, spreading out his wings to keep his balance.

'Did you say the Morrigán?'

'Yes,' Sorcha nodded. 'My companion is serving at that high office these days. That's why she left me. She's now known as the Morrigán.'

Crínóc spun around to face her mate. 'You bloody fool!' she screamed. 'Now you've offended a friend of the Morrigán, the Queen of the Ravens. You'll surely be roasted for this. I wouldn't be surprised if the Dark One had you plucked to the pink and basted over a roaring fire till your beak buckles. You old meddler. What have I told you about interfering in the doings of others?'

Crínán shrank back, settling low on the grass with his legs hugged up around him in a pose most uncharacteristic of such birds. Then he started to shake. It was a few moments before Sorcha realised he was weeping quietly in distress.

Crínóc hopped closer to the Druid woman. 'I beg you, kind lady,' she began. 'Don't be too harsh on him. He didn't mean you any harm. I've warned him time and again. I told him he'd get his comeuppance one day. But he wouldn't listen to me. I implore you not to tell the queen about all this bother. We wouldn't want her getting upset, would we? Not over such a trivial matter.'

The Druid woman rubbed her eyes. She was beginning to wonder if this whole incident was a dream-vision brought on by her extreme tiredness. But as she focused again the female Raven was still standing before her with imploring eyes.

'Please, my lady,' Crínóc begged. 'He's only a stupid old bird with an overdeveloped sense of his own importance. He isn't worthy of the baby badgers I bring him for breakfast. He's nothing but a bundle of musty feathers waiting to be stitched up inside a pillow.'

Crínán stopped his sobbing and looked up. 'What did you say?' he asked indignantly, stretching his neck to hear her.

'If I were you I'd stick a talon in his tail feathers and leave

77

it at that,' his mate went on. 'He's simply not worth your worry. You couldn't even make a half-decent soup out of his scrawny old body.'

'That's enough!' Crínán snapped, jumping forward. 'Don't listen to her. She blames me for everything. She's upset because there aren't any fledglings in the nest for her to coo over.'

'There's a simple reason for that!' Crínóc countered. 'Eggs don't just appear of their own accord. I require a little help to produce any offspring, if you take my meaning. Your active participation would do for a start.'

'I've been too distracted to think about that sort of thing!' Crínán replied. 'I've been worried about these Gaedhals and their tree-cutting ways.'

'You're past it. It's time I flew off and feathered a younger bird's nest.'

'You wouldn't!'

'Well it looks like you're going to be taking a long hot bath in a cauldron of broth,' she snapped back. 'I might as well find myself a strong willing replacement who won't waste the midnight hours annoying passers-by. I can think of better things to be doing in the dark than chastising strangers.'

'The darker the better, where you're concerned,' Crínán quipped viciously under his breath.

It was at this moment the two birds noticed that Sorcha had lain back against the rock and fallen into a heavy snoring sleep.

'Now we're both in strife,' Crínán hummed with satisfaction, glad to have dragged his mate into his dilemma. 'You've bored her into unconsciousness with your prattle.'

'If anything happens to her we'll be in terrible trouble,' his wife agreed, her voice full of nervous remorse. 'We'll have to keep an eye on her all night. But I'll be hung by my feet in a smoke-house if you think I'm taking the first watch.'

With that she spread her wings and with a mighty flap flew back up to her nest.

'Wake me just before sunrise and I'll take over from you,' she called back.

Crínán whispered several unintelligible curses as he settled down in the grass beside Sorcha.

'We'll see if you can find a younger mate,' he mumbled, or as close to a mumble as a Raven can manage.

Chapter Six

om stood naked in front of his people as the chorus of praise died away. It was then Dalan noticed an old woman appear from the edge of the crowd. She leaned heavily on a stick of carved blackthorn and hobbled a little as she walked. Under her arm she carried a long bundle wrapped in rags of no better quality than her clothes.

The Brehon wondered how she could have possibly climbed over the low circle of stones without help. Then he frowned as he tried to recall the old woman's name. He was sure he knew her but he couldn't quite place where they might have met.

She made her way to stand in front of the young man who had been confirmed as the King of the Fir-Bolg. Then the old woman looked him up and down, pausing as she inspected the area around his thighs. Her gaze lingered just a little longer than was decent for one who had ostensibly interrupted a sacred ceremony. Then the old woman smiled broadly, looked Lom in the eyes and spoke.

'Danu blesses you,' she told him.

'Thank you, mother,' he stuttered in reply, nervous about her close scrutiny of his nakedness.

She smiled again, showing her blackened teeth. Everyone nearby flinched at the stench of her breath. But Lom was intrigued.

'I have a gift for you, my son,' she laughed. 'But you'll have to earn it.'

'What would you have me do?' he asked her.

The old woman broke into uproarious laughter as she cast a surprisingly girlish glance in his direction. Then she rushed forward to whisper something into his ear. The young man turned pale as he listened to her words.

When she had finished speaking she stood back and waited for his reply.

'Well?' she pressed after a few moments of uncomfortable silence. 'You must give me your answer.'

'What gift would you give me in return?' Lom inquired, obviously unsettled by her request.

'I have something here in this bundle of rags that would certainly be of interest to a king,' she replied.

'What's your name, old woman?' Dalan called out.

'That's my business.'

'You have no right to interfere with these proceedings unless you have a just cause to prevent them,' he advised.

'Who are you?' she spat.

'Dalan. I'm a Brehon judge.'

'And you've just taken the Bull Feast,' she cut in. 'You'd do well to offer a little respect to your elders.'

She lifted her palm to the Brehon. 'Isn't it time you were resting?'

Suddenly Dalan experienced a wave of exhaustion such as he'd never known before. His head grew heavy and his shoulders sagged with the weight of too many waking hours. He'd barely taken another breath before his knees began to buckle and he fell forward, crashing onto the soft grass like a lifeless sack of oats.

A few folk raced to his aid but the Brehon was unconscious by the time anyone reached him. Lom turned to the old woman and squinted, trying to discern whether she could have brought on this convulsion through some mastery of the Draoi craft.

'Kiss me,' she begged.

'I cannot.'

'If you do I will surely reward you in many ways. If you do not I will curse your reign.'

Lom turned his face away from her and cast his gaze at the ground. 'My reign will be the last of all the Fir-Bolg kings. Is that not curse enough?' he said. Then the chieftains clothed him in a fine plain red cloak. On his head was placed a diadem of fine silver and on his wrist were armbands of the same metal wrought into twisted shining serpents.

The old woman stepped back to the edge of the stone circle when she realised she was being ignored. But she didn't melt into the crowd.

'This is your last opportunity to do as I ask,' she called out.

But the young king was already surrounded by well-wishers and he couldn't hear her.

The old woman's face grew crimson with anger. She unwrapped the parcel under her arm and in a moment she was holding a bright bronze axe above her head.

'This is the ancient symbol of the kingship of the Fir-Bolg!' she shrieked. 'And you have forfeited the right to wield it.'

The crowd gasped as she rushed forward as if to strike the new king with the ceremonial weapon. A few paces from her target the old woman melted away into the air and the axe landed squarely at Lom's feet.

Despite his initial shock the young king quickly retrieved the weapon and held it aloft while everyone around him asked each other who the woman could have been.

An answer came to many of them immediately.

The air all around the new king began to sparkle, and as Lom stepped back to shade his eyes from the light, a beautiful woman appeared. She reached out to grasp the axe and wrestle it away from the young man.

'You will not wield this weapon,' she told him. 'It is not yours. You have transgressed the laws of sovereignty even before you have had a chance to call yourself King of the Fir-Bolg. Didn't anyone warn you what to expect of me?'

'Who are you?' the young king gasped.

The lady laughed out loud and let go her hold on the axe.

'You may keep the weapon. But I forbid you to use it. I curse it with bad luck. And may you suffer from my malediction until the day you surrender the axe to me of your own free will.'

She turned to face the assembly and held out the palms of her hands to them. Bright clear water began to flow from her wrists and fingertips to cascade in a shining waterfall that soaked the ground. Then just as suddenly as she had appeared the beautiful woman melted away as if she had never been. And no one who witnessed the sight ever doubted for a moment that they had been visited by the Goddess of the Flowing Waters, the Queen of Sovereignty.

Danu.

Her appearance left the assembly in a sombre mood. Most folk began dispersing to their lodgings, but Lom remained standing in the centre of the sacred circle, defiantly clutching the bronze axe of kingship.

Dalan was lifted up by the warrior chieftains to be carried back to Dun Gur and then the new King of the Fir-Bolg followed after with his head hung low. At length only Sárán remained behind as a chill breeze rose from the north.

In the moonlight the young Druid strode out across the middle of the circle, searching for any sign the old woman might have left behind for him. At last, frustrated, cold and hungry, he decided to return to Dun Gur and seek some refreshment.

He went to the lowest of the stones and swung a leg over.

As he did so a figure appeared before him. The woman put a firm hand on his shoulder and forced him to lean heavily back on the stone.

'Your brother has been cursed by Danu herself,' Isleen informed him, her intense green eyes sparkling in the moonlight.

Sárán offered no reply. He didn't want to believe that Lom had tainted his kingship before he'd even had a chance to prove his worth.

'There is a way we can undo the curse,' the Watcher went on. 'But it will take dedication from you and determination from your brother.'

'How will we win the favour of the goddess now that she has pronounced her curse?'

'I'll tell you in good time,' Isleen promised. 'But at this very moment you have a more pressing matter to deal with.'

'What matter?' Sárán frowned.

'I'll tell you when you've rested,' she assured him. 'Go straight to bed and we'll speak in the morning. You're going to need your rest if you're going to turn Danu's curse around.'

Then she took her hand from his shoulder and helped him cross the circle. Sárán was exhausted and all he could think of was the warm dry bed of straw where he could escape into slumber for a few hours.

'I'll speak with you in the morning,' he told her.

'Goodnight,' she offered, sending him on his way. 'And remember, you are to speak to no one until you've rested.'

Without another word he was gone, striding off over the fields to Dun Gur. By the stones Isleen quietly savoured the sweetness of her manipulative game before she too melted into the air just as the old woman had done.

And on the wind that had grown from the breeze a strange unearthly song was lifted up. It was the mournful low barking of many geese as they stirred in their slumber.

Mahon slipped around to the door of the storehouse as quietly as he could. His friend Iobhar the Gaedhal followed close behind, keeping a watch to the rear. No one noticed them in the shadows but their hearts were racing for fear of discovery.

Once inside the roundhouse they helped themselves to as much oat bread and dried beef as they could fit in their packs. But to their bitter disappointment there was no mead to be had anywhere. A stinking barrel of salt pork sat near the door but they didn't avail themselves of its contents as the stench was too great.

Once they had all the food they could carry they left the storehouse and made their way around to the main hall that had once belonged to Mahon's father, King Cecht. There were no guards waiting outside so the two of them took up positions at the door where the sentries would have usually placed themselves.

After a long while Iobhar nodded to his companion to indicate he thought it would be safe for them to enter the hall without arousing suspicion. Just at that moment two servants emerged from the building complaining about the way they'd been forced to answer to Aoife.

'She's not even a Gaedhal!' the first woman hissed.

'Bloody upstart!' the other agreed.

'I wish she'd never come to Dun Gur. I haven't had a moment to myself since she set foot in the fortress. Do this. Do that. Fetch the firewood. Bring us some mead. It never stops.'

'If she disappeared this night no one would mourn her,' the second woman nodded.

'Except poor Eber. He's so smitten by her he doesn't see

she's slowly taking over the running of the household. He should leave that in the hands of his own kinfolk.'

They passed on beyond earshot and Mahon threw a glance back to his friend to indicate it was time for them to make their move.

The two warriors drew the swords they'd lifted from the two guards at the causeway and, with Mahon in the lead they entered the hall. The first thing they noticed as they passed under the lintel was that the building was brightly lit by many candles. An inviting fire was crackling away in the central hearth.

There were no other servants present. But Iobhar immediately spotted two figures seated at a low bench facing the flames. Neither stirred so it was certain they hadn't noticed the intrusion. The two warriors crept closer in the shadows to hear what was being said. And it was immediately apparent that Eber was discussing his worries with Aoife.

'If the Fir-Bolg are armed within a few days we'll be able to march north and take what food we need from the land,' the king was telling her. 'But I can't feed this force much longer than that. The land all about is depleted of game and the grain stores are almost empty.'

'Summon Lom to speak with you,' she suggested. 'Distribute whatever iron weapons are available and send my brother and his men off to fend for themselves near the border with the north. Send your warriors to accompany them. That will ease the burden on the food stores.'

Eber sighed, seeing the sense in what she suggested.

'Put every able-bodied smith you have to work,' she went on. 'You mustn't waste a moment. If your force isn't ready in a week there's a real danger that Éremon will strike first. Have you sent out scouts?'

The king nodded. 'Goll mac Morna and his Fian band are roaming the north, causing havoc where they can and keeping an eye on my brother's preparations.'

'Send word to him,' Aoife suggested. 'He must bring all the plundered weapons he has gathered back to the border to meet our warriors. That will save the blacksmiths much toil and ensure we can launch our attack as soon as possible.'

'How Éremon will be rankled when he finds out he's been defeated with his own war-gear!' Eber exclaimed, seeing the worth of her suggestion.

The king shook his head in admiration. 'You were born to the warrior path. You think just like a seasoned war-leader. Where did you learn to read a situation with such clarity?'

'My father fought the Danaans all his life. I merely observed him at his work. And perhaps it's in my blood to be a fighter.'

'You're certainly no Druid,' Eber laughed. 'We'll be a good partnership. I promise I'll listen to your advice and heed your opinion in everything.'

'And I promise to train in the warrior path to the best of my ability so that together we may ensure the stability and strength of our reign.'

Mahon squatted in the shadows, hardly believing what he was hearing. He was hurt that Aoife had so obviously committed herself to this man and so easily abandoned all thoughts of him. For a brief second he considered rushing forward to grab her and beg her to come with him.

But then he realised there was no sense in such an action. She had found her calling. Aoife was destined to be Queen of the Gaedhals. And it seemed she would be a fine ruler. It would be foolish to force her to leave if it was not her wish.

So much had changed in the few short weeks since he'd been banished from Dun Aillil at the order of her father. And he was beginning to sense that she was truly lost to him. His heart sank and he turned to face Iobhar.

The Gaedhal was kneeling close by now. 'What are you

doing?' he whispered urgently. 'We can't stay here long. It's too dangerous. Let's get moving.'

'I've decided not to bring Aoife with us,' Mahon sighed.

'What?' his friend exclaimed in surprise. 'We've risked our lives to get past the main gate and now we're just going to leave her behind?'

'She's happy here.'

'She's playing a game with Eber to make him think she's his willing wife. But Aoife would never barter her freedom with any man. We must rescue her. She's virtually a prisoner here.'

Mahon considered his friend's words for a second but shook his head. 'I don't believe you're right,' he shrugged.

But Iobhar was not going to be so easily put off. He grabbed his companion's sleeve. 'You can't abandon her. We might be her last hope of escape.'

'It's finished!' Mahon hissed. 'Let's go before we're discovered.'

At that moment a servant entered the hall carrying a large ceramic jar. In the shadows he walked straight into the pair, almost spilling the precious contents of the jar. Iobhar managed to catch the man before he fell and save the jar.

But the servant's surprise gave way immediately to terror at the sight of two unknown warriors skulking in the king's hall with drawn swords. He shrieked. Mahon punched at him instinctively and the servant reeled back, sprawling onto the floor.

In an instant Eber Finn was on his feet searching for his own blade. Aoife retreated to the far side of the fire.

'What's the meaning of this?' he bellowed. 'What are you two warriors doing here in my chamber? I didn't summon you. Did my brother send you to put an end to my life?'

The king found his blade lying by the seat. He lifted it up and levelled it at the strangers.

'Show me your faces!' he demanded.

Mahon stepped forward into the light and drew the cloak from his face. Aoife gasped when she recognised him.

'I'm not one of your warriors,' the Danaan declared.

Eber Finn squinted. 'I know you,' he said, struggling to recall where he'd met this man.

Then the memory of the night at Dun Aillil came to him and he drew a deep breath full of dread. This young man had come to his lodgings to beg his help. Mahon had intended to steal Aoife away from her father. He had no idea Eber intended to marry her himself.

'What are you doing here in my hall, armed as if for war? Have you come to murder me? Are you in league with my brother?'

'No. I came here to rescue Aoife.'

At that the young woman let her temper take her. She stormed around to where the Danaan stood and slapped him hard across the cheek, knocking the borrowed helm from his head.

'I don't want to be rescued!' she shrieked. 'Least of all by you! I'm to be married to Eber Finn. I'll be Queen of the Gaedhals. I'm not interested in you or your foolish ways. I'm tired of you.'

Eber frowned, remembering that Mahon had wanted to rescue her from Dun Aillil. There was obviously a story here he'd not been told.

'Is this man your lover?' the king inquired calmly, voicing his deepest suspicions.

'I called him that once,' Aoife replied. 'But the silly infatuations of a girl are no match for the love of a woman. And the lazy inattentive ways of a boy don't compare to the respect of a king.'

'Why didn't you tell me about him?' Eber asked with a touch of jealousy in his voice.

'Because he is not important.'

Mahon lowered his eyes, hurt beyond words. He shuffled his feet, making ready to leave.

'I won't disturb you any further,' he assured them as he leaned down to pick up the guardsman's helm. 'I was wrong to have come here. I'm sorry. We'll be going on our way.'

'Going on your way?' the king snapped. 'You've violated the privacy of my hall and the laws of hospitality by bearing blades in this chamber. Throw down your weapons and I'll see the Brehons judge you for your foolishness.'

'We're outlaws already,' Iobhar reminded Mahon urgently. 'If we give in, Eber has no obligation to summon the Brehons. By law he can deal with us in whatever way he wishes. And I'll never trust his word again after the way he betrayed us at Dun Aillil.'

'How were you betrayed?' Aoife cut in.

'Eber promised us safe passage out of the fort,' Mahon explained. 'He told us he would personally arrange our escape. But he returned with armed sentries.'

'Then he claimed that a knife he'd given to Mahon was stolen,' Iobhar went on. 'That's why your father banished us.'

'Why would you need safe passage to leave Dun Aillil?' scoffed the young woman.

'Mahon was hoping to spirit you away from the fort so that you could live your life without the Druid vows hanging over your head,' Iobhar replied.

'Is this true?' she shot back at the Danaan.

Mahon nodded but he did not lift his eyes from the floor.

Aoife came around to stand beside Eber. 'Let them go,' she said softly. 'They've done no harm. They're misguided boys who haven't considered the repercussions of their actions.'

'They've broken the law and trespassed in my hall,' Eber answered coldly. 'They must be punished. Indeed, I don't see why they shouldn't forfeit their lives to me for this crime.'

'I have taken the Quicken Brew,' Mahon replied defiantly. 'My life cannot be taken.'

'Then I shall seize your companion and deal with him. He's a traitor to his people and an outlaw.'

The Danaan raised his sword and levelled it at the king. 'I can't allow that. Iobhar came here because of his loyalty to me. I won't see him punished on my behalf.'

'Very well,' Eber shrugged. 'You leave me no option but to act.'

With that the king walked calmly forward until the point of Mahon's blade was pressing into his chest. He waited there a few moments then smiled when he realised the Danaan had no intention of taking advantage of the situation.

'Aren't you going to strike me down?' he asked, making no move to use his own sword in any way.

'No.'

'Then I promise you the day will come when you'll wish you had.' Eber brushed past the Danaan and went to the door. In a loud commanding voice he called out, 'Guards! There are intruders in the hall. Call the sentries.'

Mahon glanced at Aoife, saw the fear in her eyes and realised she was frightened for his safety. It was only a vague glimmer of love but it was enough to spur him into action.

The young Danaan warrior stepped up behind Eber, grabbing him by the collar of his tunic. But the king was also a warrior and he deftly swung an elbow back to thump Mahon in the chest. The blow was powerful enough to push the Danaan backwards and make him lose his grip. In a flash the two rivals had lifted their swords against one another. Eber laughed as he lunged at his opponent. The blades locked in a sickening clash of steel.

Iobhar went to the door to see whether any guards had answered the summons. He was certain the hall would be swarming with warriors at any moment. He turned to Aoife.

'I know you hold me in contempt,' he whispered. 'But you once told me you cared for me and made me promise to take you away from the life of a Druid —'

'Eber will have you put to death if you tarry here,' she interrupted.

'Then come with us as far as the gate to ensure I am not taken.'

Aoife hesitated for a moment then nodded before she rushed forward to stand between Eber and Mahon. Her shouts prompted them both to lower their weapons.

'He cannot be harmed by your blade,' she reminded the king. 'The Quicken Brew protects him. Put down your sword and let him be. I couldn't bear to see you wounded.'

'Did you hear that?' the king asked Mahon. 'She has taken a decision to stand by me. You're a fool for thinking she'd go with you.'

The Danaan looked into Aoife's eyes, pleading for a sign that she still held him in some regard. But her face was cold and expressionless.

'I beg you to let them go free,' she said to Eber.

'They will not walk from this fortress,' was his reply.

Aoife turned to look Mahon in the eye. 'Then I'll go with you to the gate to protect Iobhar from the king's revenge.'

'How dare you defy me?' Eber grunted.

'They've done no harm,' the young woman replied.

Eber Finn snarled and brushed the woman aside with contempt. But as he did so Mahon put a hand to the king's chest and shoved him back towards the wall. The ruler of the Gaedhals knocked his head hard against the doorpost and slid silently to the floor. Iobhar's jaw dropped in amazement.

'He'll have me flayed for this,' the warrior stammered.

In the next instant Mahon sheathed his sword, grabbed Aoife by the arm and stepped over the unconscious king.

Iobhar was by his side in an instant, still carrying the heavy sealed jar he'd taken from the servant. Then, with the young woman offering no resistance, the three of them were off into the night, skirting around the buildings in an attempt to stay concealed from the guards.

They had not gone far when the fortress erupted with the sound of horns blowing and warriors assembling. There were torches everywhere and news of the bold Danaan who'd assaulted the king and kidnapped the queen passed swifter than the wind.

But Mahon knew his way around this fortress. He'd grown up here in the days before it was ceded to the Gaedhals. In a short while they'd made their way to the back of the kitchens where few folk ever strayed. Here Mahon expected to find a gate in the walls where all the discarded rubbish was dumped down the slopes of the island and into the lough. And sure enough the gate was still there but it was guarded by two tall warriors with grim expressions and heavy swords.

Two cooks were in the process of hauling on a rope to raise the portcullis so they could dump a basket full of refuse. When they'd done that they left the gate open and returned to the kitchen.

Mahon crouched by the kitchen wall while he decided what to do next.

'We don't have much time,' he noted. 'The cooks will be back with another load soon and then the portcullis will be shut again. We have to make our move now.'

'We'll never get past the guards,' Iobhar told his friend. 'They're huge.'

'You won't get away,' Aoife agreed. 'It's better to give up now. I'll plead for you both. I promise Iobhar won't be murdered.'

'It's too late for that now,' the Gaedhal told her flatly. 'Eber isn't a forgiving man. He'll make sure I suffer for my crime.'

'There's no other way out of Dun Gur,' Mahon cut in. 'We'll

have to take the two guards on. But we'll need your help, Aoife.'

'I can't.'

Her eyes darted this way and that. She knew Iobhar would be punished for his rebellious actions.

The Danaan put his head in his hands for a few breaths then suddenly stood up, sweeping the young woman into his arms as he rose. The move was so unexpected she didn't have a chance to struggle, and by the time she realised what was happening it was too late.

Mahon strode across the open ground between the kitchen and the gate, Aoife in his arms and Iobhar following up behind still clutching the jar.

'I have an injured woman here!' he called out to the sentries. 'The renegades knocked her down as they were escaping.'

The two warriors raised their swords and approached warily, sensing something was amiss. But before they could investigate, Mahon threw Aoife down upon the ground, drew his own sword and held it out in front of him in threat.

Then Iobhar rushed up and swung the heavy jar at the sentries. It hit one of them square on the side of the head with a crunch. He fell to the ground senseless without ever having had the chance to put up any kind of a fight.

His comrade immediately brought his blade around in an attempt to strike at Iobhar's head. The Gaedhal managed to lift the jar just high enough to parry the blow but the ceramic jug shattered under the impact.

Both men were showered with a sweet sticky liquid that stung their eyes. This temporary blindness gave Mahon the opportunity to punch the guard hard in the jaw. The warrior fell backwards through the gate and disappeared into the darkness below without a word.

'That jar was full of mead!' Iobhar moaned as he licked his fingers. 'It was probably the only strong drink in the fortress and I wasted it on a sentry.'

'It saved your life,' Mahon shot back. 'And it's probably the first time you've wielded the mead jar all night and left the headache for another man to bear.'

As he spoke he went over to the gate and peered through the opening. It was large enough for two men to squeeze through side by side.

'You go first,' he told Aoife.

'I'm not going anywhere,' she spat. 'I'm to be wed with Eber Finn and you can't do anything about it. I've come this far with you because I didn't want to see Iobhar punished. Now you are on your own. My duty lies here.'

'You're coming with us,' Mahon yelled, losing his temper. 'If we don't make a good escape I'll need something to bargain with. Like you, I won't see Iobhar punished for the whims of my foolish heart.'

With that he lifted her up under the arms and shoved her through the opening. The young woman screamed with rage as she slid through and down onto the slopes below, and Mahon instantly regretted his rough treatment of her.

In the darkness he couldn't see whether she'd fared well on the slide down but he had no time to consider that now. Iobhar was slipping through the gate just as more warriors arrived, led by Eber Finn with a drawn sword and a fire in his eyes.

'Stop!' the king bawled with rage.

Mahon patted his friend on the head to push him through, then jumped into the gap. With his razor-sharp blade he sliced the supporting rope holding the portcullis open. It shuddered and fell as he disappeared through the gate.

Outside the walls Mahon clung to the little wooden portcullis as it closed behind him. He was certain the Gaedhals would not be able to raise it again without great effort. Satisfied, he hung on for a few breaths longer before he let go his hold and slid down the steep slope towards the lough.

Chapter Seven

oll mac Morna was no fool. He'd fought many battles for his king and kin and he'd always managed to come through more or less unscathed. He listened to his instincts, followed his heart and disregarded the opinions of those he considered his inferiors.

That is why the war-leader set camp fires on top of the round hill where he'd arranged to meet King Éremon but stationed his warrior Fian all around in the underbrush to bide their time. He knew the northern king would come as soon as he received the summons.

Éremon, like his younger brother Eber, was easily roused to rage. The sons of Míl were renowned for their quick tempers. He certainly wouldn't wait three days before coming to seek revenge for the raid. So Goll had resolved to be well prepared.

The war-leader had settled himself down in the midst of the prickly blackberry bushes by the side of the road which led north. Even on this dark night, from this position he would be able to see anyone approaching the ancient ruined hill fort. And he could be well enough concealed that he'd be in no danger should the northerners be ready for a fight.

His plan was a simple one. He'd decided to lure the northern king to this remote spot and dispose of him as quickly and efficiently as possible. He certainly had no intention of wasting words with Éremon.

The time for talking was past. In this part of the country he was an outlaw beyond hope of any negotiated settlement. No words would win him any advantage.

The war-leader reasoned to himself that if he could manage to kill Éremon he would be considered a hero among his own people of the south. It would not be unreasonable for him to expect that Eber should declare him his heir, since the king had no blood heir to assume the position.

Once he was affirmed as heir to the throne of the south, it would only take Eber's death to ensure Goll was installed as king. With Éremon dead, the King of the South would also effectively be the King of all Eirinn. The high-king.

It was an ambition he'd harboured ever since the battle of Sliabh Mis when he'd watched the Danaans retreat into the strange misty Otherworld they'd created for themselves. He'd never before witnessed such an act of cowardice. As he'd watched the Danaan sorcerers disappear he'd been filled with hope that his own dreams might one day become reality. He'd learned there was no enemy, however mighty, that couldn't be defeated.

The Danaans had held this island for generations. They'd fought off other invaders and won, time after time. In his eyes all it had taken was Eber's determination to bring about their defeat. Goll knew he was more than capable of the same resolve.

As he lay on his stomach with his breacan cloak spread out beneath him on the cold ground, the war-leader let his mind wander to thoughts of the future. He decided he would be a just ruler and a fair-minded king. There'd be no more war under King Goll of the Gaedhals, he told himself proudly.

No more war on this island in any case. He'd heard tell of a land called Alban which lay to the east of Eirinn. It was the perfect place for his warriors to hone their skills and vent their frustration far from his court and his peace-loving subjects.

At the same time Goll decided he would make some major changes to the way the land was governed. He couldn't see why the king had to rely on a Druid adviser in matters of law and strategy. There were no Gaedhals left to fill this post since the death of Máel Máedóc. It was wrong, he told himself, that Dalan, a Fir-Bolg, should be advising Eber Finn. Since there were no Gaedhals who could fulfil the duties of adviser, he would abolish the position altogether.

As soon as Goll made this decision he realised he would be granting himself more freedom than any other ruler had ever known. Without a Druid breathing down his back he'd be able to do anything he wished, make any changes that took his fancy and eliminate any opponent who criticised him.

The war-leader smiled to himself, secure in the knowledge that all this would come to pass. And he imagined the songs future generations would sing about him, praising his wisdom, his courage, and above all, his sharp instincts.

It was these instincts that wakened him from his reverie. There was something in the air that alerted him to danger. In a flash he sat up to get a better look at the road. But nothing stirred along its length. Then he rolled onto his side and pressed his ear to the earth but could not discern the telltale rhythm of approaching horses.

He sat up again, his cloak now entangled in the blackberry thorns. There was no sign of movement anywhere along the road. Yet he was particularly uneasy. Slowly, carefully, he drew his sword from the sheath at his side.

The air was cold and the dawn only a few hours off. There were no clouds in the sky but the sparkling stars didn't cheer him. Something was amiss. He could feel it in his bones.

Goll noticed his hand trembling slightly, then he heard a

noise behind him. He turned slowly so as not to attract attention to his hiding place. A figure was making its way through the underbrush. At the edge of the blackberry stand the warrior halted and then the war-leader heard the low cry of an owl.

Without hesitation he cupped his hands to his mouth and answered the call. Then the warrior moved closer, trying to find a path through the tangled mire of thorns. Goll relaxed a little, secure in the knowledge that this was one of his own Fian scouts.

It took Mughain a long while to find him and he didn't offer her any guidance. But when she finally lay down beside him, her face scratched and her breacan torn, he greeted her warmly.

'I'm glad of your company, sister,' he offered.

'I'm not your bloody sister,' she snapped back under her breath. 'We've bedded together too often to make any pretence at that kind of relationship.'

Her tone was harsher than usual so Goll decided to be gentle with her. The strain of all this watch-keeping was clearly beginning to tell.

'How goes the night?' he asked in a soothing voice.

'I'm tired, hungry and cold,' she retorted. 'And there's no sign north or south.'

'How are the rest of the Fian getting on?'

'They're mostly grumbling. Why can't we sit close by the fires up amongst the ruins at the top of the hill?'

'Because that's where Éremon will be expecting us to be.'

'He's not going to come tonight.'

Goll's face contorted into a knowing smile. Then he reached out to pick a ripe blackberry. He chewed on the sweet morsel before he went on.

'If I know the King of the North, he'll be here as soon as he gets wind of our raid. He's not the sort to waste a moment when his people are being threatened or his pride challenged. And I expect he'll be ready for a fight.'

'But you told the boy you wanted to talk with the king!'

'Éremon's no talker. His elder brother, the bard Amergin, might end up mediating but the king will come in force hoping to teach us a lesson.'

'We'll never hold them if they outnumber us. We're only two dozen!'

'Don't worry. I intend to have a firm grip on the kingship of this land as soon as I've dealt with Éremon. So far my good fortune has led me on and I expect it will continue to do so. I'm destined for the high-kingship.'

Mughain frowned as he handed her a blackberry. She could see the danger clearly. And she knew Goll's arrogance was legendary. But she trusted her war-leader. She asked her question before she put the succulent purple fruit into her mouth.

'What's your plan?'

'To dispatch Éremon as quickly as possible, then fetch all the Fian of the South. While the north is still choosing a replacement we'll scatter their warriors before us like snowflakes in a strong wind.'

'Then Eber will claim the high-kingship.'

'For a while,' Goll nodded. 'But the days of the sons of Míl are numbered. They've had their chance at ruling this land and they've not done a very good job of it. The day will come when I claim the leadership of our people.'

'You have the makings of a king,' Mughain agreed. 'May I live to see it.'

'If you do you'll be my queen,' the war-leader told her with a sparkle in his eyes. 'You've stood beside me through all the trials of the last few months and I've come to respect your dedication to me. When I am proclaimed king you'll stand beside me again and share the honour.'

'I don't want to be left at home to run your household

while you go on a circuit of the country bedding every country lass who takes your eye.'

'Then you shall come with me.'

That comment calmed Mughain and her face softened a little. 'May I stay here with you a while?' she asked.

'You must be keen if you'd willingly roll around in the blackberry thorns with me. And who will keep watch for you while we indulge ourselves?'

'Éremon won't come tonight,' she countered. 'Can't we relax just for one evening?'

'The Fian never rest until they're laid in the grave. And rulers often don't rest until long after their deaths. So don't expect life will be getting any easier once we have the kingship in our grasp.'

'The King of the North is far away yet,' Mughain pleaded. 'Just give me one night.'

But her plea was interrupted by a distant trumpet call. Both of them gasped and dropped flat on the ground to listen carefully. Three longs blasts rang out through the night, shattering any hope of peace.

'Who has the signal horn?' Goll demanded.

'I do,' Mughain replied, holding the bronze instrument up to show him. 'I brought it with me into the blackberry briar.'

Goll's face paled. 'Éremon has come.'

The war-leader sat up cautiously, trying discern where the sound had originated. Another series of blasts rang out and he soon realised the trumpeter was on top of the hill, standing amongst the ruins.

'Éremon is more stealthy than I imagined,' Goll admitted with just the merest hint of a quiver in his voice. But Mughain could not tell whether it was fear or disappointment that caused it. The war-leader was adept at concealing his thoughts and feelings. 'He's managed to make his way past our people without raising the alarm,' he added expressionlessly.

Then a voice rang out in the cold air. 'Éremon, King of the North and High-King of all Eirinn, summons Goll mac Morna to the place of meeting. Your fires are lit but they are unattended. Come forth now or I will send my warriors down to seek you out. And they won't be in the mood to parley, I can assure you.'

'How many are you?' Goll called back.

'As many as are the stars in the night sky. You are trapped. Lay down your weapons and come forth into the firelight. If you do as I command I may show you mercy.'

The war-leader cursed under his breath as he realised he'd been outmanoeuvred.

'I won't come to talk with you unless I have a guarantee of safe conduct.'

'I hold twenty-two of your Fian here at the top of this hill,' Éremon replied. 'I know where you are hiding amongst those blackberries. If you don't come forth immediately, I'll slit the throat of one warrior at a time until they're all gone. And then I'll come for you.'

'I wish to speak with you and offer terms,' Goll replied, desperately trying to cover the nervousness in his voice.

'Come to the top of the hill and let me see your face,' Éremon replied. 'I'll hear your terms when I can look into your eyes.'

Goll mac Morna shook his head, hardly believing that the northern king could have slipped past his sentries and captured his entire band. He turned to Mughain.

'You slip away while I go up to meet Éremon. Make your way back to Dun Gur. Find Eber and report what has happened.'

But Mughain didn't even have a chance to protest before the king's voice rang out again. 'Bring the woman with you. She won't escape and it'll be the worse for her if she tries.'

Goll cursed under his breath again but he knew he had no

choice. He might have been a tough, ruthless, scheming man but he would never put the lives of his Fian at risk in return for his own safety.

'I'll come!' he bellowed.

'We'll go together,' Mughain told him. 'There may yet be a way we can salvage this situation.'

With a nod the war-leader crawled forward through the thorns until he was clear. Then he stood up, helped his companion to her feet and together they set off through the stream towards the top of the hill.

As Mahon slid down the slope towards the lough in the dark he tried to make out where the steep path ended. He rolled over bumps and protruding clumps of grass and was covered in filth before he landed head-first and hard at the bottom in the soft slushy mud.

He lay on his stomach to catch his breath before dragging himself out of the congealing slime and kitchen leavings that had accumulated by the edge of the lough. When he found his feet he was confronted by the sight of his two companions covered in mud and scowling.

By his side lay the motionless body of the Gaedhal guard face down in the sludge.

'He must have been unconscious when he landed,' Iobhar noted. 'He drowned.'

Mahon looked up at the young woman. 'Are you hurt?'

'How dare you push me around like that?' Aoife growled from the back of her throat.

'I have to commend you. That was a bloody brilliant escape route,' Iobhar sputtered, wiping the mud from his face.

A stray pig snorted nearby. The animal made its way over

to where the Gaedhal was standing then unceremoniously knocked him off his feet. It snuffled about in the mud for scraps by his head then moved on.

When it came close to Aoife she kicked the poor beast and it squealed like a little child.

'Leave her alone,' Mahon objected. 'This is none of her doing.'

'Wait till I get hold of you, you bastard,' the young woman shrieked, pulling clumps of filth from her hair.

She lunged forward to grab at the warrior's tunic but slipped her footing and fell forward into the mud. In an instant the pig was snuffling around her hair. Aoife fought it off for a moment but then her strength failed and she lay down with her hands over her head, screaming at the animal to leave her alone.

High above at the fortress wall a warrior stood looking down at them.

'You won't get far!' Eber yelled. 'I'll hunt you down and you'll pay dearly for this breach of custom.'

Mahon looked up but offered no answer. He was fairly certain the king couldn't see them in the dark and he was reluctant to give away their position.

'By the time you swim across the lough my Fian will be waiting on the other side.'

Mahon looked out across the silvery moonlit mud and realised the king was probably right. But the Danaan was not one to give in easily. Before Aoife had a chance to protest he grabbed her by the arm and began dragging her out across the mud where once there had been a shining expanse of water.

Iobhar took a few moments to realise what was happening but he too was soon following after them. He'd only gone a few paces, however, when a thought struck him. He turned around, grabbed the pig under his arm and, with the poor creature squealing for all it was worth, set off to catch up to the others.

They were halfway across the mud when they saw in the distance the first torches emerging from the fortress at the rock ford. And it was then Mahon knew they had a chance to escape. He redoubled his efforts to reach the other side and thanked Danu that Aoife didn't have the strength to struggle against him.

By the time they came to the bank at the far side of the lough the torches were still a long way off. Mahon motioned to Iobhar to make for the woods nearby, but it took a great effort and a long while before Aoife and the pig were lifted up the steep bank.

The three of them made it to the thick cover of the woods in enough time to conceal themselves. But the pig was still screaming and threatened to give them away.

'Break its neck!' Mahon hissed.

Iobhar grasped the animal roughly around the jaw and prepared to twist its head. But the pig cried out with a higher-pitched cry that sounded like a frightened child. The Gaedhal's heart softened and he forced its mouth shut.

The pig grumbled a little more, then settled as the warrior stroked the top of her nose to calm her. As if by some miracle his touch relaxed the creature completely and in moments she was fast asleep in his arms.

Aoife had to stifle a laugh when she saw the pig slumbering happily. 'If only you'd charmed me like that,' she gasped mirthfully. 'I would have been as happy as that pig in your arms.'

'I've always had a way with animals,' he snapped back.

'Are you sure you haven't simply met your match?' she chided.

'Silence!' Mahon whispered hoarsely. 'This isn't a bloody game! If we're captured, Iobhar could lose his life. Do you want to be responsible for another death?'

'Another?' she frowned.

'How easily you've forgotten my poor brother Fearna,' Mahon shot back.

'I hadn't forgotten him.'

'Then hold your tongue or you'll have another death on your conscience.'

Aoife lowered her eyes at the reprimand, then lay flat and silent on the ground to wait until the danger had passed.

In the dark the king's warriors misjudged the place where the fugitives had emerged from the muddy lake. They didn't stop when they came to the woods but carried on further round the shoreline. Soon the torchbearer was off in the distance searching the darkness.

Just as he was beginning to think they'd eluded capture, Mahon heard a sound so dreadful it sent shivers through his body. At the ford there were more torches and in the orange light he could plainly see the distorted shadowy forms of huge hunting dogs. Their yelping cries carried across the distance to where the fugitives were hiding and set all three hearts to racing.

'We're going to have to make a run for it through the woods,' the Danaan told his companions. Then he turned to Aoife. 'If you won't come willingly we'll leave you. I haven't the strength to drag you against your will. Nor do I have the spirit to take you anywhere you would not go.'

Aoife looked him in the eye and glimpsed something of the Mahon she had been attracted to when they'd first met. This was the adventurous Mahon, the warrior, the risk-taker who'd once filled her life with laughter.

'If Eber catches you, you'll need me as a hostage to bargain for Iobhar's life.'

'That's true enough.'

'Where are you heading?' she asked him.

'North,' the Danaan replied. 'In the kingdom of Éremon my friend Iobhar will surely be given sanctuary. It's my duty to see that he comes to no harm. He offered to help me and I've put his life in danger. I won't stand by and see him come to any harm.'

'And where will you go after that?'

Mahon shrugged. 'I'd be surprised if my father, King Cecht, would have anything to do with me after this,' he sighed. 'And besides, I'm sure I wouldn't want to withdraw into the Otherworld in any case. So I can't say where I'll be headed. All I know is that I'll be free of all the rules that have dogged me throughout my life.'

She nodded and lowered her eyes. It was as if an enchantment were lifting from her and she could see her life in a new light.

'You'd be welcome to come with me,' he offered. 'If you're not tempted by the life of a queen at court.'

'There are so many rules at court. And if I'm honest with myself, the Gaedhals have a love of order that turns my stomach.'

'You might be their queen for twenty seasons before your husband became too old to rule,' Mahon added.

'And what would I do with an old man for my husband?' she laughed. 'You know well enough that I'd come looking for you in time.'

'Then why wait? Come with me now.'

'We shall see. For the moment I'll go with you to the border to ensure Iobhar is safe. I'll make my decision then.'

Mahon shrugged, conceding she had a right to make up her mind in her own time.

'Would you still have me after all the trouble I've caused?' Aoife asked.

The Danaan laughed lowly and touched the young woman on the arm with a tenderness that brought a tingling to her skin. Before another breath had passed her lips she began sobbing quietly.

'I've been so selfish, Mahon,' she cried, realising that she had endangered Iobhar's life and caused Mahon pain through her stubbornness. 'Can you ever forgive me?'

'If we don't get a move on *I* won't forgive you,' Iobhar cut in. 'Those dogs mean to find us. And I'd much rather discuss these matters by a fireside in the north.'

He stood up, slung the sleeping pig over his shoulder and set off through the tangled underbrush.

Chapter Eight

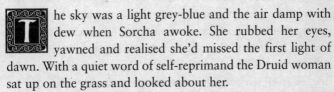he sky was a light grey-blue and the air damp with dew when Sorcha awoke. She rubbed her eyes, yawned and realised she'd missed the first light of dawn. With a quiet word of self-reprimand the Druid woman sat up on the grass and looked about her.

Then she leaned forward in a fit of coughing that cleared her lungs of soot. A great knot of phlegm rose in her throat and she spat it out onto the grass in front of her.

'Watch where you're spitting!' a crackling voice demanded. 'I don't want to be covered in your foulness.'

Sorcha shook her head as she focused on the Raven who stood only a few paces away.

'I'm very sorry,' she said with genuine remorse. 'I wasn't aware you were still here.'

'Wasn't aware?' the Raven shrieked in outrage. 'Some Druid you've turned out to be. I thought the whole point of training at the holy orders was to raise your awareness of the world!'

'I was asleep,' she protested.

'That's no excuse. A real Druid is just as awake to the Earth when they're slumbering as when their eyes are wide open. And anyway, would you sit up in your own bed and spit like that across the covers?'

The bird didn't wait for a reply. 'Of course you wouldn't. So why evacuate your mucky chest fluids all over my lawn? You Gaedhals have no respect for anything.'

'I'm not a Gaedhal,' Sorcha cut in. 'I'm a Fir-Bolg of the Burren.'

The bird hopped closer and put a beady little dark eye close to her face.

'So you say,' he nodded. 'But I still have my doubts. You're all tree-cutters and bough-splitters as far as I'm concerned.'

He stepped back and fluttered his wings. 'What were you doing wandering about at night in my woods? Have you come to scout out some timber for your new house? Or perhaps you think my grove would make fine axe handles so you can go around the countryside cutting down every living splinter. Boats. That's what it is, isn't it? You want to build a fine fleet of ships. All your people are possessed by an overwhelming greed that is only matched by the destructive nature of your souls.'

High above in the treetop there was a loud screech.

'Husband!' the other bird called. 'Are you talking to someone?'

Crínán took two sharp steps back. 'The Gaedhal is awake,' he called back tentatively to his wife.

'Then I'll come down,' Crínóc told him.

'I'm not a Gaedhal,' Sorcha protested, rolling her eyes in exasperation.

The Raven hopped forward again and spoke in a low tone so that only the Druid woman would hear him. 'You may have put the fear of the Morrigán into my old woman,' he warned. 'But I'm onto your game. I'm watching every move you make. I've been standing by you all night. I can see through your little ruse. You're no Druid woman. And you're no friend to the Dark One either. You're a Gaedhal come to steal away my tree. Well I won't have it! Do you understand?'

Sorcha sighed, realising there was no sense in arguing with this bird. Then she sat on her knees as the second Raven landed nearby.

'Did you sleep well, my dear?' Crínóc asked her politely.

'Yes, thank you.'

'And what has my meddling husband been whispering about?'

Sorcha opened her mouth to answer but thought better of it. The Raven-wife read the hesitation in the Druid woman's face well and knew she'd guessed right. In a second she'd turned on her husband, flapping her wings wildly at him to drive him off.

'I've had enough of you!' she screamed. 'Why can't you let sleeping Druids lie? Do you know what sort of trouble we could get into if this gracious lady chose to take her case to the Morrigán?'

'She's no Druid,' Crínán objected. 'She's a Gaedhal.'

Crínóc turned around to face the Druid woman. 'Forgive him,' she pleaded. 'Even when he was a young bird his brain was no bigger than a walnut. Now the nut has shrivelled and it's not worth the cracking.'

'I'm tired of your insults!' Crínán spat. 'I won't share that nest with you again.'

'Then you'll be sitting out on a limb by yourself,' his wife cawed back at him. 'I built that bloody nest and I'm not about to give it over to a decrepit, scatterbrained old dust-bucket who is only interested in trees!'

Sorcha rolled her eyes and stood up. She didn't want to seem impolite but she was anxious to get back to Dun Gur to see to Dalan. Her back ached from sleeping propped against the stone. Her bare feet were deathly cold from the night air and the chilly dew.

No sooner had she arisen than Crínóc spun around, distracted from the argument with her husband.

'You won't mention any of this to the Morrigán, will you?' she begged. 'We're both good-hearted birds really. We don't mean any harm.'

'I won't mention it,' Sorcha promised, 'but I really must be on my way. I have to see to a friend of mine who is recovering from the Bull Feast.'

'The Bull Feast?' Crínóc gasped as she turned to her husband. 'There. You see. She is most certainly a Fir-Bolg Druid. Have you ever heard of a Gaedhal taking part in the Bull Feast?'

Crínán shrugged or as close to a shrug as any Raven can manage. 'Perhaps you're right,' he conceded.

Crínóc jumped closer to the woman. 'Lady,' she began, 'it is most gracious of you to promise not to say a word of this to the Dark One. You see, we've transgressed her laws once before. My husband and I were banished from our people because of our incessant arguing. It's not that we don't share an enduring affection, you understand. It's just that we both like a good fight at least as much as we love one another.'

'The Morrigán wasn't happy with us at all,' Crínán cut in. 'She thought we needed to spend some time alone away from our kinfolk until we'd got all the fight out of our spirits. I've managed very well, of course. But as you have no doubt observed, my wife still has a long road to travel to her recovery.'

'Shut up!' Crínóc spat, but quickly gained control of herself when she realised he was baiting her. 'The Morrigán would be most displeased with us if we were to be brought before her,' she explained in a forced calm tone.

'This is all very interesting,' Sorcha interrupted, 'but I must be on my way. I don't mean to seem disrespectful but I'm sure you understand the urgency of my task. My dear friend may be in need of me.'

'Then I'll get to the point,' Crínóc cut in. 'I've spent the night trying to find a solution to our problem. If we were to offer our services to you in recompense for the terrible way my stupid husband has treated you —'

'I'm not stupid,' Crínán protested.

'Be quiet!' Crínóc shook her head to clear the interruption from her thoughts. 'As I was saying,' she went on. 'If we were to offer our services to you and serve you well, do you think you might be able to have a word with the Morrigán on our behalf? You can't imagine how much I miss my family. And you have no idea how difficult it is to wake up each morning with no one to speak to but that tedious, half-witted bone-bag I have the misfortune to call my life-partner.'

Crínán took a breath, ready to contradict her but she hushed him abruptly before he had a chance to form an utterance on his tongue.

'Please, lady. Let us be your servants for a while. One good turn deserves another. And you have no idea how useful two pairs of wings and hunters' eyes might be to you.'

Sorcha looked down at the Raven and realised there were wells of tears rolling down her beak. The pain of separation from her kinfolk was obviously tearing at her heart.

'Very well,' the Druid woman nodded, giving in at last out of compassion and in the hope they'd let her get back to Dun Gur.

'Will you talk to the Morrigán for us?'

'I will. But I can't guarantee she'll listen to me.'

Then a thought struck Sorcha. And in a hasty trusting moment she was inspired to share her own concerns with these birds.

'I'm searching for something,' the Druid woman blurted. 'Perhaps you can help me?'

Then she told her feathered listeners the tale of the Watchers, which they'd heard of course, both being as inquisitive as they were argumentative. She explained the great need to rid the land of their influence and the one hope of achieving that objective.

The Ravens nodded politely, and once in a while one or the other of them would snap a beak in sympathy or mutter approval to let the Druid woman know they were still listening.

To conclude her tale Sorcha explained that the Watchers themselves had requested aid from Dalan to find peace for their souls, and that there was rumoured to be a song, passed down through the years since the time of Balor, which had a special property. This unbinding spell was a product of the ancient Draoi craft, but because many generations had passed since anyone had sung it, the song was feared to have been lost. The only way to free the Watchers from their enchantment and liberate Innisfail from their bitter manipulations was to sing this song. The hope was that it still lived in the heart of some learned Druid.

'I don't have time to interview every holy man and woman in the land,' Sorcha explained. 'Do you know of anyone who might have inherited this learning through a wise master of the old ways?'

Both birds looked at each other and their beaks dropped.

'There's no one among the Fir-Bolg or the Danaans,' Crínán replied in a low frightened rattle from the back of his neck. 'But I know of someone who could help you.'

'Do you mean there is a Gaedhal who knows the secret?' the Druid woman gasped in shock.

'Not one of those folk, my lady,' Crínóc answered under her breath, turning her head this way and that as if she were worried someone might overhear her. 'I speak of one who lives among the Sen Erainn.'

'The Sen Erainn?'

'The small folk of the western isles,' Crínán confirmed. 'The people who call King Aenghus mac Ómor their lord.'

114

'They live on the greater Isle of Arainn,' his wife added. 'A few of their folk dwell here in Innisfail also, though they rarely leave the safety of their forests. There is a woman known as Beag ní Dé and she dwells on the island fortress of King Aenghus.'

'It will take me days to reach Arainn,' the Druid woman despaired. 'It's a long walk to the coast and the sea journey is treacherous so close to the feast of Samhain. Even if I find a boatman who will take me, there's no guarantee the Sen Erainn will allow me to speak with Beag ní Dé.'

'She is old and rarely speaks to anyone,' Crínán sighed. 'You would not likely be permitted to see her. I doubt they'd even let you make landfall on the isle. They have an old feud with the Fir-Bolg.'

'But I must discover whether this learned Druid woman knows the song.'

'Let us fly to her,' Crínóc cut in. 'We'll be back by tomorrow morning if the winds are fair to us. And then we will have done you a great service.'

'If you undertake this task I will certainly speak with the Morrigán on your behalf,' Sorcha reaffirmed. 'And I'm sure the Dark One would be impressed. She is well aware of the importance of the song.'

'Thank you, my lady,' Crínóc cawed thankfully, touching the tips of her wings to the Druid woman's legs. 'You can't know what joy you've granted me. I promise we'll both change for the better. Everything will be different from now on if only I can convince my husband to mend his ways.'

'She's living in a dream world,' Crínán cut in. 'She thinks I'm the one with the problem.'

'Keep your beak tight or I'll bend it with my own claws,' his wife shot back.

But the argument had no chance of developing further. On the brow of the hill there suddenly appeared a chariot drawn by a white horse. And holding the reins was a young man. Sorcha heard her name called out and then she recognised the warrior.

It was Lom.

'Sorcha!' he cried. 'Where have you been? I've been riding around half the night looking for you. Aoife's been stolen away from the fortress by Mahon. And Eber Finn has raised all the Fian to search for them.'

'And what of Dalan?' she called back as the King of the Fir-Bolg raced towards her.

'He was asking after you in his sleep.'

'Just call on us when you have the need,' Crínóc reminded her. 'And we'll be there. Won't we husband?'

'We will. And that errand we spoke of will be performed. We will report to you as soon as we have word.'

With that the two birds flew up into the trees just as Lom brought the vehicle to a halt. Sorcha jumped aboard, grasped the young man about the waist and they set off as fast as the horse could carry them.

In a short while they disappeared over the brow of the hill.

'They'll be back by nightfall to take our tree,' Crínán muttered in a sour tone. 'You mark my words.'

'Shut up.'

Mughain and Goll reached the summit of the hill just as the dawn sun was peeping over the far horizon. It was immediately apparent that Éremon had spoken the truth. All around the hilltop in a great circle sat the Fian of Goll mac Morna. They were cross-legged with their hands tied firmly behind their backs.

The war-leader hardly had time to take in this sight before

a tall warrior with long golden hair stepped out from behind a ruined wall and strode directly over to him.

The stranger was only ten paces away from the two southerners when three arrows shot out from the ruins and landed in the grass at Goll's feet.

'Lay down your swords,' the warrior demanded.

Mughain and Goll immediately dropped their weapons on the ground. Then the stranger became bolder. In moments he was standing face to face with Goll, surveying the southerner's eyes with an intense anger.

It was then Goll recognised the man he had not seen for more than three winters. Éremon had grown older. His beard was showing streaks of grey and the lines about his blue eyes were deeper, but he was unmistakably the elder brother of Eber Finn.

'Are you Goll mac Morna?'

'I am.'

'I don't recall your face,' the king noted. 'You must have been one of the minor Fian leaders when my father was king.'

'Are you Éremon?' Goll rejoined. 'I seem to recall he was a younger, wiser and altogether stronger man. And he had an air of confidence about him. Surely this old man who stands before me couldn't be that same king?'

Éremon's face darkened with a frowning scowl and like a flash he raised his fist and thumped the southerner hard in the jaw. Goll fell backward to be caught by Mughain.

'Watch your tongue, lad,' the king growled. 'You've caused enough trouble. If you want to live to see the sun set this day you'll keep a respectful air about you.'

As the war-leader regained his balance he noticed another figure standing close behind the king where just a few seconds earlier there had been no one. The Druid was dressed in a poet's cloak of deep blue.

The stranger laughed as he removed the covering from his

head to reveal a long white beard, bright blue-grey eyes and a head shaved in the tonsure which marked his vocation. The grey hairs were short across the front of his head from ear to ear, but his locks hung long at the back and were matted into thick ropes.

'I remember you, Goll mac Morna,' the Druid nodded. 'Your father was almost as ambitious as you are. Does treachery run in the blood of Morna's sons?'

'Amergin,' the war-leader muttered, acknowledging the renowned bard. 'My father was a loyal Fian leader who followed your father into battle without flinching.'

'Clearly you haven't been told the whole tale of your father's life,' the poet shot back. 'But that is none of my concern. Why have you fallen under the fist of Éremon?'

'This lad insulted me,' Éremon explained.

'Goll mac Morna is your prisoner,' the poet reminded his younger brother. 'You will treat him with respect or I'll lay a geis on you for the grief you cause him.'

'Yes, brother.'

The poet squinted as he observed every detail of the southerner's face.

'What are you going to do with him?' he asked at last, not taking his eyes from Goll for even a breath.

'He's an outlaw. He's ravaged one of our settlements and put fine people to the sword. His life is forfeit.'

Amergin raised his eyebrows in surprise. 'That would be a very foolish path to tread,' he noted without any trace of emotion in his voice. 'This warrior and his Fian band could prove very useful to you.'

'How so?'

'What better messenger to send to your brother in the south than one of his trusted Fian who has seen with his own eyes the strength of your resolve?'

Éremon grunted. Then he suddenly understood what his

elder brother meant. He raised two fingers to his mouth and blew a sharp whistle that hurt Goll's ears with its intensity.

Suddenly from all around there appeared hundreds of grim-faced warriors painted from head to foot in the red ochre of war. There were so many that Goll gasped in shock at their unexpected appearance. And he knew now that he was in real trouble.

'Since you won't let me take his life,' Éremon told his brother, 'will you pass judgement on him and his Fian?'

The poet nodded.

'My judgement is this,' he began without the need to consider his words. 'Goll mac Morna, you will pay King Éremon three hundred and fifty cows in recompense for the good folk you have slain. You will also pay two pigs and seven chickens to replace those your Fian killed for food while you waited here for our arrival.'

The war-leader bowed his head, relieved that the price had been set so low. But then he realised Amergin had not yet finished his judgement.

'As surety that you will pay this debt, you will return to Eber Finn and issue a challenge to him. This quarrel between my brothers has gone on long enough. I'm tired of it. The King of the South will meet the warriors of the north at this place in open battle as soon as he can raise all his Fian.'

'Yes, my lord,' the war-leader affirmed.

'You will take this message to him and let him know the strength of Éremon's following. If Eber should decide the odds are too great against him, he must come here alone and negotiate a settlement.'

'I will do my best, my lord.'

'You'll do better,' Amergin cut in with just a hint of threat in his voice. 'I've been very lenient with you. I suspect that your motives for enticing Éremon to this place were not as pure as mine are in sending you back to your hearthside.

Indeed, I'm certain you would have murdered my brother if he hadn't taken my advice and come properly prepared.'

Goll dropped his gaze so that he didn't have to meet the all-knowing eyes of the poet.

'So to ensure this is all done in an honourable fashion I will accompany you to Eber's court.'

Suddenly Amergin sighed deeply, then he turned on his heel and walked off. Ten paces away he called back to his brother.

'Now that's settled I'm going to have my breakfast.'

And then he was gone.

Éremon waited till his brother was out of earshot. Then he spoke to Goll again. 'You'll come back to the battlefield and fight alongside Eber Finn,' he said coldly. 'But in the heat of the fight when the opportunity arises, I want you to raise your sword against him and end this quarrel once and for all. If you do this I will consider the debt between us to be settled and I will honour you with a gift.'

'What gift?'

'I'll give you this ruined hill fort and all the land around.'

The war-leader bit his lip as he considered the king's words.

'You don't have any choice but to agree,' Éremon smiled. 'Either way Eber Finn will not gain the field here. And you strike me as a man who is always standing under the banner of victory.'

'I will consider your offer.'

'You have one hour. If you don't accept I will slay every one of your Fian, including this woman, before I allow you to go back to your king. Amergin didn't stipulate that any of them had to be given their liberty.'

'I don't need an hour to make my decision,' Goll answered bitterly. 'I'll do as you ask.'

'I knew you would,' the king smiled, slapping the war-leader on the shoulder. 'I knew you would.'

Chapter Nine

om told Sorcha all about Mahon's daring raid on the king's hall as they rode the chariot back to Dun Gur. She listened intently, hardly believing her ears, especially when the young Fir-Bolg king told her that Aoife had gone willingly with the Danaan and his friend Iobhar.

The Druid woman expected to find Eber Finn in a rage when she returned. But nothing could have prepared her for the sight that met her eyes as she and Lom crossed the stone causeway leading to the main gate of the fortress.

Row upon row of warriors had seated themselves on the grassy slopes below the walls of Dun Gur, waiting for orders from their king. And there were more Fian still coming in from outlying settlements. None of them carried their cooking gear or their hard-weather clothes. It was evident they meant to travel light.

That could only mean Eber intended his warriors to scour the countryside in search of the fugitives. And it was plain, too, that all other concerns had been laid aside until this matter was settled.

Lom left the chariot in the hands of Eber's stewards. Then he and Sorcha made their way to the king's hall. When they arrived, servants were rubbing beeswax into the royal armour, boots and sword to waterproof them against the weather.

A fire built of split timber blocks was blazing in the hearth. Nearby on a long bench Dalan lay wrapped in furs, still fast asleep. His face was peaceful even though his body was curled into a tight ball.

Lom made his apologies then departed to dress in his own war-gear. He asked Sorcha to tell the Gaedhal king he'd be back as soon as he could manage it. Eber Finn intended to address the warriors before the search commenced.

Sorcha thanked Lom for returning her to the fortress, then called for water to be brought to Dalan's side. Other servants fetched his Raven-feather cloak which had been dusted and brushed. Then a chamberlain came in bearing a fine set of clothes which Lom had gifted to the Brehon in gratitude for the service he had done at the Bull Feast.

Dalan, however, was lost in a deep slumber and Sorcha decided it surely wouldn't hurt to let him sleep until King Eber arrived. She sat down at the Brehon's head, stroked his hair and marvelled that in the midst of all this frantic activity he was able to rest so soundly.

As it happened, Dalan awoke shortly afterwards, stirred perhaps by her presence. With a warm smile he looked up into her familiar face. And the Druid woman could immediately see he might need some time to recuperate from his ordeal.

The whites of his eyes were red and watery. Deep dark circles outlined his eye-sockets. And the flesh of his cheeks was a pale waxy colour. Sorcha checked his tongue and recoiled at the state of it.

This worried her. Dalan had taken the Quicken Brew, and it was very strange that he should be taking so long to recover from the Bull Feast. Obviously the experience had been more draining than she could have imagined, for the Quicken Brew was such a potent healing agent that it was rare for anyone who had partaken of it to suffer any illness or injury for more than a few hours at the most. Yet there was much the Druid-Healers did not know about the Brew. Its limitations were still a mystery. And Sorcha knew that everything on Earth has its limitations.

Dalan interrupted her thoughts to ask how long he had slept. She brushed a hand over his brow to soothe him but did not reply. She didn't want him to worry unnecessarily. When she didn't speak up he wanted to know why so many folk were rushing about in the king's hall.

Sorcha explained that Aoife had run off with Mahon, and the Brehon laughed. He simply couldn't believe the Danaan would have been so foolish as to enter the fortress and steal the young woman away.

He tried to get up when he realised Eber Finn would be needing his advice. But Sorcha placed a firm hand on his chest and told him to wait a while. The Brehon saw the concern in her eyes but read it simply as an expression of her love. He relented and lay back down to rest.

Eber Finn was busy dealing with many small matters that needed his urgent attention. The flight of Mahon, Aoife and Iobhar had shaken him. He was determined not to lose this woman who had been so supportive and inspirational. And just as firm that Mahon would not go unpunished.

A monster had stirred within the king. A creature that had cursed the line of Míl for generations. And that beast was called jealousy. All his brothers suffered from it from time to time. Even Amergin the wise poet had once succumbed to the green fire of rivalry.

Vengeance was the child of jealousy and the brother of hatred. There were times in the past when the terrible influence of vengeance had almost engulfed Eber. Though he'd lately begun to believe he'd outgrown such feelings, now he felt the familiar icy grip of it curling spindly fingers round his heart once again.

This morning his soul was black with rage and his mind full of scenes in which he imagined the manner of punishment he would inflict on the renegades. And the nature of this breed of hatred was such that it spread quickly amongst the gathered Fian.

Within a short space of time every warrior in the fortress was talking about the outrageous circumstances of Aoife's abduction. The tale grew in the telling, as all good stories do. At length everyone had heard how Eber Finn had fought a long duel against the Danaan and was finally knocked unconscious and left for dead. Every ear was cocked to the tale of the two brave Fian warriors who had defended the kitchen gate against the vicious assault of the outlaws. One of them had given his life, forced face-first into the muddy sludge at the bottom of the kitchen sluice until he drowned.

Such cowardice! It stirred the outrage of everyone who heard the reports. Then of course every good Gaedhal's heart beat with passionate fury when told of the theft of Eber Finn's favourite pig. This last act of banditry had secured Mahon's place among the most hated enemies of the Gaedhal.

To steal another man's wife-to-be was one thing. It could be explained away as the result of overwhelming passion or misguided love. These were common feelings almost everyone experienced at some time in their lives.

To murder a guard in cold blood in a dishonourable fashion could be explained as a mistake made in the heat of the moment. Even the drowning of a sentry in the mud might have been an unfortunate mishap.

But the theft of a favourite pig amounted to little more than unchecked, arrogant greed.

With all this malicious talk on the wind, Mahon quickly attained the status of ruthless outlaw. This was despite the fact that he hadn't actually been the one to steal the pig and that Eber Finn hadn't actually known of the animal's existence until it was taken from him.

Such is the nature of myths. Some tales grow in the telling. Others miss the original point entirely. And only a few preserve the intent of the storyteller who first told them. In any case, all this gossip and hearsay had the result of raising the fortress of Dun Gur to fever pitch.

And Eber was making the most of his position as the hard-done-by but magnanimous ruler. By the time he made his way back into the hall he was surrounded by a group of loyal Fian war-leaders full of suggestions and helpful advice on where to seek out the runaways.

The king went straight to Dalan's bedside and knelt down by his adviser. Before he spoke he called everyone to a respectful silence and summoned Lom, dressed now in the attire of war, to kneel down with him.

'A great wrong has been done to me,' he informed the Brehon. 'A stranger broke into my hall last night. My bride has been taken away against her will.'

'A warrior has been killed dishonourably,' a Fian leader piped up.

'And the king's most treasured pig has been stolen,' another warrior added, indignation in his voice.

Eber Finn did not confirm this addition but he didn't deny it either.

'I know you must be exhausted after your ordeal,' the king went on, hushing his followers again, 'but I am in need of your wise counsel.'

Dalan sat up on his elbows and Sorcha propped his back with a bundle of furs.

'I've known Aoife for some time,' the Brehon began. 'She was my student. A poor Druid scholar she was. That young woman only ever wanted to follow the warrior path. It was her avowed ambition to leave me and live a life devoted to the arts of warfare.'

Eber glanced at Sorcha, clearly not understanding the point of Dalan's speech.

'The way of the Fian is her chosen path,' the Brehon continued. 'I was arrogant enough to believe that I could teach her to appreciate the customs and traditions of the holy orders. But I was wrong. If she had made up her mind to stay with you, no force on this Earth would have been able to tear her away.'

Now the truth was beginning to dawn on Eber. Dalan continued before the king had a chance to interrupt.

'It seems to me Aoife must have desired in the depths of her heart to go with Mahon. Otherwise she would have remained here with you. She's a difficult creature to understand in many respects, but this I can say about her: when an opportunity arises, she takes advantage of it.'

'Aoife told me she loved me,' the king spat dismissively. 'We were talking about how we could rally our forces against my brother in the north. She was offering advice and passionately interested in the affairs of the kingdom. How could she so easily abandon such thoughts to run off into the wilds with two fugitives?'

Dalan reached out and took Sorcha's hand.

'Would you do something for me?' he asked her.

She nodded.

'Fetch me my Brandubh board. I have a lesson to impart to the king and I feel the only way to make it clear is to teach him the principles of the ancient game.'

When the Druid woman was gone, Lom moved closer to the Brehon and the Fian warriors gathered in a tighter circle to hear every word the judge had to say.

'There are many influences at work in this land at present,' he told them, taking on the voice of a teacher, despite his fatigue. 'Some of these forces are as constant and reliable as the rising sun. Others are entirely unpredictable.'

Then Dalan went on to tell the tale of the Watchers. He related what he knew of their origins, their purpose and the predicament the two survivors now faced. When that part of the story was done he told of how he believed the Watchers had led the Gaedhals to Innisfail.

It was his opinion, he told them all, that the Watchers fed on conflict, though they were not perhaps entirely aware of this fact themselves. Thus the discord that had arisen between Eber and Éremon could be explained as a manifestation of their influence.

'I also believe that Aoife and Mahon may have fallen under the sway of their Draoi craft,' he added. 'If we can break the enchanting power of the Watchers then perhaps the world will be set to rights again. And all things will come back to a balance.'

'So Aoife will return to me once these spirits have been defeated?' Eber asked.

'When I first encountered the Watchers,' Dalan explained, 'I had very little understanding of their ways. I believed all I was told about them. But the truth is often hidden behind a veil of deception and misconception. The Watchers can be defeated. They must be if there is to be any hope of peace in this land.'

Lom nodded, at last comprehending some of what had happened since the coming of the Gaedhals.

'I believe Dalan is right,' he spoke up. 'For I have witnessed much of what he has related.'

As he spoke Sorcha returned bearing the Brandubh board and its pieces. She set the gaming table down between Dalan and Eber and placed the pieces in their places. When all was ready, Dalan spoke.

'Now I will explain to you a mystery which has only recently been revealed to me. In the light of all that has happened I'm sure you'll agree we have a hard fight ahead of us.'

He pointed to the Brandubh board.

'Shall we play?'

Sárán slept soundly after he returned from the king-making at the sacred circle. He had no dreams. No visions came to him in the night. And when he awoke he was thoroughly refreshed as if he had been reborn into a completely re-vitalised body.

As he lay on his back staring blankly at the thatch ceiling of the house where he'd been billeted, his thoughts returned to the previous evening. He understood that the old woman who'd visited the king-making had indeed been Danu herself, and doubts now were beginning to creep into his mind.

He reasoned that if the Goddess of the Flowing Waters had cursed Lom's reign then there was little that could be done to avoid disaster. This led the young Druid to question all the events of the past three winters. His own personal ambitions seemed suddenly shallow compared to the duty now laid before him.

The chieftains would certainly not follow his brother into battle. Before the first clash in the war with the north, the alliance with the Gaedhals was already in tatters. Sárán struggled to find a way of convincing the Fir-Bolg warriors to honour their king. But there wasn't an argument he could think of that would have swayed them.

As Lom's adviser it was his obligation to steer his king away from trouble, to guide the war-leader through the dark caverns of destiny into the light beyond. For the first time he began to doubt his own ability.

'I am not wise enough to place my hand on the tiller of Lom's life,' he said aloud to himself.

'Nonsense!' Isleen scoffed, bowing low as she stepped through the door and into the roundhouse. 'Danu isn't the beginning and end of all things. She's merely one deity in a vast hierarchy of beings who have care over this world.'

'She's the Mother of All,' Sárán replied sharply. 'There's no greater goddess.'

'Is that what they teach apprentice Druids these days?' the Watcher laughed. 'Little wonder the Danaans were so easily defeated by the Gaedhals.'

'Danu placed a curse on my brother.'

Isleen strode purposefully over to the bed and tore away the furs that covered the young man. He was still dressed in his breeches and tunic which he'd been too tired to discard before crawling into bed. There was obvious disappointment on the Watcher's face that he hadn't been naked under the covers.

'Nothing is certain in this world unless a gifted Seer has seen it,' she informed him. 'And even then there's plenty of room for interpretation.'

She frowned when he didn't move to get up. 'Shouldn't you be out and about?'

'I've been awake for two days,' Sárán complained.

'Your sister ran off with Mahon mac Cecht last night. Didn't you hear the commotion when you arrived back at the fortress?'

'I came straight to bed as you told me to do. I was exhausted.'

'You'll have to do better than that if you aspire to be a king's counsellor,' she warned him, wagging a mocking finger in front of him. 'Are you lazy or stupid?'

Sárán got up off the bed and wrapped his cloak around himself. 'I'm neither,' he replied indignantly. 'Did Aoife go willingly with Mahon?'

'That's what folk are saying, and I have an inkling she didn't have to struggle very hard with her conscience to decide between Eber Finn and the Danaan. Eber's about to send his warriors out to hunt them down.'

'The alliance will be shattered,' the young Druid sighed. 'Doesn't she understand what this means? Has she lost her senses completely? We're about to go to war. King Eber can't afford to spread his warriors out in a search when his brother is poised to attack.'

'Go to Lom,' Isleen advised. 'The two of you can mend this mess without the need for Eber Finn to send his own warriors out after the renegades. Take one of the chariots which the Gaedhals have built and I will direct you to where Mahon, Aoife and Iobhar are hiding.'

'Iobhar is with them?' Sárán asked. 'I should have known *he* would be involved. The Gaedhals can be a treacherous people.'

'Go now,' Isleen insisted. 'There isn't a moment to lose. Eber Finn will thank you, and this simple act may save the alliance. I'll come to you when I've tracked the fugitives down. You'll find your brother in the king's chamber.'

With those words the Watcher turned and walked to the door. Then a thought crossed her mind and she faced the young Druid again.

'Be careful not to mention my name to anyone,' she warned. 'There's no telling how folk would react if they knew I had a hand in all this.'

Dalan offered the opening play of the white king to Eber Finn. But the Gaedhal called impatiently for his boots and his cloak.

'I can't sit around wasting precious moments with you while Aoife is being dragged across the countryside by some outlaw. I have to go out searching for her.'

He stood up and bowed to his counsellor. 'I trust you will not be offended if I leave now,' he said with a hint of sarcasm.

'Sit down!' the Brehon demanded and the assembled warriors muttered to one another at the Druid's tone. 'I'm your adviser. It's a poor king who doesn't have time to heed the words of a Brehon. I was under the impression you were seeking my help.'

'With every breath I take Mahon puts two paces between himself and Dun Gur. I can't wait!'

'Then you will forfeit your kingdom,' Dalan shrugged with resignation. 'If you care so little for the southern lands that you'd risk them for a flighty young girl then you deserve to lose the kingship.'

'How would I lose my kingdom?' Eber scoffed, disbelieving.

'Play the Brandubh with me and I'll explain.'

The Brehon paused when he realised the Gaedhals might not know this game of strategy. 'Have you played before?' he inquired.

'My people play a similar game called Fidchell,' Eber nodded. 'I haven't taken part in a tournament since I was a lad. I'm not sure I remember all the rules.'

'A good king should play the Brandubh at least three times a day,' Dalan advised. 'It keeps your mind sharp, your senses alert and it promotes humility.'

He went on to explain that the white player's objective was to bring his high-king to one of the four sanctuaries around the edge of the board.

'It is the black Raven player's challenge to capture the high-king before he has the chance to escape.' The Brehon pointed to the board. 'White begins.'

The Gaedhal squatted down beside the board carved into a low portable table. After a few moments of contemplation he moved one of the white pieces then crossed his legs on the floor to make himself more comfortable.

They played three games in quick succession. As was the custom among both their peoples they took turns at playing white and black. But Eber Finn couldn't win, no matter which side he was given.

'Are you trying to humiliate me?' he hissed at the Brehon at last. 'It's plain you're a better player than I am. I don't see what you've proved by defeating me in front of my chieftains and my Fian leaders.'

Dalan sat up on the bench, suddenly looking refreshed. Sorcha was surprised but relieved at this quick recovery.

'Have you ever wondered why it is the custom to change sides after each game?' he pressed the king.

'No.'

'Then I'm going to reveal a Druidic secret to you,' Dalan declared. 'But I won't have anyone else but Sorcha, Lom and yourself in the room if this mystery is to be given to you. Clear all these other folk out.'

'I haven't time to play this silly game!' the king insisted.

Dalan leaned forward and touched Eber on the shoulder. 'I'm offering you the answer to all your troubles,' the Brehon promised. 'Once you've seen what I've seen, your kingdom will be secure, your duty clear and your future will no longer be in doubt.'

Eber Finn read the sincerity in Dalan's face. He thought carefully for a moment.

'Very well,' he conceded, and waved his chieftains out of the chamber. 'I'll listen.'

He looked up when none of the warriors made a move to leave.

'Get out!'

Without any further hesitation the Fian leaders and the chieftains did as they were commanded. Soon only Sorcha, Lom, Eber Finn and the Brehon were left in the king's hall.

'Now I want you to play the part of the black Ravens,'

Dalan told the king. 'You'll play until you win. And when you've won your first game we'll talk a little more.'

So the tournament began. They played a dozen games before Eber finally managed to almost surround the white high-king. But Dalan was one step ahead of Eber and he easily won the match.

'I can't beat you!' the Gaedhal complained. 'You've had much more practice at this pointless pursuit than I have. Druids enjoy a leisure of which war-leaders may only dream.'

'One more game,' the Brehon insisted. 'I find it hard to believe that a man who has spent his life training for war and fighting battles can't understand the simple flow of a board game he played as a child.'

Eber Finn grunted with disdain. 'The Fidchell has nothing to do with warfare, warrior skills or the winning of battles.'

'On the contrary,' Dalan smiled. 'It has everything to do with such things. Indeed, if you can but glimpse the hidden patterns in this game you will be granted an insight into the very essence of your life's journey. Comprehend the subtle flow of the Brandubh and you may even be able to predict the future.'

'Nonsense!'

'Play!' the Brehon snapped. 'One more game. But this time look carefully for the patterns.'

The Druid picked up a white piece and placed it down in a new position. And for the first time Eber realised that Dalan always opened with the same move or a subtle variation on that move.

The Gaedhal made a safe decision and placed one of his Ravens down to block the high-king's escape. Dalan made his next move almost without thinking. Eber Finn began to understand that the Brehon followed a strict game plan which he rarely varied. The Gaedhal began to question his own strategies. If these tactics worked for Dalan, they could certainly work for him.

Then in a flash of inspiration Eber Finn understood what Dalan had been talking about. There was a definite pattern to be discerned in the ebb and flow of the game. The only way for the Raven to win was to unswervingly adhere to the tactic of gradually surrounding his opponent's king. The temptation to take the white pieces was to be avoided until just the right moment.

He lured Dalan's pieces into brilliant traps from which they could not escape, until one by one he had dwindled their numbers from twelve to seven. Within another twenty moves, Eber Finn had won his first game of Brandubh against Dalan the Brehon.

'Do you see?' the Druid asked.

The Gaedhal nodded. 'There is a pattern. If I serve the pattern well and do not try to turn the game against the pattern, I will be victorious. If I allow myself to become distracted from the greater pattern I will be tempted into disaster.'

'Indeed you have learned a profound lesson,' Dalan smiled, slapping the king on the shoulder. 'Do not listen to your arrogant self speaking of what should be. Respect the patterns and let them lead you to your goals.'

'I have allowed my pride to overrule my good judgement in the matter of Mahon and Aoife,' the king admitted.

'No matter how important she may seem to you, Aoife is merely a distraction,' Dalan added. 'Should you send your warriors out in search of her, you will certainly risk your kingdom.'

'My brother could decide to march south at any time,' the Gaedhal nodded, understanding the Brehon's point.

'And Dun Gur would be without a garrison,' Dalan shrugged. 'What value would your queen be to you if you lost the kingship?'

'You're right,' Eber sighed. 'How far can they run? I'll catch Mahon and Iobhar in good time.'

'They're not likely to harm Aoife,' Dalan added. 'If I've guessed right, the Danaan has done this out of love for the girl. She's in good hands for the moment.'

As he spoke Sárán forced his way into the king's chamber against the objections of the warriors waiting outside. He bowed low to Eber Finn and to his own brother before he spoke.

'Forgive this intrusion,' the young Druid began. 'I've only just heard the news of Aoife's abduction.'

'Did you sleep well?' Sorcha asked with a hint of sarcasm in her voice. 'You've certainly slept long for one who had no work to do at the Bull Feast.'

Sárán narrowed his eyes in contempt. 'I've come to offer my help,' he snapped. 'Aoife is my sister. I will go in search of her.'

'What hope would you have of finding Mahon and Iobhar if they decided to conceal themselves in the forest?' Eber laughed. 'And what if they decided to put up a fight? You may have a certain skill in the Draoi craft, but you're no match for a trained warrior.'

'Then send a warrior with me,' Sárán retorted. 'If my brother King Lom were to consent to coming we would have a very good chance of bringing our sister back.'

Lom looked up, startled at the prospect of chasing off after Aoife. He knew that trouble was attracted to her like bees to the mead jar. Too many times he'd been drawn into her schemes and adventures. His instincts told him this would only end in grief.

'I should stay here with my warriors and help direct the war with Eber Finn,' he countered nervously.

But Sárán's idea had already struck a chord with the Brehon. Dalan knew that Lom had very little experience at warfare, though the risk to his personal safety in battle was insignificant because of the Quicken Brew he'd taken. But

Lom was destined to be the last king of the Fir-Bolg. And Dalan didn't want to take any unnecessary risks with the young ruler or the warriors under his command. If he could keep Lom out of trouble he was determined to do so.

At the same time Dalan had an instinct to keep Sárán as far away as possible from the coming conflict. He considered the young Druid to be little more than a boy. Even though he'd been trained by Fineen the renowned healer, Sárán had very little commonsense.

And both brothers had a reputation for poor judgement in testing times. All in all, Dalan decided, it would be best if they were sent off to look for Aoife. Eber Finn would then have a free hand to deploy the Fir-Bolg warriors as he wished and conduct the war without the interference of two untried lads who happened to hold nominal positions of authority.

'For once I agree with Sárán,' the Brehon began. 'If he and King Lom were to find Mahon they would have a good chance of reasoning with him. Lom was a good friend of the Danaan before all this trouble. I believe he would listen to the king.'

Eber Finn realised immediately that Dalan must have some unspoken motive for sending Lom and Sárán off into the wilderness with little hope of finding the fugitives. But he decided it didn't really matter to him what that motive might be. The Brehon could be trusted to follow the patterns he observed in the world.

The King of the Gaedhals felt that if he were left alone to coordinate the attack on the north he'd have a better chance of victory. The loss of Lom to his campaign would be negligible. And the Fir-Bolg chieftains would certainly feel better about fighting under an experienced war-leader rather than an untried lad.

'King Lom,' the Gaedhal announced formally, 'I would consider it a great personal favour if you would undertake this task on my behalf. Dalan speaks the truth. Éremon could attack the southern kingdom at any time. I must remain here with the greater part of the warriors in case he marches for Dun Gur.'

Lom closed his eyes and hung his head. He was overcome by a terrible conviction that no matter what he decided to do he would land himself in difficulty. He'd been drawn into Aoife's whirlpools of mayhem too many times and had no wish to become embroiled in another of her misadventures. Yet if he refused the personal request of his ally, King Eber, then his honour would be called into question. Any dishonour he brought on his people now would only compound the effects of the terrible curse Danu had laid upon him. And it would confirm the augury pronounced for him by Dalan.

He was young this king, but he wasn't a fool. He knew the chieftains of the Fir-Bolg would already be muttering about whether going to war under the banner of a cursed king was a wise plan. If Eber Finn were left in command of the Fir-Bolg, they would probably follow him willingly. At least the Gaedhal had a reputation as a warrior and had no curse hanging over his head.

The Fir-Bolg warriors had thrown their bronze weapons into the lough, rendering their fighters impotent. Now Eber Finn was forced to rearm them with iron and grant them equal footing with his own warriors. If they withdrew from the alliance for any reason, they would be defenceless when King Éremon of the North marched into their territory. And they would very likely withdraw rather than march behind a doomed king. Lom sighed, understanding he really had very little choice in the matter.

'I will go in search of Aoife,' he conceded. 'But on one condition. I insist that Eber Finn take command of the warriors of the Fir-Bolg and lead them honourably into battle.'

The King of the Southern Gaedhals stood up and took Lom's hand. 'I promise to be an honourable and just war-leader to your people until such time as you return from your quest.'

'Then we're agreed?' Sárán cut in, surprised that it had been so easy to convince them all to follow the wishes of Isleen.

'May we take one of your chariots?' Lom asked Eber. 'It would hasten our journey and help us catch the renegades.'

'You will have the finest chariot of all,' Eber replied. 'I give you my own war-cart, the first and fastest of them all. And I will see you are well provisioned for your quest. Any weapon you require will be yours.'

Lom pulled the bronze axe from his belt, the ceremonial weapon Danu had left at his feet. 'This is the only weapon I need,' he said quietly.

And then Lom, King of the Fir-Bolg of the Burren, bowed before Eber and left.

Chapter Ten

alan advised Eber to wait one more day before setting out north to counter the expected attack of King Éremon. The Brehon reasoned this would give his scouts time to scour the country in case the northerners had made incursions into the southern territory.

Dalan also argued that one more day would bring more able warriors in from the surrounding settlements. And the Druid wanted time to consult with the Fir-Bolg chieftains, none of whom were likely to be keen on going to war.

But the Brehon didn't dare mention this to Eber. He understood that there was now no alternative to conflict. If the Fir-Bolg did not stand with Eber they would be swept away by Éremon like a tower of sand built at the edge of the ocean.

As soon as the meeting ended Sorcha took Dalan aside and told him of her encounter with the two Ravens, Crínóc and Crínán. The Brehon was delighted at the news and excited by the idea that the Sen Erainn may have preserved the Draoi song which could free the Watchers.

'Now there's a good chance this conflict may be avoided entirely,' he told her.

'How?' Sorcha asked, not following his reasoning.

'We must gain the instrument of the Watchers' delivery,'

the Brehon argued. 'Once we have the song that liberates them, we can negotiate a bargain.'

The Druid woman's eyes lit up as she understood his meaning. 'They instigated this war with their interference, and so they have the power to end it favourably.'

'When will you hear from your Raven friends?'

'If the winds lift them on their journey, they might be back by dawn tomorrow.'

Dalan put a hand to his chin and thought for a moment. 'Yet we must be prepared for battle if they are unable to track down the one who has preserved the song,' he reasoned. 'So I will go to the Council of Chieftains of the Fir-Bolg and present the case for the support of Eber Finn. Now that Lom will not be marching at their head, the warriors of our people may not hold any major misgivings. I may be able to persuade them to stand with the Southern Gaedhals.'

'Do you really believe you can convince the Watchers to end this war?'

'It is within their power to influence events as they see fit,' Dalan assured her. 'And I'm sure they would do almost anything to alter their fate.'

He stroked his beard thoughtfully. 'I have no knowledge of the Sen Erainn language. All I know is that the legends say they speak an old dialect of Fir-Bolg which is now unintelligible to our folk.'

'My teacher gave me a grounding in the basics of the Sen Erainn legends,' Sorcha told him. 'The chants of the Ritual of the Sun are sung in their tongue. And if I find I can't understand their speech, the Ravens can be our go-betweens.'

'Will the Sen Erainn consent to help us?' the Brehon asked. 'They have no love for our folk, though we are cousins.'

'I can't answer that question,' the Druid woman replied honestly. 'We shall have to wait and see.'

With that Dalan invited her to attend the Council of

Chieftains with him. Then they went off together to put their case to the elders.

Even before Lom and his brother had crossed the stone causeway, leading the horse that was harnessed to the chariot, there were mutterings among their kinfolk. Many of the chieftains were openly discussing the wisdom of going off to fight in Eber Finn's war.

Despite Dalan's eloquent arguments, by sunset that day four chieftains and their warriors had simply packed up and gone home. It was evident this was the trickle that would precede the flood. And Eber was growing worried.

He stood at the summit of the hill where the king's kitchens were situated and looked out over the countryside. The night air chilled him slightly so he wrapped his cloak tightly about his body. Despair was already creeping into his soul. Without the aid of the Fir-Bolg he might as well surrender his kingdom.

The sky darkened as he shivered in the gloom. He was exhausted from a day of long discussions. The blacksmiths' forges were running hot, their hammers thudding ceaselessly on sword, spear and armour. There was to be no turning back now.

His heart was against this conflict and he was bitter that he had been left no choice. Whether or not he had the numbers to secure a victory, he would be forced to make a stand. However, Eber could see no sense in provoking his brother without enough warriors to put up a good fight. It was clear to him his reign was as doomed as Lom's. He'd lost the war before it had even begun, lost the woman he loved and lost all hope of retaining the kingdom he'd worked so hard to establish.

Not for the first time he wondered whether it would be

more honourable for him to capitulate to the northerners without a fight. At least in that manner he might save the lives of many of his warriors.

But Eber Finn had been imbued with his father's stubbornness. King Míl was renowned in his time for a tenacity that often challenged the boundaries of commonsense. Yet he'd never lost a battle or failed to achieve an objective once he'd set his mind on it. His two youngest sons were cast in the same metal as old Míl. So King Eber soon banished all thoughts of giving up and began to plan a strategy that would make the best of his available resources.

Éremon might have the numbers but Eber was determined to triumph, even if it meant resorting to some underhanded tactics that might risk his honour. For the first time in a long while he wished Goll mac Morna was by his side. If anyone had a flair for disguising a dishonourable act it was Goll.

No sooner had the thought occurred to him than a horn sounded at the causeway, signalling the approach of a rider. Eber would not usually have taken much notice. There were scouts and messengers coming and going all day. But some instinct told him to go down to the gate and meet the rider.

By the time he'd come to the place where the sentries guarded the main entrance to the fortress, the messenger had dismounted and was making his way into the citadel. Eber hailed the warrior and asked him what news he was carrying.

'My words are for the king,' the rider replied sharply. 'And for none other.'

Eber Finn snatched a torch from one of the sentries and when the warrior saw his face in the firelight he bowed respectfully.

'Forgive me, my lord,' he began. 'I was given strict instructions to speak with no one but yourself. I bring news from Goll mac Morna, Champion of the Southern Gaedhals.'

'Summon Dalan to me immediately,' Eber commanded as

he turned to one of the sentries. 'I would have him hear this news also.'

The sentry ran off into the night to bring the Brehon to the king. Then Eber Finn offered the messenger his hand in greeting.

'I'm glad to see you. Where are the Fian of Goll at present?'

'My brothers and sisters raided a dun two days march from here,' the rider declared. 'And my war-leader has sent word to Éremon that he will gladly give battle on an ancient ruined rath by the side of a stream a thousand paces from the settlement.'

'Is he mad?' Eber barked. 'He's challenged Éremon to a fight? Two dozen Fian will stand against at least five hundred?'

'Goll would have you march north to lend him your support,' the messenger added sheepishly. 'He holds this rath and is certain it cannot be taken.'

If the messenger could have known that Goll's plan had already collapsed, perhaps he would have thought differently, but he frowned to hear the king speak ill of Mac Morna. 'Lend my support? Which one of us is the king? Goll or myself? I won't lend him a single downy duckling. For all I care he can perish on the top of his little hill. Who does he think he is to command me to bring the gathered Fian of the South to a battlefield of his choosing?'

'If you knew the rath, my lord, you would understand it affords the best defensive position in all the border country,' the rider explained.

Eber turned on the warrior with a rage that forced the man to take a step backwards for fear he would be struck.

'I don't need a lesson in tactics from Goll!' the king spat. 'Much less from a mere messenger boy.'

At that moment Dalan arrived and as was his way quickly calmed King Eber with a hand on his shoulder. This skill was essential for anyone who aspired to the vocation of Brehon. After a quiet private discussion the two of them approached the messenger again and the news was repeated.

The Druid frowned as the warrior spoke and Eber noticed the lines on his forehead deepen with every word. At last the Brehon nodded to acknowledge the tidings, took the king by the arm and dismissed the warrior.

'Go find yourself a meal,' he advised. 'Within the hour you'll be riding back to your war-leader with King Eber's reply.'

The messenger bowed low to the Brehon and was gone, leaving Eber Finn and Dalan standing by the gate.

'Let us not discuss this in front of the sentries,' the Brehon advised, dragging the king away towards the royal hall. 'They've already heard enough. I expect the gossip will be all round the fortress by the time that rider sets off again.'

'Goll is no fool,' Eber shrugged as he walked beside the Druid. 'To send this dispatch with word of a victory and of a challenge to Éremon only serves to gild his reputation.'

'Do you hold some fear that Goll mac Morna may have an ambition for the kingship?'

The king nodded. 'He's coveted my position since we arrived on these shores.'

'Well he's certainly added to his prestige by this act,' Dalan agreed. 'If he defeats Éremon single-handedly, you may be sure he'll challenge you next. By that time he'll have the support of your chieftains and elders.'

'I thought he'd do no damage to me if I sent him off raiding in the north,' the king sighed. 'I hoped he'd fall in some fight before he had a chance to cause any more trouble.'

'More trouble?'

Eber stopped walking and realised he would have to tell Dalan why he'd decided to send Goll and his Fian off to the north. 'His band of warriors cut down Fergus, the Fir-Bolg champion, in cold blood during a raid on one of your settlements,' the king admitted.

'Goll murdered the champion of old King Brocan?'

Eber nodded.

'Why didn't you tell us this man was the culprit? Why did you take responsibility for his barbarous act?'

'Because I didn't want Goll to add to his reputation from the killing. The only way I could make certain he was no threat or distraction to me was to send him away. He is too popular with the young Fian and I wouldn't be surprised if he has his heart set on the kingship of the south.'

'It's too late to fence the bull in when the cow is heavy with calf,' the Brehon noted. 'There is only one course of action open to you. You and your warriors must reach this outpost before Éremon. If you don't, Goll will certainly further enhance his standing with your people, which could lead to a threat on your leadership.'

'I'll order the Fian bands to be ready to move off at first light,' Eber assured him. 'With our chariots and the warriors moving at the run, we just might make it to Goll before any more damage is done.'

'If it's two days march then you can be sure it will take at least a full day to run the distance,' Dalan calculated. 'Let us hope you don't find the warriors of the north gathered in wait for you when you arrive. No one could fight a battle after such a forced march.'

'You will come with us?'

'I am not a warrior,' the Brehon protested. 'I doubt I would be able to sustain such a run.'

'I'll give you a chariot so you and Sorcha may witness events. I may stand in need of a Brehon judge if Éremon demands retribution against Goll's raiding.'

As he spoke, both of them witnessed an unusual sight. Flying in low from the north-east came two black shapes. Most large birds were nested for the night by this time, so the arrival of the pair of Ravens was completely unexpected and sent a murmur around the fortress.

They flew up towards the king's hall where Dalan had left

his companion Sorcha. The king and the Brehon said nothing more to each other but picked up their pace until they were standing in the hall where the Druid woman was engaged in a strange conversation with the birds.

Eber would not come within the hall but stood at the door, too frightened to approach the carrion creatures. But Dalan wasn't as shy as he once would have been. After his experience with the black bird at Sorcha's house he was less frightened by Ravens than he used to be.

The Druid woman cawed and clicked her tongue to imitate the strange speech these creatures used. And once in a while one of the Ravens would scream and spread its wings as if to emphasise a point.

The conversation was long and detailed. Sorcha obviously had many questions to ask. And the two Ravens often interrupted one another. The Brehon found himself wishing he had even a basic understanding of their language but he sat patiently nearby until the discussion was concluded.

At long last, after a lengthy discourse by the larger of the two birds, Sorcha sighed and turned to her companion.

'They've found a Druid who may be able to help us,' she told Dalan. 'I had not expected to hear from them so soon. But they found this woman eager to help us and not in need of persuasion. Her name is Beag ní Dé and she dwells on the island of Arainn in the west.'

'She's the Druid of the Sen Erainn of whom you spoke?' Dalan asked.

'Yes.'

'And she's willing to help us?'

'Her people are aware of the terrible war we fought against the Gaedhals. So far they've been spared the ravages of invasion. She's willing to help us if King Eber Finn will guarantee the sovereignty of her people over the fortress of Dun Aenghus and the surrounding islands.'

'What kind of help are these folk offering?' Eber cut in.

'They've consented to teach us a song,' Sorcha replied.

'A song?' the king repeated incredulously. 'They would barter my claim over those islands for a song?'

'This song will send the Watchers on their way,' Dalan explained. 'The Watchers are desperate to be released from the binding enchantment that has imprisoned their souls on this Earth for generations.'

'How does that help my cause?' Eber spat.

'The Watchers are very powerful,' Sorcha informed the king, urging him with a gesture of her hand to keep his voice low so he didn't upset the Ravens. 'They would surely intervene if we forced their hands.'

'How will you do that?' Eber Finn asked.

'They would do almost anything in return for being released from the bind of their enchantment,' Dalan explained. 'I'm certain they could, if pressed, be persuaded to intervene in this war.'

'If they are such powerful beings, why don't they simply steal the song from you and use it themselves?'

'For the enchantment to be broken they need a Druid who is skilled in the Draoi craft,' Sorcha replied. 'They can't sing the song themselves. They need us.'

'How do we know this song will indeed do as you say and rid the land of the Watchers?'

Both Druids caught each other's glance, silently recalling their experience within the stone hut of the Bull Feast, which had ended in failure.

'I can't be entirely certain the song will do as is intended,' the Druid woman admitted.

'So if you convince them to help me and the song doesn't release them from their bindings, they will likely take their frustration out on me?' Eber shrugged. 'I'm not sure you've found an answer to my problem. Indeed, I'd trust my sword arm before a song any day.'

Eber ventured further into the hall to steal a better look at the Ravens. 'Will these folk from the Isle of Arainn send warriors?' he asked.

Sorcha glanced at the Brehon but didn't answer.

'The Sen Erainn are ancient enemies of the Fir-Bolg,' Dalan explained. 'I doubt they would support us. And I'd be surprised if they committed their warriors to war on your behalf. They are a reputedly savage people who drink the blood of the slain on the battlefield and take heads as trophies.'

'Ask the Ravens,' Eber insisted.

Sorcha hesitated but after a few moments turned to address the birds. When she had spoken with the creatures at length she faced the king once more.

'King Aenghus mac Ómor, their ruler, expected that you would make such a request,' she explained. 'His people have already set out in boats and are marching to meet with you. He offers his warriors but there is a price to be paid for their service.'

'What price?'

'A very high price,' the Druid woman answered.

'What price?' Eber repeated in frustration.

'The secret of the Quicken Brew.'

Dalan shook his head as she spoke, masking his surprise at the suggestion. 'The secret of the Brew may not be revealed to anyone,' he said sternly.

'But if it means ridding the land of the Watchers and averting this war, it's a small price to pay,' Eber argued. 'I'm not asking for this secret to be given to my people. But if it guarantees the goodwill of the Sen Erainn, then surely it's a price worth paying.'

'Among our folk only Fineen the healer had the craft of brewing the Quicken juice,' the Brehon explained. 'And he has withdrawn behind the veil of the Otherworld as far as we can tell for he hasn't been seen since we entered the Aillwee caves. There is none who could perform the task.'

'I have the knowledge,' Sorcha cut in. 'I understand the secret of the Brew. I have stirred the broth myself and administered it to some of my fellow Druids who live solitary lives in the forest. And I have in my possession all the makings of it.'

'Then there is no reason to withhold the potion from the Sen Erainn,' the king pressed.

'They are not our people,' Dalan argued. 'We can't simply hand it over to them. They're savages.'

'They're our cousins,' the Druid woman corrected him. 'If we secure a lasting peace through the gift of the Quicken Brew, the old enmity between the Fir-Bolg and the Sen Erainn may be ended once and for all.'

One of the Ravens cawed loudly then chattered excitedly. Sorcha caught her words and passed them on as soon as the bird finished speaking.

'Beag ní Dé, their chief Druid, will meet us at a place one day's walk to the north at sunset tomorrow evening. We will have an opportunity to negotiate with her then.'

'There's no time,' Eber shook his head. 'A decision must be made now.'

Dalan looked from one to the other, realising the responsibility fell to him. As the last senior Druid of his people remaining on this side of the veil to the Otherworld, there was no one else who could decide this matter.

He understood there was a chance the Draoi song would not free the Watchers from their enchantment. On the other hand, the arrival of reinforcements from the Sen Erainn would ensure a victory for Eber. Thus if the song was not effective, at least there would be time to find another such Draoi chant while the future of the Fir-Bolg and the Southern Gaedhals was secured.

'Tell the Ravens we will give the secret of the Quicken Brew to the Sen Erainn if they will send their warriors to the aid of Eber Finn,' the Brehon sighed at last.

'And tell them I will guarantee the sovereignty of the Sen Erainn for all time if they lend their aid to me in my time of need,' Eber added.

Sorcha turned to the birds and passed on the king's words in a speech they could fully understand, then wished them a safe journey. Without any further cawing the Ravens were gone into the night.

After they'd departed the Druid woman turned to Dalan and smiled. 'You've made a very wise decision.'

The Brehon nodded gravely. 'I hope so.'

Sorcha frowned at the deep dark circles under his eyes and the grey pallor of his skin. Suddenly Dalan seemed very tired and drawn again and looked as if he was almost asleep on his feet.

'Now we must all rest,' Eber interrupted. 'No matter what the outcome of all this talking, there is much to be done tomorrow. We are all about to face some stern challenges and I for one would rather have a fresh mind when the dawn sun climbs into the sky.'

'Yes,' the Brehon nodded feebly. 'I believe it is time to take some sleep.'

Sorcha came and took his arm. 'We can't sleep in our camp tonight,' she whispered as they made their way to the door.

She turned to the king. 'Will you grant us a room in the fortress this night, my lord?'

'Gladly.'

With that Eber summoned a servant who showed them to a warm room attached to the king's hall. Dalan was asleep before he'd even undressed and fallen onto the straw mattress. His companion wrapped the blankets round him, even more concerned for his health.

There she sat for a long while wondering what could have brought this exhaustion on him. The Bull Feast was a test of any Druid's endurance but the Quicken Brew should have allayed any ill effects.

After a long while she left to fetch her herb satchel and travelling gear from their camp at the side of the lough. And by the time she returned she was beginning to feel a little tired herself. This surprised her but she didn't pay too much attention to it.

Sorcha lay down beside the Brehon, put her arms about his neck, and in moments she was breathing low as sleep engulfed her.

Chapter Eleven

alan and Sorcha rode on the back of one of Eber Finn's chariots all day long. Sometimes one or the other would stand up to stretch their legs but for the most part they sat with their backs to the charioteer, looking out at the war-cart that followed them.

In that chariot rode the lame blacksmith and the blind wheelwright who had constructed these vehicles. Eber thought it prudent to bring them should any of the war-carts need repair during the journey to the battleground.

The Brehon said little during the journey. He was still exhausted, despite having rested deeply the previous night. Ever since the Bull Feast he'd felt drained and drawn. And for most of the morning, as they made their way north, he'd dozed with his chin on his chest.

Sorcha kept an eye on her companion, concerned that his health seemed to have waned since his ordeal. She refrained from inquiring after him, however, suspecting he would not appreciate the fuss.

Though Dalan hardly spoke all morning, his mind was alert. They stopped to rest at midday and he ate some oatcakes with butter and drank deeply from a stream. When they set out again, he seemed to be a little refreshed.

The chariots were forced to slow down after the rest stop

so that they didn't get too far ahead of the Fian warriors who were making their way on foot. This relaxed pace was more conducive to rest for the Brehon and he found himself drifting off into a strange sleep, jolted now and then by the uneven track.

An hour passed and then another as all consciousness fled from his eyes to be replaced with a shroud of drowsiness. Now and then Sorcha grabbed at his belt just as he would have tumbled off the back of the cart, but Dalan didn't seem to notice. The Druid woman understood that the Watchers had established a very strong connection with him. Whenever he drifted into a trance it seemed one or the other of them was waiting to pass on some news or some threat.

Her instincts were correct. As Dalan gently swayed with the cart, eyes staring at the ground, he was being drawn in by the force of his trance. The chariot slowed to a walking pace as it struggled up a steep hill, and some of the passengers from other war-carts took the opportunity to stretch their legs.

Sorcha also saw her chance for some exercise and jumped off. Eber Finn was walking up and down the line, giving words of encouragement to his warriors, and the Druid woman followed him for a while, leaving Dalan to his daydream.

It was at this point that the Brehon stirred himself from the strange state which had overcome him. He stretched his arms high, yawned and sighed loudly. Then he scratched his beard and looked about him. He felt a little better but his legs were numb from sitting in the one position for too long. He decided to get off the cart and walk to pump some blood through to his feet. Just as he was about to jump a hand pushed into his chest and a pair of bright green eyes appeared before him.

'Don't move.'

It was Lochie.

The Brehon looked straight into the Watcher's face then

shook his head and tried to remove the restraining hand from his chest. But Lochie had no intention of letting him go.

'Don't move,' the Watcher repeated in a gentle but firm tone.

Dalan tore his eyes from those green orbs of fire, hoping to break the bond between them. He saw Eber and the warriors of the Fian talking and joking as they climbed the hill beside their chariots. And he saw Sorcha taking part in conversations along the way. But he knew they couldn't see Lochie. Nor did they have any idea what was happening to him. He turned his gaze back to those eyes, ready to hear whatever the Watcher had to say and hoping he would be allowed to rest afterwards.

'I'm exhausted,' the Brehon stammered. 'I've been so since the Bull Feast. Please let me rest.'

'I will not speak too long with you,' Lochie soothed. 'I've come to thank you. Is it true you may have found the song which will save us from our fate?'

The Brehon nodded, lacking the energy even to open his mouth.

'You've often asked me about the origins of my kind,' the Watcher went on. 'And now I will share one of the secrets of our beginnings. This tale has been shrouded in the mists of the passing generations. For Isleen and our companions were not the first Watchers. And neither will we be the last.'

With these words Lochie leaned forward with his eyes fixed on the Brehon's until their foreheads touched lightly. And the very moment that happened Dalan's mind was filled with explosions of light and music the like of which he had never known before. He shut his eyes but the rainbow colours burned into his mind nevertheless. His ears rang with the chanting of a hundred voices raised in a joyous harmonious song that lifted his soul into a state of indescribable bliss.

'This is what I seek,' Lochie whispered. 'This is what has been denied to me.'

Dalan nodded, understanding at last. For the experience stirred an unusual memory in the Brehon. A recollection came to him of his first breath and his first glimpse of consciousness in this life. And even though he could not clearly define this experience, he knew it was pivotal to everything that had happened to him in the seasons since his birth.

'What is happening?' Dalan managed to whisper.

But Lochie hushed him with a soothing sigh. 'You'll see.'

The Brehon's consciousness was still full of light but now it was concentrated in a single beam of pure golden sunshine which seared his mind like the touch of a red-hot iron. Then Dalan perceived that the beam of light was shining through a doorway of some sort to illuminate a dark chamber. He recognised this place and this feeling but he had no idea why. The whole experience was unfamiliar to him, yet at the same time it seemed as if he'd witnessed it a thousand times before.

In the next instant he had become part of this beam of light. His soul travelled along its length until it burst out into the dawn and soared above the Earth towards the sun. Dalan looked back at the world he'd left behind and clearly saw that the beam of light on which he was riding pierced the entrance to a mound. The man-made hill seemed to sparkle with a stunning white radiance. Then he was drawn into the golden warmth of the sun. Like a stone tossed high into the air, he reached the apogee of his flight and began to fall again.

As his spirit plummeted earthward Dalan sensed he had been refreshed by this experience. His heart was brimming with joy and his laughter filled the air. Ahead of him he saw the shining mound with its dark entrance.

This was his goal. Someone from beyond this doorway was calling his name. Dalan the Brehon had been summoned and he felt compelled to answer the call. The beam of golden light suddenly seemed as solid as the ground beneath his feet.

As Dalan came closer he heard the chanting again, though

now he discerned only one voice where there had earlier been a hundred. He fell faster, sliding along the path of light towards the opening in the mound with unstoppable certainty.

Just as he arrived at the hill he found himself standing still, observing the spectacle taking place around him. His spirit was still bathed in the glorious light of the golden sun, which he now understood to be the very essence of his deeper self. Before him a great stone lay on its side in front of the doorway to the mound. And every available surface of this stone had been covered with carved designs of spirals and zigzags, dots and circles.

The Brehon tried to recall where he'd seen these motifs before. And then the answer came to him. Near to where he'd been born on the Burren in the west of Innisfail there was an ancient mound. No one had ventured into the chamber for generations for it was held as a place sacred to the ancestors.

But there was a stone which lay at the entrance to the underground passage and it was very similar to this one he could see before him now. In the next instant he was granted a profound and unexpected understanding of the symbolism on the stone. Three spirals were closely interwoven at the centre of the monument and with a strange insight he knew they stood as motifs representing death, rebirth and the natural cycle of the returning soul.

Though this concept was clear, Dalan would have been hard-pressed to put into words what had entered his consciousness. Yet he did not question the truth of the understanding. Indeed he laughed at himself a little for imagining that there was anything to question.

In that moment his own foolish thoughts, wishes, desires and worries seemed so insignificant, so petty. He was amazed at his own arrogance in believing he could somehow bend the world to his will.

He no longer felt separate from everything. Dalan knew he was simply one small part of all things. Then he realised the distinction between himself and the world was so blurred as to make it impossible for him to distinguish himself as an individual entity.

The light pushed at his back then, and it was like the rush of a river carrying him along whether he wished it or not. For a short while he fought the force that urged him on into the doorway of the mound. But he soon realised he was only resisting because he was frightened. And there was no need for fear in this place.

He allowed the current to take him up to the entrance and he peered in, following the distinct outline of the golden beam of light. Before him he saw the great walls of the passage constructed from massive boulders larger than the one which lay on its side at the door. Like that entrance stone each of these was covered in intricate designs. The tale these pictures told concerned the journey of the sun and stars across the heavens. They spoke of the changing seasons, the phases of the moon.

Depicted side by side with these stories was the epic journey of the soul through the many circles of existence. Though he wouldn't have recognised the meaning of the motifs if he hadn't been in this dream trance, the message they conveyed was clear.

Dalan took a few tentative steps into the passage, still following the beam of light. Ahead of him he could just discern the shape of an old man in long flowing robes of green, an impossibly overgrown beard almost completely covering his face. He was standing beside a stone basin in which a naked woman was squatting. Her arms rested on the sides of the basin and her face was cut in deep lines of agony.

Abruptly the Brehon was pushed by the current from behind so that he had no choice but to move closer to the woman. At her side the old man was chanting a beautiful beckoning melody full of joy. But Dalan paid no attention to him. All his senses were focused on this woman.

Suddenly he realised why she was suffering so much pain. She was in the act of giving birth. With overwhelming certainty Dalan knew he was looking at the woman who would be his mother. It was his soul being drawn into existence from beyond the grave to take a new form.

The old man stopped singing and his gaze fell directly on the Brehon, though how he could have seen the floating spirit was not clear. He held up a skull and spoke a name which Dalan recognised as having once been his own. The empty lifeless skull must have also once belonged to him. This was a ritual to call him back from beyond the grave to finish his work amongst these people. And the Brehon knew this had happened many times down the generations.

The woman screamed in unimaginable pain as Dalan experienced a tearing of his soul. He understood then that he was beginning to share her feelings through every stage of the birth.

'The longer you tarry the more she will suffer,' the old man told him sternly.

The Brehon was overcome with fear at that second but he was shoved towards the basin by a force he could not resist. Before he could tell what was taking place the world had faded into darkness, the light of the sun withdrew and he was deathly cold.

Then he heard a song, felt a slap on his back and took his first breath in this new body. His eyes were wide with wonder as he looked up at the face of his mother, a face he'd seen countless times before.

She smiled down at him and spoke in a language he had never heard before in his waking life but understood perfectly. When she had greeted him he was wrapped in furs and carried outside by the old man.

To Dalan's surprise the ground was covered in snow and there was a great gathering of folk there, some of whom he recognised as his close kin. The old man held him up high and proclaimed his return into a new body. When that was done Dalan lapsed into a deep and restful sleep.

'That is what I have been missing,' Lochie told the Brehon as he gently shook him by the shoulder to stir him. 'The round of birth and death.'

'Is that what the Sun Ritual represents?' the Brehon asked.

'The ritual Sorcha practises is but a dim memory of these things. It is a dim reflection of a half-forgotten wisdom. Few folk nowadays know the truth of the matter.'

Dalan opened his eyes and stared into Lochie's for a few breaths. All of a sudden the fierce green fire seemed to subside. It was replaced by a gentleness the Brehon had never expected to see. There was compassion in Lochie's expression and Dalan could only wonder why this enchanted spirit might have such a feeling for him. Then the answer came to him in a flash and the realisation struck a painful blow to his heart.

'I will never know again what it is to be reborn,' the Brehon stated with a terrible certainty. 'You may one day be free of your enchantment. But I will be a prisoner of the Quicken Brew throughout eternity.'

Lochie nodded, averting his eyes. 'It is true,' he confirmed. 'In the ancient days when folk still understood the workings of the sky mounds there was a name for those who sought rebirth through the power of the sun and the passing seasons. These folk observed the heavens carefully and chose their time with care, understanding that they could choose the moment of their birth as surely as they decided the time of their death.'

'And they considered themselves immortal?'

'Yes,' Lochie nodded. 'They were immortal as all souls are. But their immortality stemmed from a continuous unbroken cycle leading from life to life. These folk called themselves the Watchers.'

'And now my people have become the Watchers,' Dalan realised. 'When you are gone you'll pass the burden to my folk.'

'You've helped me,' Lochie said, his voice choking with gratitude. 'If by some miracle Isleen and I are freed from our enchantment, you will have our eternal thanks.'

'Eternal,' the Brehon echoed with a smile.

'I will do what I can to ease your passage through the generations,' Lochie promised.

With that he took the Brehon's hand, kissed it lightly and faded into the air as if he had never been.

Chapter Twelve

fter Éremon released them, Goll mac Morna and Mughain made their way towards Dun Gur. They had been disarmed and relieved of their armour and packs, so the going was relatively easy.

They hardly spoke to one another for the first part of their journey until they rested by a pool long after sunset. Goll lit a fire, rolled onto his side and grunted when Mughain asked if he was hungry. It wouldn't have mattered. The King of the North had not given them any food or means to hunt.

She awoke the next morning to the war-leader shaking her out of sleep. His face had hardened with bitterness at being forced to run messages for King Éremon. They were on the road again just after sunrise, making good time on their journey south.

It was late afternoon before Goll finally slackened his pace a little and turned to his companion who was lagging behind. They hadn't stopped for food or drink all day and she was showing the signs of exhaustion.

'Shall we stop soon?' he asked.

Mughain shook her head and carried on, walking past him with a grim determination on her face.

'I'm sorry for my silence,' he called after her. 'I've been trying to hold my anger in. I didn't want it to spill over.'

The woman stopped in her tracks and turned around. There was rage in her eyes.

'This is no time to start feeling sorry for yourself!' she bellowed. 'We have a job to do and our comrades' lives to save.'

'I've let you down. All of you,' Goll admitted. 'I shouldn't have been so arrogant to think I could outwit the wily Éremon.'

Mughain growled under her breath then stormed back to where he was standing, a new-found energy in her stride. A pace or two away from him she let fly with the back of her hand and slapped him across the face.

'Don't ever let me hear you speak like that again,' the warrior woman warned through gritted teeth.

The war-leader touched his stinging cheek with the tips of his fingers and winced slightly.

'I've been a loyal warrior of your Fian band since we landed on these shores,' Mughain went on. 'But I swear I'll desert your leadership if you ever show such a sign of weakness again.'

'And if you ever strike me like that again, I'll have your hide,' Goll answered in a low menacing tone.

'That's what I like to hear,' she smiled. 'That's the voice of Goll mac Morna.'

Mughain turned around to continue the journey but she hadn't gone two steps when she froze and hushed her companion.

'What's that?' she whispered urgently.

The war-leader crept up by her side. 'What did you hear?'

'Voices in the woods.'

Goll cocked his head to one side. He could hear the leaves rustling in the breeze and the birds calling to one another. But through all this he couldn't make out the sound of any voices.

'Are you sure?' he asked.

'Certain.'

It was at that moment the war-leader spotted a movement on the path ahead of them. It was already too late to hide themselves in the underbrush so he took a deep breath and decided to face these strangers.

'Let me do the talking,' he told Mughain as he strode purposefully along the track.

He hadn't gone far, though, when his stride became less confident. After a mere twenty paces he came to a halt. The party he saw before him was huge. There must have been three hundred or more warriors dressed for battle.

Now it is true that Goll had fought against the savage tribespeople of the southern desert lands before he'd come to Innisfail. He'd battled the Fir-Bolg and the Danaans and witnessed their savage ways at close hand. But these people were unlike any folk he'd ever seen before.

They were tiny, though well proportioned. None was taller than a large child. Each warrior wore a tight bright red cap on the back of the head. They carried long spears, bows of incredible size, and strange short fat swords. Their clothes were brown, as was their armour which Goll guessed must be bronze. Their speech was an unintelligible gabble that made no sense to his ears at all. And every one of them spoke excitedly and over the top of one another, until their leader spotted the two Gaedhals on the road ahead.

All these strangers were unusually short but it seemed their leader was slightly taller than his comrades. He carried a great heavy club with a bronze axe-head wedged into the end. He raised this weapon high in the air and gave a high-pitched cry that hushed his company instantly.

The red-capped strangers stood utterly still as they stared wild-eyed at Goll and Mughain. It was obvious they were just as surprised to encounter the Gaedhals on the path as the two Fian were to see them.

They did not stay still for long. Their chieftain lowered his club — obviously the signal to advance with weapons at the ready — and in a matter of seconds Goll and Mughain were surrounded.

Spear points were waved about at them, shouts hurled into their faces and handfuls of dirt cast at their clothes. Though none of these folk was taller than Goll's shoulder, they were fierce and defiant. Their war-leader pushed his way through the crowd and thrust his club high into the air again. There was immediate silence. Their leader squinted, sizing up the Gaedhals from head to foot. He uttered a few guttural words and suddenly there were hands searching the two Gaedhals.

'Don't resist them,' Goll advised. 'Remember, we are unarmed and pose no threat.'

Mughain replied with a silent nod.

After a few moments it was clear that neither of the Gaedhals was carrying any weapons, so the war-leader lowered his club again. As he did so the ranks parted and four strangers approached, bearing a wooden chair on their shoulders.

Seated in this chair was an old woman with a deeply wrinkled face and the same tight red cap stretched over the bald crown of her head. The chair was lowered to the ground and the old woman sat forward to get a better view of Goll and Mughain.

Her face was etched with blue lines that had been cut into her skin in various designs. This gave the impression of fierceness. But her eyes betrayed a certain gentleness.

At last she beckoned with her finger for her war-leader to come close. They whispered some words between them before the woman pointed directly at Goll.

'Gaedhal?' she wheezed and it was apparent the word was foreign to her.

Goll mac Morna nodded.

'Eber Finn?' she pointed.

The war-leader shook his head.

'Éremon?'

Again the Gaedhal shook his head.

This seemed to puzzle the old woman. She frowned deeply and put a hand to her mouth to show she was having trouble communicating her question.

'Are you a follower of Eber Finn?' she asked emphatically, and Goll was shocked that she spoke his language after all.

He nodded and smiled. Almost immediately there was a general sigh of relief from the gathering. Weapons were sheathed and everyone relaxed, though Goll had no idea why.

The war-leader coughed to get the attention of the old woman, and when the chieftain noticed this he raised his club again and silenced everyone.

'Who are you?' Goll asked, pointing to the old woman.

Her grey-blue eyes sparkled with mischief as she sat back and laughed. Then she said something to the gathering and they all laughed in uproar. When they had settled again they started breaking off to continue their journey eastwards.

The four strange warriors lifted the old woman in her chair and she beckoned to Goll and Mughain to follow. But the Gaedhals could not understand why she might want them to go with her.

'I'll visit Eber,' she stated in her thick accent.

And then the old woman pointed east in the direction her people were headed. 'Eber.'

'She must be going to meet with the king,' Mughain said excitedly. 'Perhaps these folk are kin of the Fir-Bolg come to aid us in our fight.'

'You might be right,' Goll agreed. 'They dress like the Fir-Bolg of the Burren, except for the red hats. And they carry bronze weaponry.'

'Should we go with them?'

'We must hurry,' the old woman told them as her bearers

broke into a trot. With one more wave of her hand she urged them to follow and then she was gone as the ranks of Red Caps swarmed around them.

The two Gaedhals looked at each other, shrugged and silently agreed to go on after these strangers. In a few moments they were picking up the pace in an attempt to catch up to the old woman. But they were too exhausted to maintain it, and within an hour they'd lost sight of the unusual company of warriors.

Not long after Dalan awoke from his trance the chariots reached an open, cleared area where there was a well and a good stock of hay for the horses. There they halted. And Eber Finn decided to wait here until the rest of his warriors arrived on foot. Even though the Fian were travelling as fast as they could, the war-carts had gained quite a lead on them.

The king was too experienced to allow his force to be split. If the Sen Erainn proved to be difficult to deal with, he wanted to be certain he was in no danger. There was something about this whole business that disturbed Eber. And he knew his brother well enough to expect treachery at every turn.

Eber ordered fires to be lit, for though there had been no rain all season, the days were growing cold as Samhain approached. Dalan wrapped his Raven-feather cloak around him and sat by the largest blaze to ponder all that had been revealed to him.

He said nothing to Sorcha about the trance, knowing she was already very worried about him. She heated some mead for him in a bronze cauldron and gave him a cup. The Brehon thanked her, pulled his cloak up to cover his head and sipped his liquor.

The Druid woman sat by him for a while, but she sensed he was too tired to talk so she eventually let him be alone. She decided to fetch some water from the well which was a short distance from the place the warriors had halted. It was the custom in those times not to stand horses too close to a source of water lest they foul it. And with the lack of rain in the past months everyone was that much more respectful of the wells and springs which dotted the countryside.

The Druid woman picked up a water skin and wandered back up the road to fill it. She'd just plugged a cork into the neck of the full skin when she heard the caw of a Raven. She immediately looked up to the west, knowing her birds would be returning from that direction. The dying sun forced her to shade her eyes but she squinted and managed to make out two black dots soaring low over the treetops.

She answered their cries with a Raven-like call of her own and in seconds the pair of birds were sailing down towards her, their beaks clacking in excited greeting.

'The Sen Erainn are coming!' Crínán screeched. 'They'll be at the well before sunset.'

'Be quiet, you foolish bird!' his wife spat. 'Do you want all the creatures of the forest to hear you?'

'What matter if they do?'

'There are some who might not scruple to pass such news on, and before you know it Éremon of the North would hear that the Red Caps will march with Eber Finn.'

'He'll know it in any case, won't he?' Crínán frowned, or as close to a frown as he could approximate.

'It would be better if it were a surprise,' Crínóc admonished him as she landed softly by Sorcha's side.

'You just like to hear yourself telling me to be silent,' her husband complained as he came to rest a short way off. 'And you'd like this Gaedhal to think I jump at your every command.'

'I'm not a Gaedhal,' the Druid woman intervened, rolling her eyes and silently praying he wouldn't start on that subject again.

'But those folk you're travelling with are Gaedhals and no mistake,' Crínán pointed out, lifting a wing in the direction of the crossroads. 'I hope you're not getting too friendly with the tree-killers.'

'Shut up!' Crínóc shrieked. 'We've got important news to share. We haven't got time for your foolishness now.'

'You're always telling me to be quiet,' he sulked.

'If you don't keep your beak closed I'll tie it shut with a thread from your own sinews!'

'Very well.'

'Good.'

'I'll be silent now,' Crínán nodded. 'Absolutely quiet.'

'Thank you.'

'I won't speak until you give me the nod.'

His wife would have turned purple with rage if Ravens were able to blush. But to her credit she didn't rise to his challenge. She looked up to the sky, which was slowly growing pink with the sunset, and waited until her husband had finished his little game.

At last he stopped talking and hopped over to the well for a drink. As he sat up on the retaining wall, sipping from the bucket now and then, Sorcha tried not to show her impatience. At length she could stand the silence no longer.

'Are you going to tell me what happened?' she asked.

'Only if I can be sure Crínán won't interrupt me,' Crínóc replied sullenly.

'I won't,' he promised cheerily.

'Very well then,' his wife began.

'Not a word shall I speak,' Crínán chortled. 'Not a murmur.'

'Be quiet!' the Druid woman and the Raven-wife bellowed in unison.

'The Sen Erainn will be here soon,' he reported, stealing his wife's news and obviously unperturbed by the anger in their expressions. 'But Eber Finn's warriors will be here first. I saw them making good time up the hill as we came in to land.'

'And is the King of the Sen Erainn willing to enter into an alliance with the Gaedhals?' Sorcha pressed.

'He has terms to offer,' Crínóc cut in before her husband could go on. 'But he has brought the old woman, Beag ní Dé, with him so there is a chance you may gain the knowledge you've been seeking.'

'Are you tired?' the Druid woman asked urgently.

'Exhausted!' Crínán huffed. 'Don't tell me you've got another message for us to carry.'

'Not a message,' Sorcha told him. 'I want you to find Aoife, Mahon and Iobhar for me. Keep an eye on them if you come across them. And don't let them come too close to the battleground.'

'As you wish, my lady,' Crínóc bowed. 'How will we recognise them?'

'How many folk are travelling by night and resting by day? Make enquiries of everyone you meet.'

'I haven't slept for two days!' her husband cried. 'We can't keep going on like this. We need to rest.'

'I'll rest when I'm back amongst my kith and kin,' his wife shot back. 'This duty will earn us the privilege of returning to the nesting trees of our clan.'

'If the Gaedhals leave us any trees to nest in,' he sighed, shaking his head.

'Then stay here, you lazy bastard!' she squawked and was gone to do as Sorcha had asked.

'What did I say?' he shrugged, though Ravens throw the tips of their wings up in the air when they're puzzled, so it wasn't really a shrug as you might know it.

'You might try being a little more cooperative,' the Druid

169

woman suggested. 'I must admit you're really starting to annoy me too. Imagine what your wife must feel like having to put up with you day in, day out, season after season.'

'I believe I see your point, you don't need to go on,' he grunted.

'Well it must be a terrible burden,' Sorcha added. 'Perhaps she will find a younger mate to nestle with.'

'Yes, I think I can see where your reasoning is leading.'

With those words Crínán shook himself and spread his wings.

'Well I must be off,' he told her in a very formal tone. 'If we're going to complete all the tasks you've set us, we'd best be getting on our way.'

'Crínóc has already gone,' Sorcha reminded him.

The Raven fluttered his wings, preparing to fly away.

'I'll meet you at the hill fort where Goll is waiting,' Sorcha told him.

'If we aren't all murdered by those troublesome Gaedhals first,' the bird sighed as he took off in pursuit of his wife. He called back a few words as he departed and the Druid woman had to smile.

'Tree-butchers and bird-murderers the lot of them.'

Sorcha watched the two black specks until they disappeared in the crimson sunset sky. Then she shouldered the water skin and went to tell Eber Finn the news.

Chapter Thirteen

t was a little after dawn when Aoife awoke abruptly, startled by a shuffling sound in the fallen leaves nearby. Her mouth was dry, her vision blurred, and there was a terrible stiffness in her neck.

She coughed up smoke from the fire and decided that her discomfort had woken her. As the young woman rolled over onto her back to stretch she heard the shuffling noise again. It was louder this time and there was a hint of threat in it.

This made her sit up sharply as she remembered the dogs Eber Finn had set to chase them the night before last. But she had hardly moved when a wet hairy muzzle was thrust into her face and instinctively she screamed.

Aoife heard Mahon laughing as she cowered behind her arms. Then Iobhar spoke, barely able to contain his amusement.

'It's all right,' he giggled. 'Molly won't do you any harm.'

'Molly?' Aoife shrieked. 'What are you talking about?'

'The pig,' Mahon sputtered as he rolled about laughing for all he was worth.

The young woman looked up as the sow tasted her cheek again and grunted. But Aoife pushed her away before the pig could offer another kiss.

'She's just being affectionate!' Iobhar protested.

Aoife stood up and pointed a stern finger at the Gaedhal. 'Keep that animal away from me.' Then she stormed off to find the stream so she could wash and alleviate the dryness of her mouth.

After she had gone Mahon sat up and stretched. He cast an admiring glance at the sow when he thought Iobhar wasn't looking.

'I know what's on your mind,' the Gaedhal snapped. 'I can see in your expression what you're thinking.'

'What do you mean?' Mahon protested.

'There's a hunger in your eyes for the flesh of my pig.'

'And what if there is?' the Danaan shrugged. 'It's a pig and we're all hungry. We have a fine fire here for roasting and we've given our pursuers the slip, so we've plenty of time to prepare our feast.'

'Molly's my friend,' Iobhar shot back. 'She's intelligent and sensitive. And I have to look after her.'

'Did you bump your head when you slid down the kitchen sluice at Dun Gur?' Mahon asked incredulously. 'Or have you always had a touch of madness about you?'

'I've grown attached to Molly,' Iobhar replied, taking her in his arms and hugging her close. 'She's a sweet soul without a malicious thought in her head.'

At that very moment the pig let out a loud and noxious gust of gas from her rear which made Mahon groan and hold his nose. The Gaedhal hardly flinched but it was soon apparent he was holding his breath.

'I'm not sleeping another night with that going on upwind of me,' the Danaan declared. 'I couldn't sleep a wink for the stench of that creature's bowels last night. It's another good reason to stick her on a skewer and be done with it.'

'Don't talk so about my Molly,' Iobhar sobbed. 'She's a gentle spirit who was abandoned to the cold muddy edges of the lough without a thought for her welfare.'

'I imagine she was pushed down the kitchen sluice arse-first,' Mahon quipped.

'I rescued her from that lonely existence. I've carried her under my arm right across the countryside.'

'You've lost your mind.'

'Let's see what Aoife says,' Iobhar retorted. 'I'll bet she won't want to see anything happen to my lovely sow. Molly adores Aoife.'

At that moment the young woman returned, cast her eyes from the Danaan to Iobhar then asked, 'When are we going to eat that pig? I'm so hungry I could probably finish her off all by myself.'

'She's not for eating,' the Gaedhal stated with finality.

'Not for eating?' Aoife asked, stunned.

'She's his friend,' Mahon explained. 'She's smart and emotional. And it's his duty to take care of her.'

Once more Molly's bowels let loose their store of putrid gas. All three companions gasped in disbelief at the powerful foulness that filled the air.

'Perhaps you're right,' Mahon conceded. 'I don't know if I could bring myself to eat a creature that has such an odour leeching out of its body every few minutes. It's not healthy.'

'She's just upset at all this talk of butchering and eating,' Iobhar nodded. 'I told you she's a sensitive soul.'

But that was as far as his protest could progress. Mahon hushed them with a raised hand and a startled expression.

'Did you hear that?'

'Another fart?' Aoife laughed.

'No!' He pointed with his right hand while his left shaded his eyes. 'There's something in the forest across there on the ridge we crossed yesterday. King Eber and his dogs must be onto our scent.'

All talk of feasting on pigs was forgotten. Without another word they gathered the few things they carried, including

Molly, and were off down the hill in the opposite direction to the sound. In their rush they didn't bother to conceal their camp site. There was no time for that. Their only hope was to reach the stream where Aoife had been washing. They all knew the dogs would lose the chase among the rushing waters. Once they came to the stream they followed it towards the rising sun until they came to a bend which turned south.

At that point they turned north, forcing their way through the virgin underbrush until they came to open ground again. Before them there was an open bog which was quite springy underfoot but not very wide. At the other side of this there were more trees. A wood stretched out across the floor of a low valley bounded on two sides by bare round-topped hills.

'We'll make for that one,' Mahon decided, pointing again and shading his eyes from the sun. 'It looks like an old hill fort. We should be able to get a good view of the whole valley and know if we've been followed.'

It was at that moment the Danaan realised he'd left his cloak behind at the camp site. He cursed his foolishness but shrugged off the loss, knowing there was nothing he could do about it now.

Iobhar brushed his brow to mop away the sweat and as he did so he put Molly down on the ground. In an instant she was off into the woods as if she was possessed by some demon. Her fat little legs tore up the soft bog as she ran, leaving deep marks in the ground.

Before Mahon could stop him Iobhar was off after her shouting her name without a thought for who might hear him or where she might be heading.

'What's he doing?' Aoife asked. 'Has he gone completely mad?'

But by the time the words were out of her mouth Mahon had made off after the Gaedhal as fast as a fox after a rabbit. When she realised she'd been left alone, Aoife followed as quickly as she could, hampered by the heavy warrior's cloak Iobhar had loaned her.

The two young men were too swift for her, however, and despite her best efforts she soon lost both of them in among the closely gathered trees. A few times she thought she heard the squeal of a pig or the shrill cry Mahon used when he was out hunting deer. Once or twice she was certain the Danaan called out her name. But she couldn't find any trace of either companion until she stumbled on a clearing just after midday.

The circle of soft lush grass was bounded on all sides by mighty oaks which shaded the perimeter perfectly. In the centre of the sun-drenched area among the bright grasses Aoife caught a flash of reflected silver and she ran towards it with her heart in her throat.

She was no more than ten paces away when she plainly saw it was a sword of steel such as the Gaedhals often carried. The weapon had been broken halfway along the haft so the only part remaining was the hilt and a length of blade. Aoife was certain this was the sword Mahon had stolen from the guards at the ford, although there were no distinguishing marks on it. At first this was just an intuition, but the more she stared at the weapon the more convinced she became that this indeed was Mahon's sword.

She cupped her hands to her mouth to call out his name, but before she'd made a sound she thought better of it. Her eyes strayed back to the shattered blade. Steel was harder than bronze, so what could have broken a weapon made of the tempered iron of the Gaedhal.

Aoife spun around, searching the perimeter of trees for any sign of movement, frightened now that she may have been apprehended by King Eber and his men. But nothing stirred except the breeze flowing down from above the trees to tickle the uppermost leaves.

In her heart she sensed that Mahon was safe. But that

didn't ease her concern for her own welfare. She turned and picked up the broken blade, then threw off her heavy cloak. There was still a lot of weight to the weapon, even though it was only half its original length. Aoife balanced it carefully in her right hand, supporting her wrist with her left so that her arm would not tire too quickly. She'd seen hardened warriors do this in the thick of battle when their sword arms became weary. Then she waited in a half-crouching stance until she thought she heard a sound at the edge of the trees.

'Who's there?' she demanded. 'Come out and show yourself.'

The forest was still.

'Did you hear me?' she bellowed and her voice echoed through the woods. 'I'm waiting for you.'

As she issued her challenge for the second time there was a great crashing behind her. She spun around as a black shape rushed out from beneath the shade of the trees into the shining circle of sunlight.

The creature moved so quickly that Aoife could hardly focus on it before another noise distracted her. Directly behind her again she heard a strange high-pitched whooping cry.

It was answered immediately by the snorting of a pig. And Aoife recognised the black shape as Molly, Iobhar's sow. She was so glad to see the pig she might have hugged her just then if it hadn't been for the other sound.

With the sword held high now she turned to face the noise. What she saw almost made her drop the blade.

Running across the grass with a long spear in his hand was an unusual little warrior no taller than a child of twelve winters, though he was certainly well proportioned. His skin wasn't the healthy pink colour of the Fir-Bolg, it was a light tan. But his clothes were typical of her people.

However, it wasn't any of these details that shook her. What surprised her so much was his shaved head and long face. In the depths of his almond-shaped eyes there was a wit and wisdom far beyond his apparent age.

His wispy beard was greying and she wondered whether he might be quite old. But he wore upon his crown a bright red densely woven woollen cap. Aoife wasn't sure whether there was a delicate design worked into the weave but it was certainly beautifully crafted.

The stranger smiled at her, lowered his spear point to show it was not a threat to her, and then stalked slowly round until he saw the pig again. Then he gave out another ear-splitting call of exultation which Molly answered with a frightened squeal. Within a few breaths he'd stabbed at the little sow six or eight times but Molly was too quick for him. She dodged around his little legs and knocked him over.

He lay there shaking his head as the sow made a run for the woods and was gone. Aoife stood with her mouth open, unable to believe the scene she'd just witnessed.

What finally woke her from this state was another cry.

'Molly? You've murdered my Molly, you bastard!'

It was Iobhar and he was charging out from the edge of the trees with his sword raised above his head ready to strike. The little stranger looked up in seeming disinterest then finally rose to his feet as the Gaedhal got closer.

Iobhar swung his weapon at the strange warrior and missed. Then before he knew what had hit him the red-capped fighter struck the Gaedhal with the butt of his spear and knocked the poor warrior senseless.

This spurred Aoife into action at last. She rushed at the enemy with the half blade held above her head. The strange warrior turned, threw down his spear and held his hands out, inviting her to attack him with little movements of his fingers.

The young woman halted just out of reach while she tried to get herself a closer look at this enemy. He wore a string of spiral shells about his neck and his head was shiny under the cap. He was barefoot. His feet were broad and obviously toughened from walking the forest paths.

'Who are you?' she asked.

He stopped, frowned and cocked his head to one side as if he was surprised she could speak at all. Then in one swift graceful movement he stepped up to Aoife, grabbed her sword arm and twisted it till the blade dropped onto the grass.

He stepped back again and looked into her eyes. And as she opened her mouth to speak he turned to strike her across the face with a backward sweep of his elbow. The young woman took the savage blow, her head jolting back as she fell to the ground. Then the soft warm grass caught her in a gentle embrace and she surrendered to unconsciousness.

Lom had always been a good hunter. Since childhood he'd studied the many signs that lead an able warrior to his prey. So it was no surprise to Sárán when his twin brother picked up the trail of Mahon, Aoife and Iobhar.

Luck may have had something to do with it, but once he knew which direction they were headed, Lom was careful not to lose them. All day they followed in the chariot Eber had given them. Then, confident they would soon catch up with the fugitives, they rested just after nightfall.

The next day they lost all trace of the party for a while where they'd crossed a stream, but Lom was not easily fooled by such an elementary trick and was before long following the traces of their passing again.

And thanks to Lom's skill and the speed of the war-cart they would have caught them that very afternoon, but two hours before dusk their horse threw a shoe. The animal would not go on and the brothers were forced to abandon the chariot.

The going wasn't hard but it was much slower on foot and by sunset they were both exhausted. They marched on until Lom could no longer be certain he was following the trail and there they stopped for the night. They had no way of knowing that they had camped but a bowshot from the renegades. Only a valley separated them from each other that night. But it might as well have been an ocean.

When the sun came up, the two brothers sat at their fireside and ate a breakfast of porridge and butter. By the time they had cleared up the cauldron and packed their gear, the sun was already climbing into their part of the valley.

Lom was distressed by the late start and Sárán was ill-tempered after the loss of the chariot. As they walked he argued they should return to Dun Gur to fetch another, until his brother pointed out that all the war-carts would be heading off to battle.

He had just explained this when he stumbled on the place where Mahon, Aoife and Iobhar had spent the previous night. He was so surprised that they'd been camped so close, he couldn't believe his eyes at first. The fireplace was still smoking. There was travelling gear all around. Mahon's cloak was still spread out on the ground. Indeed it seemed as if all three had simply wandered off for a while and could return at any moment.

'They can't have gone far,' Sárán surmised. 'The Danaan didn't even take his cloak with him.'

'There's something wrong here,' Lom replied cautiously. 'I can't understand why they would have just up and left the camp without putting the fire out and covering it over. Surely Mahon wouldn't have left his cloak lying on the ground like that.'

'We'll wait,' his brother decided, sitting down by the fireplace and placing a log on it to burn. 'They won't be long. You'll see.'

Lom searched the camp site and soon found tracks leading down towards a stream. He told himself they must have heard Sárán and himself approaching and made a hasty retreat.

While his brother waited at the fireplace Lom followed the stream a short way east, guessing this would be the direction they'd headed. It wasn't long before he came to the place where they'd left the stream. Here he noticed the bog was torn up by the tracks of an animal. This confused him but he was certain from the other footprints in the soft ground that he'd discovered their whereabouts. He turned to fetch his brother and then had second thoughts. It would be just as easy to go on without him. And it would be a waste of time to go all the way back to the camp site to get him. On the other hand, the renegades were not too far ahead and there was no telling how they would react when confronted. And he knew his brother would be furious at being left out of this adventure.

The truth was Lom didn't particularly want to catch up with Aoife, Mahon and Iobhar. He was happy to let them go. They were free of all obligations, unburdened by duty. They'd been brave enough to throw aside all other concerns and take what they wanted from life.

He was beginning to consider joining them. If he let Sárán sleep by the camp fire, his brother might not wake until late afternoon. And Sárán certainly didn't have the skills to track any further. Indeed, it would take his brother at least several days to find his way out of this forest. By that time he and the fugitives would be far away in the north, perhaps feasting in the court of King Éremon.

Then Lom remembered the war that was about to be fought. His people had sided with Eber Finn. He was the King of the Fir-Bolg and it was his duty to keep his word to his kinfolk and his allies. His reign had already been cursed. He didn't want to make things worse by acting foolishly.

So Lom turned regretfully around, stepped back into the

stream and went back to find his brother. But he didn't hurry. He had lost the stomach for this chase. Now his sympathies lay with the fox, not the hounds.

When Aoife began to regain consciousness she had no recollection of anything that had happened that morning. She opened her eyes, yawned and looked about her, expecting to see the camp where they'd rested the night before.

The first sign that something was wrong was that the sky was darkening and the sun had set. This made her frown with confusion. Surely she couldn't possibly have slept that long.

Then she noticed the fire was burning brightly, even though Mahon and Iobhar were fast asleep. She nudged the Danaan but he just grunted and rolled over. Even Iobhar's pig was snoring gently, lost in a deep slumber from which nothing would wake her.

When she couldn't rouse her companions Aoife looked about her and was surprised to find she didn't recognise her surroundings. As far as she could recall they'd made their camp on the top of a little rise where they could keep a watch on the surrounding countryside.

But this camp was set by a flowing river which ran through a dark forest. The air was cold and dank as if it had been raining for weeks, though Aoife knew there hadn't been a drop of rain since before midsummer.

'Where am I?' she wondered aloud.

'Welcome to my forest,' a female voice replied and Aoife was on her feet in a flash.

A red-haired woman dressed in a long green cloak stepped out from the trees and walked towards the fire.

'I trust you slept well,' she offered.

The young woman nodded. She was completely confused but kept her senses enough to remain polite. There was danger here. The air was full of the scent of it and the young woman was unwilling to tempt fate.

'Surely you have nothing to fear from me,' the stranger laughed. 'You've taken the Quicken Brew, haven't you?' You're immortal. Nothing can touch you.'

'I beg your pardon, lady,' Aoife cut in, shaking her head to clear the confusion. 'I don't believe I know you. And I'm not sure how you would know anything about me.'

'We've met before, though I don't believe more than a few words have ever passed between us.'

With that the stranger came closer to the fire so that the young woman could see her face.

'Isleen?' Aoife gasped.

'Yes.'

'Why have you brought us here?'

'I'll tell you that in good time. Do not fear. No harm will come to you if you do exactly as I tell you.'

'I've taken the Quicken Brew. No harm may come to me.'

Isleen smiled and pointed to the sleeping forms by the fire.

'But that one is a Gaedhal. And he hasn't tasted the Brew. You will do as I request or Iobhar will suffer for you. Do you understand?'

Aoife nodded as the Watcher smiled and turned around to face the trees.

'Very well,' she called out. 'I'm very happy with the bargain.'

From behind the trees there appeared three strange creatures, two men and a woman. They were as short as any Fir-Bolg children and their heads were shaved clean. On the crowns of their skulls they wore tight-fitting red woollen hats that must have served to warm their hairless scalps.

The men both wore short, neatly trimmed pointed beards. And the woman had an elegant shape to her face and gorgeous almond-shaped eyes. Their clothes were exactly the same style as any of the Fir-Bolg of the Burren. That is, except for the colour. All their garments were dyed a nut-brown.

'Who are they?' Aoife asked, recalling the warrior she'd encountered in the clearing.

'Sen Erainn,' Isleen told her. 'They brought you to me. We have had a long association. They're a gentle people. One would hardly believe they could be cousins to the Fir-Bolg.'

'You paid them to hunt us and bring us here?'

'They consider me a holy being,' the Watcher explained. 'They're simple fisherfolk. They do as I ask them. Now and then I send them plentiful fish for their curraghs to net, or make sure the harvest isn't spoiled by bad weather. Without me they might not have survived on those barren islands they call home.'

She turned to the Red Caps and spoke a few words in a language Aoife could not understand, though she thought she caught a word here and there. The three strangers removed their hats and bowed and the young woman saw they were indeed completely bald.

'I've never seen creatures like them,' Aoife whispered, though she was certain they couldn't understand her.

The Sen Erainn replaced their hats and Isleen clapped her hands. In the instant her palms met, a small barrel of apples appeared in front of the Red Caps. Their eyes lit up with joy as they took the gift and departed quickly into the depths of the forest.

'They worked hard to bring you here,' the Watcher explained, turning to face her prisoner again. 'They deserve to be rewarded.'

'In ancient times a child was born to the Sen Erainn,' Isleen told her. 'His head was long and it was thought he would not survive. But he did and lived to become one of the wisest chieftains and Druids of his people.'

'A chieftain and a Druid?'

'Amongst the Sen Erainn a Druid may also follow the warrior path. A king must also be a trained and practising poet.'

The Watcher took Aoife by the arm and led her back to the fire.

'He wore a red cap on the back of his head to cover the shape of it. Ever since the time of that deformed Druid-chieftain the folk of Sen Erainn have venerated this fashion. Anyone born of their people is instantly recognised by their headgear. A red cap is a sign of great wisdom.'

Aoife stared down into the fire. 'They thought you were a goddess,' she remarked.

'To them I am a deity,' Isleen shrugged. 'Their people have known me for generations. I'm immortal. I have a certain skill granted to me by the enchantment which burdens me.'

'I have heard Dalan speak of it as a burden also. But I don't understand why it must be so.'

The Watcher laughed. 'When you are older you'll understand. Much older.'

She wafted her hand over the flames and the fire roared. 'But I haven't brought you here to discuss my plight. I have another little matter to discuss with you.'

'What matter?'

The Watcher pointed to the sleeping Mahon. 'Him.'

With that she sat down at one side of the fire and politely asked Aoife to join her. The young woman did as she was asked, surprised at her own lack of fear under the circumstances.

'Where shall I begin?' the Watcher asked herself aloud.

Then she produced a pair of mead cups and a jug from the folds of her cloak and poured two drinks. Aoife took the offered cup and drank down the contents quickly.

'That's better, isn't it?' Isleen soothed. 'Now you'll be able to relax a little.'

Aoife immediately felt giddy. Her heavy eyes were drawn to the flames of the fire and there they remained fixed while Isleen hummed a calming lullaby.

'Do not fear, child,' the Watcher sang gently. 'No harm will come to you.'

Before Sorcha made it back to where the chariots had halted, the first of Eber Finn's foot soldiers arrived. They were all exhausted from the pace of their journey but exhilarated as only warriors can be before a fight.

There was excited talk about who would lead the various Fian and what part of the field would be given to the Fir-Bolg. It was a matter of honour for the finest fighters to be given the right-hand flank of the king, who always fought in the centre, surrounded by his own household guards. This honour would usually be given to an ally. But the Fir-Bolg were fighting without their king and it was thought best that they stand with the king in the centre.

Eber Finn had already decided to give the right flank to the Sen Erainn, though he hadn't told his chieftains of this plan because he had not yet negotiated a firm alliance. If he failed to win the Sen Erainn to his cause, the king would have little hope of defeating his brother in open battle, so it hardly mattered how the warriors were arranged.

The northern folk who fought for Éremon were mostly veterans of the wars that had taken place in Iber before the Gaedhals set out on their voyage to Innisfail. The oldest and most experienced fighters had opted to remain with Éremon, while many of the younger, untried warriors had taken up arms alongside Eber.

The best blacksmiths also lived in the north, and the south

was suffering a severe shortage of arms and armour. After issuing new weapons to the Fir-Bolg Eber had found he had barely enough shields to go around his force. He'd taken swords from his warriors to equip the Fir-Bolg with blades because they had no experience with the bow. Fortunately he had an ample stock of bows. But his warriors would only be able to shoot five volleys before they would have to begin scrounging for arrows.

He was hoping and praying the northern warriors used their arrows early in the fight so that his own bowmen would have a stock of missiles to shoot back. If not, his archers would quickly become useless.

The king was seated on the back of his chariot, contemplating the coming fight and calculating the size of his force, when Sorcha approached him.

'I've had word from the Ravens,' she reported. 'The hosts of the Sen Erainn are not far away and should be here by sunset as arranged.'

'That's a blessing,' Eber sighed. 'Is there any other word?'

'None.'

'I must admit something to you,' the king went on. 'I fear I will lose this battle. And I already regret the life of every warrior who will fall today, whether they be from the south, the north or the Fir-Bolg peoples who are under my care.'

'Have you seen your own death?' she asked.

He shook his head. 'But I don't care that much for my own life.'

'That's foolishness! If you don't care for your own safety, how can these warriors hold any faith in you?'

'That's not what I mean. I wish I could find a way to avoid this conflict,' Eber stressed.

'That may yet be possible,' Sorcha assured him, placing a hand on his shoulder to offer comfort. 'This night Dalan and I will do all we can to bring a peaceful resolution. But it is well that you continue to plan the battle. Put your mind to your skill as a war-leader and don't think about what may be or should be.'

The king nodded, accepting the advice with humility.

'If you are not determined and ready for battle, all our efforts may be in vain,' she went on. 'If Dalan and I should fail and Éremon should gain the victory, the Watchers will visit their vengeance on this island for many generations. Of that you can be certain. The Fir-Bolg will be scattered to the four winds. The Danaans may stay safe in their Otherworld paradise, but your people will endure suffering until time overtakes the Watchers at last.'

'I am a good warrior,' Eber nodded. 'I'm a better war-leader. So I will do my best to gain the victory. But this will be my last war. I've lost the will to fight. I have no wish to see good folk perish by the sword. I don't relish the bloody work of battle.'

'Yet this is what you were born to do. So do your best.'

Again he nodded as trumpets sounded further up the road to announce the approach of the Sen Erainn.

'They'll be here among us soon,' Sorcha told him. 'Take off these mud-stained, travel-worn clothes. Dress in your finest battle array. Stand proud and make a good show of yourself. For if things go badly you may not live to see another week.'

The king was shocked that she spoke to him with such familiarity and honesty but he knew she was right.

'Remember the Brandubh game,' she told him sternly. 'Don't be distracted from the patterns by some small diversion or petty fear. Hold fast to your strategy and adapt where necessary, but don't lose sight of your goal.'

'You're right. I might as well enjoy being king while I may,' Eber Finn shrugged. 'There's no sense in worrying about what might be. I will hold to my strategy. You can be assured of that.'

'My people have placed their future in your hands,' Sorcha reminded him. 'That is a heavy responsibility. I hope you can live up to the faith they've placed in you.'

'I will honour the trust they have placed in me.'

With that the king stood up, smiled at the Druid woman to show his gratitude, and went off to find his chamberlain and a clean set of clothes.

Chapter Fourteen

t was after midday by the time Lom returned to the bog with his twin brother. Sárán refused to get his feet wet, so he walked along the bank of the stream which was overgrown in parts with blackberry briars. Lom was a patient man but his brother often tried that patience to its limit.

They found the clearing where Aoife had encountered the Red Cap. Sárán found the broken sword lying in the thick grass. Lom realised there had been a brief struggle, but to his intense frustration he couldn't find a clue to the direction his sister had been headed when she left the clearing.

While Lom was searching the outer edges of the circle of trees Sárán lay down on his back, his hands cupped behind his head, and waited. After a few minutes he began to doze and he was soon snoring in the warm sunshine.

He was abruptly awoken by a shadow blocking the light and he opened his eyes to see what it could be. Above him stood the form of his brother outlined in the sunlight.

'Get up and help me,' Lom growled.

'You're doing fine by yourself,' Sárán sighed dreamily. 'I'd just be getting in your way.'

'I've had enough of this!' his brother exclaimed. 'Two pairs of hands halve the harvest. Get up.'

'I'm a Druid. I have no expertise in these matters.'

'Then it's about time you bloody learned,' Lom told him sternly.

With that his brother reached down, grabbed Sárán by the tunic and hauled him to his feet.

'This is outrageous! I'm a member of the holy orders. How dare you treat me in this fashion.'

'This was all your idea, this chasing our sister around in the forest. So get on your feet and help me find the trail.'

'I won't do anything if you're going to treat me with such disrespect.'

Lom grunted, overcome with rage at his brother's arrogance. He pushed him away. 'You're no Druid,' he spat.

'And you're no king.'

That was the moment Lom saw red. The world turned scarlet. Everything before him was the colour of raging anger and he could restrain himself no longer. With a mighty punch such as he hadn't landed in many seasons, he thumped his brother hard in the jaw.

Sárán flew backwards and landed in the grass, clutching at his face where the blow had connected.

'That's for all the foolishness, the mischief, the selfish adventure and danger you've got me into since Fearna's death. It's for the snide little comments you've made about me just within my hearing, and the glib judgements you've passed on my friends. It's for the contempt you openly showed our father and the insufferable manner in which you've taken to the role of Druid adviser.'

'You'll regret this behaviour,' Sárán warned him. 'I'll have you judged by the Brehons and I'll have my honour price paid for this outrage.'

Lom walked up to where his brother lay and kicked him hard in the ribs. 'Then I'd better get some value for the cows it'll cost me.'

'Are you mad?' his twin screamed. 'I'm no warrior! I'm a Druid. I can't defend myself.'

But Lom was deriving great satisfaction from this beating and he leaned over to punch Sárán several times in the head, making his brother cower behind his hands.

'I should've done this a long time ago!' Lom shouted. 'By Danu's Holy Well, you deserve it. When I think of all the lies and petty deceptions you've heaped on me, I just want to beat you till I get it all out of my system. When I recall all the sanctimonious snivelling you've indulged in, I don't know how I put up with it for so long. You pretend to be so spiritual. You mask yourself behind a cloak of holiness. But you're less of a man than that boy Fearna was when he rode drunkenly to his death.'

'I'll have the Brehons take your throne from you for this!' Sárán spat back.

'Do it! None would be happier than I if you would. I never asked to be king. I was content with my life as a warrior of the Fir-Bolg. I never had any of your ambition. I'd resign tomorrow if there was anyone who could take the reins.'

'You can't resign. You've made a vow. The future of your kingship has been augured by the Bull Feast. There's no honourable way for you to abandon your duties until the prophesies and curses bear fruit.'

'This is all your fault! I never wanted the kingship. You did. But since a Druid can't be king, you decided to become the next best thing — the king's adviser.'

Suddenly Lom saw clearly what had driven his brother to advocate his kingship. He understood why Sárán had been so keen to become his counsellor.

'You thought you'd be able to manipulate me, didn't you?' he hissed.

Sárán blushed but didn't answer. So Lom kicked him again to stir some reply.

'You and Aoife have always considered me feeble-minded. You've always believed you could turn me to your will. Well I'm the bloody king now! And you'll do as I say or I'll have you replaced. And I'm sure Dalan will side with me. The Brehon would relish any excuse to have you packed off to some Druid island to live out eternity in holy isolation.'

'You wouldn't!' Sárán protested. 'You'd be lost without me. Just remember who saved your honour by bringing you on this expedition. If it hadn't been for me, you would have gone off to fight in Eber Finn's war and none of our chieftains would have dared to follow you. Our people will always be on the brink of deserting you unless you accept my guidance.'

'Get up and help me search for Aoife. If we find her and resolve the matter of her stupid flight with Mahon, then perhaps I will be allowed to fight in the battle. I've trained for war all my life. Now I'm burdened with an unwanted kingship and a lazy brother who is no better than a lead weight round my neck.'

'If you're seeking glory in battle, you'd better think again,' Sárán snapped. 'Have you forgotten the Quicken Brew? What honour will there ever be for a warrior who can't be killed? What glory can you claim if you have no life to offer up to your people?'

He had no wish to admit it, but Lom knew his brother was right. The Brew had taken away the danger that comes with an ordinary life. Not only had the thrill of battle been diminished, the excitement of all the little everyday risks had faded also.

There was a time when he would have been out every day racing horses with his friends or climbing the cliffs of the Burren to fetch the eggs of seabirds for his mother's breakfast. He didn't even bother to practise his swordsmanship these days. The invincible can afford to make mistakes in battle.

The strange thing was that he'd felt more invincible before

he'd taken the Brew. He rarely took any notice of fear then. In those days he really didn't believe he could be injured. Now that he was an immortal he'd lost his passion for life. And that was in some ways more frightening to him.

Lom gave a last half-hearted kick at his brother, then turned around to head back to the edge of the clearing. He heard Sárán offer a few parting insults but he ignored them. He knew his twin always had to have the last word but he just couldn't be bothered answering back.

He stormed off into the forest to find some peace and to sit and think a while.

It was a long time before he heard Sárán calling out to him in an urgent voice. And it was longer still before he decided he'd better go and find out what the fuss was about.

When he crossed the clearing his brother was standing up, pointing to the skies.

'Look!' he cried. 'There are two Ravens circling high above the trees over in the north-east.'

'Ravens!' Lom gasped, fearing the worst. 'Iobhar must have been hurt.'

'We're not searching for the Gaedhal,' his twin reminded him. 'We're looking for Aoife.'

Lom ignored his brother. 'We'd best be heading off over there,' he decided. 'I can find no trace of them in the forest. Those two carrion birds are our best hope for finding Aoife. Though I pray that all we find is the carcass of a stag which has expired from old age.'

He didn't wait for Sárán to offer any more advice or opinions, instead he strode off in the direction of the birds. His brother followed on behind, keeping a distance between them in case his brother flew into a rage again.

When Aoife looked up from her mead there was a duck spitted over the fire, being slowly turned by unseen hands. She raised an eyebrow at this but made no comment.

'Do you like roasted duck?' Isleen asked.

'Yes.'

'Aren't you impressed with my skills?' the Watcher pressed. 'Most of your kind would be thoroughly awed by having their favourite food produced for them in less time than it takes to conjure the thought.'

'It's just a trick,' Aoife replied.

'A trick?'

'Dalan taught me that there is nothing beyond the ability of a determined mind. Persistence is the key to success in any venture. He told me that there are many talented folk in the world but many of them are afraid to share their talents. There are also many who have spent their lives learning all there is to know about the world, yet they never make use of their knowledge. They hoard it like some precious treasure and rarely share it with anyone.'

Aoife took another sip of her mead and then went on.

'Of all these gifted and talented folk, of all who are learned, it is only the persistent who achieve what they set out to do.'

'Dalan is very wise,' Isleen agreed.

'He told me once about a Druid he had known in his youth,' Aoife continued, emboldened by the easy manner of the Watcher. 'This wise woman one day decided she wanted to learn how to fly through the air. Perhaps she thought it would make journeying around the countryside easier.'

'And did she learn to fly?'

'She spent forty winters locked away in a cave without light or sound or any contact with her kinfolk except for the food they passed through to her on a long wooden spade. And at the end of that time she emerged from her self-imposed exile.'

'Could she fly?' the Watcher asked eagerly.

'She could fly or float around as was her will,' the young woman nodded. 'But she'd spent half her life on this quest. Most of her old friends had passed away. Her family were too much in awe of her to have her stay in their settlement and she was forced to take to wandering the country on foot.'

'On foot?'

'Can you imagine how much a flying Druid woman would have upset the cattle?' Aoife countered. 'One look at her floating through the air was enough to stop the cows giving any milk for days.'

'So her life was mostly a futile squandering of time?'

'Dalan told me she had learned a great lesson from that experience. The last time he saw her she was quietly laughing at herself for her own foolishness. She realised she'd wasted her precious life in mastering a useless trick.'

Then the young woman remembered the point she had being going to make. 'Of course that was before the Quicken Brew,' she told the Watcher. 'So this Druid woman passed away as folk did in those times. You've been alive for a great many seasons. So I suppose you've come to master many tricks. I suppose there was little else to do.'

'You have no idea how time drags on without sickness or death to cloud the horizon,' Isleen sighed. 'It's been so many winters since the enchantment was put on me, I can't even recall when or where I learned all my little tricks. I mastered my mind quite early in the piece. So did Lochie. Perhaps that's why we were always the most formidable of all the Watchers and why we alone remain.'

'What happened to the others?'

'They became bored or disgruntled with life,' she shrugged. 'They grew tired. In the end they became one with the circle of standing stones.'

'Are you tired?'

'I'm exhausted. My spirit is ready to sleep for a thousand summers.'

'Then why don't you sleep? Why do you continue to cause havoc in the world?'

'I have seen what happens to my kind when sleep overtakes them. Watchers turn to stone. They retain a consciousness of sorts but they are imprisoned in an impregnable slumber which is painful and unending. Lochie and I spread mischief to keep ourselves interested in the ways of the world. Without our little intrigues we'd soon degenerate into the form our brothers and sisters took.'

'I've not thought much about this gift of immortality until now. You've made me begin to wonder whether it is as fine a thing as the Druids say. Will we share your fate? Will my folk be cursed with boredom or exhaustion?'

'You have taken the Quicken Brew,' Isleen told her. 'At least for Lochie and myself there is some hope of being released from our enchantment. I haven't heard of any potion that will reverse the effects of the Brew.'

'But the Brew was never used before. Perhaps the Druids will find a way to release us from eternal life.'

'The Brew has most certainly been used before,' Isleen countered. 'Though it was long ago and the story may have been forgotten. The Druids of your day did not invent it. It came from the people who are our ancestors, the folk who lived on the Isles of the West before the stars fell and the waters rose. Danu was one of their number. And she is still among us. If there was a cure for the effects of the Brew, Danu would have found it.'

'But you're one of the Fomor!' Aoife exclaimed. 'Our peoples are not related.'

'I was a Fir-Bolg before I took the side of Balor, Lord of the Fomorians. He promised to bestow upon our little company the wisdom and immortality of the ancient Watchers from the time before the floods. But he lied to us. His enchantment was but an empty reflection of the Quicken Brew. And so we are fated to fade from the world slowly and painfully unless we find the song that breaks our enchantment.'

Aoife took another sip of her mead and considered everything the Watcher had told her.

'Why have you brought me here?'

'Lochie and I have an old game we play to keep ourselves amused,' Isleen admitted. 'I know it probably doesn't sound very bright for two beings who've gathered a wealth of knowledge and wisdom about them. We like to indulge in wagers. It's one of the diversions that keeps us from falling into the oblivion of sleep.'

'Wagers?'

'I made a bet with Lochie that you would never wed Mahon. He, on the other hand, was certain you would.'

'You mean to tell me my life has been influenced by a wager?'

'Yes. Indeed the wager has influenced a great many of our decisions of late.'

'And what if it so happened that I did intend to marry Mahon?'

'Are you serious?' the Watcher sputtered. 'He's an oaf. He's nothing but a foolish boy who loves to show off. He's no match for your wit or learning. You surely can't be considering wedding him. He's hopeless in the bedchamber.'

'How do you know?'

'My dear,' Isleen sighed, seeing there was no way of breaking this gently, 'I spent quite a long while at the Danaan court before the Quicken Brew was consumed. I came to know Mahon and his father Cecht on intimate terms, if you know what I mean. The two of them are among the most fumbling, uninspired lovers I've ever flattened the furs with.'

'Truly?'

It was at this moment the Watcher realised Aoife was not as experienced as she had at first assumed.

'Surely you've had other lovers?' Isleen asked.

The young woman shook her head. 'Father was always careful to keep the young lads at a distance,' she admitted. 'He was always talking about saving myself for a suitable alliance. And my mother was always trying to tell me that males in general were a waste of energy.'

'She was a wise woman,' the Watcher noted. 'Though I can't entirely agree with her.'

'I never got to know another man as well as I know Mahon, if you take my meaning.'

'Aren't you curious?'

Aoife looked down at the fire and thought about the question for a while. She helped herself to another cupful of mead and then gave her answer.

'I am curious,' she admitted. 'And I very nearly allowed my curiosity to lead me into marriage with the King of the Southern Gaedhals. If Mahon and Iobhar hadn't come to rescue me, I would have ended up married to a man who would be old before I had a chance to get to know him.'

She took a mouthful of the honey liquor before she went on.

'Mahon has his faults. He's sometimes selfish and he's often a little dim. But he has a good heart and he's loyal. I can't imagine a better friend. He knows all there is to know about me. I've never kept any secret from him, until lately. And if I'm going to live an unnaturally long life I can think of no one I'd rather share it with. Don't you feel the same way about Lochie?'

'Lochie?' Isleen laughed. 'Come now, child. Lochie and I would hardly describe one another as friends. We're not in the least compatible. It was fate that threw us together, nothing more.'

'I'm sorry to hear that,' Aoife sighed. 'I'm just beginning to realise how lucky I am. Tell me truthfully, though. Would you miss him if he was taken away from you?'

'After a while perhaps. He is a very good Brandubh player.'

Aoife noticed that the duck was nearly done and pointed to the spit. But the Watcher stood up and dusted off her cloak.

'Enjoy your meal,' she told the young woman. 'I have some preparations to make and will return shortly. Don't think to wake those two. They're resting under the effects of a sleep potion. And don't try to escape. You wouldn't get very far in this forest.'

'What have you got planned for me?'

'All in good time, my child. All in good time. You have nothing to fear.'

Dalan leaned on Sorcha's arm as they waited to greet the Sen Erainn. He was still very tired and uncharacteristically silent. The Druid woman could sense a great emptiness in him but she knew it was more than the Bull Feast that had brought it on.

The Brehon had up till now resisted all attempts she made to quietly broach the subject. So Sorcha held her tongue for the moment, resolving to confront him after the formal greetings were done. It would not do, she told herself, to have the chief Brehon and adviser to the king wandering about in a daze as if he'd suffered a head injury.

Just then Eber Finn stepped up beside them. He was dressed in a polished mail coat which sparkled over a dark blue tunic. His cloak was of dark blackberry red and his breeches were of the finest doeskin.

He nodded to Dalan and placed a hand on his shoulder. The Brehon grunted a reply that was neither polite nor appropriate. Then he moved his shoulder to shake away the king's hand.

'I trust you'll be more diplomatic with the Sen Erainn,' the king noted dryly.

Dalan did not acknowledge the reprimand. It was all he could do to stay alert and focus his attention on the road along which they expected the strangers to appear. He did not have to wait long. A scout driving one of Eber's chariots appeared from around a distant corner and sped towards the well at a fearful pace.

By the time he'd reached the king, the hosts of the Sen Erainn were already visible on the road. In their distinctive red headgear they looked like a distant field of mushrooms that had decided to take to the march as one company.

'How many would you say there are?' Eber Finn whispered to Sorcha.

'Three hundred. Maybe more.'

The king sighed with relief. He would have estimated only a hundred or so but his eyes were not as sharp as Sorcha's so he discarded his own pessimistic reckoning.

As the warriors came closer it was clear their number was more likely around four hundred. Eber's blood began to pulse faster and his excitement was clearly visible.

'They look like strong men and women,' he said loudly. 'There's no doubt they'll be a great help to us in the field.'

Dalan grunted again, wishing the king would keep quiet so he could concentrate on trying to spot the old woman known as Beag ní Dé. The hosts of the Sen Erainn were quite close before he saw a figure being carried on a chair. He guessed this must be her.

As the strangers drew close they fanned out across the road in their battle array as was the custom when two kings met in the company of all their warriors. This was not a gesture of threat but rather a sign that there was no trickery involved.

All the Sen Erainn warriors turned the points of their spears to the ground once they were in place.

Almost immediately Eber Finn's Fian rushed to their battle positions and mirrored the gesture, with swordsmen leaning on their blades and bowmen laying their bows upon the ground.

Then three warriors stepped out from the Sen Erainn. One of them raised a club high in the air as the other two, a man and a woman, chanted the opening verse of a war cry. All the warriors behind them joined in the refrain and then there was a sudden silence as the three warriors openly laid down their arms.

That done, they made their way swiftly to where the King of the Southern Gaedhals and his entourage were waiting. Dalan roused himself from the cloud of exhaustion hanging over him and tried to concentrate on observing every detail of these people.

The caps they all wore were dyed a bright red and about a tenth of their number had elongated heads that swept back to a point behind their crowns. The rest wore flat red hats shaped like mushrooms. Their clothes were all greys and browns, no bright colours. Their skin was slightly darker than the Gaedhals or the Fir-Bolg.

Just as the three strangers came close Sorcha remembered the Ravens. She knew some among Sen Erainn understood the Raven tongue, so if they had trouble with the Fir-Bolg speech or the language of the Gaedhals they could resort to that.

In the event she didn't need to concern herself. The Sen Erainn king walked straight up to Eber Finn, grasped his hand and greeted him in a strong but understandable accent.

'My name is Aenghus son of Ómor,' the short, stout old warrior declared with a broad smile. 'I am a king, a fighter and a poet. Are you the one they call Eber Finn?'

'I am.'

The little king turned around to face his two companions and they all laughed together.

'Are you a Gaedhal?' he asked.

'Yes.'

Once again he turned around and shared some private joke.

'We were under the impression your people were much taller and broader about the shoulders. But you're actually quite a scrawny looking folk, if you'll pardon me saying so. How did you come to defeat the Danaans and the Fir-Bolg in open battle?'

'They have a weapon which cut through our swords and shattered our axes,' Dalan piped up, summoning all his strength.

'It is called steel,' Eber confirmed.

'Steel, is it?' the King of the Sen Erainn asked and the mirth dropped away from his face. 'Show us this steel.'

Eber Finn called for his blade and the giant Naithí rushed to fetch it. As soon as Eber had it he drew the weapon from its scabbard and passed it over to the Red Cap king.

Aenghus weighed the sword in his hand carefully before examining the metal and the workmanship.

'Take this as a gift,' the Gaedhal offered.

But the Sen Erainn king frowned and handed the weapon back. 'I was led to believe you had asked the assistance of my folk in a fight with your brother in the north. Is that true?'

Eber Finn nodded. 'It is.'

'I'll be honest with you,' Aenghus sighed with a sudden familiarity that broadened his accent. 'As we three walked up here and took a look at your warriors we said among ourselves it would be a small matter for our people to trounce yours on the field. So we reckoned this trouble with your brother would be easily resolved.'

He took a few breaths while his companions nodded their heads to confirm he was speaking the truth.

'But if the northern Gaedhals are armed with swords such as that, I'll need more than one if I'm going to do the job properly.'

'I have no more swords,' Eber protested. 'My armourers have been working for days without rest and we have barely enough weapons for our own folk.'

'In that case I wish you the best of luck on the battlefield,' Aenghus said gravely. 'For my folk cannot accompany you.'

It was at this instant Dalan laughed. Both Eber Finn and Sorcha turned sharply towards the Brehon. The Gaedhal's face showed his patience was at an end; the Druid woman was confused and concerned.

'You know well enough that we have the secret of the Quicken Brew,' he reminded the Red Cap. 'Our messengers have told you we are willing to offer you the secret of it in exchange for your aid in battle.'

'Since when do Brehons negotiate on behalf of kings?' Aenghus replied, barely disguising the outrage in his voice at being scoffed at by a Druid.

'Since when do warriors claim the status of a poet?' Dalan countered. 'Have you trained in the Druid ways?'

'I have learned the art of poetry in the schools of Arainn!' Aenghus snapped. 'Among our people it is not uncommon for a king to be of the poetic class. I will recite one of my compositions for you as proof.'

The King of the Sen Erainn cleared his throat before he began.

'A fisherman caught three sizeable sea-going fish,' he began. 'They were long and salty smelling. Their gills flapped wildly. And they had silvery parts around their enormous black eyes. I would give those three fish and a dozen more like them if I could be a herring.'

Dalan stared blankly at Aenghus, unsure whether he was serious.

'If you could have understood it in my own language you would probably have appreciated it better,' the Red Cap explained.

'Among our peoples it is customary for Brehons to negotiate on behalf of their kings,' Dalan went on, deciding the less said about the poetry of Aenghus mac Ómor, the better. 'I am chief adviser to King Eber. He trusts my judgement in all things.'

Eber Finn did not protest, even though he was less than happy with Dalan right at this moment.

'Then you will give me the Quicken Brew?'

'If we do you will have no need of steel weapons,' the Brehon reasoned.

'We will need to see some proof of the Brew's worth,' the Sen Erainn king pointed out.

'Naturally,' Dalan agreed. 'I was expecting as much.'

The Brehon turned to Sorcha. 'Can you prepare a small portion of the Brew for us?'

She nodded. 'It will take me an hour or two at the most.'

'There you are!' Dalan exclaimed. 'You shall have your demonstration later this evening.'

'But I will require weapons made of steel as well as a guarantee of sovereignty over the islands of Arainn.'

'Eber Finn does not at present have enough steel blades to issue any of your warriors with them,' the Brehon reasoned. 'But if the battle is won I'm sure he would be happy to supply the weapons to you at a reasonable price.'

'We'll pay for them with our sword arms,' Aenghus growled. 'Or we'll take our strength over to Éremon. I'm sure he wouldn't deny us the steel.'

Eber felt the sweat break out upon his brow. The situation was turning the worse with every word.

'Steel is no use to you,' Dalan reasoned. 'You are an island race who live close to the sea.'

'What of it?'

'Sea salt weakens iron and steel. In time weapons and implements fashioned from it corrode away to nothing. You're better holding onto your bronze. It's easier to maintain and will serve you well even when it's been in the water a while.'

'Is this true?'

'I'll show you. Bring up King Eber's chariot!' Dalan commanded.

As they waited for the war-cart Dalan asked a question that had been intriguing him. 'You speak the Fir-Bolg tongue quite fluently. I was led to believe that our languages had diverged generations ago. Where did you learn our speech?'

'I was caught in a storm while fishing when I was young. I was washed up on the shores of Innisfail. A Fir-Bolg family nursed me until I was able to leave. They taught me your tongue.'

The war-cart drove up just then and the King of the Sen Erainn whistled through his teeth when he saw it. It was clear he was impressed.

Eber Finn pointed to the wheels. 'Do you see the rims which bind the timber wheels and protect them from the rough ground?'

Aenghus nodded.

'Do you see how they have started to rot and turn red?'

'Yes.'

'That is rust,' Dalan cut in. 'It is the one weakness of steel and iron. It's caused by water. And the damage is worse from the salt sea. If you still don't believe me then take some swords home after the battle and you can witness the corrosion for yourself.'

'I'll speak with my chieftains on this matter,' the king replied cautiously.

'The offer of the Quicken Brew is still open to you if you

would take it,' the Brehon went on. 'But in accepting it you must also promise to observe a peace-making and an eternal truce with the Fir-Bolg folk.'

'That also will have to be put to the chieftains,' Aenghus informed him as he walked around the chariot inspecting it. He kicked the wheels once or twice then jumped up beside the driver and looked back at Eber expectantly.

'Take him for a ride,' the Gaedhal commanded.

The driver acknowledged his king then gave the horse the order to move on. The war-cart went down towards the ranks of the Sen Erainn, who raised their voices in salute to their king as he rode triumphantly past them.

'He's like a little boy with a new pony,' Eber whispered with a smile.

'Shall we let him play for a while?' the Brehon inquired, casting a glance at the king.

When the war-cart driver returned, Aenghus leapt from it as it came to a halt. He was howling with joy and exhilaration.

'Give me a chariot,' the Red Cap king demanded. 'Give me a chariot and I'll convince the chieftains to fight for you.'

'It's yours,' Eber Finn replied without the slightest hesitation.

'I will go speak with my people now. I can already feel a poem beginning to take shape in my mind in celebration of this alliance.'

Then Aenghus mac Ómor turned to his companions and spoke a few words in his own language, at which the two of them departed immediately. The Red Cap king mounted his new war-cart.

'There are no fishes so swift as those who swish their tails like a leather boat in a large sea-swell,' he recited in his best poetic tones. 'They cook quickly and their bones are few. When you go out fishing, catch me one for my supper.'

With that he rode off, whooping and calling at the top of his lungs while his warriors shouted encouragement to him. Dalan was left frowning for a few moments, unable to decide whether the poem had been rather witty or just plain nonsense.

As the chariot was crossing the field towards the ranks of the Sen Erainn, four folk emerged from the battle lines bearing the chair Dalan had spotted earlier. The Brehon stood up straight. The old woman's skin was pale and heavily lined, and her bony features made her face look drawn and withered. It was immediately apparent that she was not long for this world. The Brehon thanked Danu under his breath that she had lived long enough to pass on her knowledge.

'This is Druid business,' Eber Finn stated. 'I will go to await the word of Aenghus mac Ómor.'

'Very well,' Dalan replied sharply. 'Go then.'

The king hesitated then added, 'Thank you for your words to the Sen Erainn. You may have saved me a great expense.'

The Brehon grunted again. The king, puzzled, glanced at Sorcha then turned and walked away.

'Why are you treating Eber with such contempt?' the Druid woman hissed. 'You're supposed to be his adviser.'

Dalan frowned. 'I don't mean to be rude. I'm incredibly tired,' he sighed. 'It seems to be making me a little short-tempered.'

'Then guard your tongue when dealing with this Druid. We don't want to risk losing the secrets of the Watchers' Draoi song because you're tired and irritable.'

Beag ní Dé was set down in front of the Brehon and he took a few steps towards her, showed the palms of his hands in friendship and bowed low. The old Druid smiled and caught his glance. Her eyes were bright, blue and clear, full of mirth and wisdom. And her face was etched with hundreds of fine blue lines that had been pricked into her skin in ink. Three spirals on her left cheek were the freshest of these and seemed to have been added recently.

Dalan was surprised at how refreshed he immediately felt in her presence.

'You are in need of rest,' she observed. 'Has Aenghus been reciting his poems?'

Sorcha smiled. 'Indeed he has.'

'He is a man obsessed,' the old woman sighed. 'But he has been waiting a long while to meet the King of the Fishes.'

Then, without explaining what this might mean, she turned to one of her bearers and issued an order. He ran off down towards the Red Cap warriors to carry out her command.

'I've sent him to fetch my herbs. I'll make you a tea that will clear your head and soothe your troubled mind.'

'Thank you,' the Brehon stuttered in surprise. 'You also speak the Fir-Bolg tongue.'

'I'm a Druid,' she shrugged. 'I know many things. Can we sit by a fire and talk? My old bones ache in the open air.'

She stood up and placed her hand on Dalan's arm and he led her over to the main fire. The warriors who were gathered there politely departed so the Druids could confer in private. Sorcha placed a three-legged stool close to the coals. Then Beag ní Dé sat down on it and thanked her for the courtesy.

'I believe I may be able to help you,' the old woman began, coming straight to the point.

'We're seeking a song that will free the Watchers from their enchantment,' Sorcha explained. 'We've heard tell that you have some recollection of this song.'

'Indeed I do,' Beag ní Dé replied with a nod and a smile. 'But I'm not sure I should share it with you. Why would you want to know such a secret?'

'It is our intention to break the enchantment which Balor of the Evil Eye placed on the Watchers generations ago,' Dalan told her. 'In this way we will free them from their bondage to this world and cleanse Innisfail of their influence.'

The old woman raised an eyebrow and smiled from the

corner of her mouth. 'You must understand that I have been given this song as a safeguard,' she informed him. 'You see, my people venerate the Watchers as powerful deities. They've aided us on many occasions when hunger, storm or pestilence has struck the islands. You're asking me to banish the beings who have saved my folk from destruction a hundred times.'

'The Watchers themselves have requested this be done,' Sorcha cut in.

'They've enlisted our help in breaking the enchantment,' the Brehon added. 'They fear they will become like their brethren.'

'Do you mean that awful circle of stones?' Beag ní Dé asked. Dalan nodded.

'But that is their fate. They cannot escape what was set down for them from the beginning. When they are tired they must turn to stone. That is the nature of the enchantment.'

'But no one's fate is certain,' Sorcha argued. 'And if you know a song that might free the Watchers from their fate there is the proof of it.'

'The song was passed down to me as a secret,' the old woman told her. 'Not even the Watchers are aware I possess the knowledge of it. In ancient times when they first came to our people they caused a terrible fight between our folk and our cousins the Fir-Bolg. Our king at the time promised to serve them faithfully if they would make an oath to protect our kindred forever.'

The old woman looked around and made a complicated gesture with her hands to one of her bearers, indicating she wanted some water boiled. He went off straightaway to fetch a cauldron.

'If it wasn't for the Watchers we would have been overrun by the Fir-Bolg, the Danaans or the Gaedhals long ago,' she went on. 'So if they leave, our islands will be defenceless. You must understand I cannot support such a possibility.'

'Have they always kept their word?' Dalan inquired.

'Indeed they have. But our Druids thought it best to preserve this song just in case they stirred up trouble again. I have promised it will not be used unless the Watchers bring danger to our people.'

'They are bringing danger,' the Brehon insisted. 'If they are not appeased I believe they may become extremely dangerous. They have already threatened me and Sorcha, even though we are working to help them realise their dream.'

'They've stirred up this war,' Sorcha agreed. 'They inspired the Gaedhals to come to this land. And that is just a small example of their capabilities.'

The three of them fell silent as the bearer put a cauldron of water on the fire and handed them cups. Then the other Red Cap returned with a leather satchel. Beag ní Dé searched through it and quickly located what she was looking for.

'You'll find this will help to ease your tired mind,' she told Dalan as she threw a handful of herbs into the cauldron.

When she saw that the herbs had settled to the bottom she looked up at the Brehon and went on. 'My king wants to possess a secret that you hold,' the old woman shrugged. 'I've tried to dissuade him but he's determined to know the mystery of the Quicken Brew.'

'The Brew would certainly return you to the full vigour of your youth,' the Brehon assured her.

But Beag ní Dé just laughed. She laughed so hard that she had to put down her satchel and wipe the tears from her eyes.

'You must think I am an utter fool,' she cried. 'Why would I want to live forever? I count myself lucky it won't be long before I pass over to the Halls of Waiting and drink from the Well of Forgetfulness. I've seen enough pain, fear, suffering, sorrow and selfishness in this lifetime. I have no wish to be subjected to it for an eternity. I pity you if that is your fate.'

Then she picked up her cup again and stirred the water in the cauldron with it.

'I know the Quicken Brew cures all manner of physical sickness,' she told them. 'But can it cure a black heart or a greedy spirit? I don't believe so.'

She pointed down to the ranks of Sen Erainn warriors. 'King Aenghus is a good ruler. He has a kind heart and the door to his feasting hall is always open. But he's also a selfish man who loves gold above his own kinfolk. To him the Quicken Brew is just a means to gather trinkets endlessly. It will bestow power on him which he could otherwise only dream of. And it will lead to bitter wars that will split our folk into factions. I am a seer of the Frith-craft. The mushrooms have spoken to me and I have seen exactly what would happen if Aenghus were to have his way.'

Dalan stared off into the fire and did not speak. He knew she was probably speaking the truth.

'Of course you understand that under no circumstances should Aenghus be allowed to take the Brew before the battle,' the old woman added. 'There'd be all sorts of trouble if he did. What makes you think I'd want my kindred to end up fighting one another over such a silly thing?'

'You may be right,' the Brehon admitted. 'But you must understand I wouldn't be asking for this song if the Watchers themselves hadn't begged for my help. Somehow the Quicken Brew has been brought in as a bargaining piece and the impending battle has confused the situation completely.'

'I'll give the song to you on one condition,' Beag ní Dé said firmly, holding up her hand to silence him. 'Summon the Watchers to this place and let me hear from their own lips that they have asked for this. And then I want to see the power of the Quicken Brew for myself.'

'Very well,' the Brehon agreed. 'I'll do what I can to bring the Watchers here, though I can't promise they'll come when I call.'

'When will this battle be fought?' Beag ní Dé asked him.

'In the next day or so. If we wait much longer the snow will come and there will be no resolution of this problem until the late spring. That will annoy the Watchers and complicate the situation even further.'

'Éremon will have time to raise a larger fighting force and train them through the winter,' the old woman nodded. 'Yes, it is better this is resolved quickly. You'd best summon the Watchers then and offer me your proof.'

She held up her finger in warning. 'But don't let them know I hold the secret of the Draoi song. Do you understand?'

Dalan assured her he would not. The water was beginning to boil so Beag Ní Dé filled a cup with the tea and handed it to him.

'Drink this. It will take the fire from your head and soothe your soul.'

The Brehon accepted the cup and as he did so he noticed the old woman was watching him intently.

'Don't mind me,' she told him. 'It's rare for me to meet one who has recently undergone the Bull Feast.'

'How did you know?'

'It's written in your eyes,' she winked. 'And it just goes to prove there are some ailments which the Quicken Brew cannot cure completely. Ailments of the spirit can never be alleviated by it. For it is said that weariness of the feet lasts an hour. Weariness of the soul lasts a lifetime.'

Dalan took a mouthful of the tea, thanked her for her thoughtfulness and then excused himself, explaining he needed to be alone to summon the Watchers. He went off into the forest, leaning heavily on his staff as he went. As Sorcha watched him depart, her heart went with him.

Beag ní Dé noticed the longing in the Druid woman's expression and smiled as she sipped her tea.

'You'll have the rest of eternity to enjoy his company,' she told Sorcha. 'Don't fret after him. He'll not come to any harm. Now drink the brew I've made for you. It won't cure everything but it will calm your spirit for a while.'

CHAPTER FIFTEEN

hen Aoife had finished eating she felt extremely tired so she lay down beside Mahon and covered herself with the cloak Iobhar had given her to keep her warm. It never occurred to her that her host might have slipped a sleeping potion in the mead so she wasn't anxious at her sudden drowsiness.

Her last conscious thought was that Isleen didn't seem to be at all evil. She'd heard Dalan say many times that the Watchers were neither good nor bad. In his opinion they simply followed the dictates of their hearts without the restraint of rules or laws. He regarded them as lawless and lacking a moral code but also capable of great compassion.

The young woman dismissed every opinion she'd heard of the Watchers. To her, Isleen seemed to have good intentions. She was warm and sympathetic in a maternal way. Then Aoife's thoughts strayed to her own mother and she drifted into slumber.

Her mother's face appeared in her imagination and her features were as real as if Aoife had been standing right in front of her. Riona, former queen of the Fir-Bolg, was sleeping peacefully on a bed of thick straw. In her dream state the young woman tried to wake her mother but Riona hardly stirred.

The strange thing was that Aoife understood she was

dreaming, that what she was experiencing wasn't real. She was too aware for it to be anything other than a sleep vision. Once she'd settled this in her mind, she decided not to be too worried by anything she might witness.

She stepped back from the sleeping form of her mother and looked around the room. She found herself standing in the centre of a vast chamber where countless beds were arrayed. And each bed cradled the sleeping form of someone she knew. There was Cecht, King of the Danaans and father to Mahon. Beside her mother's bed slept her father, King Brocan of the Fir-Bolg. Nearby were Fineen the Healer and many others she recognised from the days before the Quicken Brew and the coming of the Gaedhals. Most of these folk had decided to retreat into the Otherworld with King Cecht, yet here they lay sleeping.

Aoife had to remind herself that this was just a dream. She reached out to touch the covers on her mother's bed and the furs were soft, warm and inviting. Then, as is the way with dreams, she knew how they had all come to be here.

'It is my gift to them,' Isleen soothed. 'I have granted them sleep so they will not have to endure the endless round of seasons without death. It is better that they lie here and dream, beyond all cares and safe from the withering of the spirit that would surely plague them if they were awake.'

The young woman turned to face the Watcher but Isleen was nowhere to be seen.

'Are they at peace? Will any harm come to them?' she asked.

'They are sleeping peacefully and their souls are free to dance together in the Land of Dreams, the Land of Eternal Youth, Tir na nÓg. In that place they can forget the cares of this world and find true happiness of the spirit.'

'You didn't answer me. Are they in danger?'

'Whatever happens to them in Tir na nÓg they will always return to their sleeping bodies. There can be no death for them but I have eased the burden of immortality on them.'

Aoife looked at all the faces of the folk she knew so well and thought she'd never seen any of them looking so healthy, content and peaceful.

'Will they ever wake from their sleep?' she ventured.

'They may be woken,' Isleen replied. 'Love can awaken them. But why would you wish them to be awake when they are enjoying such a joyous sleep? They are sleepwalking in a most glorious dreamworld. It is a finer place than you can even begin to imagine. '

She looked on the faces again and found she had to agree with Isleen. But a doubt crept into her mind and it would not go away.

'How do I know you're telling me the truth?'

'Wake one of them and ask for yourself.'

Aoife stepped forward to her mother's bedside and took Riona by the hand. The queen stirred but did not wake. So the young woman tried speaking to her.

'Mother? Can you hear me? It's your daughter Aoife. Wake up, Mother, I wish to speak with you.'

But still Riona didn't open her eyes. So Aoife leaned in close and kissed her mother on the cheek and as she did so her thoughts were full of fond memories of her childhood. And she knew immediately that this had been enough to drag her mother out of her dreaming.

'Aoife?' Riona yawned. 'Is that you?'

'Yes, Mother.'

'Why did you wake me up? I was having such a wonderful dream. Now I don't know if I'll ever be able to return to it.'

'You can go back whenever you wish,' Isleen soothed. The Watcher placed a gentle hand on the top of Riona's head.

'It's you,' the queen sighed. 'Is Lochie with you?'

'He's off away on other business,' Isleen explained. 'No need to worry about him.'

'It's a wonderful gift you've given us,' the queen said with sincere gratitude in her eyes.

'What would you say to your daughter if she were considering taking the long sleep?'

Riona turned to the young woman and clasped her hands tightly.

'Aoife, my darling girl,' she began. 'I thought the Otherworld was a wondrous place when I first travelled there. And it will always be a divine sanctuary for all who have taken the Quicken Brew. But the Land of Dreams is far better.'

'Why?'

'The Otherworld is intricately linked with the world of mortals. Whatever happens in Innisfail is mirrored in that other place. So the temptation is to interfere in the world of mortals. But in the world of dreams anything can happen. There is no unhappiness there.'

'Are you content?'

'If I were to live in the mortal world I would grow weary in the soul before a cycle of the seasons had passed me by. In the Otherworld it might take longer but I would certainly grow weary. In this state of sleep I am free of all pain. I harm no one and no one harms me.'

'Would I be happy there?'

'If happiness is what you seek then you shall find it,' Riona told her sincerely. 'None of us is abandoned to our own dreams alone. We share the joy of the vision world and walk together in that place. I can tell you with my hand on my heart that I have never known such euphoria. I have never experienced such a sharing of bliss. Come with us and sleep and you too will know the joys of which I speak.'

Then the queen turned to face Isleen again. 'May I return now?' she asked. 'I don't want to miss anything.'

'You won't miss a moment,' Isleen assured her. 'Time passes differently in the world of dreams.'

Riona took her daughter's hand again and squeezed it tightly. 'Farewell, my dear. I must return. I hope you'll join us soon. You've been missed. We often talk about you.'

With those words the queen lay down and closed her eyes as the Watcher touched her forehead. In moments she was soundly asleep again.

'Will you join them?' Isleen asked.

'What of Mahon? Will you allow him to accompany me?'

'That is his decision to make,' the Watcher shrugged. 'It would be wrong of you to try and influence him.'

'I'm sure he'll join me once he realises how happy everyone is in that place,' she reasoned. 'I will go to the Land of Dreams if you would be so kind as to lead me there.'

The Brehon wandered out among the trees and sat down alone for a long while. He finished the concoction Beag ní Dé had given him and he began to feel better almost immediately.

He had to concede there was probably some truth in what she'd said about the Quicken Brew not being able to cure maladies of the spirit. And he began to regret the harsh way he'd treated Eber Finn. Dalan resolved to apologise to the king at the first opportunity.

With that settled in his mind, he leaned against a tree in a squatting position such as he found best for meditating in the forest, and put all his thoughts to the Watchers. In his mind he conjured a clear picture of Lochie and Isleen and held their images in his consciousness until he was certain they must know he was thinking of them.

Then he put out a call to them through his thoughts, though he hardly expected them to acknowledge the contact.

So it was a great surprise to him when he distinctly heard Lochie promise to be at the camp with his companion after the moon had set behind the distant hills.

The Brehon opened his eyes and looked around to reassure himself that Lochie wasn't actually present. Then he stood up, shook himself to release the nervousness he'd felt, and made his way back to the camp.

Along the way he reflected on how easy this had all become. It seemed that the more he accepted the Watchers' ways, the more able he was to deal with them as equals. He began to wonder if that was what they had really wanted all along.

He returned to camp just as the forge was being unpacked. And he stopped for a short while to watch. The secret of the ironworkers was fascinating to Dalan. All his life weapons, farm implements and cooking utensils had been cast in bronze. When the Gaedhals arrived all that had changed forever.

Tuargain the wheelwright was blind but his workmanship was renowned among the Gaedhals both north and south. His best friend, Méaraigh the blacksmith, was a cripple. Together they had fashioned the chariots that were the pride of Eber Finn's Fianna. While the warriors rested, polished their mail coats or prepared their spirits for the coming battle, the two comrades set up their travelling forge with their small company of assistant smiths.

Dalan shook his head in wonder at all the activity, then went off in search of Sorcha.

It was already dark by the time they set the fire going, but hammers started to ring upon anvils. Eber would need every weapon his warriors could lay their hands on, so the work would likely continue even up to the moment the battle began.

The moon was in their favour for it was three nights before the full. The land was brightly lit by a silvery glow unhampered by clouds. And close to the forge no one would have guessed how cold the evenings were becoming in the approach to Samhain Eve.

Aenghus mac Ómor and his two bodyguards came to watch the work for a while, fascinated by the process of blowing up the fire with a bellows. At length Eber and Naithí of the Golden Hair came to stand beside the King of the Sen Erainn.

For a long while no words passed between them. They were content to watch as the blacksmith sat on a log to supervise the forge and the wheelwright checked the chariots one by one with the aid of his sensitive hands.

Finally Eber could stand the silence no longer. He was desperate to know whether the Sen Erainn chieftains had come to some agreement. He coughed to clear his throat before he spoke.

'Have you made a decision?' he asked.

Aenghus raised his eyebrows and turned to face the Gaedhal. 'We have.'

Then he returned all his attention to the forge. Eber Finn began to feel as if the Red Cap was playing some sort of game with him. His palms began to sweat and his breathing was becoming shallow. He simply had to know whether the Sen Erainn would fight beside him.

'And what was the decision?'

'There is still some room for negotiation,' Aenghus told him. 'I'm wondering whether your brother, Éremon, might make us a better offer.'

'The northerners don't have the secret of the Quicken Brew,' Dalan interrupted as he returned to the forge. 'They may have weapons but Sorcha is the last Druid remaining in Innisfail who knows the manner of brewing the potion.'

He smiled to see the expression of defeat on Aenghus's face.

'But if you believe Éremon of the North will offer you fairer terms, then by all means go to him.'

'I'm not used to dealing with Druids where there is a king

and equal in my presence,' the Sen Erainn war-leader retorted grumpily.

'Eber Finn is not your equal,' the Brehon pointed out. 'This Gaedhal rules the south of Innisfail by right of conquest and under the terms of a treaty. If he so wished he could sail his longboats over to your islands and install one of his own chieftains in your place. And believe me, there would be little you could do about it.'

Aenghus was beginning to turn red with rage. But Dalan was enjoying himself and feeling much better after Beag ní Dé's tea.

'You've sailed past the islands of Arainn, Naithí,' the Brehon went on, addressing the chieftain who stood at Eber's side. 'Tell me. Would it be difficult to take those islands and hold them?'

'I could do it with a hundred warriors,' the chieftain replied.

'I have four hundred,' Aenghus spat.

'Naithí has steel swords,' Dalan pointed out, holding up a finger to emphasise the advantage the Gaedhals would always retain.

'This is getting us nowhere!' the King of the Sen Erainn exclaimed.

'What did the chieftains of your people decide?' Dalan asked.

'In exchange for our support in battle we will take the secret of the Quicken Brew, a guarantee of sovereignty over our islands forever, ten chariots and a sword for every chieftain of my people.'

'How many swords is that?' Eber winced.

'One hundred.'

The Brehon laughed again, this time in a most dismissive manner. 'Two chariots and ten swords.'

'Eight chariots and fifty swords,' Aenghus shot back.

'Three chariots and twelve swords,' Dalan replied as he held his palm up in the air. 'And that is our final offer.'

'Five chariots and twenty swords,' the King of the Sen Erainn pleaded, beginning to feel he'd let the treasures slip through his fingers.

'Very well,' the Brehon nodded, clapping his hands. 'Let the alliance be concluded on those terms.'

Aenghus let the hint of a smile pass over his lips. This Brehon had earned his grudging respect.

'If I were a fish,' Aenghus began, composing a poem off the top of his head, 'I would certainly want to swim with an eel like yourself. But not too far. I am a fish who prefers to keep his scales fresh and sparkling. Dine with me on the bottom of the ocean and we will pass wind together.'

Dalan frowned, momentarily off guard.

'I give that poem as a gift to you, Brehon. It is in honour of your great skill at bargaining.'

'Thank you,' Dalan replied cautiously.

The Brehon was beginning to suspect that the humour of the Sen Erainn folk was unimaginably obscure and extremely subtle.

'Now I wish to see proof of the power of the Quicken Brew,' Aenghus insisted. 'Without proof I cannot confirm our deal.'

'And what would constitute proof?' Dalan asked.

'I would see a wounded warrior returned to health by the Brew.'

'Are you asking that we deliberately injure someone then force them to drink the potion just so you can be assured it does what we claim?'

'Nothing less will do.'

The Brehon paused for a moment, considering the implications of such a display. While he was sure there would be no danger to the warrior who was chosen, he wasn't keen to grant immortality to anyone. He'd had the opportunity to consider the consequences of eternal life and didn't want to be responsible for imposing them on anyone else.

'Would it not be enough if a wound were to be inflicted on me and the healing properties observed?' he asked.

'Forgive me,' Aenghus frowned, suspecting a trick. 'You are a Brehon Druid. You have many skills of which a humble poet-warrior such as myself knows nothing. Choose someone who is not a member of the holy orders for this test.'

'There is only Sorcha and myself in this camp who have taken the Brew and we're both Druids,' Dalan explained.

'So a warrior must be wounded,' Aenghus shrugged.

The Brehon paused again, unwilling to hand immortality to either a warrior Gaedhal, who would most certainly use it to seize the kingship from Eber, or one of the Sen Erainn, who might do something similar.

Then his gaze strayed across to the forge and he noticed the blacksmith and the wheelwright working away at their tasks. And a possibility came to his mind.

'I will need a short while to consider a suitable candidate for the Quicken Brew,' he declared. 'This is not a matter that can be considered lightly.'

'Very well,' Eber cut in. 'Aenghus will accompany me and share my table. When we've eaten supper we'll return to the forge and you'll give your demonstration.'

Dalan bowed low as the two kings departed. As soon as they were gone he went to speak with Tuargain and Méaraigh at the forge.

By the time Lochie tracked down Isleen the moon was already high in the sky. She was seated at her fire in the depths of the woods, with Mahon, Iobhar and his pig all sleeping soundly nearby. He stood at the perimeter of the clearing for a long while, wondering whether his companion had managed to find Aoife as well.

'Why don't you come closer where I can see you?' Isleen called out. 'I know you're there.'

Lochie smiled to himself and walked slowly into the firelight.

'It's a pity you weren't here earlier,' she stated. 'I had young Aoife here as well. But she's gone now. She decided to take the sleep.'

'The sleep?' Lochie spat. 'But that nullifies our wager!'

'Not to my understanding,' Isleen replied. 'You bet me that Mahon would wed Aoife and that she'd take him willingly for her husband. I asserted she had better sense than to marry such an oaf and that she would never consent to be his wife.'

Isleen stood up and handed her companion a cup of mead. 'Well she can't wed him if she's asleep. Can she?'

'You cheated! This is outrageous. I refuse to concede defeat.'

'We agreed that we should resolve this wager before Samhain,' she reminded him. 'And it seems to me you can't possibly win the bet before that time. There's only twelve days left until the wager expires.'

'I won't accept that you've won,' Lochie asserted, shaking his head. 'I call for an extension of time to settle this matter once and for all.'

'How much time would you like?' she laughed.

'They're both immortal,' her comrade reminded her. 'Why don't we make this bet a little more open-ended?'

'But if all goes according to plan we won't be around much longer,' Isleen pointed out.

That reminded Lochie of the real reason why he'd come in search of her. 'Dalan is summoning us. We're to meet him after the moon has set tonight.'

'Tonight? Do you think he's discovered the song?'

'I believe he may have done.'

'I don't trust him,' Isleen confided. 'Those two tried to work a song on me while he was in the trance of the Bull Feast and it was an utter failure. He and that woman he wanders around with are both incompetent, if not plain stupid.'

'There's no need to take that tone with me,' Lochie warned her. 'I'm not at fault here. If you'd waited until we were both present, perhaps the Draoi song might have worked. The trouble with you is you're becoming impatient. It's affecting your judgement.'

'You're getting soft,' she laughed, realising that a change had come over her companion. 'You're beginning to feel sympathy for them! I don't believe it. Is this the same Lochie who has enticed a thousand warriors to their deaths, one way or another. Is this the same Watcher who once swore that the Fir-Bolg would always be his enemies and that he would seek to destroy their people whenever the opportunity arose?'

'That was a long time ago. Balor has been dead for generations. I have no quarrel with these folk. They are our only hope of salvation.'

'I'd sooner put my trust in that pig,' she screamed, pointing to where Iobhar's pet lay snoring.

'Nevertheless, Dalan and Sorcha have been working hard on our behalf. It's time you acknowledged that.'

'I'll recognise their hard work when I'm dead. When I'm sitting in the Halls of Waiting chatting with my ancestors I'll be sure to mention that I only managed to make it because of two Fir-Bolg Druids.'

'Where's Aoife?' Lochie asked, changing the subject. 'I demand to know her whereabouts.'

'I told you she is sleeping with the rest of her folk. There's no use trying to wake her. She went to sleep of her own free will. She as good as begged me to place her in the slumber. So you won't be able to wake her. There's no love in your black heart. And even if there were, you wouldn't know what to do with it.'

As she was speaking Mahon began to wake up. He rolled over, yawned and then stretched his legs out towards the fire. Iobhar the Gaedhal and his pig, Molly, slept on undisturbed.

'Where am I?' he asked in confusion. 'Who are you?'

'Don't you recognise me?' Isleen teased. 'I once dwelt at your father's court. We became quite close for a while.'

The young warrior sat up and frowned. 'What are you doing here in the forest? How did I come to be here?'

'You wandered off from your friends. That was very silly.'

'Stop teasing the lad,' Lochie hissed. 'Can't you see he's confused?'

'I know you,' Mahon frowned. 'You're Isleen. You're a Watcher. And that's Lochie. He's one as well.'

It was in that instant the Danaan noticed Aoife was missing. 'What have you done with her?' he bellowed, getting to his feet.

'Who do you mean?'

'Aoife.'

'She's gone to sleep with her father, mother and a great many of the Danaan court as well. Would you like to join them?'

'No! I'll not fall for your tricks. And I'll not waste the gift I've been given with useless slumber.'

'I didn't think you would but I promised her I'd ask you anyway,' Isleen smiled. 'You'll find Eber Finn and his warriors waiting over in that direction. But if you want to make it to the battle you'd better set out now. They'll be striking camp in the morning.'

'Where will I find Aoife?'

'That's a very good question,' the Watcher smiled. 'But if I were to tell you that, it would take the enjoyment out of the chase for me. And I'd lose my wager as well. But I'll give you a hint. She's in an underground chamber. It's a palace of crystal where the sun shines but once every cycle of the seasons.'

'Tell me where she is!' Mahon shrieked as he charged towards Isleen, ready to strike her.

Lochie stepped into the path of the young Danaan and put a hand on his chest to stop him making a deadly mistake.

'Calm down, lad,' he whispered. 'There's no sense in this. She's enjoying every moment. Don't give her the satisfaction. When we're gone, gather your possessions and leave this place. You'll find her if you look in the right places.'

'Do you know where she is?'

Lochie opened his mouth to speak.

'I forbid you to tell him,' Isleen cut in. 'Unless you want enmity between us, Lochie, you will stay silent.'

'I can't tell you,' he admitted. 'I am close to realising a goal that I've worked towards for many generations. If I earn Isleen's contempt she could make it very difficult for me.'

'You won't help?'

'I'll tell you this,' he conceded. 'Beneath the crystal palace you'll end your quest. And if your heart remains true she will awaken to you.'

Then Lochie turned to Isleen.

'Let's go. There's no more damage you can do here.'

She smiled, bowed to Mahon and together they melted into the air like the smoke from the fire carried away on the night breeze.

Chapter Sixteen

t was late that evening before Lom and his brother found the clearing where Mahon and Iobhar had been held captive by Isleen. They'd marched on under the light of the nearly full moon until they saw the flickering fire in the distance.

Sárán didn't want to get too close, fearing the Ravens he'd seen circling earlier that day. He counselled his brother to stay within sight of the fire and rest the night. It was his opinion that they'd be better able to deal with any danger by the light of the sun rather than the moon.

But Lom was determined to find out whether Aoife was safe. The Ravens had been a terrible omen for him. There was only one meaning he could attach to their presence and that was death. They rarely wasted their energy on the living.

So when the two of them walked into the clearing at last, Lom was relieved to find Mahon and Iobhar but concerned that his sister was nowhere to be seen. Mahon explained all that had happened to them since they left the fortress of Dun Gur, while Sárán sat scowling at him by the fire.

When Iobhar awoke at last from his deep sleep he was startled to see the twins by the fireside. Then part of the story had to be told again to satisfy the Gaedhal's curiosity as to how he came to be sleeping by a fire in the middle of the forest.

The involvement of the Watchers was a terrible blow to Lom. He'd always suspected his sister would continue to put herself in danger, but he had no idea she'd end up a permanent prisoner of Lochie and Isleen. However, he was warmed by Mahon's determination to find her, and seeing the sincerity in his face he managed to forgive the Danaan for stealing her away from Dun Gur. He knew, too, that Aoife would have run away one day in any case. She was a woman who was too easily bored and Dun Gur would not have offered her much in the way of entertainment.

But his brother Sárán was not so forgiving. He wanted every detail of what had happened repeated to him over and over as if he was waiting for Mahon to trip up with his story. He swore the Danaan would be brought before a Brehon judge and recompense would be made for the loss of Aoife.

Mahon, for his part, was truly remorseful that he'd run off into the woods after Iobhar. He acknowledged that if he'd waited with Aoife they might not have all been separated and she would still be with them.

Sárán took this as an admission of guilt. 'We who are her kindred will seek her honour price,' the young Druid declared. 'And you can expect that Eber Finn, her betrothed, will likely seek a similar amount. Where are you going to find that many cows? Even the clothes you're wearing were stolen.'

Mahon explained that it would not come to that. He was confident he would be able to track her down in a very short while if left to his own devices. But neither Sárán nor Lom would allow him to go off on his own again.

They insisted that Mahon and Iobhar accompany them to the camp of Eber where they would have to tell their tale to Dalan, Sorcha and the king. The Brehon would decide whether they were to be trusted. And there was the life of one of Eber Finn's warriors to be accounted for as well. The man who had drowned in the mud of the lough had been but twenty-five summers old. He'd left a wife and three children behind, Sárán pointed out, and they would have to be provided for in the future. Mahon had a duty to see to their wellbeing before he went off chasing around the countryside.

The Danaan acknowledged this debt but expressed the feeling that Sárán was more interested in revenge than in finding his sister. Of course that was too much for the young Druid. He lost his temper completely and vowed he'd seek a blush fine for the injury to his pride.

Now, as a Druid and a young man of royal kinfolk, he was entitled to seek recompense when his honour and good name were insulted. A blush fine was a perfectly reasonable expectation for anyone who had the respect of their peers. The problem was that Sárán wasn't widely respected and he knew it well enough. So he accused Mahon of being a party to Aoife's disappearance. In less time than it takes for a pig to fart the Danaan had drawn his sword and there was a terrible yelling match going on.

Lom held his brother back, though it must be said he didn't have to struggle too much. And Iobhar managed to calm Mahon down. At length, with all their energy spent on fighting amongst themselves, the four of them watched the sky grow dark as the moon slipped behind the hills.

There would be no more travelling that night. Not even blind badgers venture out when there is no moon to guide them. The four settled down by the fire and stared distrustfully at each other until a noise startled them all.

High above in the treetops they all clearly heard the cawing of two Ravens, a most unusual sound in the middle of the night and quite chilling. So they resolved to build the fire up, take turns at the watch and rest as much as possible.

Mahon claimed to know in which direction they would have to journey at daylight to find Eber Finn and the place where the battle was to take place. But Lom didn't think to ask him how he'd come by this information.

Iobhar took the first watch because he claimed he was feeling more refreshed than he had in weeks. He sat by the flames, carefully tending them, until the others were fast asleep and then he dragged his snoring pig close. As he held her in his arms like a baby he wondered what Eber would say when they turned up at his camp without Aoife. He prayed silently that Dalan the wise Brehon would know where to find her. And he hoped above all else that the king would not want his pig back.

'What are we going to do, Molly?' he asked her.

But alas she had no answers.

Dalan consulted Sorcha, who approved of his idea. But she insisted that every detail of the Quicken Brew be explained to the blacksmith and the wheelwright. For she knew only too well that the Druids who had originally prepared the Brew had not given full consideration to the consequences of immortality.

The two of them told Beag ní Dé of their intentions. She gave her approval but insisted that the two craftsmen not be coerced into making a decision either way. And she reminded Dalan to tell the men they would probably be banished from their people after a time, for there is nothing so divisive as jealousy.

Sorcha assured the old woman that Tuargain and Méaraigh would always be welcome among the Fir-Bolg and the few Danaans that remained on this side of the veil of the Otherworld. Then Beag ní Dé promised they would also be welcomed among her people and suggested in fact that they return with the Sen Erainn to their island home.

When the three Druids had agreed the plan was a good one, they took their proposal to the two craftsmen. This pair had been fast friends since childhood. They'd both been incapacitated for most of their lives and relied on one another completely.

Tuargain the Wheelwright was blind but he had powerful arms and shoulders. His comrade, Méaraigh the Blacksmith, was crippled in the legs but his eyesight was excellent. So they were usually seen together, the wheelwright carrying the blacksmith who'd had a special harness made so that he wouldn't fall.

When the offer was made neither man could believe it was genuine. Then they both suspected the Brehon's motives. When it was explained to them that the King of the Sen Erainn had demanded a display of the powers of the Quicken Brew, they both had to stop and consider the proposal.

King Eber had been very generous to them during his reign. Even before the journey to Innisfail Eber Finn had argued that these two skilled artisans were too valuable to be left behind in the lands of Iber. They understood that Aenghus mac Ómor would not commit his warriors to an alliance unless this test took place.

So in the end they agreed to take the Brew. But their reasons were not selfish at all. For both men the only thought they had was for the debt they owed their king. Even when Dalan and Sorcha spoke to them of the terrible burden which immortality might place upon them, neither man was perturbed.

'Our lives have been hard,' the blacksmith explained. 'We've had precious little time to think about ourselves and no expectation of ever having a moment to consider our future. So this is a great gift you're giving us.'

Beag ní Dé assured them they would always be welcome with her folk and they were grateful to her for the courtesy.

'But we'll remain with Eber until he passes on, if you don't mind,' Tuargain told her. 'After he's gone we'll come for a visit, to be sure.'

With that matter settled Sorcha went to fetch the cauldron in which she'd prepared the Quicken Brew. The others waited by the forge fire for her return. But it was Eber Finn and Aenghus who arrived first.

'Are you ready to demonstrate the effectiveness of the potion?' the King of the Sen Erainn asked.

Dalan told them he was ready but that he had to seek the leave of King Eber first.

'These two loyal servants of yours have offered to take part in this test,' the Brehon told Eber. 'The consequences of their decision have been explained to them and they are well aware they may not be able to dwell among your people once it is realised they are no longer subject to death.'

The king nodded to show he understood what was being said to him.

'I seek your permission to administer the Quicken Brew to two of your subjects,' Dalan concluded.

'If they are willing, I will not stand in their way,' Eber Finn told him. 'These two are the finest craftsmen I have ever encountered, despite their disabilities. If you can cure them it will make my heart glad to see it.'

Just then Sorcha arrived carrying a small steaming cauldron which she placed down by the fire. She filled two cups with the Brew and there was just enough liquid to do that. Then she handed the cups to Méaraigh and Tuargain.

'Watch these two men carefully,' Dalan advised. 'Méaraigh's legs have been withered since he was a boy. The wheelwright has been blinded almost as long. This night they will be healed.'

The Brehon nodded to the blacksmith who was seated on a bench beside his friend.

'The Druid says we should drink it now,' Méaraigh whispered.

His comrade nodded and together they swallowed the contents of their cups. At first Méaraigh screwed up his face with disgust at the taste of the concoction but this changed to alarm a moment later.

As the blacksmith looked down at his legs they were already growing and strengthening. The muscles were bulging out and forming into well-shaped limbs. His toes were moving and he found he could wriggle them at will.

'I don't believe it!' he exclaimed. 'My legs have returned to me.'

'I can see it and I don't believe it,' his friend sobbed as the first tears he'd cried since he was a lad poured out from his healed eyes. Then he blushed and admitted something to Méaraigh. 'You're not as ugly as I imagined you to be.'

'You have a more active imagination than I realised,' the blacksmith laughed.

But that wasn't the end of the miracle. For both men had had greying hair and wrinkled faces, but now Méaraigh's hair returned to the rich red curly lustre of his youth and the wheelwright's was jet black again.

Tuargain stood up and looked about him. Then he pointed at the king.

'Are you Eber Finn?' he asked.

'I am,' the king choked as he fought back tears of joy.

'I thought you must be. You're just as I pictured you.'

'He's just as I described him,' Méaraigh corrected his friend.

Then Tuargain turned to the blacksmith and took him by the hands. His legs and feet were perfectly restored but Méaraigh was nervous about standing up. It took a few minutes for him to summon the courage but at last he was standing with the help of his friend who'd once carried him everywhere on his back.

The blacksmith's legs were unsteady and it was clear he would have to learn to walk all over again, but it was a miraculous cure nevertheless. Dalan came over to wish the two men well and share their joy. They thanked him with all their hearts and then they hugged Sorcha too and called for mead to be passed around to everyone.

'Excuse me, my lord,' Méaraigh bowed, realising his presumption. 'We didn't mean to be rude. It's just that we're both quite overwhelmed.'

The king laughed and repeated the call for strong drink. For a long while no one even noticed the awe-struck King of the Sen Erainn sitting down cross-legged on the grass, his mouth wide open.

'What breed of fish is this I see before me?' he pondered in poetic amazement. 'Cut off its tail and it grows another. I'll make sure every fish I haul in with my net is properly bludgeoned from now on.'

Chapter Seventeen

nvisible to all, Lochie and Isleen hovered around the camp, observing the comings and goings of the Sen Erainn and the celebrations Eber Finn seemed to be hosting for two of his servants. When the moon disappeared and the sky grew black the festivities came to their natural conclusion. Folk drifted off to find themselves a warm place by the fire.

Dalan and Sorcha padded through the darkness to the well, accompanied by the old woman of the Sen Erainn. Lochie was waiting for them when they arrived and offered a cup of clear water from the depths of the well.

Beag ní Dé took the cup gratefully and bowed to the Watcher.

'She knows who I am,' Lochie commented. 'Have you told her?'

'She's a wise and gentle Druid of the Sen Erainn,' Dalan explained. 'Sorcha and I have asked her advice on this matter and she has shared her wisdom with us.'

'Will Isleen join us?' Sorcha asked, and as she spoke the other Watcher stepped out of the darkness, throwing back a cloak from her head.

'She will. Why have you summoned us?' she demanded.

'We have discovered the Draoi song you've been seeking,'

Dalan informed them. 'And now we'd like to discuss the terms under which you will be released.'

'Terms?' Isleen spat. 'How dare you talk to me of terms? I've witnessed your expertise with the Draoi craft. You are in no position to speak terms with me.'

'Calm yourself, my dear,' Lochie soothed. 'Let us hear the Druids out before we dismiss their words completely.'

'Is it still your wish that we sing the song that will break your enchantment?' Sorcha asked.

'Are you trying to provoke me into anger?' Isleen sneered. 'Because I should warn you that I am not in any mood to be played with. You are the one who brought me so close to freedom at the Bull Feast and who dashed my hopes. Consider your words carefully or I will unleash my vengeance on you for your failure.'

'Please excuse Isleen,' Lochie begged. 'It is still our wish to be released from Balor's enchantment if you have the means to do that.'

'We believe we do,' Dalan informed him.

'You believe?' Isleen mocked. 'You don't have a good reputation with me. You've let me down once already. I've wasted both time and effort with you. And I'm in no mood for any more failures.'

'I'm not afraid of what threats you may direct at me,' the Brehon replied calmly. 'But you've already disrupted the lives of many people and brought on a war that was needless and will end in disaster if it's allowed to continue.'

'What are you trying to say?' Lochie cut in, sensing there was something Dalan had not told him.

'We will sing the song for you on one condition.'

'Condition?' Isleen screamed. 'You dare to place conditions on us? Have you lost your reason? We're immortal beings with unlimited power at our fingertips. You can't just impose conditions on us. Who do you think you are?'

'I've taken the Quicken Brew,' the Brehon stated passively. 'I'm an immortal being. You inhabit the world of the spirit. You came to us asking for help because your state of existence is not sustainable. You told me you would be subjected to a terrible fate if I didn't find some way to help you. I have found a way. But before I sing the song that releases you I demand you undo all the evil you have done.'

'Demand?' Lochie whispered, wincing as he spoke the word.

'Respectfully request,' Dalan conceded.

'And what specifically would you like us to undo?'

'This war,' the Brehon replied. 'There is to be a terrible battle in the next day or two and it could be averted with your help. Do this and we will sing you the Draoi song.'

Lochie smiled and walked over to where Dalan was standing. He clasped a hand on each of the Brehon's shoulders and smiled as he looked into his eyes.

'I underestimated you, dear judge. I thought you'd bring me the secret of the Draoi song and free us without any hesitation. I never considered that you might want something from us in return. You're beginning to understand what it really means to be immortal.'

He held out his hand to Sorcha and she took it. Then his smile dropped away.

'But let me show you both a glimpse of your future,' he said.

With that, the two Druids were engulfed in a bright white light and when this faded away after a matter of seconds their features had changed. Dalan looked at the Druid woman and gasped in astonishment.

'What have you done to her?'

'This is how time will treat you,' the Watcher replied. 'Isleen and I may be merely disembodied spirits but that means we don't have bodies that will change over time. You, on the other hand, are living, breathing creatures. Nothing is more certain for you than change.'

The Brehon held his hand up to Sorcha's face. Where the skin had been weather-tanned and healthy it now had a grey pallor to it. Her eyes had grown enormously large and black, like two dark stones lying side by side on a beach. Her nose had flattened. Her skull had transformed into a strange, thin, Otherworldly shape.

Then the Brehon noticed his own hand. The fingers were spindly and gnarled, the nails green and waxy. The skin was dry, papery and stretched. He touched his own face and it was unfamiliar to him. His beard and stubble were gone and his cheeks felt as though they were draped in dead leaves.

'This is what you will become,' Lochie told them. 'Not within five generations but certainly before a thousand summers have passed. We can offer you an alternative to this awful decay. We can offer you sleep.'

'Sleep?' Dalan asked. 'What do you mean?'

'Many of the Danaans have already gone to sleep. And many of your own kinfolk too. Join them in the Land of Dreams and you can leave the worries of this world behind you forever. We offer this as a gift in exchange for the Draoi song of our deliverance.'

Sorcha stared disbelievingly into the strangely misshapen eyes of her friend. Despite the changes she recognised him and smiled. And the gesture was full of love. In an unspoken moment they both agreed that their outward appearances would never change who they were underneath.

Dalan knew then that they would spend the rest of their lives together and that they had two gifts that few folk would ever know. The first gift was the whole of eternity. The second gift was to know that no matter what happened they would remain firm friends and a solid support for one another.

He sensed some thread of truth in what he had been shown but he held no fear. The Brehon turned to the Watcher and gave his answer.

'No. The price for the Draoi song is peace.'

'You'll be very sorry for this,' Isleen hissed. 'I'll make you regret this decision for the whole of eternity. There'll be a war tomorrow and folk will blame you for every death, for every maiming, for every missing son and husband. And then we'll see what other mischief Lochie and I can get up to. In the end you'll sing us the song just to be rid of us.'

'I'm afraid I must agree with my dear companion,' Lochie shrugged. 'She's put it rather crudely but then that's just her charming way. My patience with you is at an end. The next time you summon us you'd better be ready to sing the song. Believe me, there are more terrible disasters we can heap upon the mortals of this island than just war. There's pestilence, to start with. That's so nasty even Isleen is loath to indulge in it.'

'And then there's famine,' his companion added. 'Famine's one of my favourites. There's nothing as certain to bring a people to their knees as hunger.'

'And we haven't even begun to list some of the unimaginable horrors we could conjure up,' Lochie assured them. 'We're both quite inventive souls, after all.'

'Think about it,' Isleen hissed. 'We'll visit you after the battle and discuss it again then.'

And in that instant they both disappeared. Dalan knew they had indeed gone, perhaps to stir up the fight between Eber and Éremon even further.

Beag Ní Dé stood up once the Watchers had departed and took the hands of the other two Druids to clasp them to her breast.

'I believe you,' she told them. 'It is time the song was sung. And I commend your bravery in rejecting the temptation of sleep.'

Dalan looked down and spoke in a defeated tone. 'But we haven't achieved anything. The battle will take place no matter what we do. We weren't able to save a single life or alleviate the suffering of one wounded warrior.'

'Yet I believe the Watchers have had their day,' the old woman told him. 'A change has come over the land of Innisfail. A new generation of Watchers is abroad and you are but two of them.'

'I'm worried that Eber has bartered the Quicken Brew for the sake of his alliance with Aenghus mac Ómor,' Sorcha confided. 'I'm not sure I want to be responsible for the Sen Erainn gaining the secret. It could so easily be misused.'

'Don't you worry about Aenghus,' the old woman smiled knowingly. 'I've known him since he was a small child who wet himself at every opportunity. He'll take heed of me.'

She went to the well, drank down the rest of the water in her cup and turned back to face Sorcha and Dalan.

'Let us go to work,' she told them. 'You have a song to learn and we don't have much time.'

When Sárán awoke just after dawn everyone was sleeping soundly. Iobhar had nodded off, still hugging his beloved sow close to him. Mahon was lying on his back with his mouth open, snoring.

The young Druid counsellor rolled over slowly to check on his twin brother and as he did so he got the shock of his life. A great black bird was standing near his brother's head as if it were about to strike at him.

The Raven stepped back a pace when Sárán moved, and ruffled its feathers, but it made no sound at all. It was obviously reluctant to draw attention to itself in this vulnerable position.

A cold chilled passed through Sárán. What could this bird

be doing here staring at his brother so intently. The Raven caught his eye and the two of them looked into each other's souls.

In his youth Sárán had been nicknamed the Young Raven by his father. Perhaps it was his dark hair and eyes that prompted this comparison. But Lom was his twin and no one ever referred to him by that name. Sárán had always assumed it was some private joke of his father's and he took it with good humour. But he'd had a fascination with these birds ever since. Over his lifetime this had almost, but not quite, become an affinity.

This was the closest he'd ever come to a living, breathing Raven. They might be fascinating but there was something about these creatures that filled his soul with fear. He couldn't explain his fright so he had always kept it secret, even from his brother. Now, staring into the eyes of this Raven, he was able for the first time to appreciate the beauty of these birds. The subtle rainbow shifts across the black feathers were unlike anything he'd ever known.

It was one thing to see these feathers on a dead bird or making up the fabric of Dalan's cloak. It was another thing altogether to observe them in life. The Raven shifted its head and the colours shifted across the shimmering surface of its feathers, taking Sárán's breath away.

And a strange wish filled his heart. Here was a gloriously beautiful creature. Here was a bird free to fly wherever it willed, unfettered by obligation or kinfolk or duty. This Raven took what it needed from the land and neither asked nor needed any help from another living soul.

Sárán imagined what it would be like to soar above the forests, carried on the wind from one corner of Innisfail to the other. And then he wondered whether Ravens ever crossed to the lands beyond this island.

No sooner had the thought struck him than he saw in his

mind's eye just such a journey. He saw the vast rolling sea beneath him as he rose higher and higher on the breeze until at last he glimpsed a far-off country of green hills and untouched forests.

Seagulls squawked madly at him as he flew on, warning him of the dangers of flying too far from home. But Sárán soared on to the east, revelling in the kinship he shared with the seabirds. It was a feeling of belonging he'd never known in this life.

The Raven shifted its feet slightly and this was enough to wake the young Druid from his delightful daydream. His heart beat faster but now it was fear that drove it on at such a pace.

Sárán was lying on his arm and the limb was beginning to go numb. He moved his body slowly so he'd be more comfortable. As he slid his arm out from under his body the bird shuffled closer until it was close enough that it could have struck at him with its beak if it wanted to. At the same time the young Druid's hand brushed against the haft of his brother's ceremonial axe. Sárán found his fingers gripping the wooden haft with all his might, though he never intended to use the weapon. It was just comforting to know it was there in case he needed it.

The young Druid held his breath, unwilling to so much as blink in case the Raven should take the opportunity to attack. He'd heard tell of birds that had taken the eye of a sleeping man and suddenly he was certain this was what the Raven intended.

He struggled not to shiver with fear, reasoning to himself that if the bird knew he was frightened it would take advantage of his state and launch a swift attack. But the Raven didn't make a move. It stood with an expression of mirth on its face. In fact, if a Raven could have smiled with amusement, this bird would have sported a wide grin. As

Sárán watched, the creature slowly lifted a claw to its beak and scratched its leg. Never for an instant did it take its eyes from him.

The young Druid realised the bird was playing with him now. The Raven knew full well that he was frightened and it was enjoying every moment of this game. When it placed its foot down on the ground again, it took a half-step closer just to test the boundary.

But this was too much for Sárán. His hand still had hold of his brother's axe. He knew this would be his last chance to attack the bird or drive it off. The Raven twitched and shifted its head, and it seemed to the young Druid that the bird was about to peck at his eyes.

The next few moments were a strange blur of fear and panic. Sárán swung the axe around from behind his body and brought it down onto the head of the bird with all the force he could muster from this horizontal position.

The Raven half spread its wings in response to the attack but the blow was so unexpected, so swift, so deadly that it never had a chance. There was a frantic caw and then silence. The bird lay in a crumpled heap upon the grass.

The noise of its call woke Lom, Mahon and Iobhar immediately and in the distance another bird cried out.

As Lom stood up and grabbed the axe from his brother's hand, the Raven circling high above them gave another sickening cry and there was so much anguish in its voice that Lom was moved to tears.

'What have you done?' he managed to ask after he'd stared at the Raven's body in disbelief for what seemed many minutes.

Sárán did not answer him. He was still shaking with fear and the tension of the attack.

'What have you done?' Lom repeated, screaming the words so that the whole forest echoed with his outrage.

'The bird was about to take out my eyes,' his brother ventured.

'What kind of a Druid are you?' Lom shouted. 'I've always known you were a self-centred coward, but to strike down a creature of the woods, a Raven, leaves me lost for words.'

Then the King of the Fir-Bolg noticed that his own tunic had been spattered with the bird's blood. He looked down at the stains in disgust and tore the garment off over his head. He threw it into the fire without a second thought.

'As children the Druids taught us the sanctity of all living things,' Lom went on. 'They told us to hunt when we needed food but never take more than was necessary for our survival. The meat of a Raven can't be eaten. They're carrion birds. There was no reason to kill this creature!'

The king's voice cracked as he spoke these last few words and Sárán bowed his head in shame.

'I was defending myself,' the young Druid muttered. 'I was defending you, my king.'

'You are no longer my counsellor,' Lom declared. 'I won't have one such as you offering advice at my court. Perhaps you're the reason my reign has been cursed.'

'I'm your brother,' Sárán appealed. 'Don't cast me out from your hearth fire.'

'From this moment on you are no longer my brother,' the king stated coldly.

Mahon noticed a hard stare in Lom's eyes which he'd never seen before. And he thought that the young Fir-Bolg had never looked so much like a king.

'You're a coward,' he went on. 'You're a liar and you use your office to play out your own little games with me. I won't have you in my retinue a moment longer. You've defiled the axe that is the symbol of my office.'

As Lom looked down at the ceremonial weapon a great sadness filled his soul and he understood for the first time what it meant to have a broken spirit. As he tried to stop the tears welling in his eyes again he sighed heavily and hardened his heart.

But before he could speak again, a terrifying sound descended on the clearing. It was a wild vengeful shriek and it pierced the eardrums of all who heard it. Lom looked up to the sky and saw to his amazement a great black shape falling to Earth like a stone cast down from the heavens.

It was another Raven and it was swooping down with wings folded close to its body in a death-tempting attack on the one who'd murdered her mate. Crínóc opened her beak wide as she fell on Sárán.

She was determined to offer no mercy. She'd already decided to take both his eyes and as the ground rushed up at her she knew she was on target. He was still seated on the grass and had no idea she was coming for him.

At last he looked up and with satisfaction the Raven-wife saw his fear, smelled his terror and tasted his dread. He put his hands up to defend himself. Crínóc sneered at this feeble attempt. And then she screamed with all the force of her lungs.

Lom watched the falling bird spread her wings wide so she could control her descent and he knew she intended to strike hard and heavy at his brother. And despite all his bitter words and sentiments he simply could not stand by and let his twin be attacked.

Surprised by the swiftness of his own reflexes Lom swung his ceremonial axe around, aiming to knock the bird out of the air before it struck Sárán. The next few moments were like a dream, as if the passing of time had been tampered with and the world had slowed its pace.

Only one thing kept its natural pace. Lom's mind. Thoughts flashed through his head like lightning bolts compared to the subdued pace of those about him. He glanced at Mahon whose face had twisted into a frightful and monstrous shape which reflected the horror of what he saw. Iobhar was looking away, unable to watch the terrible events as they unfolded. And the Raven screeched louder, falling like a great black boulder that would smash Sárán's skull open if it could.

Torn between his duty as king and his obligations as a brother, Lom closed his eyes for a split second as his heart wavered. In the next breath they were open again and he watched his hand swing the axe around as if it belonged to someone else.

As the weapon flew above his brother's head the black shape of the Raven flew straight into it and suddenly there was blood and feathers scattered everywhere. There followed a profound silence, broken only by the last twitching gasps of the black bird as it lay on the grass dying a painful death.

Without hesitating Lom walked over to it and clubbed it twice across the skull until it stopped moving. He turned to make sure his brother had not been injured, then picked up his cloak which had been lying on the grass.

Quickly he wiped the axe blade clean and then tossed his cloak into the fire. With solemnity he placed the bodies of the two Ravens in amongst the flames and soon the air stank with the smell of burning wool and feathers.

Iobhar coughed, a hand to his nose and mouth. Mahon turned away and tried not to retch. Sárán curled up with his head hidden under his cloak and didn't move for a long while.

'I should have let it attack you,' Lom whispered. 'You would have healed and learned a lesson.'

With that he paid his silent respects to the birds as their corpses were consumed by the fire. That done, he stormed off into the forest to find a stream to wash the blood from his hands.

Chapter Eighteen

nce, when winter was on the wane, I watched a woman hack her husband in half with a hatchet. Now, let me assure you that a Raven wouldn't usually flinch at the sight of bodily fluids splashed about in anger. But I freely admit to being touched by a hint of queasiness as she gleefully hung the poor fellow's bloody entrails high on hooks around the house.

It wasn't that he'd forgotten to remove his boots at the door. It wasn't that he had the stench of strong drink about him either. She'd long since learned to live with those little quirks of his.

No. The truth is such petty indiscretions would never have inspired this old girl to such an act of unbridled butchery. And she wasn't the type to teeter on the edge of madness in the manner of many housebound folk. She'd lived a challenging life and was possessed of more than a measure of commonsense.

However, even for one who is wise in the ways of the world there may come a time when reason flees before the onslaught of passion. In the case of this good lady it was jealousy that sparked her off to slice open her spouse.

He was a bit of a lad, her old man, if you know what I mean. On the morning of his dismemberment he'd been off down the valley with a widow woman renowned for luring old men off down the valley away from prying eyes.

And the two of them weren't picking blackberries either, I can promise you. There isn't much this old bird misses.

I didn't have to say very much to his wife about what I'd seen. The grass stains on his cloak and the uncharacteristic smile upon his face were enough to condemn him to his fate. Before he could utter a word of explanation, he was decorating every corner of the house. Not that an explanation would have softened the blow or blunted the axe at all.

Once she was done with him I was left to clean up the mess. Of course I couldn't sit back and let the miscreant rot away before my eyes. I can't abide waste. I'm a carrion creature. I simply cannot refuse a meal offered in the true spirit of hospitality.

As I recall he was a bony fellow, not much flesh about him. And he could have done with a wash as well. To be honest, I don't know what the widow saw in him.

What's the point of my gruesome tale?

Passion.

It's the poison that brings most of us into the world and the nectar that can snuff us out just as easily, if we don't keep a lid on it. Of course, when you're overwhelmed by bliss or belligerence, the last thing you want to do is hold a tight rein on your feelings. All you desire is to indulge yourself in the rising wave of whatever happens to be washing over your spirit at the time. Love. Infatuation. Lust. Hunger. Joy. Rage. Hate.

For some folk it's music that sparks their fire. For others it's the quiet contemplation of the soul or the unity of all things experienced through the spirit of godliness. For me? I like to watch a bloody good battle.

It's on the battlefield you folk exhibit your true nature for all to see. What other creature on this Earth can set out on a sunny morning intending to slaughter as many of his fellow beings as possible before nightfall?

It's usually over nothing more than a few harsh words or a thousand paces of earth. And this behaviour is considered a boon to the community! It's often even rewarded. Yet it's not too far removed from what that old housewife did to her husband.

So consider what I've said while I tell you about this battle. Some folk find killing easy, but the Gaedhals seem to have a real talent for adding treachery and torture to the mix.

It was an hour before dawn when Goll and Mughain stumbled into Eber Finn's camp. They'd been following the Red Caps but the hosts of the Sen Erainn marched fast and the two weary Fian warriors could not keep up with them.

They'd rested for part of the night in a valley not far off and set out again before the sky had begun to signal the sunrise. The king was woken as soon as the sentries discovered their identity, but Eber Finn took his time rising.

They'd eaten and had a chance to wash at the well by the time the king was ready to see them. And it was immediately evident he was not overjoyed at their arrival. Eber offered no greeting when they met. Instead he only said a few short words.

'Walk with me down towards the Sen Erainn camp.'

The king strolled slowly so as not to give away just how angry he was with the war-leader Goll mac Morna. But Mughain could sense a storm brewing and she fell back a few paces behind the two of them. Not for the first time she was glad she had no rank or responsibilities beyond those of an ordinary Fian warrior.

At last, when they were halfway between the camp of the

Red Caps and the well, Eber stopped walking. He turned towards Goll and waited for the war-leader to speak.

'Are you not pleased that I have returned?' mac Morna asked.

Eber Finn raised his eyebrows and considered telling him the truth. He wondered what the war-leader would say if he knew he despised Goll, distrusted him and with the slightest excuse would banish him from the realm.

'I'll need every sword I can muster in the coming battle,' the king stated flatly and truthfully. 'And yours will be welcome.' This was the only reason he hadn't stripped mac Morna of his status and position the moment he'd walked into the camp.

'Éremon ambushed us,' the war-leader blurted, coming to the point of his report quicker than he'd intended. 'We were outnumbered and surrounded. The Fian surrendered their arms rather than perish in a senseless show of honour.'

'I received a messenger who informed me you had sent out a challenge to my brother,' Eber frowned, holding his rage at bay. 'Is this true?'

'I captured a settlement just over the border,' Goll nodded. 'Then I sent out word to Éremon that I would meet him there. It was my intention to fight him in single combat and settle the matter of the kingship once and for all.'

'Single combat?' the king repeated.

'I am your champion,' Goll reminded Eber. 'I was only thinking of saving the lives of our warriors and the honour of my king.'

'You were only thinking of bolstering your own reputation among the Fian warriors!' Eber Finn shouted, unable to contain his fury a moment longer.

The king turned to Goll and stood so close that their noses almost touched. 'You've had your eye on the kingship of the south since before the Battle of Sliabh Mis,' he growled.

'You've continually worked to undermine my leadership and enhance your own position. Now you've gone too far! You've openly declared war on my brother. Even if I wanted to I couldn't find a peaceful solution now.'

'Why would you want to?' the war-leader frowned.

'Because even in the unlikely event that we should emerge from this fiasco as the victors, the battlefield will be strewn with the corpses of my people,' the king spat. 'I have no desire to send good-hearted men and women to their deaths. And I have to think about who will bring in the harvest next summer.'

'We will triumph over Éremon,' Goll assured him. 'He has less than three hundred warriors in his camp.'

Eber stepped back a few paces and considered the war-leader's words. 'His camp?'

'The King of the North is encamped within the rath where I intended to battle him.'

'Are you telling me my brother has the ground?'

Goll nodded.

'And you still think we can beat him?' Eber asked incredulously.

'Give me command of all the warriors of the Fian,' mac Morna begged. 'I'll gain that hill for you. I'll sweep your brother and his warriors aside like as much tall grass falling to the keen edge of my blade.'

'You will stand in the centre beside me,' Eber announced coldly. 'You won't stray from my sight for an instant. Do you understand? After this latest misadventure I wouldn't trust you to bring in the goats for milking.'

Goll grunted in response but Eber stepped closer again. 'Go on,' he whispered. 'I dare you to strike. You wouldn't live to walk twenty paces. My guards would be down here so fast you wouldn't have time to see your life pass before your eyes. If you so much as threaten me you'll find yourself seated amongst your ancestors telling them the tale of how you bumbled your way into the afterlife.'

'I'm your champion,' the war-leader protested.

'In name only. And you had better prove yourself on the field against my brother or I can promise you a swift judgement of banishment.'

'You wouldn't dare!' Goll spat.

'I'll do it now if you like,' the king replied. Then he turned to face the well. 'Naithí!' he bellowed. 'Naithí, Chieftain of Dun Gur! Come here!'

In a matter of moments the tall broad-shouldered chieftain was running down to them as fast as he could.

'I'd be very careful if I were you,' Eber advised. 'Naithí doesn't like you very much.'

'I'm unarmed!' the war-leader hissed. 'This is outrageous!'

Eber Finn smiled as he unbuckled a long knife from his belt and threw it to Goll. 'Now you seem to be armed well enough.'

The war-leader unsheathed the knife and for a brief moment considered plunging it deep into the heart of the king. The temptation was so great he had to clench his teeth and berate himself for entertaining such a foolish thought. But the knife was there. Perhaps this was fate lending a hand. After all it was his destiny to rule the Gaedhals as their king. He raised the weapon to strike but his hand was shaking.

Naithí saw the war-leader poised to attack the king, and with a ringing of metal he drew his sword from the scabbard at his belt. Then he gave a blood-chilling cry so full of hate that the Red Cap warriors on sentry blew their trumpets and sounded a call to arms.

Goll could plainly see that if he murdered the king now he would lose his own life and Éremon would be named High-King of all the Gaedhals. This way he would lose everything he'd planned for. This way was failure.

He told himself to be patient. He told himself to wait until the heat of battle. He promised to savour the moment when he finally ended Eber's life. And he vowed that the king's death would be to his own advantage.

At the last possible moment Goll dropped the knife and fell to his knees before Eber Finn. Naithí rushed down and kicked the war-leader in the head, knocking him to the ground. Goll lay dazed for a moment, then looked up, spitting out a tooth.

The chieftain stood with his sword still drawn between the war-leader and his king.

'That should have damaged your prestige among the Fian,' Eber noted dryly. 'Tongues will certainly wag about why you had a drawn knife pointed at your king and why you had to be restrained by one of the chieftains.'

Eber coughed to clear the least hint of fear from his voice. 'You should have killed me when you had the chance,' he went on. 'Believe me, you'll never wield authority among our people again. You may be a gifted war-leader but you have no integrity. Or as Dalan would say, your dreams are not honourable.'

Eber turned to Naithí. 'See that he is equipped for the battle. But stay close to him at all times. I don't like the idea of him wandering around behind my back with even a meat knife. To say nothing of a sharp blade.'

'You're going to forgive him?' Naithí asked in confusion. 'I saw him raise a knife to you.'

'By tomorrow evening this little argument will be forgotten,' Eber assured the chieftain. 'He has a strong sword arm. I'm trusting you to see that he uses it for the good of my cause.'

At last Eber Finn faced the disgraced and dishonoured Goll. 'If you serve me well in the coming fight, I may forgive you. If you prove to be invaluable I will reinstate you to your former titles. But from this moment you will relinquish all the honours I have bestowed on you. Your Fian will be disbanded and dispersed and I will seek a hundred cows from you as recompense for the insult you have done to me today.'

Goll mac Morna sat up on his knees. It flashed through his mind that he should beg forgiveness but his tongue was stilled by hatred.

Before the king left he picked up the little knife. 'Take this. It's a gift. Remember me by it.'

Eber dropped the knife in front of Goll then turned and walked back up to where his warriors were already gathering to discuss the attack.

The former war-leader wiped the blood from his chin with the back of his hand and made a move to stand. But before he'd got to his feet Naithí kicked him hard in the head again and put the point of his blade to Goll's throat.

'You're a coward,' he hissed. 'I'll kill you without hesitation if you ever threaten the king again.' Then he sheathed the sword and turned away. 'You'll follow me now to be issued with armour and weapons for the coming fight,' the chieftain barked over his shoulder.

Goll struggled to his feet, shook his head to clear it, and stumbled the first few steps towards the well. He hadn't gone but a few paces when his legs gave way under him and he lurched forward. Mughain was there to catch him before he landed in the grass again.

'You bloody fool,' she said quietly. 'Look what you've done to yourself.'

Dalan and Sorcha had left the main body of warriors and gone to camp in the forest for the night. The Druid woman hated being surrounded by people all the time. She was used to the solitary life she'd lived out in the woods in her little cottage.

The Brehon had never minded being amongst the throng until he'd come to know Sorcha. Little by little she'd convinced him that his thoughts would be clearer and his heart purer if he took himself away from the folk it was his duty to judge.

Indeed, these days he seldom rested well when there were a lot of people about. His dreams were always disturbed by some noise or another. And his patience was tested by selfish requests for his advice without regard for the time of day.

This morning he woke up feeling more refreshed than he had since before the coming of the Gaedhals. He couldn't be sure whether it was the herb concoction Beag ní Dé had given him the previous evening or the solitude of their camp fire, but he had slept soundly and deeply.

He rolled over to pull Sorcha to him but his arm reached out to empty furs. The Brehon opened his eyes wide and yawned as he looked about.

'I've found a spring,' the Druid woman called. 'Come and wash your cares and worries away.'

Dalan laughed and realised he hadn't felt such a sense of joy for a very long time. His head had been cluttered with his duties and the problem of the Watchers. He hadn't allowed time purely for himself.

The air was bitterly cold and he thought twice about leaving the warm cocoon of furs he been wrapped in all night. The sky was clear but Dalan could smell the scent of snow in the air. He knew from experience it would be only a few days at the most before the first falls.

Sorcha called out to him again to come down to the stream. The Brehon groaned but threw off the furs. He pulled on his boots and cloak and wandered down the hill to where the Druid woman was washing. His breath was thick and foggy and the cold was catching at his throat, so he was shocked to find her swimming in a deep dark pond.

'Come in,' she called. 'It'll wash your troubles away.'

'I'll catch my death from cold,' he replied with a shiver in his voice.

'That's one thing you won't catch,' Sorcha laughed.

Dalan had to laugh too. He still hadn't become accustomed to his newly acquired immortality. The air was freezing cold but as there was no danger to him of illness, he threw off his clothes and was soon up to his neck in the icy pond. At first it stole his breath away and he recoiled with a gasp, but the Druid woman placed a hand on his arm and encouraged him to stay a while. Once the initial shock had passed and he was able to relax a little, Dalan began to realise the cold wasn't really all that unpleasant. He'd learned to avoid extremes of heat and cold when he was a mortal. Now he would be able to learn to enjoy extremes.

'You'll appreciate the fire when we get back,' Sorcha giggled.

Just then they heard their names being called. It was the summons to return to Eber Finn's camp. Dalan turned around in the water and there was disappointment stamped all over his face. Sorcha swam close and held him in her arms as he lay back to enjoy the warmth of her body.

'Soon enough we'll be free to do as we wish,' she promised. 'We'll go to live in my little house in the middle of the woods where the world can forget about us.'

'For now we have a job to do,' the Brehon sighed.

'But we've a good incentive to get it over with quickly.'

The Druid woman turned him round to face her and put a hand under his chin so he would have to look into her eyes.

'When all these kings and warriors are no more than dust, we'll still be here,' she told him. 'When no one remembers the war between Éremon and Eber, when even the Fir-Bolg, the Danaans and the Watchers have passed into legend, we will remain.'

'You're right,' Dalan replied as he kissed her tenderly on the forehead. 'In future we must not allow ourselves to be distracted from the joy of life by mortals for whom death is a great release. Our only release will be sleep. We must be careful to care for one another lest we end up like Lochie and Isleen.'

'I have nothing but pity for them,' Sorcha agreed. 'They've learned much but they've squandered their lives in vengeance and hatred. They may be able to take on beautiful forms but underneath they are the ugliest creatures I have ever encountered.'

'It doesn't concern you that we may one day be too awful for mortals to look on without fear?' Dalan asked.

'If anyone should look at us and be frightened, it will be because fear dwells in their own heart,' she assured him. 'We are good people. No one will ever have anything to fear from either of us.'

'How will we cope with all these tiresome mortals who seek our help?' Dalan sighed.

'Let's try laughing at them,' Sorcha suggested. 'Most of their worries are pretty silly in the end.'

The Brehon smiled and then broke out into a hearty laugh. 'Take that, King Eber,' he mocked. 'That's what I think of your silly war.'

Once again they heard their names echoing through the forest. Reluctantly they left the sanctuary of their freezing pond and went back to their camp fire to get dressed. They gathered their furs and few possessions and made their way back to the camp.

By the time they arrived, their hair still dripping wet from the swim, Aenghus mac Ómor was waiting impatiently by the forge. Eber sat beside him, watching as the blacksmiths packed the wagon in readiness for the day's journey.

The King of the Gaedhals raised an eyebrow when he noticed the Druids were dripping wet. He wrapped his cloak a little tighter round his body but he had other, more important matters on his mind.

'The King of the Sen Erainn tells me he's ready to take the Quicken Brew now,' Eber Finn informed them, drawing them aside, away from Aenghus. 'His warriors are waiting for their portion also.'

'How many warriors are in his retinue?' Sorcha asked glumly.

'Four hundred and fifty!' the Gaedhal exclaimed with excitement. 'With so many warriors behind me, Éremon may just concede victory without a drop of blood being spilled.'

The Druid woman coughed nervously and put her leather bag of herbs down on the grass. For a little while she made a show of searching through the bag, but it was obvious something was amiss.

'What's wrong?' the king asked. 'You have the Quicken Brew, don't you?'

'I have enough with me for one more person,' Sorcha admitted. 'Do you know how many berries it would take to feed four hundred and fifty warriors?'

'You don't have enough?' Eber gasped, trying to keep his voice down to a whisper. 'Why didn't you say so last night?'

'No one asked her,' Dalan smiled as he shrugged his shoulders.

And then the two of them broke out into a giggle.

'Are you drunk?' Eber asked them.

The pair struggled to control their amusement.

'I'm sorry,' the Brehon offered, stifling his mirth. 'We've been under a lot of strain the last few days. I've been very tired, you know. But I'm feeling much better.'

'You are drunk.' Eber Finn moved in closer to them and his face was suddenly pale. 'Are you going to help me or not?' he pressed. 'Aenghus is expecting to be given the Quicken Brew before the battle. And he also expects that you'll bestow the

Brew on his warriors. Now, if that doesn't happen he's going to march off and raise his standard beside my brother's.'

'I didn't say I'd give him the Brew,' Sorcha protested. 'I promised I'd give him the secret of the Brew.'

'What do you mean?'

'Last night Beag ní Dé taught us the Draoi song of the Watchers and I taught her the secret of the preparation of the Quicken Brew,' the Druid woman explained. 'All she needs is the berries and then she can easily prepare the potion for all the hosts of the Sen Erainn.'

Eber cast a quick glance from one Druid to the other, wondering whether they were telling him the truth.

'You should perhaps explain that to Aenghus,' the king said at last.

'Beag ní Dé will do that,' Sorcha assured him, nodding politely to the old woman as she approached.

'Where's the Quicken Brew?' Aenghus demanded, impatient at the delay. 'I've composed a poem in honour of you for making it available to our people.'

He cleared his throat. 'A fish is a small animal. Little wonder we catch them in nets and eat them for our supper. If I had a snout like that I'd expect to be fried in butter or perhaps salted and kept in a barrel.'

Eber stared sternly at Sorcha and Dalan, silently commanding them not to laugh. They both turned away, struggling to suppress their giggles.

'So now I've given you my poem, in return you should give me the Quicken Brew,' Aenghus stated cheerily.

'I have the knowledge of it,' the old woman declared. 'And I will decide who is deserving of it. And after I'm gone my successor will decide. This is not a matter to be handed over to any warrior. The first thing you'd do is go about slaughtering everyone who'd ever offered you an insult. Then you'd probably let your greed get the better of you.'

'I was promised the Quicken Brew,' the Red Cap king retorted. 'I gave them a fine poem.'

'You were promised the *secret* of the Quicken Brew,' Beag ní Dé corrected him. 'Our people have that secret. You can rest assured it is in our possession. I will keep it safe.'

'I'll take my warriors to the King of the North!' Aenghus bellowed.

'You gave your word that you'd lend your sword arm and those of all your warriors to the cause of Eber Finn,' she reprimanded him. 'Is your word worth nothing? Is it time I called a Council of the Chieftains and had a new king installed?'

'I am the King of the Sen Erainn!'

'Not if I decide to depose you,' the old woman pointed out. 'I can guarantee that your warriors would follow my advice over yours. If I told them you had broken your word, you would be immediately replaced.'

'I won't send my warriors into battle without the protection of the Quicken Brew,' he stated bluntly.

'Why not?' Beag ní Dé asked. 'You've done so a hundred times before when it suited you. And I must say, those fights were over petty matters. If Eber loses this fight Éremon will take our islands from us and scatter our people before his steel swords.'

'How do we know Eber Finn will not do the same?'

'I am a Brehon judge,' Dalan cut in. 'I will enforce his promise to preserve your sovereignty.'

'I'd rather trade with your people than fight with them,' the Gaedhal admitted. 'I've had enough of war. I can offer you steel and iron goods. What can your people offer me?'

'Fish,' Aenghus replied without hesitation.

Eber paused, expecting that perhaps there might be something else the isles of Arainn could trade. But when Aenghus didn't add anything to his list, the Gaedhal went on.

'Fish,' Eber Finn nodded, trying not to sound too disappointed. 'Food is the basis of all trade. I'm certain we can establish the foundations for a very long and mutually beneficial friendship between our peoples.'

Aenghus realised he had little choice but to march with Eber, or else be ridiculed by Beag ní Dé. Still he reasoned she would not be around for very much longer. She was old. All he had to do was be patient and win her successor over to him.

He was, however, a stubborn man. 'My warriors will need swords of steel,' he ventured.

'That bargaining was done yesterday,' the old woman berated him. 'You've got a promise of sovereignty and trade from King Eber. And you managed to win the secret of the Quicken Brew for our people. Into the bargain you've been granted some chariots and swords. Are you such a greedy man? When have you ever been better paid for taking part in a battle?'

'I have never been paid to fight,' the king objected. 'I am an honourable man.'

'If that's how you wish to be remembered, I suggest you gather your warriors for the march north,' the old woman advised. 'There is much to be done. I may be just an old Druid who knows nothing of war, but even I can see that we're wasting precious time with all this talk.'

'Very well,' Eber cut in. 'Are you going to march with us?'

The King of the Sen Erainn growled under his breath, disgruntled that he'd been so cheaply bought. But in the end he nodded and called on his trumpeter to sound the assembly for the march.

Within an hour the entire force was making its way towards the rath where Éremon and his warriors were waiting. Goll mac Morna acted as the guide, assisted by Mughain and shadowed all the while by the watchful Naithí.

Chapter Nineteen

ber Finn's scouts arrived at the rath an hour or so before sunset. The king arrived a short while afterwards and quickly sized up the situation.

It was soon apparent the hill fort could only be assaulted from one direction. The other sides were too steep for warriors in armour to climb, or simply too thick with impenetrable blackberry bushes. At the foot of the hill was a wide shallow stream which had to be crossed before any attempt on the fort could be made. The rocky bottom was littered with many loose stones, most of which were no bigger than a fist but which rendered the chariots useless. Any war-cart trying to cross the water would have soon damaged its wheels. The defenders, on the other hand, had the perfect vantage point to rain down a torrent of arrows on their enemies.

Eber cursed his luck. There was one feature of this landscape that was in his favour, however. On his side of the wide stream there was a flat grassy expanse of land that lay just out of range of Éremon's archers. Here he would be able to assemble his warriors in relative safety.

Eber ordered a tent be erected for him at the far edge of the field because, like Dalan, he could sense there was soon going to be snow. The nights were already bitterly cold and he wanted some shelter from the howling wind at midnight.

When Sorcha and the Brehon finally arrived they found the king seated on a bench at the door to his leather tent. He was staring across the stream as if the answer to his problem was about rise up out of the waters and wave to him.

Eber Finn asked them for their assessment of the situation, but both Druids pointed out they had little experience in these matters. This plunged the king into a long stony silence from which he did not emerge until a messenger arrived from his brother's camp.

'You are trespassing on the territory of King Éremon, ruler of the North and High-King of Eirinn,' the young man declared.

'High-king?' Eber repeated in shock. 'How long has he been using that title?'

The messenger didn't answer but continued as he'd been ordered to do.

'Éremon will accept your heartfelt apologies on the condition that you come alone to the summit of the hill fort and beg his forgiveness. Failure to do so by sunset this afternoon will see his wrath descend upon you.'

Eber Finn sighed heavily then told the messenger to go away without an answer.

'What are you going to do?' Dalan asked after the young man had departed.

'I'm not going to wander up there so my brother can separate my head from my shoulders without anyone to intervene on my behalf,' he replied. 'I intend to sit here until I come up with a strategy that will assure me victory.'

'Search for the patterns,' the Brehon advised. 'Don't try to bend them to your will, or arrogance will be the end of you.'

Eber smiled, recalling the Brandubh game immediately. He thanked Dalan heartily, obviously cheered by those few words.

But by the time the sun had set, Eber Finn had still not come up with a solution to his problem. He knew it was senseless to send his warriors to a certain death in a full-frontal assault of the fort. And he was convinced his brother would never send out his warriors to fight on even ground when they could sit on the top of their hill quite safe from any attack.

At last he decided to send Dalan and Sorcha as his emissaries to Éremon. They were given strict instructions not to divulge the size of Eber's force and to scout out the numbers of the enemy as best they could. At first the Brehon objected. His status as a judge prohibited him from taking part in battle. Eber Finn, however, was quick to explain that it was more than the kingdom of the south that was at stake here. The future of the Fir-Bolg, Dalan's own people, was also in the balance.

So the Brehon and Sorcha trudged to the top of the hill to meet with Éremon. Their Druid robes guaranteed them safe passage, though the northerners marvelled at the Raven-feather cloak which Dalan wore. And more than once the Druids heard the word 'barbarians' used behind their backs.

They returned with the entire Fian band who had been captured with Goll. Éremon had graciously released them, without the return of their weapons of course. He also requested that a truce be held in place until dawn the following morning.

'There's roughly four hundred manning the top of the hill,' Dalan reported. 'One hundred and fifty of those would be archers positioned to bring their missiles to bear on anyone fool enough to cross the stream.'

Aenghus of the Sen Erainn was seated with Eber and he openly scoffed at the reluctance of the Gaedhal to storm the hill in force.

'One hundred and fifty archers?' he laughed. 'We are nearly six hundred. How long does it take an archer to shoot an arrow?'

'One every thirty seconds if they're shooting for accuracy,' Eber replied.

'How long to reach the summit?'

'Five minutes, maybe six,' the Brehon estimated.

'That's between fifteen and eighteen hundred arrows falling on the attackers,' Aenghus calculated. 'With shields raised, not many of those missiles will find their mark. I believe it's worth the risk.'

Eber Finn shook his head firmly. 'There has to be another way.'

Dalan and Sorcha excused themselves from this council of war. Druids rarely involved themselves in such matters in those days. They went out into the moonlight and stood by the flowing stream, looking up at the hill fort.

Both were silent, deep in contemplation of the terrible fight that would surely take place the next day. The Brehon closed his eyes and bowed his head, and as he did so he had a clear insight into the mayhem that would engulf this small corner of Innisfail.

'This stream will run red with the blood of the slain,' he said at last. 'And that hill will be secured at a terrible price.'

'I don't know how he is going to do it,' Sorcha added. 'But I hope Eber Finn will gain the victory here. And that his brother will fall.'

Dalan took her hand as they kicked off their boots and waded into the icy waters. After a long while he spoke what was on his mind.

'Now that I'm no longer concerned with the passing of time I have begun to feel a strange sensation, something like a unity with all things which extends beyond the confines of the past, present or future.'

'I believe I understand what you mean,' the Druid woman replied. 'It's as if we are standing in the midst of the battle at this very moment, even though not a single blow has yet been struck.'

The Brehon hummed lowly to indicate he agreed with her.

'We've become like the stream we're standing in,' Sorcha laughed. 'We will flow on over the same course for ever and ever. And if we step back to look we can see what's just around the corner.'

'Let's go to sleep now,' Dalan whispered. 'There will be wounded warriors wanting our aid tomorrow. And I fear we will have enough work to keep us busy until late into the night.'

While Eber's warriors were marching to the rath, Lom, Mahon, Sárán and Iobhar were also making their way in that direction. They cut across country through the woods and over bogs until they reached a rough road that took them to the north-east.

They came across a small settlement but made a wide circle to avoid it, since Mahon and Lom judged they were probably already travelling within the boundaries of Éremon's kingdom.

Sárán did not speak throughout this long and arduous march. He was resolutely silent, planning with every step his revenge on all who had wronged him. And no one bothered to speak to him either.

An hour before the sun set they stopped by the road and rested, though Lom was eager to press on into the night. He convinced the others they would reach the hill fort before midnight if they kept up this pace and so would be unlikely to miss the battle.

Mahon, who knew this territory well from his youth, agreed, but just as they were preparing to set off again they noticed a party approaching them on the road. Three carts guarded by four warriors were making their slow way north.

'They're headed for the rath,' Mahon declared confidently. 'Loaded with supplies, I'll wager.'

'Can we take them?' Lom asked his friend.

'There's only three of us,' Iobhar pointed out. 'They number four warriors and three drivers. We'd better be smart about it.'

'I haven't had a decent meal in days,' the Danaan noted. 'If I'm going to fight a battle tomorrow, I'll need a good feed. And I dare say that if we arrived in Eber's camp with three captured enemy wagons he might soften his attitude to us a little.'

Mahon urged them to get out of sight among the trees. As soon as they were concealed they started formulating a plan of attack. Even Sárán was given a part to play, in the hope that his presence would balance the odds.

It was a long while before the slow-moving wagons approached the spot where the travellers had been resting. As they came up to the stand of trees they found Sárán seated by the side of the road, a pig on a long leather lead beside him.

'Are you going north?' he asked.

'Well, there's a sight you don't see every day!' the old warrior riding on the front wagon called back to his comrades. 'It's a Druid leading a pig.'

He turned back to Sárán and greeted him politely. 'I don't mean to be rude but we haven't encountered many folk on this journey. This would have to be the most dismal duty I've ever been assigned.'

'Perhaps I could tell you a few tales to lighten the road?' Sárán offered.

The old warrior's eyes lit up. 'We're going off to a battle,' he warned. 'I can only take you as far as the rath where my king is waiting for these supplies.'

'I'd be glad of a ride,' the Druid assured him. 'And so will the pig.'

'It's a good while since I tasted roast pig,' the warrior hummed. 'Are you thinking of eating that animal in the near future?'

'We could share it, I suppose. But aren't you in a hurry to reach your king?'

'We'll never make it before tomorrow at this pace anyway,' the warrior shrugged. 'So we might as well stop for a few hours and eat.'

He called the wagons to a halt and jumped down. Then he told the other three warriors to go off into the woods and collect firewood for the feast while he went round to the rear wagon.

'We'll put your little friend in here until I get the fire started,' the old warrior told Sárán.

Then he gathered some kindling and got out his tinderbox. By the time he'd lit a small blaze the sun had disappeared below the horizon. The warrior was warming his hands when he suddenly realised his warriors were taking an awfully long time to gather firewood.

He stood up and was about to call out when a blade was placed at his throat. He may have been an old warrior but he was certainly experienced. With a fighter's skill he thrust his elbow into the stomach of his attacker. Iobhar fell to the ground, badly winded.

Before he'd hit the ground the old warrior had drawn his sword and was ready to take on all comers. He did not have to wait long. Mahon stepped out from the darkness, blade at the ready. The warrior lashed out with his sword, but the Danaan easily deflected the blow and punched the Gaedhal with his left hand as he recovered from the parry. The old warrior was quick, though, and with a vicious upward thrust of his sword he stabbed Mahon in the stomach.

Blood flowed over his blade and the Danaan stepped back, stunned. As the old Gaedhal was watching his defeated foe he was disarmed by Lom who grabbed his sword arm and twisted it until the blade fell down on the grass.

In seconds he was bound and laid up against the wagon while Lom and Iobhar saw to their friend's injury. Mahon managed to drag himself over to the fire and lie down while he recovered. The wound was not deep so the Quicken Brew set to work swiftly. The blood stopped flowing as Mahon tore off his tunic to expose the injury. Then the flesh began to fester around the cut as if it were badly poisoned. Pus poured from the wound and then, miraculously, the flesh knitted itself together. Within a few short minutes the injury was completely healed. Only a faint scar remained.

The old warrior sat leaning against the cart with his mouth wide open.

'Who are you?' he gasped in awe.

'I am Mahon, son of King Cecht of the Danaans.'

'Danaans?' the old warrior stammered. 'Have the Danaans sided with Eber Finn?'

'Every one of them that I know has,' Iobhar lied. Though it was only a white lie. The only Danaan he knew well was Mahon.

'Then Éremon is lost,' the old warrior sighed. 'And you'll take these provisions to your king?'

'Yes,' Lom nodded.

'Well I don't feel so bad for losing the wagons,' the old Gaedhal stated. 'Éremon couldn't have defeated the Danaans with their magic a second time. I've fought them. I know they chose to retreat into the mists. But if they've come out in support of Eber, then the north may as well fall back in disarray.'

Iobhar got the old warrior to his feet and led him away to sit with his comrades by the side of the road. All the warriors and drivers had been accounted for, so Lom thought it was time to inspect the supplies they'd captured.

He and Mahon went to the rear wagon and released Molly the pig. Sárán stood behind them, curious as to what food they might be dining on this night. But the wagon was only stacked with bundles of arrows.

They went then to the next wagon. It, too, was full of arrows. A search of the front wagon came up with the same result.

'Arrows!' Mahon spat, bitterly disappointed. 'I'm so hungry I could eat one of these horses.' He stormed over to where the warriors and drivers were gathered. 'Didn't you bring any food with you?' he demanded.

'What we had we ate an hour ago when we stopped,' the old warrior told him. 'We're due in at the rath by midnight, though I admit we'd be pushing it to make it by morning. The wagons are loaded to the brim and the horses can only take so much weight at a slow pace.'

'We have to get moving,' Lom pressed, placing a hand on Mahon's shoulder. 'The longer we wait here, the more likely we'll run into one of Éremon's patrols.'

'You'll never get away with this,' the old northern warrior grunted. 'There'll be a full Fian of fighters following behind us on the road. You might be able to deal with four of us quite easily, but you'll never defeat twenty-four.'

'He's right,' Lom agreed ruefully. 'But it's too late to worry about it now. We'll have to deal with that problem when it arises.'

'Give yourselves up,' the old warrior pleaded. 'Éremon is a forgiving king. I'm sure he'd find a place for you in his ranks.'

That gave Lom an idea. He took Mahon away out of earshot and when they returned they forced the old warrior to his feet.

'You're coming with us,' Lom informed him. 'Your friends will have to be left in the forest out of sight of the road.'

The old man was placed on top of the front wagon, his

271

hands tied in front of him. Then, with Lom at the reins of the first supply wagon, Mahon at the second and Iobhar at the third, they set off. Sárán sat on the back of the last wagon with Molly and kept lookout.

Eber Finn slept fitfully. He hadn't come to a resolution about how to fight this battle and the responsibility of kingship was weighing heavily on him.

He had refrained from drinking any mead before he lay down to sleep and now he was regretting the decision. He tried to rest for an hour or so then rose from his straw bed to get a drink. He stood at the door to his tent, sipping the honey brew and looking out at the fires and the shadowy forms of his resting warriors.

His mind drifted back to the Aillwee caves and to thoughts of his old Druid counsellor, Máel Máedóc, who had perished in the depths of the caverns. He recalled how the old man had tried to convince him that war with his brother would bring nothing but sorrow.

Now Eber wished he'd listened to Máel Máedóc. The king's perspective on the world had changed dramatically since that time, when he had been eagerly building his forces for a confrontation with Éremon.

'Perhaps it was fated that I should go to war against my brother,' he said under his breath.

'It was destiny,' a familiar voice cut in. 'Not fate.'

The king spun round and there in the shadows of the tent he could make out the form of an old man.

'Máel Máedóc? Is that you?'

'I have shed that name now,' the voice replied in a firm, fatherly tone. 'But I was called Máel Máedóc once.'

'I knew you'd come,' the king told the spirit.

'I was obliged to,' the ghost confirmed. 'With my dying breath I placed a geis upon you. And I've come at this time of test to remind you of the prohibitions I set against you.'

'I was just thinking that you were right to berate me for being so warlike,' Eber admitted.

'That is neither here nor there. I am merely here to remind you.'

'I have not forgotten your words. They have been burned into my memory.'

The shade said nothing, but hovered closer. Eber wasn't afraid but the sudden chill in the tent and the soft blue luminescence which bathed the ghost nearly snatched his breath away.

'If your brother should come with the blade of battle lust you will not draw a weapon against him. If your brother should denounce you to your kinfolk you will make a gift of two portions of your land to him. No black pig shall perish within the borders of the country which you rule. No bird will feast within your hall. No woman shall have cause to call you miserly. No rival will ever suffer hunger while he dwells on your land. You will devise the Code of the Fianna, so that folk in future will remember you for your wisdom.'

'The Code of the Fianna will be finished as soon as this battle is done with,' Eber explained.

'You will not draw a blade against your brother,' Máel Máedóc reminded him.

'Will I win the field tomorrow?' the king asked.

'Do you really want to know that?' the ghost asked.

'Will I be the victor tomorrow?'

'No.'

'Will I perish in the fight?'

'No.'

'Will my brother show mercy to me?'

'No.'

'Is there nothing I can do to avoid my fate?'

'No.'

Then Eber Finn frowned, recalling the way Máel Máedóc had always loved to play with words. He always told the truth when asked a question, but often he didn't explain what he meant. It was easy to gain a false impression from him if he wished.

'Have I asked the right questions?' the king ventured.

'No.'

And Eber Finn could have sworn he glimpsed a smile on the face of the spirit as the light brightened then suddenly dimmed. In a few breaths Máel Máedóc's shade had disappeared completely and he was gone.

It was after midnight and the supply wagons driven by Lom and his companions still had a long way to travel. If they'd been approaching the rath, Lom reasoned to himself, they would have encountered scouts or guards traversing the roads, searching for the enemy.

But the road was deadly quiet, and until after midnight they saw no sign of the warriors of Éremon. It was just as the moon was setting that Sárán caught a glint of steel reflected in the silvery light. He called to Iobhar who passed the word to Mahon. The Gaedhal stood up at the reins and looked back for confirmation. Sure enough, he spotted a band of Fian making their way with great haste along the road.

'We've seen them!' he told Lom. 'They'll be catching up with us in a short while. They're travelling at a furious pace!'

Lom turned to the old Gaedhal who sat beside him and covered his bound hands with his cloak.

'Now you just do as you're told,' he warned the old man. 'We're all Fir-Bolg and Danaan so we can't be hurt by swords and such. So if you betray us, the first one to lose his life will be you. Let them pass us by. Wish them a safe journey. And say no more.'

'I will do as you say,' the old warrior promised. 'I've seen that Éremon's cause is lost. And I have a family I wish to see again.'

'You're very wise,' Lom commended him.

It wasn't long before the band of Fian warriors caught up with the wagons. Sárán waved to them in silence as they passed on by, and a few of them wished him a safe journey. Mahon likewise didn't say a word though he was wished well by the Fian. But when they came to Lom's wagon the war-leader of the Fian hailed the old warrior as an old acquaintance.

'What are you doing guarding provisions, Scian? Have you been retired?'

'I'd rather be seated on this wagon than rushing off to fight the warriors of Eber Finn,' the old man shot back, beads of sweat gathering at his brow.

'The southerners don't stand a chance against us,' the war-leader shot back with a laugh. 'They'll have to scale the hill before they can reach us, so I'm told.'

'I've heard tell the Danaans have sided with Eber Finn,' Scian confided.

Lom nudged the old man, urging him to be silent.

'The Danaans is it? Well we've defeated them before and I suppose we'll have to beat them again.'

'May the Gods who watch over you watch over you this night and tomorrow on the field of battle,' Scian offered as a blessing.

'And the same to you,' the war-leader replied, but there was a hint of suspicion in his eyes as they darted between Lom and the old warrior.

'Tell good King Éremon I'll have these arrows to him before dawn,' Scian added.

'Good King Éremon?' the war-leader laughed. 'If I find one who can be addressed as such I'll let him know.'

By this time the Fian had passed on by and so the

war-leader waved to the old warrior and picked up his pace so that he'd catch his band. Within a short while they'd disappeared into the darkness. The moon dropped behind some clouds and then the countryside was black.

'You did well,' Lom thanked Scian. 'But I hope you didn't give us away.'

'If I did it was unintentional,' the old warrior sighed. 'I was very nervous.'

The night grew colder just before the dawn and all of them were shivering by the time the sun rose. Lom was tempted to stop and light a fire many times, but he knew these arrows would prove as precious to Eber as they would to his brother, so he pressed on.

The sky was brightly lit by the time they caught sight of the rath in the far distance.

Lom halted the wagons and conferred with Mahon about the best way to avoid being captured. The Danaan suggested they should continue straight along the road. There was only one entrance to the hill fort, as he recalled, and he expected that Eber would be waiting there blocking all entry and exit. But Lom was not so sure. He couldn't imagine that Éremon would have sent for arrows if he had no hope of getting them past his brother.

'We'll wait until we get a little closer,' he decided. 'Then we'll see whether it's safe to continue down this road. Keep a good watch.'

He'd just finished speaking when they all heard the cry of many warriors shouting in unison. It was the opening taunts of the battle and it turned their blood to ice.

Chapter Twenty

The field in front of the stream was dotted with fireplaces and littered with the slumbering bodies of countless warriors. A thin mist hung over the water and the hill fort was hidden from view. As the warriors of Éremon began their war-chant many of the Fir-Bolg, Sen Erainn and Southern Gaedhals stirred from their sleep to listen. The battle-hardened veterans cursed under their breath. The untried fighters looked to arming themselves with eagerness.

But Goll mac Morna had been awake for a long while. And just now he was finishing his breakfast. Mughain sat beside him, though she had no stomach for any food at all. She never ate before battle. And she found it difficult to understand how Goll could bring himself to eat so much.

After he had finished his first bowl of porridge and butter he helped himself to another serving and she had to turn away, unable to stand the sight of the warrior gorging himself. It was then she noticed a familiar face among the warriors gathering in their Fian groups for battle.

'Conan!' she called out with excitement. She turned to Goll. 'It's your brother Conan.'

The warrior grunted and continued to stuff porridge into his mouth without looking up.

Conan waved when he saw Mughain and headed over to where his brother was seated.

'Éremon released you!' Mughain exclaimed, hugging the younger warrior and spinning him round in a joyful embrace.

'Yes, he let us go,' Conan replied, casting a dark glance at his brother. 'The northern king told us Goll was off performing an important duty for him and he'd earned our freedom.'

Goll grunted as if he didn't know or care what was meant by that.

'Some of the Fian thought the worst,' Conan went on. 'But I had faith in my elder brother. I've worshipped him since I was old enough to hold a wooden sword. I've followed him through flood and folly.'

There was bitterness in his voice and Mughain hugged him closer so as not to look directly into his eyes.

'When I came to this camp I was told the Fian of Goll mac Morna was disbanded,' he went on, clenching his teeth. 'I was ordered to tag along with one of the other Fian bands. Then I heard that my brother had raised his hand to the king and that his hand had held a knife at the time.'

Conan pushed Mughain aside and stood over his elder brother. 'Is this true?' he asked in a small voice, as if he feared that he already knew the answer.

Goll belched and helped himself to another bowl of porridge. Naithí looked away in disgust. But Mughain could not stay silent.

'It is true,' she confirmed.

'I had a dream last night,' Conan whispered hoarsely, through a stream of tears. 'I dreamt my brother tried to strike down the king. I saw my own broken body among the slain. And the good name of our kinfolk was lost forever.'

'I've heard enough of dreams,' Goll growled under his breath. He stood up and threw his bowl into the fire where it smashed. 'Ever since you were a boy you've been talking about your bloody visions. Well if you're so frightened of dying, don't take the field today. Stay here and put on holy robes. Join the Druids and watch the whole fight from the safety of the king's tent.'

'I'm not afraid of death,' Conan retorted sharply. 'I'm afraid of what our father will say when I meet him tonight in the Halls of Waiting.'

'Give him my love!' Goll laughed.

'I'm frightened I won't be able to look him in the face when he asks me why I didn't slit your throat in the dark when I had the chance.'

Goll mac Morna contemptuously spat a wad of phlegm at his brother's feet. 'The battlefield is a dangerous place,' he grunted. 'Anything can happen. A warrior can't be blamed if he makes a mistake in the heat of the fight.'

He turned to face Conan and pressed home his point. 'If you know what's good for you, you'll stay well clear of me today. My eyesight isn't as good as it was.'

Goll wiped his mouth with the sleeve of his tunic, belched loudly and strode off to put on the armour he'd been issued, with Naithí close behind.

Mughain and Conan stood for a long while in stunned silence until the younger mac Morna finally spoke.

'Come with me,' he began. 'I've joined a Fian band of younger warriors who formed their company at Dun Gur. They're so inexperienced they consider me a veteran.'

'I'll stay by Goll,' Mughain told him. 'There's no telling what will happen today. I'd just like to be sure he doesn't bring any harm on himself.'

'No one would blame you if you left him now,' Conan assured her.

'Nevertheless, I'd prefer to be close to him when the fighting starts,' she replied.

'You're a loyal friend.'

'Am I?' Mughain whispered. 'I'm loyal. I suppose you could say that.'

And with those enigmatic words she left Conan and went to find his elder brother.

Sorcha went down to the stream just after dawn, picking her way between the men and women of the various Fian. She greeted any Fir-Bolg she recognised along the way and stopped to chat now and then.

When at last she got to the water there was barely room for her to sit down to wash her face. So she decided to wander upstream where she could have a little privacy. A couple of hundred paces or so took her to a spot where there were no warriors and the stream hadn't been fouled by the host.

She splashed water on her face and sucked up a deep draught from a place where the stream was flowing fast. The sharp iciness stung her skin but she threw another handful of water over her head and soaked her matted hair.

When she looked up into the mist that hung around the trees, a black shape shuffled on a branch and she heard a deep exhalation of breath. The Druid woman instinctively stood up and retreated to the bank.

As she reached the grass shore the black shape spread its massive wings and flew down from its perch to land on the ground nearby.

'Sorcha,' the bird said in a crackling, aged voice. 'It warms my heart to see you.'

'Morrigán,' the Druid woman bowed respectfully. 'I'm honoured that you should visit me.'

'That's enough formality,' the Raven snapped. 'You know I don't like it. It often smells of insincerity. Anyway, I know you too well to let you treat me with anything but familiarity.'

'Thank you,' Sorcha replied with a smile. 'I've missed you.'

'After this business is done with we should spend some time together,' the Morrigán suggested.

But Sorcha recognised the urgency in her tone. 'To what do I owe this visit? Surely you didn't come here to while the minutes away in idle chitchat?'

'You always were very perceptive,' the Raven noted. 'I've come because my people are restless.'

The Raven clicked her beak, then carefully checked that no one could overhear them. 'Éremon of the North has been cutting the forests at an alarming rate. Already the great woods of the east are gone. The forests of the north-east where I was raised are nothing but bare smouldering hills. The Ravens are angry.'

'The Gaedhals seem to have no sense of the sanctity of life,' Sorcha agreed.

'Is Eber any better than his brother?' the Morrigán asked. 'If we threw our support behind him would he keep his word?'

'Eber Finn is much the same as the rest of his people,' the Druid woman admitted. 'But he does listen to Dalan and myself and I believe he is at heart an honest man.'

'Go to him,' the Raven begged. 'Tell him I seek alliance with him if he will guarantee the safety of the forests. Tell him my kindred will gather from every corner of the land to fight on his behalf to rid the land of Éremon.'

'Eber Finn seems to gather allies like other men collect mushrooms,' Sorcha noted dryly. 'There seems to be a new one waiting in every field.'

'The Ravens are ready to fight,' the Morrigán pressed. 'I won't be able to calm their rage if they should loose it upon the Gaedhals. At least this way we have a chance of protecting some of our trees from the axeman.'

'I'll do as you ask,' the Druid woman assured the bird. And then she remembered the pair of Ravens that were off searching for Aoife. 'I promised I'd have a word to you on behalf of two friends of mine. May I broach the subject now?'

'Yes.'

'Do you know Crínóc and Crínán?'

'I know them too well.'

'They've been of great assistance to me,' Sorcha went on. 'I promised I'd speak to you on their behalf and secure their return from exile.'

'They're still fighting?'

'With a breathtaking passion. Yet I believe they are well-meaning souls.'

'I've tried everything I can think of to cure them of their fighting,' the Morrigán said. 'I suppose we'll just have to put up with them. I will grant your request if you are successful in negotiating a treaty for me with Eber.'

'I will do my best.'

'You'll have to do better than that,' the Raven told her sharply. 'If I can't find a suitable target for their anger, my kindred will certainly go on a rampage. There will be warfare between the Raven kind and the Gaedhals and I fear many of my kinfolk would perish in such a battle.'

'I will go now to speak with Eber Finn,' Sorcha promised.

'And I will go to gather my kin. I will bring them back before sunset. I hope the battle isn't over by then.'

'I hope it is,' the Druid woman stated bluntly.

The Raven took off, her wings spread wide, and soared off to the north. Sorcha didn't waste a moment. She headed straight for Eber's tent.

By the time she got there most of the warriors were awake and readying themselves for the first assault. From the snatches of conversation the Druid woman overheard it was evident the king had decided to attempt a frontal assault on the enemy position.

'Madness!' she hissed to herself.

Chapter Twenty-One

om halted his wagon the very second he spotted warriors on the road ahead. These fighters weren't travelling anywhere. They were waiting for someone or something. And Lom had a terrible feeling they were here expecting to escort three wagonloads of arrows into King Éremon's camp at the top of the hill.

'Is this your escort?' he whispered to Scian, the old warrior who sat next to him.

'That'll be them,' he nodded. 'Their job is to guard the wagons around to the stairs where our warriors will haul them up to the hill fort on their backs.'

'Why not take the wagons straight on up to the top?'

'I expect that Eber Finn has blocked the main path to the summit,' Scian explained. Then he thought for a few seconds. 'I don't suppose it'll do any harm to tell you, since you'll shortly be my prisoners. To the rear of the hill fort, concealed by a wooded grove, there are stairs cut into the hillside. The stairway is steep but it keeps the supplies moving in case of a siege. It's easily defended and an attacker would probably not guess its existence until too late.'

Lom shook his head, realising he'd been stupid not to send Sárán on ahead to scout out the road. Now there seemed to be no alternative to capture.

'You might as well untie my hands now, son,' the old warrior told him. 'You did your best to get these arrows through to your king. You're to be congratulated. Now you have no choice but to give yourself up.'

The young Fir-Bolg passed the word back that there were warriors waiting ahead of them. 'I'll keep you bound for the moment if you don't mind,' Lom told the old man. 'And I remind you that I have a sword here in case you're thinking of making any foolish gestures.'

Then he touched the whip to the horses' rumps and the wagon pulled ahead with a jolt. Within a hundred paces they were surrounded by northerners.

Mahon counted them quickly. 'There's no more than eight,' he called out to his friend in the forward wagon.

'What kept you? We've been waiting all night for your arrival,' the leader of the northerners called out.

'Lay down your arms!' Lom cried, holding a sword to Scian's throat.

There was immediate confusion. Éremon's warriors were caught completely by surprise. Each of the Gaedhals looked to the other in shock, unwilling to make a move lest the old man lose his life, but unsure whether they should drop their weapons.

'Kill him!' the leader shouted back. 'He's just an old man. That's why he was put in charge of the wagons.'

'You bastard!' Scian shot back. 'I'm a veteran of the king's wars in Iber! I'm entitled to a little respect.'

'I'll say a prayer over your grave,' the warrior retorted.

Scian's face turned red. 'Wait till Éremon hears about this!' he bellowed.

'You mean wait till he finds out you let three wagonloads of arrows fall into the hands of Eber Finn's fighters? He's not renowned for his stable temperament, our king. At least this way you'll die an honourable death at the hands of the enemy. That's better than a dishonourable death at our hands.'

Bows were drawn and swords raised ready to strike when a most unexpected thing happened. Sárán strode purposefully around to the front wagon and quickly sized up the situation. Then he stormed straight up to the warrior who seemed to be in charge.

'Call off your guards!' the young Druid commanded. 'You have no idea who you are dealing with here.'

'They're making Druids younger and younger,' the warrior laughed as he placed the point of his sword squarely at Sárán's throat.

The young Druid swallowed hard and his face was soon sparkling with beads of sweat. But he was determined to press his point.

'This is King Lom of the Fir-Bolg,' Sárán declared. 'And I am his twin brother, the renowned Draoi master, Sárán of the Bloody Raven.'

The warrior frowned, clearly impressed by the title the young Druid had bestowed upon just himself. But then he noticed a flash of fear in the young man's eyes and, being a veteran of several battles, he read this speech as bluff.

'You're no Druid!' he hissed.

As he spoke he thrust his sword at Sárán. The blade pierced the young man's chest and cut deep into the flesh between his ribs. Sárán let out a pathetic squeal and clutched at the wound as he fell to his knees.

The warrior laughed, placed his foot squarely on the young Druid's chest and withdrew the weapon. Sárán's face turned pale. He looked at the blood on his hands, smiled and fell onto his side, seemingly dead.

The warrior paid him no more heed.

'Are there any more Draoi masters among you?' he spat contemptuously.

'All of us are masters of the Draoi craft,' Mahon spoke up. 'You've made a terrible mistake that will cost you dearly.'

'Step down from that wagon, I'll put a sword through you and you can prove to me that you're a master of the craft too,' the warrior guffawed.

His comrades closed in, laughing with him.

'They speak the truth,' Scian spoke up. 'I've seen it. They are Draoi masters. I'd advise you to give up and just go home if you know what's good for you.'

'Shut up, old man! You're with them. You're a bloody traitor.'

'This is your last chance,' Lom advised. 'Lay down your arms or you'll surely perish at our hands.'

This brought a fresh bout of laughter from the warrior. 'What are you going to do? Kill me with boredom, or are you hoping I'll die of exhaustion from listening to your foolish tales?'

Still laughing, he turned around to where Sárán had been lying on the road. 'Or perhaps you're going to throw yourselves on our swords and —'

The warrior stopped midsentence as he realised the young Druid was standing right in front of him with a broad smile on his face.

'I thought I killed you?'

'You can't kill me,' Sárán shrugged. 'I'm a Draoi master.'

With a deep frown the warrior turned back to Lom and his captive.

Scian had a look of resignation on his face. 'I told you so.'

The leader spun round to stare at Sárán again. Then he cautiously placed his fingers on the spot where he'd stabbed the young Druid. There was no wound, just a very slight scar and even that was fading before his eyes.

'Throw down your arms, lads,' the warrior ordered. 'Let them pass. They're Draoi masters.'

His fighters did as they were told then gathered at the side of the road to watch the wagons pass.

'You couldn't direct us to Eber Finn's camp, could you?'

Sárán asked casually as he returned to his seat on the rear of the wagon.

'Straight down that road four hundred paces and you'll be stopped by the southern sentries,' the warrior replied, still stunned.

'Thank you,' the young Druid said cheerfully. Then he gave a cheerful wave. 'You've ruined a fine tunic. If I meet you on the field you will pay dearly for it.'

And the eight warriors from Éremon's Fian stayed right where they were until the wagons were out of sight. Then they picked up their weapons and, after a brief discussion among themselves, decided the battle was already lost.

The northerner was right about Eber's sentries. Within four hundred paces the wagons were surrounded again. Eber's grim-faced Fian guards levelled swords and aimed bows at each of them, warning them not to make a move.

Once Lom had identified himself he handed his prisoner over to the guards. Scian clapped his captor across the back. 'So you're a bloody king, are you?' he laughed. 'Well it's been an honour. I've never been captured before, so I'm happy to say 'twas a king who caught me.'

With that settled, Lom demanded to be taken to Eber Finn and an escort was arranged for him across the densely packed field. Sárán and his brother led the way, followed by Mahon and Iobhar, who still carried his pig.

Despite the urgency of their news, the smell of meats cooking and porridge oats boiling soon had the four travellers distracted. They begged the sentries for leave to have a bite to eat. Mahon explained he hadn't put a scrap of food in his belly for days.

The sentry looked him up and down and then asked whether they had ever met before. Mahon said he thought not but Iobhar recognised the warrior as one of the two they'd fought with at the kitchen sluice.

'Thanks for your help,' the Gaedhal cut in quickly. 'But we'll find the king ourselves if you don't mind. You make sure you tell him about those arrows while we get ourselves something to eat.'

'Where did you get that sow?' the sentry asked with a frown.

'It was my mother's,' the Gaedhal explained.

'Nice pig,' the sentry complimented as he stroked Molly gently across the nose.

The Gaedhal took his leave politely and grabbed Mahon's arm.

'What was that all about?' the Danaan hissed as Iobhar dragged him away.

'Have you forgotten what happened the night we stole Aoife away?'

Then Mahon realised the danger they were in if they were recognised by the mob before they had a chance to speak with Eber Finn. Indeed Iobhar was in the most danger. It was likely he was being touted as a traitor. And after all, he was the only one of them who was mortal.

In minutes they'd found a fire, scrounged some porridge and filled their bellies. They drank their fill from water skins then lay back to quietly discuss their next move.

'Whatever we do we must stay out of trouble,' Lom told his companions.

In the event they need not have bothered discussing a strategy. The decision was taken out of their hands. Molly had been wandering about snuffling in the grass and occasionally snuggling close to Iobhar. But after a short while he realised she was missing.

While Lom was suggesting they simply walk up to Eber

and tell him everything that had happened, Iobhar stood up and had a quick look for his beloved pig. But she was nowhere to be seen.

'Molly!' he called out.

In that instant he glimpsed her black form scurrying between two fires. There were three burly, hungry-looking warriors chasing her.

'Molly!' he cried and there was a hint of panic in his voice.

Then, before his companions could restrain him, he was off after her, jumping fires and leaping feeding fighters. Lom was up in an instant and Mahon was close behind. Sárán breathed deeply in frustration then stood up to trail along at his own pace.

'So much for staying out of trouble,' he sighed.

Chapter Twenty-Two

ber Finn was already dressed in his finest mail coat over the same dark blue tunic he'd worn to impress Aenghus mac Ómor. He'd chosen a fine sword for the battle, the same one he'd carried at Sliabh Mis. His mind was now easier. He had devised a strategy of battle, and though he had some reservations, his confidence was returning.

Gathered outside his tent were the chieftains of his people, representatives of the Fir-Bolg and the King of the Sen Erainn. Cups had already been filled with mead when he stepped out, lifted his to the sky and spoke.

'May the Gods who bless you bestow their blessings on you today. To victory!'

'To victory!' every voice replied.

The king handed his cup to a chamberlain and took Aenghus by the arm. When they were out of earshot of the crowd, Eber Finn leaned in close to the Sen Erainn king.

'We will try a frontal assault first,' he explained. 'I want to gauge their strength and the accuracy of their bowmen.'

Aenghus's eyes lit up with joy. 'I knew you'd see reason in time,' the Red Cap king smiled. 'My warriors will be up that hill in no time.'

'I don't want you to do that,' Eber explained. 'I want you to follow my warriors to within range of their archers. Then you'll hold up a shield wall and stand until the trumpet call is given. After that you will withdraw to the safety of this side of the stream.'

'Withdraw?'

'Yes.'

'And then what?'

'We shall see.'

The King of the Sen Erainn made it plain he thought this was a dishonourable way to fight a battle, but in the end he acquiesced. Then Eber summoned Dalan to his side and made his way towards the stream.

Sorcha ran into them before they'd traversed half the distance across the field.

'I've heard there's to be a frontal assault!' she exclaimed.

Dalan nodded but begged her with a gesture to be quiet for the moment.

When they reached the water Eber stopped, his toes touching the stream. 'How did you know there was to be a frontal assault?' he asked the Druid woman, and there was intense frustration in his voice.

'I heard the warriors talking about it,' she replied. 'The whole camp is buzzing with the news.'

Eber Finn shook his head, unable to understand how this had happened since he'd taken great pains to tell no one but Aenghus. And that was less than two minutes earlier. The king looked up at the hill which was still shrouded in a light mist. He realised then that it was natural for the warriors to be passing such a rumour around. There really was no alternative left open to him but a frontal assault.

'I didn't get to sleep till very late,' he told them both. 'I've tried to come up with another solution to this problem but the answer has evaded me. So I'm going to test their defences.'

'It seems to me you don't have to do anything,' Dalan observed.

'What do you mean?'

'There's only one way in or out of the hill fort,' he noted. 'If you and your warriors sit here and blockade the entrance, you could starve them out.'

The king raised his eyebrows at the suggestion. He could see the sense in it but he knew that boredom would soon set in with all his fighters who were primed for a battle. Once that happened, Éremon would be able to break out and take the offensive. There was also the coming snow to consider. Even though the sky was clear, the clouds would surely be gathering very soon. There was an icy bite in the air that spoke of a heavy fall well on its way.

'I'll test their defences first,' the king declared. 'Then we shall see what action I take.'

A sentry interrupted the king then with the news that three wagonloads of arrows had arrived as expected.

'I didn't expect any arrows!' Eber Finn exclaimed. 'In fact I was just wondering how we were going to get by with so few missiles. Who brought these arrows to the camp?'

'Four men,' the sentry replied. 'They have a beautiful black pig with them.'

'A pig?' Eber spluttered. Part of his geis was that no black pig should perish within the borders of his country. The king felt his heart begin to waver that this sign should come just before the battle commenced.

At that very moment there was a terrible commotion in amongst the fires as two men hastily dodged between the warriors.

'That was Lom!' Dalan cried, hardly believing his eyes.

'And that was Mahon, too, unless I'm very much mistaken,' Eber added.

Before they'd taken another breath they were off pushing their way through the throng to find the two men.

'Stop those two!' the king commanded.

But his warriors were already distracted by the thrill of the chase and the prize pig that couldn't be caught.

At the other side of the field Mughain had tracked down Goll. He was already dressed in a coat of mail and had slipped his boots on over his wool breeches. He'd tied his hair back, intending to fight without a helm, but his leather gloves were discarded by the fire.

'I won't be needing them,' he told her when she turned up. 'You're welcome to wear them. I know you like the feel of leather against your skin.'

'No thanks,' Mughain replied sourly.

Then she set about putting on her leather undertunic in readiness to place a mail coat over the top. She'd just finished adjusting the tunic when a strange and unexpected sight caught her attention.

A small black pig came running across the field, dodging between the camp fires and the warriors. It was squealing for all it was worth and occasionally it snapped at a hand or leg that came too close.

Warriors reached out for it from every direction. Some chased it until they tripped and fell; one or two suffered injuries that would surely handicap them in the coming battle. All across the camp laughter spread like a ripple on a pond and the pig slipped through a dozen hands. Then Goll saw the sow. With an easy confidence he bent over and snatched up the animal as if it had been running to him all along.

The creature looked into his eyes and squealed even louder. Pigs are very good judges of character and this one was better than most.

'Molly!' Iobhar called out desperately. 'Molly, where are you?'

Led by the pig's cries, the Gaedhal soon came face to face with Goll mac Morna. By this time the former war-leader was holding a knife to the little sow's throat and joking with

Mughain about what a fine feast would be waiting for them when they returned from the battle.

'I'll spit her now and she'll be sweet and tender when we get back,' he grinned.

Iobhar sized up the situation very quickly. He knew Goll's reputation for butchery well enough. If he thought nothing of killing innocent fishermen or farmers, he certainly wouldn't think twice about the life of a pig. This matter would have to be handled very delicately.

'That's my pig! Hand it over or I'll give you the thrashing you deserve,' the Gaedhal bellowed.

'It's not yours any more,' mac Morna growled, sticking his blade into the flesh at her neck.

Three drops of blood ran down onto the shining steel and spotted Goll's hand. At that very instant Eber Finn appeared from the midst of the surrounding observers.

'Put that pig down now or I'll have you slain where you stand,' he quietly commanded.

Goll turned to the king, surprised that he was making such a threat over a black sow. But before he could protest, Mughain had stepped in. She snatched the animal out of his hands and handed it to Iobhar who immediately cradled Molly close to his breast and hummed a slow melody to soothe her.

Eber Finn looked from Iobhar to Mahon, then across to Lom. 'I think we had better have a talk,' the king suggested. 'Guards! Bring them to my tent immediately.'

'I wish we'd left that bloody pig to wallow in the mud of the lough,' Mahon hissed as they were marched to Eber's tent.

The king wasted no time once he had the four of them alone. Dalan and Sorcha were there to act as witnesses but everyone else was kept out on the king's strict instructions.

'Where is Aoife?' Eber demanded. 'What have you done with her?'

Mahon stepped forward with his head bowed. 'The

Watchers have her,' he replied solemnly.

'The Watchers?' Dalan interrupted.

'Isleen took her and has refused to return her to me. The Watcher said there was nothing she could do because Aoife had taken the long sleep of her own free will.'

'The long sleep?'

'She offered the same to me but I refused. Lochie advised me to search for Aoife. He seemed to think I'd be able to find her and rescue her.'

'Is there nothing that can be done?' Eber asked Dalan with concern. He had only a vague understanding of what had happened but he knew it was something terrible.

'There's nothing we can do until Sorcha and I have had a chance to speak with the Watchers. That will certainly not be until after the battle.'

The king nodded then turned his attention back to Mahon and Iobhar.

'I will have to punish you severely,' he told them in a cold tone but everyone could see his heart wasn't in it.

'If it weren't for them I wouldn't have been able to bring three wagons of arrows to your camp,' Lom interrupted.

'So it was you who brought the arrows!' Eber was struggling to keep up with everything he was being told.

'I'm grateful for the arrows,' Eber admitted after Lom had explained what had happened. 'And I'll be thankful for every blade lifted up in my name against my brother. There is a bitter battle about to be fought here. I have no time for any feelings of vengeance or regret. All my thoughts must be focused on the coming conflict.'

The king turned to Mahon. 'What have you got to say for yourself?'

'I will fight alongside you today if you will have me, and then when this war is won I will submit to the judgement of the Brehons.'

'If I live to see the day I will certainly seek compensation for the life of the warrior you took and for the way you treated me in my own home,' Eber Finn stated coldly. 'But I welcome your support. Your actions will go some way towards soothing my injured feelings.'

'I offer my sword also,' Iobhar spoke up. 'If you will forgive me.'

'You're a traitor,' the king told him. 'I expect a Danaan to be somewhat barbaric in his behaviour. But you are one of my own people. I can only imagine that in the time you spent as a fosterling with the Fir-Bolg you forgot the ways of your people. I have a task for you more important than lending your hand to the fight.'

'I will do as you ask.'

The king pointed to the black sow in his arms. 'Guard that pig with your life.'

Iobhar frowned, unsure whether Eber Finn was serious. But he saw the unwavering determination in the king's eyes and realised that for some reason this was a very important matter.

'I will take care of her as if she were my own,' Iobhar promised.

'See that you do. If any harm comes to her I could well lose this battle, my kingdom and my life. I'm under a geis.'

With this explanation Iobhar understood the enormous significance of the task that had been put to him.

Eber moved to the entrance of the tent. 'I think we've all done enough talking. It's time to begin this business. I can't put it off any longer.' He turned to Mahon. 'Will you see to the issuing of those arrows to my archers?'

The Danaan bowed and went off immediately to perform the task.

'Will you stand beside me, King Lom?'

'I will, my lord,' the young Fir-Bolg king replied. 'Though I fear my people will be unhappy to see me.'

'Nevertheless I would have you by my side,' Eber assured him. 'If there is nothing further to be said, then let us go.'

'I have a message of support for you,' Sorcha cut in. 'The Morrigán, Queen of the Raven kind, visited me this morning. She will rally her people to your cause if you can guarantee the forests will not be destroyed in your reign. Éremon has been wantonly cutting down the woods and the Raven folk are enraged.'

'I will welcome whatever help is offered,' the king stuttered, clearly astonished. 'But I can't imagine how the Raven kind could help in this fight.' Seeing Sorcha's stern expression, he added, 'When Queen Morrigán returns I'll speak with her.'

Then the King of the Southern Gaedhals strode out to the stream to wait until his warriors were ready for the first assault.

As Eber left the tent Lom glanced across at Sorcha. The Druid woman was looking at him as if she had guessed something about the incident with the two Ravens. The young king was suddenly overwhelmed by the terrible crime he had committed. If the Raven queen discovered he had been responsible for the death of one of her folk, she might not be so eager to ally with Eber Finn.

Lom took a deep breath and told Sorcha that Sárán had killed a Raven that had ventured too close to their camp. Then, with head hung in shame, he related how he had struck at the second Raven as it swooped down to attack his brother.

'You killed one of these birds?' Sorcha asked.

'I did.'

The Druid woman was too shocked to speak for a few moments. The Raven kind were already disgruntled at the way Éremon had been destroying their forests and their homes. They saw no distinction between Gaedhal, Fir-Bolg or Danaan. If word of this crime got out before the battle, the

Ravens could well turn against Eber Finn and all the two-legged creatures of Innisfail.

'You must say nothing of this to anyone,' she insisted. 'I will pass this news on to the Morrigán. I cannot say how she will take it but I feel certain you and your brother will be called to account.'

'I expect no less,' Lom sighed. 'I don't know what came over me. It was a flash of protectiveness for my brother.'

'And what of his killing of the first bird?'

'I can't explain his reasons for that,' the young king replied, shaking his head.

'Go and fight,' Sorcha advised him. 'Stand by Eber Finn and put this out of your mind for the moment. I fear I knew those two birds. They were doing my bidding in searching for Aoife. This is as much my fault as anyone else's.'

With a heavy heart Sorcha went outside to help the Brehon prepare a place to tend the wounded. She found Dalan by a large fire over which a cauldron of water was boiling. Beag ní Dé was there also, ready to lend a hand to the gruesome work that was always the result of such a conflict.

While the warriors were waiting for the order to advance there was little for the Druids to do, so Beag ní Dé made up some of her refreshing tea and asked the other two if they'd ever played Brandubh.

Dalan was delighted to find that the Sen Erainn had a tradition of playing and he went off to fetch his board. By the time he returned, Eber's warriors had only just begun their war-chant so the Brehon knew they would not be launching their attack for a good while.

The war-chant was an essential part of any battle. Its purpose was not only to intimidate the enemy. The feeling it inspired of belonging to a whole band of warriors who shared a common goal was also a very powerful tool for building morale.

Death waited for many of them on the field. This might be the last chance some had to sing alongside their friends and celebrate membership of the Fian. For it must not be forgotten that these folk were proud to be warriors. Most of them were descended from long bloodlines of warrior men and women. Their heritage was war. Their entire lives had consisted of training for this moment. Every painted line or spiral on their bodies had significance. Every item of war-gear had been sanctified to its purpose.

In the same manner every word, every note of this chant had been passed down through the generations maintaining a mystical hold over the singers. Each clan had its own song and the tribe had another which combined the themes and melodies of all the individual clans.

It was Eber's folk who began the chant, for they held the centre of the line and the king himself stood at that place. His standard was raised the moment his kinfolk began to sing. It was waved from side to side until the instant the song ceased. Then it hung limp in the still air.

By tradition the song then passed to the right of the line which was a position of honour and was usually set aside for allies. The Sen Erainn king raised his standard and his folk started to chant their own strange songs. The right of the line was responsible for protecting the centre. The warriors there were expected to stand fast, and never, no matter what the odds against them, were they to retreat. This ensured that even if the battle went badly for the king, he still had a chance to escape with his life.

On the left were placed the reserves who could be called on in an emergency to rally to the support of the main force. This morning the left was peopled by warriors of the Fir-Bolg supported by Fian bands made up of the younger warriors.

With the war-chants as a background, Beag ní Dé and the Brehon commenced their game of Brandubh. From the opening gambit they both had a sense that their game was a mystical reflection of the battle about to take place. Beag ní Dé played white, which Sorcha commented could represent Éremon who was defending his own territory against an invader and had already declared himself high-king in anticipation of victory.

Dalan agreed, for Éremon was surrounded on a hill, mirroring the layout of the pieces on the board. Eber's warriors, on the other hand, had cut off all escape routes. It would be a challenge for the northern king to break out from this encirclement and achieve victory.

It was a fast-paced game. The old woman was a very skilled tactician. Dalan's Raven pieces were on the run from the very beginning trying to outmanoeuvre her. In twenty moves she had stretched his pieces out so that he barely had a chance of defeating her. But the Brehon had been playing this game since he was a lad. He knew a trick or two himself.

In ten more moves he'd managed to pin the white high-king against one side of the board so that it couldn't move. Beag ní Dé laughed when she realised what he'd done, but Dalan frowned, not understanding why being trapped would lift her spirits.

The old woman gave her four white pieces away in what seemed silly, wasteful strategies until the only white piece left on the board was the high-king. It was her move and this one piece was still surrounded.

'You've lost sight of the patterns,' she gently rebuked the Brehon. 'The game is a stalemate. I cannot move.'

Dalan looked down at the board. A stalemate was a very rare occurrence in this game and for it to be achieved successfully required great skill on the part of the white player.

'You have handed me the victory,' she smiled.

'How so?' the Brehon asked.

'In the context of this game we have ended without either side achieving their objective. But in the context of a battle a king who has not been captured will go on to fight another day.'

'Is this how the conflict will go today?' Sorcha cut in. 'Do you think the day will end without a clear victor?'

'Since Eber has begun without a fixed strategy I wouldn't be surprised if both sides failed to achieve their objectives,' Dalan replied.

As he spoke the last war-chants ended and the centre ranks of the force moved forward. They crossed the stream with bristling spears and the sound of armour rattling, but not one warrior among them so much as uttered a word.

There was a strange eerie quiet as the first three ranks set foot on the grass on the other side. The mass of warriors formed into a great square fifteen ranks wide by fifteen ranks deep, representing almost all the Fian warriors of the Southern Gaedhal.

In a carefully executed move the front ranks closed their shields to cover their advance while their comrades behind locked shields to deflect arrows falling from above. The sides of the square were not so well protected but there was not as great a danger from that direction. Immediately behind, the Sen Erainn began forming into two similar squares as if preparing to march up the hill.

The three Druids watched as Eber's fighters exhibited their skills, and they commented with admiration on their discipline and skill. This was all the more remarkable because none of these warriors had been gathered together in this fashion since the Battle of Sliabh Mis more than three winters ago. The war-leaders of each of the Fian bands had done a fine job of drilling their individual groups to fit into a plan. Each band made up a small part of the square. Their position never varied and the knowledge of it was passed down from one war-leader to the next. This square had probably not changed its composition or order in generations.

There was a long pause before the sound of trumpets rang out from the top of the hill. Then a great shower of arrows rained down upon the attackers. Their steel points sparkled like the dew on spiderweb in the bright sunlight from the east. The missiles found their marks in leather and wooden shields. The noise must have been terrible for the warriors crouching underneath the shield wall, but from where the Druids stood the noise was like the sound of hundreds of stones being pelted down from above.

Eber's warriors all unexpectedly gave out a low humming grunt as the square moved forward a dozen steps. Then the first casualties were brought out. To Dalan's surprise there were only a few wounded warriors who left the square and they came mostly without the need for any help.

Only one had to be carried out by his comrades. And it turned out he had been rendered senseless not by the sharp point of an arrow but by the blunt end of a mead cup the night before. His friends were good natured about it but the poor fellow was distraught at being left out of the fight. He wouldn't have been much use though. He could hardly stand. Beag ní Dé gave him some of her tea and he slept through the remainder of the day.

The trumpets blew from the top of the hill again and another storm of arrows sailed down to stick out of shields at odd angles. There were only two wounded this time. The warriors had swiftly plugged any gaps they'd discovered after the first arrows had struck.

The three Druids tended their wounded charges and kept an eye out for the next fall of arrows. From their position they had a clear, uninterrupted view of the action, and all three understood it was their duty to record the day for future generations.

Dalan was glad there were three of them present. It would result in a balanced and well-versed story-poem. He was especially pleased that the responsibility for this would be shared between the Sen Erainn and the Fir-Bolg who had been enemies for so long and were now fighting side by side.

For a long while no more trumpets sounded and the squares made no further moves up the hill. Sorcha mused aloud that the fighting seemed to have stopped.

'Éremon isn't going to waste arrows on the shield wall,' one of the wounded warriors told her. 'And Eber isn't willing to commit himself to climbing the hill.'

'Why not?'

'It may not look very steep from here but it certainly is and the ground is uneven,' the warrior replied. 'It's a challenge to keep the shield wall together when you're on the move over a flat field. But it's nigh on impossible up a steep slope with clods of grass poking out everywhere to trip you up.'

Dalan had seen a similar situation once in the many fights between Cecht of the Danaans and Brocan of the Fir-Bolg in the days before the coming of the Gaedhals. He explained that Éremon was waiting for his enemies to advance so he could exploit their difficulty in moving.

Sure enough, as soon as Eber's warriors took a few steps forward the trumpets sounded from the summit again. Moments later another hail of deadly wooden needles fell upon the fighters of the south.

This time there were more casualties. But as they were being helped off the field there were two short sharp blasts from the trumpeters concealed somewhere on the hilltop. Then a mighty shout rose up and there was a great din of clanging metal and mingled voices.

Sorcha was confused. There had been no movement from either of the squares. She couldn't make out what had happened. Dalan, too, was frowning, unable to offer an answer.

But Beag ní Dé stepped forward, shaded her eyes and gave a mournful cry.

'They've stopped playing with each other,' she wailed. 'Now the battle will start in earnest. And we will have work enough to keep us going until long after sunset.'

Chapter Twenty-Three

p on the hillside Eber heard the short sharp trumpet blasts and he braced himself for the next fall of missiles. But it never came.

Then he heard the cries from above and ventured to look out from under his shield. What he saw turned his blood to ice. He caught his trumpeter by the arm but was so shocked it was a few moments before he found the words to give the order.

'Sound the signal to form a crescent line!' he shouted.

Those warriors closest to him were already pushing their neighbours aside to do as he commanded. His standard-bearer, gripping the staff of a long dark-green banner unadorned by any device, shuffled to get closer to the king. The command had passed on through the two dozen warriors of the bodyguard by the time the young trumpeter put the bronze horn to his lips.

Rippling out at the order, the formation collapsed. It took what seemed to Eber to be an age for the warriors to re-form in a wide crescent with the horns pointed forward. This defensive line was called the Bull by the veteran fighters. It was the only effective way to counter a downhill charge by a determined enemy.

Eber stood beside Lom in the second rank of three and stared disbelievingly at the warriors who were charging down the slope with wild reckless hatred in their eyes. The trumpets sounded again but the king left it to the commonsense of his fighters to ready themselves for more arrows. Most of them were veterans and raised their shields, but they need not have bothered. A sudden gust of wind blowing up the hill caused most of the arrows to fall harmlessly short.

Eber struggled to make sense of his brother's unexpected strategy. There was no sense in his sending warriors out to fight beyond the safety of the natural defences of the hill fort. Just out of range of a spear cast the enemy halted and formed a long line to stand against the southerners.

'What are they playing at?' Eber wondered aloud, but before he'd finished speaking the answer was presented to him.

On the hilltop where the mist had only just started to clear there stood three ranks of chariots six abreast. Each war-cart carried two or three spearmen and the standard of King Éremon fluttered above one of the leading vehicles.

Eber's heart skipped a beat. This was the last thing he'd expected. A mad charge down the slope was unnecessary. If he'd wanted to, his brother could have stayed put within the confines of his defences and showered arrows down on his enemies all day long. There could only be one reason for this desperate tactic.

'My brother has almost run out of arrows,' he told Lom excitedly. 'You must have captured nearly his entire store.'

In the next second his thoughts had moved on to how he would deal with this problem. If the chariots were allowed to come down on his line at speed, his warriors would be scattered and cut to pieces by the foot soldiers following on behind.

Eber hesitated, his throat dry, his hands shaking. Then he turned to Naithí who stood on his left. 'Run to Aenghus!' he screamed with urgency. 'Tell him to be ready to charge forward with his warriors when he hears three sharp short blasts from the trumpet. Tell him he is not to move so much as a step forward until he has that specific signal.'

'I must stand by you!' Naithí protested, anxious about losing track of Goll mac Morna.

'Do as I say or the day will be lost.'

'Yes, my lord.'

'Then you are to cross the stream and bring the archers across. I want you to command them yourself. If Éremon tries to retreat up to his fort I want a steady pelting rain of arrows to fall down upon his head. And no matter what happens, don't shoot into the fort itself. If his archers want to replenish their arrows they'll have to come out and get them.'

He patted the chieftain on the back to send him on his way. Then Eber turned his attention back to the waiting enemy. In a few minutes he'd passed his orders down the line in both directions so that every man knew what to do when the signal was given.

He thanked the gods that his brother's warriors seemed to be going about their preparations very slowly. He reckoned there must have been some reluctance from them to carry out this daring plan. And he decided to take advantage of their doubts by delivering a trouncing defeat.

The next few seconds passed in a blur as the northern chariots began their run down the slope. Soon they were hurtling towards the backs of their own line of warriors at a dangerous pace. One war-cart toppled before it had travelled more than fifty paces. The driver was thrown clear but the two warriors clinging to the back were crushed as the vehicle rolled over and splintered. The horse fell and tumbled but it soon regained its feet and thundered off towards the summit and safety.

More than one of Eber's fighters turned away from the sight in disgust and disbelief that a war-leader could waste his warriors in such a reckless fashion. The southern king placed a hand on his trumpeter's shoulder and told him to be ready for the first signal.

The young lad licked his lips, praying this would not be the day his skill or his breath failed him. He put the instrument to his mouth and realised he was shaking so much he could hardly hold the trumpet still. He didn't want the king to notice his fear so he put the instrument down until he'd drawn half-a-dozen deep draughts of air into his lungs. At last he put the trumpet up to his mouth again. He was no longer trembling but his mouth was so dry he doubted he'd be able to blow with enough force to be heard all along the line.

One hundred paces separated the front line of the northern foot soldiers from Eber's warriors. So when Éremon's line collapsed, the young lad knew the chariots would be upon them soon. He gathered his courage and prepared to do his duty.

Eber squeezed the trumpeter's shoulder as the war-carts passed by the warriors who would back up their charge. The king called out to his fighters to hold their ground.

'Stay till the last!' he bellowed. 'Stay!'

Then when the chariots were less than thirty paces from the front rank he yelled in the young trumpeter's ears.

'Blow! Blow for all you're worth!'

The lad took a great breath and coughed. Eber glanced at him. And in that silent plea the trumpeter found the strength to give the call. He swallowed his cough and the air was torn apart by two short blasts of the war horn.

The signal was expected. Most of Eber's warriors were moving before the second note had been sounded. In what must have looked to Dalan and the Druids as a smoothly executed movement but was in fact haphazard and chaotic, the line split in two.

The warriors fell back to let the chariots run on past them. And as they sailed on down the hill Eber Finn caught the first glimpse of his brother. The northern king was standing proudly on the back of his war-cart, defiantly pouring out insults to the southerners who'd shattered his strategy.

When they had passed, Eber's two hundred closed ranks behind them. Then they faced uphill again to deal with the second wave of foot soldiers. Their spear points bristled at the ready. But it seemed the foot soldiers of Éremon were not willing to follow their king into this trap. They hesitated. Eber ordered the trumpeter to blow again. This time three short bursts rang out and the Sen Erainn gave a terrifying shout as they rushed forward into the affray.

In their haste to bring the war-carts to a halt, many of the drivers lost control and came to grief. But a handful managed to turn their chariots around to head back up the hill. Then the chieftains of the north rallied their foot soldiers and charged down to rescue their king.

Eber had not counted on the charioteers being able to bring their vehicles back up the hill behind him. Suddenly it was his warriors who were being assailed on two sides. Their horses were almost spent but Éremon's war-carts drove into the back of Eber's line with surprising force.

There were only half-a-dozen but they pushed the southern warriors out of the way and there was suddenly a perilous break in the line. Just at that moment the northern foot soldiers crashed into the front ranks of Eber's formation.

All the previous order that had reigned on the field disintegrated in those few seconds as the Sen Erainn rushed up to support their comrades. In the centre where Eber stood surrounded by his bodyguards there was barely room to swing a sword. But his loyal warriors formed a circle to keep him from being crushed.

Men and women fell without ever having raised a blade in anger or received a blow. The melee was so tight some were simply trampled underfoot and left for dead. Horses screamed, men wept and women shouted obscenities above the awful din of steel striking steel.

But the only real fighting took place at the outer edges of the crush. In the middle it was almost impossible to tell friend from foe. Eventually a small group of determined northerners forced their way to a spot close to where Eber's standard was still held high. They were soon cut down by the king's bodyguard, several of whom fell wounded. Their comrades had to be quick to save them from being kicked to death or crushed beneath the feet of many fighters.

Amid all this panic and confusion Goll saw his chance. Naithí was gone. There was no one to watch over him now. He threw down his sword. At such close quarters he'd never have a chance to raise it against the king. He drew the knife Eber had given him and held the weapon close to his body. Then he pushed with all his strength to make his way closer to the king. Eber's guards were set upon by another onslaught of northerners.

Eber must have sensed the danger to his life for at that very instant he turned round and caught Goll's eye.

'Come here and lend your hand!' the king bellowed above the din.

And mac Morna smiled at the irony.

'I'll lend my bloody hand all right,' he growled under his breath.

But as he was making his way towards Eber he was pushed aside by a warrior who fell back hard against him. Goll saw by the rich mail coat he wore that this fighter was one of Éremon's personal guard come to rescue his king.

The wounded man rolled onto his back, exhausted. Then he looked into the fierce bloodthirsty eyes of Goll mac Morna and thought his life was over. He put up his hands to fend off the attack he knew must surely come.

When the death blow didn't arrive he dropped his guard. 'Have mercy!' the warrior cried.

The son of Morna laughed, elated to have such an easy target, but he knew that this fellow was not actually his foeman. In reality they both desired the same thing. The death and defeat of Eber Finn. If he spared this fellow's life he might be able to rely on him at some future time.

So, much to the northerner's surprise, Goll mac Morna offered his hand and helped the injured man to his feet. Then he pointed him in the right direction to escape the throng and turned his attention back to the task at hand.

When he searched around for the king he discovered Eber had been pushed further down the hill under the press of the northern foot soldiers. To his frustration Goll had to retreat in a wide circle and come up behind the warriors of the king's bodyguard. This took him some time but suddenly the chance he'd been hoping for was presented to him. As several of Éremon's warriors fell back in disarray, a gap opened in the ranks of Eber's guard.

This was Goll's moment. He rushed at Eber Finn with the knife raised. The same instinct that had alerted the king earlier must have screamed out to him again, but by the time Eber turned around the warrior was too close to be fended off with a sword.

So the king grappled with the hand that held the knife. But Goll was the stronger of the two and he was driven by an unrelenting hatred and revenge for the dishonour Eber had heaped on him. All the frustration and bitterness of the last few months suddenly burst forth from him in an unstoppable outpouring of malevolence.

Eber knew his time had come but he refused to give in easily. It simply wasn't in his character to capitulate under the weight of such a threat. The crush nearly knocked them over but Goll was strong enough to keep his feet. His blade edged closer to Eber's chest and the king tensed in preparation for the pain he was sure would follow. Just then Goll mac Morna let out a cry and stepped back.

Eber saw blood flowing from the back of the disgraced war-leader's head. Someone had struck him a heavy blow from behind. And though the attack would have knocked most warriors senseless, Goll was made of stronger stuff.

Conan waited for his brother to turn, then he thrust his sword into Goll's chest, aiming through a gap in the mail coat designed to allow the wearer unrestricted arm movement. But even this attack hardly seemed to quench the fire of passionate hatred in mac Morna's eyes.

With a savage slashing sweep he cut his brother across the throat. Then he stabbed him three times in the chest, watched him fall and kicked the lifeless corpse for good measure. By the time he turned round to deal with the king, Eber had gone.

In his place stood Mughain, the woman who had once considered him a mentor and had long been his devoted lover. She swallowed hard and raised her sword as Goll laughed. There was blood all over his hand where he'd struck his brother. His eyes were wild.

This was not the Goll mac Morna Mughain had worshipped. This was a monster, a traitor and a kin-killer. With a swiftness that surprised even her she brought her blade down hard on mac Morna's shoulder. The blow knocked him backwards and he stumbled over the body of his brother.

There he lay with the wind knocked out of him and his vision blurring. It took a few moments for his eyes to focus again but when they did there was another warrior standing before him.

The grey-haired stranger was vaguely familiar but Goll couldn't place him. The noise and confusion of battle had suddenly dissipated. There seemed to be silence all around and the sweet scent of fresh mead.

'Don't you remember me?' the warrior asked.

Goll struggled but he couldn't recall having ever known

any Fir-Bolg warriors. Then a strange and fearful recollection struck him.

'You do remember me,' the stranger smiled. 'This would have been a wasted effort if you'd spent your last breath and not recalled one of the most unjust crimes you ever committed in your life.'

Goll frowned but he couldn't summon the breath to speak.

'I am Fergus mac Roth,' the warrior declared. 'You murdered me one morning during a raid on my mother's settlement. I was on my way to see your king with a gift from Brocan, war-leader of the Fir-Bolg.'

The stranger squinted, trying to discern if mac Morna was taking all this in. Then Goll swallowed hard and a hint of panic appeared on his face.

'You do remember,' Fergus nodded. 'I'm so glad.'

Then the spirit knelt down and took Goll's chin in one hand, forcing him to look into his ghostly eyes. 'Do you recall the geis I laid upon you?'

Goll's eyes widened in despair as he struggled to breathe.

'You'll never sleep in one house more than three nights in a row. That was the first part. It certainly came true. But that one was easy to arrange. I'm not very proud of that. The next was that you must never show mercy to a stranger as long as you live. Foolish man. Only a short while ago you allowed one of Éremon's bodyguards to slip through your fingers.'

The ghost held mac Morna's chin tightly when he tried to turn away.

'Let me see if I can remember what was next?' Fergus murmured, teasing the warrior. 'If a black pig should come into your possession, not a drop of blood must fall from its body. Now that was a difficult one to get right but I managed it this morning. You'll never know how hard it was to bring that pig to you just in time. I almost thought I wouldn't make it.'

Fergus dropped the smile. His expression showed he was becoming bored with this game.

'If your king summons you, you must not tarry but travel to him by the most direct road,' he went on quickly. 'That was easy enough to set up in the heat of this battle. No woman may come between you and your next meal. I believe I owe a debt of gratitude to that pig. Twice she helped me today. Was it your woman, Mughain, who snatched the animal away from you?'

Then the ghost forced Goll to look down at his feet where Conan lay dead.

'The last geis I set was almost the most satisfying to bring to fruition. I told you your brother would be the instrument of your downfall. You tripped over him just now, didn't you? All the prohibitions have thus been fulfilled.'

Goll mac Morna struggled to free his head from the unrelenting grip of his tormentor. When he conceded to himself he could not break free, he began to sob. At last he managed to say just one word.

'Why?'

Fergus frowned and let go of the warrior's chin. Goll's head fell back hard against the ground.

'How else are you going to learn to respect others?' Fergus shrugged.

The warrior frowned in dismay. He'd been taught a terrible lesson. Now he was about to pass on to the Halls of Waiting where he would have to recount the deeds of his life to his ancestors. He struggled to raise his head to take one last look at the Fir-Bolg spirit.

But Fergus was gone.

Mughain was standing over him now. He smiled up at her, relieved to see her familiar face. But her gaze was empty of all emotion. Then he realised she was holding her blade high in both hands ready to thrust it into his chest.

Goll made a frantic attempt to get up. But before he could move she swiftly plunged the cold steel through his mail coat hard into his heart. The very last thing Goll mac Morna saw was the stern tear-stained face of the warrior woman called Mughain.

Eber Finn stumbled about after he'd watched Mughain dispatch the traitor. Then he found himself a sword and stood ready to defend himself. The battle had degenerated into a wild melee with no purpose or objective.

The king saw there was nothing to be achieved from this chaotic pushing and shoving. So he searched about for his trumpeter with the thought to order a general withdrawal of his forces from the field. But he couldn't find the young man anywhere nearby. Nor could he see his own standard flying. A cold panic set in when he realised he'd lost his bodyguard in the ebb and flow of the fight.

The thought came to the king that if he could make his way back to the stream he'd be safe. He turned to face downhill and as he did so the crowd ahead of him thinned. Out from the crush of warriors who pushed this way and that stepped a figure he'd hardly expected to meet face to face ever again in this life. The warrior spotted him immediately and threw off his helm to show his face.

The two men stood breathless and exhausted as they faced each other down. Neither had the energy or the will to raise a weapon. All around them the fighting continued unabated. It was as if some magic circle had been drawn around the two brothers which no one else could penetrate.

Eber looked into those eyes he knew so well. He marvelled at how much his brother had aged. Éremon's hair was grey, his features drawn. Even the once straight back was slightly stooped with the passing of the seasons.

An unbidden memory came to him of a young lad who liked to play at warriors. Eber glimpsed that little boy with the wooden sword and the mischievous grin. His joyful laughing spirit was still buried somewhere under the façade of the warrior-king who stood before him. The King of the North had become a shrunken old man weighed down with his responsibilities, bowed with the burden of ruling his kingdom. In a passing instant Eber felt an enormous pity for this man he'd grown to hate without ever really coming to know.

His brother's eyes flashed fire as their father's had done whenever he was in a rage. Then Eber clearly understood that it had been Míl, their sire, who had set them on this path to rivalry and war. He'd taught them how to fight, how to wage war against an enemy. But he hadn't taught them to share in one another's successes and triumphs. This battle had begun when they were children learning the craft of kingship from their father.

Éremon strode towards his younger brother, raised his sword and with a well-aimed stroke slashed the blade at his brother. The blow struck Eber hard across the back as he turned to avoid the full impact of it.

It was a powerful stroke. It knocked Eber Finn down onto his knees. And as he fell the words of Máel Máedóc echoed in his mind.

'If your brother should come with the blade of battle lust you will not draw a weapon against him.'

Éremon raised his sword again to deliver the fatal blow. Eber lifted his blade to parry the attack, but he knew for certain that if he tried to resist this assault he would break the geis prohibition that had been placed on him. In so doing he would bring about his own downfall.

So Eber Finn, fighting against his deepest instincts, dropped his sword and smiled at his brother. Then he threw his arms wide and bared his neck, inviting his brother's blade to do its work.

Éremon paused for breath. Perhaps he too saw the little boy in his brother. Perhaps some memory of childhood also returned to him then and he was overcome by the futility of this quarrel. Or perhaps he simply didn't have the stomach to strike another man down that day. Whatever the reason, King Éremon of the North let the blade slip from his hands and turned to stumble away into the melee.

Eber saw him a few moments later holding on tight to the chariot that rescued him. Then he heard a trumpet sound and watched dumbfounded as the warriors of the north fell back up the hill. Another horn blew and he recognised the call. It was his own trumpeter sounding the command for a general withdrawal.

Suddenly Eber Finn found his armour had grown impossibly heavy. He was more exhausted than he had ever been in his life. All thoughts of his own safety now melted away and he succumbed to the temptation to lie down on the patch of grass beneath him. On the entire battlefield this seemed to be the only spot that was untouched by the fighting. It had not been churned up. There was no blood spilled here.

And so he stretched out on his back and stared at the sky. After a few moments his thoughts wandered away from the field and he no longer heard the sounds around him. Then directly overhead a forest of arrows flew like a mighty war-band of angry birds flying to peck the eyes of their enemies.

In a short while another mass of arrows sailed overhead and this time Eber heard the distant triumphal cry of many voices joined together in exultation. The king closed his eyes then. He'd seen enough. And he promised himself that one day, when this fighting was done, he'd come back to this beautiful place and lie down to sleep.

Chapter Twenty-Four

hen the king awoke he was lying on his back covered by furs, under the cover of his own leather tent. For a long while he stared at the hide canopy stretched over him. Then slowly he began to recall snatches of the battle.

He realised there was a fire set in the centre of his tent and that the light from it was dispelling the darkness. He tried to sit up but an intense pain stung him sharply behind the eyes and he had to lie back again and close them.

When Eber found the courage to open his eyes again there was a familiar face looking down at him with a broad smile.

'You'll probably have quite a headache for a day or so,' Sorcha whispered. 'It's only to be expected. You took a nasty knock on the head.'

'Is the battle over?' the king managed to say, even though every word was a stabbing agony across his forehead.

'The fighting has concluded for the day,' Dalan replied quietly.

Eber turned to see the Brehon sitting close beside him on a low stool. There was a cup in his hand and he offered it to the king. With Sorcha's help Eber sat up and drank his fill of the cold water.

'Beag ní Dé is making a tea for you if you think you can

stomach it,' the Druid woman told him. 'It will ease the discomfort in your head and help you to sleep.'

'Did we win?' Eber asked.

The two Druids glanced hesitantly at each other.

'This is not the time for talking,' Sorcha told him. 'Now you should rest.'

'Tell me what happened!' the king demanded, struggling to sit up again.

Dalan put a gentle hand to his chest. 'You must rest. Your warriors will be needing your leadership tomorrow.'

'Has Éremon beaten us then?'

'There were losses on both sides,' Dalan told him. 'But neither you nor your brother would be able to claim a victory. When you have slept we will discuss it further. The sun has just set. Take the tea that is given to you and I will watch over you this night. Before dawn we will see whether you are fit to continue the fight.'

Eber would have argued if it hadn't been for the searing agony that pulsed through his head. He gratefully drank every last drop of the old woman's tea. Then he lay back down and slipped into a deep and lasting sleep.

He stirred again just before dawn. The Brehon was still seated beside him on the short stool.

'Are you feeling better?'

'Yes,' Eber replied. His head still ached but with none of the ferocity of the night before. The king sat up cautiously and found that it was not too much effort. Dalan placed a bundle of furs behind his back to support him, then poured him a cup of water.

'So tell me what happened,' Eber asked when he'd finished the water.

The Brehon built up the fire to warm the tent then placed a small cauldron over the flames. 'There's some more tea for you when you're ready,' he noted.

'Tell me.'

Dalan sat down on the stool again and commenced to relate all the events of the battle. He told how those watching in the camp had thought Éremon had surely gained the victory when they saw his chariots charging down towards the lines of Eber's warriors. The Brehon praised the king for his quick-witted response to what should have been a disaster. Then he explained how the battle degenerated into a bloody confusion in which both kings were lost by their bodyguards.

In his best poet's voice he told how Éremon's charioteers bravely cut a path out of the melee and rode up to rescue their king. Then he related how Naithí, in charge of the company of archers, had kept up a steady rain of arrows until the northerners had retreated into the safety of their fort to lick their wounds.

'It was early afternoon when we first considered the possibility that you might be dead,' Dalan told him. 'Your bodyguards had been separated from you early in the fight and no one had confirmed a sighting of you after the charioteers began their desperate counterattack.'

'Goll,' the king whispered as the memory returned to him.

'The woman who brought you back slung over her shoulders explained all about Goll's cowardly actions,' the Brehon confirmed. 'She was wounded herself but she stayed by you until she felt strong enough to carry you across the stream.'

'How could it have taken so long to find me?' Eber frowned in confusion.

'The battlefield was a terrible sight,' Dalan explained. 'I've never seen anything like it in my life. Where your front line stood against Éremon's foot soldiers there was a wall of corpses. Strewn behind that for two hundred paces down to the water were hundreds of wounded or dead.'

'What are our losses?'

'I have to say that it is remarkable they were not higher,' the Brehon told him. 'There are sixty wounded and nineteen dead of the Fianna. The Sen Erainn lost forty-five killed and sixty-two who were injured. The Fir-Bolg and the reserves were not called upon. Lom and Naithí managed the battle after you fell and they kept these warriors from the fight, realising the conflict would not be decided that day.'

'So I have fresh fighters to send out today?'

'It seems so.'

'And the weather?'

'There are clouds gathering,' Dalan told him. 'The first I've seen in many months. But I don't think they're carrying rain. It's to be snow.'

'Then this day may be our last chance to defeat Éremon,' the king sighed. 'And what of my brother's losses?'

'That is a sad tale,' the Brehon replied with his head bowed. 'One hundred and eighty of his warriors were killed. Fifteen were wounded. These few are in my care. They were captured.'

'How is it there were so few wounded among the northerners?'

'The Sen Erainn are not accustomed to showing any mercy on the battlefield,' Dalan explained with a grimace. 'And after you went missing some of your warriors became enraged. There was a slaughter of wounded northerners.'

The king sat back hard against the furs, his mouth open in shock. He could hardly believe his ears. Indeed, if it hadn't been the Brehon breaking the news to him, he might not have believed it at all.

Then he realised that he would be remembered for this terrible murderous outrage. 'This is all my fault,' he muttered.

'You must not think that,' Dalan soothed. 'In the heat of battle folk are apt to commit acts of hatred that they would not otherwise countenance. The very act of war is an atrocity. But it is a fact of life and it seems it cannot be avoided.'

'It will be shunned in my kingdom ever after this day,' Eber shook his head. 'I will end all battles. I want the poets to sing of this fight as the last time blood was spilled on this island.'

The Brehon smiled indulgently and got up to fill a cup with tea from the boiling cauldron.

'You have a good heart,' he assured the king. 'But unless you decide to take the Druid path you should leave the peace-making to others. You're a warrior and a king. War is one of your tools, just as the harp is one of mine. It has taken you a lifetime to learn your craft.'

The Druid passed the cup to Eber Finn and sat down again.

At that moment Naithí appeared at the tent flap. The king beckoned him to come in and thanked him for his part in the battle. The warrior knelt down and placed his hand in Eber's.

'I would have been beside you when Goll tried to murder you, but you insisted I go to the archers.'

'It all turned out for the best,' Eber Finn smiled. 'I got a good knock on the head to remind me to keep you at my side at all times.'

'Are you well enough to receive a visitor?' Naithí asked.

'That depends on who it is,' Dalan cut in.

'It's your brother,' the chieftain replied.

'Éremon?' the king gasped in surprise.

'No. Amergin. He's been sent as an envoy from the King of the North.'

'Bring him in,' Eber replied without a second thought.

Dalan warned the king that he should not be coaxed into another fight if he did not feel well enough. He reminded Eber Finn that the hill fort was surrounded and that Éremon had suffered huge losses. He was in no position to make demands.

As the Brehon finished speaking the tall grey-headed Druid

322

was led in by Naithí, Aenghus and Lom. The three warriors stayed by the tent flap to make certain the king was not under any threat.

'I will speak with my brother alone,' Amergin declared imperiously. 'This is a matter between us. You others may leave.'

'There are more folk involved now than just we three brothers,' Eber stated. 'The Fir-Bolg and the Sen Erainn are my allies. Whatever you would say to me you can say in front of these folk. Two of them are kings. The other is a loyal chieftain.'

'Very well,' the poet dismissed. 'I won't waste words. Éremon offers you peace.'

'We've won!' Lom whispered to himself.

But Eber knew his brother better than to expect capitulation so easily, even after the loss of so many of his warriors.

'You will have peace,' Amergin went on. 'But these are the conditions. First, you will withdraw your warriors from this place to your own stronghold. Second, you, Eber Finn, son of Míl, will submit yourself to the judgement of the Brehons for the dishonourable manner in which you have treated your wounded foes. Third, all your household, all your warriors, all your followers, all those who have allied themselves to your cause will swear an oath of allegiance and peace to Éremon, son of Míl, High-King of Eirinn.'

Lom laughed and the poet turned sharply to face him.

'Surely you're too young to be a king,' he said with venom. 'Do you not know to keep silent in the presence of those who have conquered you?'

'I am the King of the Fir-Bolg,' Lom stated proudly. 'I have a treaty with Eber Finn. My people were never conquered.'

'You seem to have some trouble brewing with the natives,' Amergin told his youngest brother.

'The trouble broth is boiling and you are the fire under the cauldron,' Dalan cut in. 'I suppose you've come to stir the pot.'

'Do I know you?' Amergin spat.

'I am Dalan. I am a Brehon judge of the Fir-Bolg of the Burren. I am the king's counsellor.'

'You have surrounded yourself with subject peoples,' the poet snapped at Eber. 'Little wonder you have turned to barbarous ways. Now I have seen the company you keep and the advice you receive, I'm not surprised you started this war.'

'This war was in the making when Éremon and I were children,' Eber scoffed. 'You saw how old Míl pitted us against each other at every opportunity.'

'Now you defile the name of our father!' Amergin bellowed. 'It's clear you have no respect for anyone. Your brother Éremon nurtured you to his bosom. He brought you here to Eirinn so that you might share the opportunities in this new land.'

'This is an ancient land,' Dalan corrected him. 'You are new.'

'Be silent!' the poet spat. 'I will not have an underling speak to me in that manner.'

'I'm more than your equal,' the Brehon countered calmly. 'You are chief Druid of your people simply because no other folk of learning survived the sea voyage.'

'You will silence this person,' Amergin demanded of his brother. 'I am a noble of the royal house of the Gaedhal. I refuse to be treated like a native.'

'These natives have more nobility about them than our blood will ever be able to bear,' the king snapped. 'If you've finished the message you were sent to deliver, then leave. I am only sorry it appears I have lost two brothers this day.'

Then, as if he had witnessed this scene a hundred times, Eber watched his brother turn his back on him. The king knew Amergin was about to denounce him. The opening lines of his diatribe were already echoing in Eber's head, even though they hadn't yet passed his brother's lips.

The king recalled the second prohibition Máel Máedóc had placed on him. 'If your brother should denounce you to your kinfolk you will make a gift of two portions of your land to him.'

Amergin struck his staff three times on the ground and spoke. 'Here is a warrior who falsely claims to be king. He has forsaken his duty to his kinfolk, to his brother and to his own people, the Gaedhals of the land of Iber. Any who follow him will be subject to my judgement.'

'And what is that judgement?' Dalan interrupted.

'They shall be outlaws. Any who give Eber Finn aid will share his fate. I outlaw him.'

'Your authority is not recognised,' the Brehon stated. 'You are a poet, not a judge. I am the only Druid here with qualifications at law. Be careful I don't pass a judgement against you.'

'How dare you?' Amergin raged. 'You are nothing but a savage. If you imagine I would accept any judgement of yours, you're very much mistaken.'

'Just try to enforce your judgement then,' Lom scoffed. 'The battle is soon to be joined again. And Éremon is sure to be defeated.'

'You are a lesser people,' the poet replied, obviously struggling to keep himself under control. 'You have no part to play in the future of this land. You will be subjugated by the Gaedhals and you will be grateful for what we have to offer you.'

The Brehon let his disgust show clearly in his eyes. Lom was speechless. Naithí swallowed hard, ashamed to call himself a Gaedhal. Only Aenghus mac Ómor seemed unmoved.

The King of the Sen Erainn stepped forward and drew the axe he carried at his belt.

'In my country a Druid who speaks like that is soon

enough found floating face down in the water. Food for fishes,' he informed the poet with a wink. 'Come outside with me. Let's take a wee walk by the stream.'

Amergin was a Druid. He was not used to being threatened. And when he saw no one in the tent was going to stand in the way of this little man in the red cap, he began to sweat at the brow.

'I'm a poet of the holy orders,' he stammered.

'Then stay out of the business of war,' Aenghus warned. 'Or else this warrior will compose a poem for you.'

Dalan looked up, somewhat surprised at the Red Cap king's sudden stand in support of Eber Finn. The Brehon knew it wasn't the proper thing to do in this situation but he couldn't stop himself smiling broadly.

Aenghus cleared his throat. 'I had a fish once,' the Red Cap king began. 'A strange fish he was. He told me he was witty and also learned in the ways of his kind. Indeed he often claimed I knew little of the world and that I should honour him for his watery wisdom. Then, at supper, as I recall, one of his bones got stuck in my teeth. I should have fried him, I know that now, but like a fool I put him in the soup.'

Amergin frowned, hearing only nonsense but uncertain whether there was a veiled threat implied. Dalan nodded to Aenghus to show his admiration for a poem that made a point. At last the Brehon was beginning to appreciate the subtleties of Sen Erainn poetry.

Eber Finn sat up and called for his armour. 'There'll be no wandering out by the stream with your axe in one hand and my brother in the other,' Eber told the Red Cap. 'If anyone is to go around drowning Druids it will be me. I'm the King of the Gaedhals.'

Amergin swallowed hard, realising a protest would be futile.

'Tell Éremon I will bring battle to his door every day until he comes to me in all humility and asks for forgiveness,' Eber

Finn declared. 'Tell our brother I will not leave this field until he surrenders the kingship of the north to me.'

'You will pay dearly for this outrage!' Amergin exclaimed. 'I have been mocked in your hall.'

'Then take two parts of the south in recompense,' Eber offered.

'What?' the poet asked, unsure whether he'd heard correctly.

'Two portions of my land is yours,' Eber repeated. 'I hope that is sufficient to ease the insults you may feel you've suffered.'

'It will do to start with,' Amergin replied, somewhat surprised at the sudden generosity of his brother.

'Now come and share a meal with me before you go,' the king offered, quietly relieved he had been able to deal so easily with the second prohibition of his geis. 'We have only porridge and butter but there's plenty. You and I haven't had breakfast together since we set sail for this land.'

The poet agreed, though he made a show of appearing reluctant. After they had eaten, the king stepped out into the dawn with his brother only to face a sight both shocking and heartening.

On every tree and scattered all round the field were countless hosts of Ravens. A few looked up when Eber appeared but most of them were content to preen themselves or sit silently waiting for the battle to begin.

'They've come,' Sorcha reported. 'The Queen of the Ravens is not here yet. I'm told she's gathering more of her kinfolk from the east.'

Amergin was clearly upset at this strange development. He took his brother's sleeve and whispered urgently into his ear. 'You must be very careful. You are allying yourself with forces you do not understand. I strongly advise you to think again about this enterprise. Look to your heart and ask yourself whether you should be turning for friendship to your brother, King Éremon, or this motley collection of creatures who call themselves your allies.'

'I will think carefully on your words, brother,' Eber replied. 'Now if you will excuse me I have a battle to begin. It is time you returned to the hill fort with my message.'

'You already know what his answer will be?'

'Of course I do,' the king answered. 'I know as well as you do that our brother is too proud to admit defeat.'

'Then I hope you won't live to regret this decision,' Amergin ended.

The poet strode off, leaning on his staff. He crossed the stream and climbed into the thick morning mist that had engulfed the hill fort in the hours before dawn.

Dalan and Beag ní Dé played another game of Brandubh that morning as the warriors of the south were dressing for battle. But they kept the result a secret, refusing to divulge the outcome even to Sorcha.

They tended the fire after their game and spoke of the fire ritual which had fascinated the Brehon since he had first seen Sorcha performing it. Beag ní Dé explained that the Ritual of the Sun was of great antiquity. It had been preserved among her people because the folk who lived on the isles of Arainn had a very deep affinity with the elements. She laughed as she told Dalan he would have to visit her home to understand just what she meant by that statement.

Her knowledge of the ritual had been passed down to her from her teacher in the same way Sorcha had been instructed. However, they each preserved divergent traditions which in isolation were difficult to interpret. Beag ní Dé explained that since she and Sorcha had shared their knowledge both had come to understand their own path a little better.

'I have no intention of taking the Quicken Brew,' Beag ní Dé stated again. 'I've told you this before and I trust that you will respect my wishes.'

Then she looked the Brehon squarely in the eye and concluded, 'I will not die. There is no death. Though it may seem that I am gone, you and I will meet again. You may recognise me by the glint in my eye. If I should pass away the Ritual of the Sun will herald my return.'

Dalan begged to know what she meant but the old woman laughed and told him to be patient. The Brehon promised he would try to keep his curiosity in check. He further vowed that he and Sorcha would be guardians of her spirit in the days near to her passing and the forty days after. The old woman thanked him with a smile and a mischievous wink.

'I've already passed most of my knowledge on to my successor,' she told him. 'He's a bright young fellow with a strong sense of what is right and wrong. But he could do with a little guidance here and there. Will you consent to be his mentor?'

'I would be honoured,' the Brehon replied.

Dalan was beginning to think this conversation had the ring of finality about it. He was too polite to ask but he resolved to watch Beag ní Dé carefully and listen well to everything she said in the next few days. He had an instinct she was preparing to depart for the Halls of Waiting.

Sorcha interrupted their discussion when she noticed the five chariots of King Aenghus being led down to the water. Beag ní Dé stood up as soon as the younger woman spoke, and whistled through her teeth in surprise.

'Old Aenghus hasn't taken my advice in a long time,' she hummed, obviously overjoyed. 'I'm truly overwhelmed that he listened to me on this occasion. Well, I'm off.'

'Where are you going?' Sorcha asked in surprise. 'We need your help here at the fire to tend the wounded.'

'You'll manage without me,' the old woman told her with a patronising pat on the back of the hand. 'I'm off to ride in the chariot beside Aenghus. I won't be coming back so I have a favour to ask of you.'

'You won't be coming back?' the younger woman gasped.

'This is the completion of my geis,' Beag ní Dé explained. 'To ride on a chariot into battle beside a fish-poet. It's the last prohibition I have to face. I'm tired and rather relieved I've been given the opportunity.'

'What would you have us do for you?' Dalan inquired with a gentle hand on her shoulder. 'Ask what you will, and if it is in our power we will grant it.'

'My granddaughter has a child in her belly,' Beag ní Dé told them. 'It will be a lad. He's due to be born at midwinter. I would have you take my bones back to Arainn and place them in the Crystal House. Then I'd have you play the harp for the boy's birthing.'

The Brehon promised they would do this for her.

'You have no idea how important this is to me,' she stated sternly. 'But you will understand when the time comes.'

Then she had another thought. 'There's a bag of those herbs that help your weariness.' She handed over the pack that had been lying at her feet. 'You'll find some other useful remedies in there also.'

The Brehon took the bag and weighed it in his hand. 'A lifetime supply!' he joked.

'You'd need a lot more than I could carry to see you through your lifetime,' she laughed. 'My young student will give you whatever quantity you require. He's expecting you.'

'Expecting us?'

The old woman put a hand on his arm to hush him. 'You ask too many questions! You worry too much. Even for an immortal life's too short to be concerning yourself with strife and bother. A light heart lives long, as they say. I advise you to keep your heart light for your life will certainly be a long one.'

'Aren't the seas rough in winter?' Sorcha cut in.

'Now don't you worry about the ocean. A good boatman will bring you across to Arainn. You can teach the Quicken Brew to my apprentice while you're there. He's a fine young man who can be trusted to use the secret wisely.'

'That will surely put Aenghus in a nasty frame of mind,' Dalan frowned.

'Aenghus won't mind too much,' she laughed. 'Indeed he will probably never know of it. His geis is nearly complete too. Once he's brought his boat round in the storm and looked on the King of the Fishes, he'll have finished his time as king. I've seen it.'

Then the trumpets of the Sen Erainn blew and the old woman hugged her two fellow Druids.

'May we meet again soon in the golden chamber of the silver fortress. You may not recognise me but I'll be the one wearing a new suit of clothes.'

And with those mysterious words Beag ní Dé, High-Druid of the Sen Erainn, made her way as quickly as she could down to the water where the war-carts were waiting for her. Dalan and Sorcha went with her and watched her climb aboard one of the chariots.

She chose a spear from a bundle offered to her. It was the tradition of her people that Druids be allowed to fight alongside warriors. The old woman waved the weapon above her head and the Red Cap warriors who were gathered round cheered her on.

Aenghus took the reins of the war-cart and called his warriors to silence. 'Today,' he proclaimed, 'I am going fishing.' He gave a yell and the five chariots led the way across the water, followed by the vast host of the Sen Erainn.

Dalan and Sorcha stood on the banks watching for a short while before they realised none of Eber's fighters were following the Red Caps into battle. The Brehon looked around for the king but couldn't see him anywhere.

Just then Naithí appeared. There was confusion and despair on his face.

'Where are they going?' the chieftain asked in a frantic voice.

'To the battle,' Sorcha replied.

'But our warriors aren't ready! They can't just go off like that without orders from the king.'

'Aenghus is also a king,' Dalan pointed out.

'What did he say? Why is he doing this?'

'He told us he was going fishing,' the Druid woman replied.

'Fishing?' Naithí muttered. 'I'd best go find the king. He'll want to know about this.'

But Eber Finn was already emerging from his tent where he'd been resting away from the prying eyes of his warriors. His face was pale and his eyes bloodshot but when he saw the Sen Erainn crossing the stream he forgot how badly his head hurt him.

Eber ran down to the water, bellowing at the top of his voice. 'Where do you think you're going?'

Aenghus stopped his war-cart and turned back to face the southern king. He spoke one word but Eber Finn couldn't hear what it was over the din of the warriors and the chariots.

'What did he say?' the king cried in a panic. 'What's he saying? Where's he going?'

'He says he's going fishing,' Dalan coughed, trying to give the expression the significance he felt it deserved.

'Fishing?'

Eber's face turned red and the veins stood out on his neck. He waded into the water and held his fist in the air.

'Not without me, you bastard!' he screamed.

Then Eber turned to Naithí. 'Sound the assembly. I want every able-bodied warrior here and ready to move immediately.'

'What about the reserves?'

'Everyone!' the king shrieked. 'This is my battle! It won't start until I give the order.'

But even as he spoke a few arrows fell down on the Sen Erainn from the hill fort. These must have been among the last missiles in Éremon's store because in the next breath a formation of northern warriors appeared. A massive square of them was edging into view just below the line of mist. In the midst of the throng the red and white standard of the northern king fluttered freely in the breeze.

Eber's trumpeter blew his horn to pass on the order to assemble. But on the slopes of the hill fort the trumpets of the Red Caps and the northerners were already blowing high and shrill in the chilly air.

As the note pierced the air the gathering of Ravens took to flight as one. They circled the stream three times and soared off to the south without ever once making a sound. The king watched them go and wondered whether they had decided his cause wasn't worth supporting after all.

Lom and Mahon were at Eber's side almost as soon as the trumpet called to the warriors. They'd been dressed and ready for battle an hour before the dawn. Dalan and Sorcha greeted them and inquired what part they'd played in the previous day's fighting.

The Danaan described how he had been helping unload arrows when the real fighting had begun. By the time he'd finished issuing missiles to the archers and struggled into his mail coat, most of the fighting had been done. He was determined to be in the thick of it today.

Lom was also keen to be at the heart of the fighting and openly stated that if it weren't for the fact he was King of the Fir-Bolg he would have been riding on the back of one of the Sen Erainn war-carts.

These words were greeted with a dark frown by Eber. 'You'd be better putting your energy into finding a way to avert disaster,' he snarled. 'I hope it hasn't escaped your attention that Aenghus is indulging in a foolhardy act that could cost him many warriors and gain not ten paces of ground.'

Eber sighed heavily and rubbed his forehead with the heel of his hand. 'The snow is coming,' he hissed. 'This is our last chance. If only I could get around behind the hill fort. If only there was another way to assault this fortress.'

Mahon looked at Lom and the light of recognition was mirrored in their eyes. How on Earth could they have forgotten to mention the stairs on the other side of the hill? In the confusion of the pig chase and Eber's subsequent anger, they had forgotten all about it.

'I believe there is a way,' the Fir-Bolg king spoke up.

'There's a stairway cut into the side of the hill,' Mahon confirmed after Lom had explained. 'And though it's concealed by bushes, I'm certain we can find it again.'

Eber listened carefully to their report. And their words filled him with such a new-found vitality and strength that he forgot to demand why they had kept this from him for so long.

'We'll attack from the rear,' he decided. 'Let's hope Aenghus can hold the northerners on the slopes while we take our warriors around by the road.'

'Leave the archers here to offer support to the Sen Erainn,' Naithí suggested. 'They'll keep Éremon busy.'

So it was decided. The Gaedhals and Fir-Bolg withdrew in good order to the road. High on the hill there was a great cheer as the northerners watched the retreat, assuming Eber was running from the battlefield. Under the cover of the forest, however, the warriors were able to cut around to where the road led north.

There were a dozen of Éremon's fighters waiting there to guard the stairs, but they soon threw down their weapons when they saw the size of the force that was arrayed against them. When the concealed path to the fort was found Lom and Mahon went with a dozen warriors to scout ahead up to the summit. Eber Finn was unwilling to commit all his fighters to such a narrow path if there were too many guards at the top.

After the scouts had been gone a long while Eber glanced up at the sky. He knew snow clouds when he saw them. And these dark masses were loaded with it. The king realised the path was too steep to climb once the snow began to fall. His warriors would have been slipping and sliding all over the place.

So he was forced to make a terrible decision. To wait here could prove disastrous. If he was to take advantage of this wonderful opportunity he had to act. Then he recalled Dalan's words regarding the Brandubh.

'I will stick to my strategy,' he told himself aloud. 'I've found my enemy's weakness and now I must exploit it.'

In that instant he put aside all thoughts of the danger which faced his fighters at the top of the hill. He passed the word along the line of waiting warriors.

'We're going up,' he declared.

Chapter Twenty-Five

árán had watched the first day of battle from the safety of the camp. He had no intention of approaching Dalan, Sorcha or Beag ní Dé and he knew he wouldn't have been welcomed. His teacher had been a great healer but Sárán was not inclined to share his knowledge with any of these folk. The Brehon, for his part, did not seek the young man out either. He had developed a distaste for Sárán and preferred not to be forced to share his company.

However, at the end of the first fight he found he was bored just sitting around waiting for the battle to end. So he resolved to go out and find something to keep himself occupied the next morning.

The young Druid was particularly fond of blackberries and had been since he was a little child. When he was a boy he used to go out for days, living rough in the wilds of the Burren, hunting for the sweetest fruits. He never tired of them and his stomach never suffered from overindulgence.

If it weren't for the fact that blackberries began to go bad on the bush after Samhain he would have lived on them as long as could find them. He calculated that there was about a week remaining until the festival of the turning of the great wheel of the seasons. So he decided to spend the morning out on the slopes away from the battle, gathering as many of the dark red fruits as he could eat and carry. To this end he found himself a basket small enough to sling over his shoulder but still large enough to hold a good supply of his treasure.

He recalled that he'd spotted many bushes from the road as he travelled on the back of the last arrow wagon. They'd obviously been planted in ancient times high up along the sides of the hill to slow any warriors who might try to assault the hill from below.

He'd already set out by the time Aenghus took his chariots across the stream and he was stuffing fruit into his mouth when the warriors of Eber Finn crept by below him on their way to the stairs. Sárán guessed their destination immediately. Indeed, he was surprised they hadn't gone round that way the day before. He sat watching them and eating his fill until the last fighters had passed. Then he decided he'd like to get a view of the stairs they were going to climb up.

He could see a thick stand of bushes further around, so he headed in that direction, stopping now and then to sample the blackberries. In the distance he could hear the war trumpets and the general noise from the main battlefield. But he paid no attention to any of that. He wasn't interested in whether or not Eber gained the victory. He'd realised after the wound he'd received at the hands of the northern sentry that he had a very long life ahead of him

He was determined to live for himself, not for any foolish ideals such as he was sure were the motivation for folk like Dalan and Sorcha. And this blackberry feast was his own private ritual marking this change in his focus.

He'd just popped a particularly juicy blackberry into his mouth with ecstasy when he heard a groan on the other side of the bushes.

'Who's there?' he ventured.

'Help,' a man's voice cried pathetically.

Sárán cursed his flapping tongue.

'You must help me!' the man wheezed. 'I'm dying.'

For some reason this caught the young Druid's interest. He hadn't actually witnessed a death since he'd taken the Quicken Brew. He recalled that he'd always been overwhelmed by the experience before he'd been granted the potion of life. Indeed he had to be honest with himself and admit death had filled him with fear. It wasn't just the thought of his own death that disturbed him. The whole process of passing on was so filled with pain, remorse, regret and sadness that it generally drained everyone who witnessed it as well.

Sárán decided to see whether his attitude had changed at all. He took his physician's sickle from his belt and, just as though he were cutting herbs for his healer's bag, carefully plucked away at the bushes until he saw the bloodied face of a warrior who'd rolled down from the top of the hill.

The fighter glimpsed the movement and tried to turn his head. But the side of his face had been cut as he fell and the flesh was hanging limply.

'A healer!' he cried. 'Thank you, Druid. You've saved my life. I thought I was going to bleed to death here at the bottom of this ditch. How did you find me?'

Sárán did not answer. He was fascinated that he was able to look on the warrior's wounded face and feel absolutely no disgust. Not even a hint of queasiness touched his stomach. The Quicken Brew had many benefits, he decided.

The warrior tried to raise himself up but his chest seemed pinned down by something. Sárán cut away a few more small branches and soon understood what had been holding the fighter down.

An arrow had embedded itself in his chest and as he'd rolled down the hill he'd become tangled in the blackberries.

'Help me,' he begged.

The young Druid picked a berry and placed it in the wounded man's mouth. The warrior chewed the fruit and

338

swallowed, but the frown on his face showed he didn't understand what was happening to him.

Then Sárán smiled and the fighter squinted, trying to get a closer look at the face of this Druid. In a flash the warrior came to a realisation that seemed to give him some comfort.

'I'm already dead,' he whispered.

'Yes,' Sárán soothed.

'It won't be long,' he stated hopefully.

'Not long,' the young Druid assured him.

The warrior smiled. He closed his eyes, banished all pain from his mind and within a few minutes his breathing had slowed then finally stopped. All the while Sárán sat watching, carefully observing every detail of the passing.

At last he was satisfied that death no longer held any fear for him. And he reasoned that if he could conquer his fear of death he could abolish all fear from his life. Such a prospect astounded him. As long as he could remember he'd been ruled by fear, though he never would have admitted that to anyone, least of all himself. In the next breath, however, Sárán was forced to reconsider whether he had been a little hasty in dismissing fear.

Before his disbelieving eyes the corpse of the warrior began to decay as if time had taken its toll over a full cycle of the seasons rather than just a few minutes. The lifeless eyes sank back into the skull to become two dark hollows. The cheeks withered as the flesh dried. The lips drew back in a ghastly smile to reveal two rows of blackened teeth. But strangest of all, the hair on the rotting body continued to grow until what was a short crop had become shoulder-length curls.

The young Druid felt his guts start to tremble as the stench of death teased his nostrils. He had to stand up and turn away or else he would have been retching blackberries all over the place.

But as soon as his stomach was settled again his fascination drew him to take another quick glance at the unnatural corpse. Disgust gave way to utter astonishment as his eyes locked with Isleen's. She was lying where the warrior had been and she had a broad grin on her face.

'It's one thing to be able to strike a Raven dead,' the Watcher commented, 'but it is another thing entirely to be able to observe a fellow being passing from this world and not lift a finger to help. You're changing faster than the others, Sárán.'

'What do you mean?' he shot back, angered that she'd played such a trick on him.

'You've already begun to realise that empathising with mortal creatures is a waste of energy for an immortal,' she explained.

'I haven't the faintest idea what you're talking about,' Sárán replied.

Isleen patted the ground beside her, indicating that he should sit down with her.

'I have to be going,' the young Druid told her. 'I'll be expected back at the camp. I don't want to be separated from my fellow Druids for too long. They may need me.'

'Nonsense!' Isleen laughed. 'You came out here to ease your boredom. Stop thinking you can get away with those little lies with me. Believe me, when you've been around as long as I have you'll be able to look at anyone and understand their every thought and desire.'

Once again she patted the earth with her hand. And this time Sárán came to sit beside her.

'You're different,' she told him. 'You've already begun to mature in ways the others who took the Quicken Brew may never understand. I'm proud of you. It takes a certain courage to be able to disregard life the way you just did. It takes a certain understanding of the true cycles of life. An acceptance of the great wheel of existence.'

'I knew there was nothing I could do,' the young Druid shrugged. 'Even if I saved his life he would have certainly perished one day. Perhaps he would have died a painful, lonely death on some other battlefield. Who can say?'

'Fineen the Healer was your teacher, wasn't he?'

'Yes.'

'You've been taught well,' Isleen nodded. 'It is strange, isn't it, that you had to be granted immortality of the body before you understood that immortality of the spirit is given to every being. Beware lest the Quicken Brew should rob you of your spirit.'

'As Balor's enchantment stole yours away,' Sárán noted.

'My spirit has been imprisoned,' she admitted. 'But there is a chance my soul can escape and be free again to wander from one body to the next. For you that is unlikely. My prison was a song of the Draoi craft. Yours is your body. I am beginning to feel a genuine pity for you.'

'I'm not frightened of the future,' he replied defiantly. 'I'll serve my king and my people and I'll be respected for my wisdom. I'll use my time wisely and I will answer to no one.'

Isleen laughed. 'You poor misguided young lad!' she gasped, hardly believing her ears. 'Can't you see that though you may have conquered your fear of death you haven't faced the demon that haunts you?'

'What demon?' he frowned.

'The fear you have of living.'

This time Sárán laughed. 'You're toying with me. I'm beginning to understand the way you work. You convinced me to take Lom and go off looking for Aoife. I don't know how this suited your purpose but I've been a playing piece in your hands. As surely as if you'd been sitting at the Brandubh table you've moved me to your will back and forth. And I've been foolish enough to accept that.'

'I wanted to be certain those arrows made it into Eber's hands,' Isleen admitted. 'I certainly didn't want Éremon to win this battle.'

'Will Eber be the victor?'

'The King of the North will be dead shortly, if he isn't already. Lochie promised he'd see to that.'

'Why would you want Eber to triumph?'

The Watcher looked down at her hands. 'Let's just say I have a special interest in what happens to Eber,' she whispered, reluctant to reveal that she had been his lover. 'I have no idea how all this will turn out, so it's best I support those I know well and feel I can trust.'

She caught his eye again. 'You'll learn that in time.'

'What have you done with Aoife?'

'She's taken the long sleep.'

'What's that?'

Isleen explained that she and Lochie had originally thought of the long sleep as a way of ridding themselves of the troubling influences of Brocan and Fineen. But as it turned out they soon realised that the sleep state eased the souls of those who had taken the Quicken Brew. In the end they had come to think of it as their rare opportunity to show compassion for their fellow beings. For the first time in many generations they felt a kinship with the folk of the Danaan and the Fir-Bolg who had been granted immortality.

'But Aoife was also the subject of a wager,' Isleen added. 'Lochie always believed she'd wed Mahon. I thought she was too smart for that. So I placed her in the sleep in order that I would win the wager by default.'

'What will become of her?'

'She'll sleep, that's all. She's perfectly safe. And if Mahon ever tracks her down he'll be able to wake her again. Only love will stir the sleepers. If he ever loved her then he will prove it and they will be wed. If he abandons his quest then it was never meant to be.'

'That is rather cruel,' Sárán noted.

'How is it any different from what most folk experience?'

she countered. 'Life after life we seek to rediscover the souls with whom we've shared a deep affinity or love. Until that happens it is as if we've been asleep. You really must begin to think beyond the boundaries of this life if you're ever going to earn your death.'

'What do you mean, earn my death?'

'That's what I've come to tell you. I believe it is possible for you to find death one day. But you must understand that life may not turn out exactly as you've expected. You will have to answer for the murders of those two Ravens for a start.'

'I'm not afraid.'

'Then remember this,' Isleen pressed. 'When the day arrives when you find you're tired of life, that is the day to start earning your death. You'll understand when the time is right.'

Then she sat up, kissed him lightly on the forehead and brushed back his black hair with her fingertips.

'You never taught me the Ogham as you promised,' he sulked. 'You never initiated me into the Druid orders.'

'You've been initiated,' she assured him. 'Don't you think you've earned the right to call yourself a Druid? You were stabbed through the heart by a sword. You suffered the little death. You are a Druid.'

'And the Ogham signs?'

'I don't know they would be much use to you. I've heard you killed a Raven. Is that true?'

He nodded.

'You'll have to answer to the Morrigán. You won't be needing the Ogham. That's for certain.'

'What do you mean?'

Isleen shrugged her shoulders.

'You'll find out in good time. Let's go now.'

'Where?'

'To see how Lochie is coping with the battlefield.'

The chariot carrying the King of the Sen Erainn and the Druid woman, Beag ní Dé, led the charge up the slope towards the wildly screaming warriors of the north. Behind them were four other war-carts and nearly four hundred Red Cap fighters.

The old woman clung tightly to Aenghus as he reined in his horse and brought the chariot round in a circle to halt it. The hill was too steep here for the animal to continue drawing the cart at speed. From here they would have to fight on foot.

By the time Aenghus had brought the war-cart to a standstill and jumped off the back, the other chariots were gathered round. Already his foot soldiers were rushing past to attack the orderly formation of King Éremon's warriors.

The great square of the fighters of the north halted a mere fifty paces from where Aenghus had stopped his chariot. The Sen Erainn king, however, was not going to be drawn into making an assault on the battle formation. Instead he had his trumpeters give the command to form their own square. It took quite a while for this to be achieved. The trumpets had to give the order a dozen times for the Red Cap warriors were eager for a fight and many simply ignored the command. Aenghus himself had to step out to grab the odd disobedient fighter and drag him back into the square. And a few fighters insisted on running out to cast their spears at the enemy.

The northerners took little notice of the Red Caps until one got too close, then an axeman strode out from Éremon's line and cut him down. The Sen Erainn erupted in rage at this and their king despaired of being able to keep them under control.

The last thing Aenghus wanted was a disorganised attack. He could see that Éremon had disciplined his troops well. They would likely hold their ground against any assault. Filling his lungs with air, Aenghus bellowed out the first notes of a chant. Soon all his men joined in the war-song, and anyone who broke ranks during the chant was derided by his comrades, as was the custom. In this way the situation was soon calmed.

Aenghus was left with the problem of how to break up the tight formation that was blocking his way to the top of the hill. He saw Éremon's battle standard flying in the midst of the square and he realised that the northern king had no choice but to stand his ground. If his warriors charged down the hill as they had the day before, all would be lost. If they retreated to the top of the hill they would be picked off by archers, spearmen and the determined fighters of the Sen Erainn.

Aenghus recognised this day could easily end in another stalemate, and he wasn't prepared to allow that to happen. The air was full of the promise of snow. The Red Cap king had to act quickly. If the snow came it would be a terrible struggle to bring his warriors to the summit of the hill fort.

He turned to see Beag ní Dé still standing on the back of the chariot. Her gaze was stern. She was counselling him to take action. He knew what he had to do. He was about to fulfil his destiny and complete his geis. In the next instant he'd grabbed half-a-dozen casting spears from nearby warriors. He made sure his axe was secure in his belt then he leapt up onto the chariot in front of the old woman and drove it through the press of his fighters and out into the open.

'There's a lovely shoal of silver fishes,' he told her, pointing to the northern warriors in their gleaming mail coats. 'Out there where the waters are treacherous they're begging us to chase them. See how their pretty scales glisten. Wouldn't you like to catch a few of those beauties in your net?'

In answer Beag ní Dé gave a hooting howl that was picked up by the Red Cap fighters. When they'd calmed again Aenghus spoke the last line of his poem.

'Let's take the boat out, you and I, and see how many we can fetch for supper.'

Then Aenghus gave the horse a slap with the reins and the animal jolted the chariot forward. In moments they were close enough to cast their spears at the enemy. The first two found their mark, much to the delight of the Sen Erainn warriors who watched in awe as their king and High-Druid took on the enemy host like two fabled heroes of old.

Aenghus brought the cart in closer and called out a challenge to the northerners. 'I am the King of the Sen Erainn!' he declared. 'Show me your king!'

The warriors hummed and hissed their defiance.

'Where is he?'

The standard moved from the centre of the square until it was near the front. There were three warriors around it and any one of them could have been Éremon. Aenghus hesitated, unsure which one he should try to strike at. Then he saw a tall warrior dressed in a silver coat made of tiny scales. His helm had crowning it a crest that looked like the fins of a merman.

'The King of the Fishes!' the old warrior gasped.

While Aenghus was awestruck at being faced with the completion of his own personal geis, Beag ní Dé didn't have to stop and consider which fighter she'd cast her spear at. She knew it didn't matter which of them was king. There was one warrior whose death would certainly stir up the northerners.

She raised the spear to her shoulder and cast it. As it sailed the short distance into the square some warriors fell over rather than chance being touched by it. But none attempted to put a stop to its flight. The weapon disappeared into the mass of jostling fighters and in the next instant the king's standard fell. The old woman had found her mark. The standard-bearer was dead.

In a great outpouring of rage the northerners turned as one and threw a hundred missiles at the chariot. Aenghus held his shield to protect them as best he could and hauled on the reins, but to no avail.

The horse was already falling to its knees in the throes of death, struck by many spear shafts. Beag ní Dé was wounded, a short spear shaft wedged in her shoulder. The king grabbed her round the waist as other chariots rode out to rescue them. Before Aenghus had carried her a dozen steps, however, they were overwhelmed by the enemy. In seconds the Sen Erainn witnessed the awful sight of the old woman's head being thrust into the air on the point of a long spear shaft.

The warriors of Éremon were jubilant at the death of the Red Cap king and his High-Druid. They danced and taunted their enemies, and when the Red Caps grimly held their ground, the northerners broke ranks.

The king's trumpeter blew the signal to re-form ranks. Then Éremon ordered a general retreat. But the damage had been done. These few hundred warriors had suffered a near defeat the day before. They were not going to be denied a victory now.

'The Red Cap king and his grandmother are dead!' they sang as they advanced towards the enemy lines.

And the Sen Erainn let them come.

Éremon screamed at the top of his lungs, begged, commanded his troops to withdraw, but either they did not hear him or they did not want to. At last he realised he had no choice but to join them.

He hung his head, biting his lip. He knew this moment would be remembered down the generations as the turning point in the history of this land. He knew he had lost. But he didn't want the song-makers to accuse him of cowardice or indecision. He resolved his death would be heroic.

'Sound the attack,' he said in a subdued tone.

His trumpeter just shook his head, unable to hear a word over the noise of battle.

'Sound the attack!' Éremon cried.

The horn rose up above the din of the cursing warriors and the northerners cheered as one. And suddenly Éremon began to take heart. The Sen Erainn were withdrawing to avoid his charging fighters. They were running. His eyes lit up with the hope of victory.

'Onward!' the northern king bellowed. 'Chase them back to their islands in the west!'

Chapter Twenty-Six

hen Lom and Mahon had climbed to the top of the stairs they found an open flat circle of ground dotted with mostly unattended fires. There were tents and a few temporary lean-to shelters among the ruins, and a few dozen cattle wandering around eating their fill of the lush grass at the summit.

There was a ruined wall near the top of the stairs which was high enough for a warrior on horseback to hide behind. The young King of the Fir-Bolg decided to make this place the rallying point for his scouts.

'Keep out of sight,' he advised the fighters. 'I don't want anyone raising the alarm. Return here with a good estimate of the enemy strength.'

The dozen or so warriors who'd accompanied Lom and Mahon fanned out swiftly to scour the entire area within the walls. It was soon established there were only between thirty and forty archers on the hilltop and they had only a few missiles each.

Lom guessed that Éremon had given the other archers swords and sent them in to fight with the foot soldiers. The young king resolved it would be best to take the summit before the main force of the northerners returned to their stronghold. But there wasn't time to send a warrior down to fetch Eber Finn and he couldn't spare anyone in any case. So he decided he'd take the hill with the few fighters at his disposal.

When the scouts had all reported in he told them his plan. Their first target had to be any trumpeters who might give Éremon a warning of what was taking place on the summit. Mahon pointed out that there was a good deal of open ground between the ruined buildings and the defensive wall where the archers were stationed. He suggested he might be able to arrange a diversion. Before Lom had a chance to object, Mahon was off, saying that he'd call for them when the ground was safe to cross.

The Danaan went round the summit gathering the cattle together and driving them towards the open ground. The archers were watching the battle so intently they hardly noticed the sudden appearance of all the garrison's cattle on the one patch of clear ground on the whole hilltop. One thing the Danaan had not reckoned on, however, was the call of nature. As he was driving the last few cattle into place a lone archer came up behind him. The warrior, certain he wouldn't be missed for a few minutes, had been away to the latrines to relieve himself. As he was returning he spotted Mahon and raised the alarm.

Immediately the trumpeter put the horn to his lips and blew a terrible blast, full of frantic terror and pleading for help. The Danaan pushed his way between the cows, making straight for the musician. He drew his sword as he ran.

Half a dozen archers shot missiles at him but at that close range most had no hope of hitting him. Two arrows struck though. One pierced Mahon's left thigh and the other his left shoulder. This didn't stop him dispatching the trumpeter swiftly with one stroke of his blade. One brave woman archer stepped up to Mahon and stabbed him in the chest, lodging her blade between his ribs.

The Danaan plucked it out almost immediately and calmly handed it back to her.

'I'm returning this to you so you may have the opportunity to lay it down,' he told her. For though he felt pain he knew it would pass under the healing influence of the Quicken Brew. So he could easily dismiss it. There was blood all over his tunic and more poured out when he withdrew the arrow from his shoulder. Then he moved to extract the last missile from his thigh. It had a barbed point and tore the flesh as he pulled it out.

Mahon threw the arrow on the ground in disgust and only then did he notice that all the archers had laid down their weapons at his feet in utter shock that he was still standing. By the time Lom and his dozen warriors arrived, the hill fort had already fallen.

This of course was too much excitement for the cattle. The entire herd somehow found their way to the main rampart which led to the entrance of the fort. To escape the warriors and their howls of delight the cattle ran off down this rampart out of sight.

Lom and his warriors were still searching the prisoners before taking them to the rear of the fortress when King Eber and the main body of the force arrived. They'd been halfway up the stairs when they'd heard the horn blast and had rushed to aid their scouts.

'I feared the worst!' the king told Lom, slapping him on the back to congratulate him.

'It's Mahon you should thank,' the young Fir-Bolg king told Eber. 'He took this hill single-handedly.'

As they spoke Eber Finn's standard was lifted above the fort so that everyone on the battlefield could plainly see the fortress had fallen. If that wasn't enough of a disappointment for the northerners, the sight of their own herd charging down upon them must have made them despair.

While the warriors of Éremon were fleeing, throwing down their arms, the snow began to fall at last. In a very short while the air was thick with huge snowflakes each the size of a fingernail. It was thick, too, with countless black shapes dipping and diving this way and that.

'Ravens,' Lom gasped in awe.

Isleen led Sárán across the hill to a point where they could watch the battle without being observed. They arrived just in time to witness the front line of the Sen Erainn falling back in seeming disorder.

The young Druid was surprised at this until he glimpsed a tall figure in the midst of the Red Caps urging them to retreat. It was Lochie. Sárán frowned, hardly understanding what was happening.

The standard of the King of the North, the huge red banner with a double spiral emblazoned upon it in white, was moving swiftly down the hill, surrounded by Éremon's warriors.

'Why is Lochie ordering a retreat?' Sárán asked.

'The Sen Erainn do not see him,' Isleen explained. 'If any of them ever think back on this battle they will put it down to luck or instinct. But they are being led by Lochie. He is springing a little trap for the northerners.'

She laughed. 'It's the same trap they fell for yesterday, near enough,' she added. 'But warriors don't have the sharpest minds or the keenest intellects.'

'I wish I could get a better look at the fighting,' Sárán complained.

'Why don't you?' the Watcher asked. 'You're dressed as a Druid. No one's going to harm you. And even if they did, you're under the protection of the Quicken Brew. You've nothing to fear.'

The young Druid ran forward, anxious not to miss anything. Before he'd gone too far, though, he stopped and called back to the Watcher.

'Are you coming?'

'I'll hover above and keep an eye on things. Don't worry, you'll be safe.'

With that she faded into the chill air and Sárán turned around to run off into the thick of the fighting. It was only a short distance but he was panting heavily by the time he came to where the northerners had suddenly and unexpectedly come to a halt.

The young Druid strained to see what could have stopped their advance but the ranks were six deep. He saw the king's standard flying ahead of him and resolved to push his way to there so he could see what Éremon saw. Before he'd got very far he heard a strange foreign shout go up. He looked about and realised the Sen Erainn had managed to bring their line around in a pincer to surround the warriors of the north.

Northerners at the rear of the formation were already throwing down their arms and retreating for fear of being completely encircled and cut down. But the warriors at the front, including the king, were stuck by the press of fighters behind them. Sárán was overwhelmed by the fear that pervaded these desperate folk. Most knew they were about to face death. It was obvious to all that there was to be a slaughter.

The air was thick with curses, crying and the smell of men and women so frightened they'd loosed their bowels in panic. Here and there a warrior fell over without a scratch on them, fainting from the intensity of their fear.

A spear cast flew by him but Sárán was unmoved. He'd never been this close to the heart of such a vicious fight before. When he was younger he had dreamed of being a warrior. Now he was glad his path had taken him to other destinations.

The northerners suddenly broke and ran as if they were all of one mind. Sárán recalled Dalan speaking of the fish poems of King Aenghus. And he wondered whether people were capable of acting like a shoal of fish, a swarm of bees or a flock of birds.

In the next instant there were warriors tripping over each other in the rush to escape. But the Red Caps had already closed the trap around their unfortunate victims.

The little men and women of the Sen Erainn were screaming with delight. Some were literally drenched in northern blood. Others sang songs in their strange language as they rhythmically slashed away with their bronze axes. Not even the tempered steel of the northerners could save them from the determined assault of the Red Caps.

Quite unexpectedly Sárán found himself standing beside Éremon's standard-bearer. The warrior was a grim-faced veteran who was nevertheless shaking with fear. The young Druid asked where the king was but the old man didn't answer. His gaze was fixed on the hundreds of Sen Erainn who were closing in fast.

Just then Éremon came and snatched the standard away from the warrior. The old man fell forward, a spear in his back. It was then Sárán noticed the field was drenched in blood.

Éremon was wounded in the leg and he leaned heavily on the staff which bore his standard. With a quick look about him he realised there was no chance of escape. At that moment he noticed the young Druid standing beside him.

'Tell my brother I will meet him in the Halls of Waiting,' the king stated coldly. 'And in the presence of our ancestors he will answer for this outrage.'

Sárán promised to pass the words on but he was never sure whether Éremon heard. For at that moment a trumpet call rang out from the hilltop. The king turned all his attention to the fortress walls. He threw off his helm and frowned, knowing that the desperate call could only mean the summit was under attack. He slumped a moment against the standard staff.

Sárán watched speechless as the Sen Erainn rushed through a gap in the line formed by the king's bodyguard. A spear struck Éremon just below the left collarbone and he screamed in agony. His loyal warriors managed to beat off the attackers and formed a tight circle around him. Sárán, coming to his senses, tried to reach the king but was pushed aside.

'I'm a healer,' the young Druid pleaded.

'He doesn't need a healer,' one of the northerners growled. 'He needs an honourable death.'

The king heard this and rallied himself, ignoring his pain. He shoved his guards aside and pressed forward at the Sen Erainn lines. Almost immediately three spears struck him in the upper body and another in the back. But he didn't fall.

Éremon fixed his eyes on the summit of the hill, intending to defend to the last. He caught sight of the beautiful broad green banner which flew from the battlements. And then he allowed the last breath to pass out of his body.

Almost at that very instant the snow began to fall as if it had been holding off for the death of King Éremon. Sárán had enough experience of the Watchers to recognise their handiwork. The snow would have appealed to Isleen's sense of the poetic.

Another remarkable thing happened when the king fell. A cloud darkened the sky. At first Sárán assumed this must be the snow clouds closing in. But the darkness was like evening. When the young Druid looked up he gasped in shock. The air was filled with Ravens.

Éremon's bodyguard saw them too. And when they did they threw down their weapons and begged for mercy. For the most part the Sen Erainn granted it to them. For they had seen the loyalty these men and women had retained for their king up the very instant he drew his last breath.

At length the young Druid left the dead and dying and wandered down to the stream, crossing over to the camp. He went straight to the fire he'd been sleeping by and found himself a small cauldron.

Then, with the memory of the battle still fresh in his mind, he calmly set about boiling up a meal from the fruits he'd collected. It was going to be a cold night and Sárán knew that nothing warmed the body like a feast of sweet hot blackberries.

As the snow began to blanket the land in white, Eber Finn decided it would be wise to send envoys to the northern chiefs while the roads were still open. Naithí was chosen as his representative and given a half dozen of the best chariots to accompany him. The giant had instructions to summon the northern chieftains and the elders of Éremon's people to Dun Gur four days before Samhain. At that time a treaty would be agreed between all the peoples of the island and the festival of the turning of the seasons would be celebrated.

'And tell the chieftains I will come north at Beltinne to claim the royal enclosure at Teamhair for my own.'

He gave orders that Amergin be found and taken to Teamhair to bear witness to the death of Éremon. The poet assented to this, though he refused to return at Samhain, claiming old age and a hard road would keep him by his own fireside.

Finally, when all his warriors were gathered around him, Eber paid tribute to Aenghus and the people of Sen Erainn before he asked the question he'd been waiting so long to put to them.

'Will you have me as your king?'

Every one of them raised their voices in a resounding answer. 'Aye.'

Then Naithí stepped forward and spoke. 'Long life to King Eber, Lord of Teamhair and Dun Gur, High-King of Eirinn, Protector of the peoples of Innisfail.'

'Long life!' was the refrain and it echoed across the stream.

'I name Naithí as my steward at Teamhair,' Eber declared. 'And he will make decisions in my place until I come there at Beltinne. I name Iobhar as marshal of the north, responsible for keeping the peace. Without these two I would have no kingdom and no life to call my own.'

Iobhar was also named Keeper of the Black Pigs. It was his duty to gather every such creature in the realm and ensure its safety. This was Eber's way of making certain his geis wasn't unexpectedly fulfilled.

Iobhar was surprised at the honour but Eber was firm in his decision. He knew that mercy and loyalty go hand in hand. And the duties of his new office would surely keep Iobhar out of mischief.

Dalan and Sorcha stayed a while longer, listening to the Gaedhals paying respect to one another and to their allies. But the snow was already beginning to cover the corpses and they had a grim duty to perform. They slipped away to seek out Beag ní Dé's body.

The task was more difficult because Éremon's warriors had severed her head. Though one of the Sen Erainn fighters had rescued this gruesome artefact, it took long hours of searching before the two Druids located her corpse.

She was lying near the body of Aenghus, King of the Sen Erainn. Both corpses were carried by the Red Caps to their camp on the back of a war-cart, the only one of their chariots to remain intact.

The Brehon returned to help tend the wounded and Sorcha followed a short time after. They had much work to do if they were going to save lives. Now the snow had come there were many who would likely not survive the night.

Much later Eber Finn came to speak with them. He told them there would be wagons waiting in the morning to carry the injured back to Dun Gur where they could be cared for in some degree of comfort. Then he asked to be shown to the warrior woman known as Mughain. She was sipping a bowl of soup and tried to stand when she saw him, but he put a gentle hand on the top of her head to stop her.

'Stay where you are. You've paid me enough respect by saving my life. I saw the way you dealt with Goll. I should have done the same thing myself long ago.' He noticed the bandages securing her left arm against her chest. 'Were you badly hurt?'

'A scratch,' she replied. 'I'll mend.'

'When you're mended I'd like to appoint you to my bodyguard. I was hoping you'd accept the position of standard-bearer. When we march into Teamhair I want everyone to see the woman who saved my life.'

'Thank you, my lord.'

'There's a meal waiting for you in my tent,' he went on. 'I'll be sleeping among my warriors tonight. That is, if we actually sleep. We've a lot to celebrate. You will have the royal tent tonight. I don't want a chill getting into that wound.'

'Yes, my lord,' she replied.

Eber Finn helped the young woman to her feet and realised she was incredibly thin for a warrior. 'You're half-starved!' he exclaimed.

'The life of a Fian warrior is hard, my lord.'

'Well I'll be making a change to that. There are some traditions we can do without,' he assured her. 'This is a new land. We can afford to make a few adjustments to the way we do things.' The king paused a moment. 'I'm going to devise a new set of laws for the Fian. Would you help me?'

'I'd be honoured, my lord.'

'We'll start the moment we return to Dun Gur.'

The Brehon caught Sorcha's attention as the king helped Mughain to his tent. 'What do you think of that then?' he asked the Druid woman.

'They'd be well suited,' she replied. 'She's a warrior, isn't she?'

'I hope all's well with Aoife, but I must admit I never liked the idea of her becoming Queen of the Gaedhals.'

'We'll see she's safe when we speak with the Watchers,' Dalan assured her.

'She's safe,' Lochie declared, suddenly materialising behind them. 'I've just been to visit her. She's sleeping peacefully.'

'How long have you been there?' the Brehon asked.

'A few minutes.'

'I'll never get used to the way you appear abruptly like that. It's unnerving.'

The Watcher laughed. 'It's just a trick. One day you might learn it for yourself. It comes in very useful at times.'

'But it's disconcerting,' Sorcha reprimanded him. 'And impolite to just leap into people's lives like that without any beg pardon or excuse me. Couldn't you wear a cow-bell round your neck to give us some warning?' Lochie dismissed the comment with a wave of his hand.'

'Aoife will sleep until Mahon awakens her,' he went on. 'And I can promise you the same restful peace if you wish it. You have nothing to fear from me. I'm grateful for the work you've done for us.'

'You've done a lot of damage,' Dalan replied. 'I don't doubt you were standing behind Éremon whispering in his ear the whole time, spurring him on to revenge. And what of Goll? Did you have anything to do with his attempt on Eber's life?'

'I had nothing to do with either of them,' the Watcher protested. 'They were both quite capable of creating this terrible mess without my intervention. Perhaps you'll understand one day when you've had a bit more experience of life and the frailties of your fellow beings.'

'What do you mean?'

'Wars don't start because there are hidden beings secretly pushing the contenders into conflict. I could be held responsible for introducing the Gaedhals to this land, that I admit. I showed them glimpses of this land in their dreams. But it was up to them to build a fleet of ships and go off sailing to the ends of the known world searching for it.'

The Brehon was about to launch into an objection but the Watcher held up a hand to stop him. 'I merely set in motion a chain of events that led to this battlefield,' Lochie went on. 'Isleen and I steered things a little as time passed, but that was because we didn't want this war to happen too quickly. If we hadn't been offering distractions the conflict would have escalated in a flash.'

He put his hands out to warm his fingers over the fire. 'We had to give you time to find the Draoi song which would save us. We had to be certain you would have enough incentive to search thoroughly.'

'But inspiring the Gaedhals to come here has shattered the peace of this island,' Sorcha protested.

'They would have come here anyway in time,' the Watcher shrugged.

As he spoke a cloaked woman walked across the field towards the fire. As she came closer she removed the hood covering her head and bowed to each of the three gathered at the fire.

'Hello, my dear,' Lochie bowed.

'Greetings, my friend,' Isleen replied. 'Is the song ready yet?'

'We were just coming to that,' her companion informed her.

'We have a few questions to ask first,' Sorcha interrupted.

'What of the Quicken Brew?' Dalan inquired. 'Would the Danaans and the Fir-Bolg have been exposed to that if there had been peace in this land?'

'That was a little piece of revenge which both Isleen and I regret very much,' Lochie sighed.

'I don't regret it!' Isleen protested. 'I think it's only fitting that you people should carry on the fine tradition of the Watchers.'

'What tradition?' Sorcha gasped in surprise.

'Before our time there were folk who studied the heavens,' Isleen explained. 'The Fir-Bolg of old knew the changing sky as well as they knew the changing seasons. They built monuments to the path of the stars, the sun and the moon. These are the stone circles and the hill-houses that still remain.'

'But surely those Fir-Bolg were not immortal?' the Brehon cut in.

'In a sense they were,' Lochie answered. 'They knew that the spirit passes from one form to the next after a short period of rest. They had the skill of calling a spirit into a new body at the moment of birth. In that manner they ensured birth into the same clan and a continuity of vocation which engendered great wisdom.'

'How was this knowledge lost?' the Druid woman asked.

'The Quicken Brew was discovered,' Lochie shrugged. 'The journey between life and death is arduous, even for one who is wise in the ways of creation. The two most painful experiences for most folk involve birth or death. The Brew promised to put an end to that.'

'I understand that it puts an end to the pain of death,' Dalan told him, 'but how does it alleviate the pain of birth?'

'You will never suffer birth again,' the Watcher explained. 'Nor will any woman who has taken the Brew ever be able to conceive a child by any male who has tasted it.'

'No children?' Sorcha cut in. 'Are you certain?'

'The first Watchers were not unhappy that this turned out to be the case. They were interested in ending the cycles of birth and death. They saw this as a kind of freedom. Indeed, as one who has been an immortal for some time now, I must admit there is a great deal of freedom to be had from the gift of eternal life. However, freedom has come to mean something different for me. I see death as freedom. My soul is ready to travel on and forget the things I have seen. My memory is ready to be washed clean in the Well of Forgetfulness.'

'So in a sense you'll take our place,' Isleen told them. 'Until you find a way to undo the Quicken Brew or simply accept your destiny as others have done before you.'

'What happened to the first Watchers?' Sorcha inquired.

'Some retreated into the bowels of the Earth to hide from everything,' Lochie replied. 'Others learned how to use their immortality for the good of all and so became part of the land. A few learned how to manipulate the elements and are venerated today as deities.'

'Was Danu one of these folk?'

'Most certainly. You might be surprised. One day mortal folk may look on you as gods.'

'You have spoken of how you've influenced affairs in the lives of the Gaedhals, the Fir-Bolg and the Danaan,' Dalan observed. 'So it is within your power to bring peace?'

'It is.'

'Why then didn't you interfere to stop this battle? You know we have the Draoi song. Yet you refused to stop all this killing.'

'You will understand one day,' Isleen advised him. 'Events had already progressed to the point where certain folk would have taken matters into their own hands. Then the situation would have spiralled out of control. Take the warrior Goll. He could have murdered Eber and seized the kingship. I mean to say, we may be known as Watchers but we can't be watching everyone all of the time.'

'It was better to allow this natural resolution to come to pass,' Lochie agreed. 'You'll see for yourself that there will be a long period of peace after this chaos. I'm very proud we managed events so well.'

'Now it's time to talk of our reward,' Isleen declared. 'We've brought peace. Now we want our freedom.'

'Sorcha and I are in the position to grant that to you,' Dalan nodded. 'But I wish to wait until Eber's treaty is agreed at Samhain. If all goes well and the peoples of Innisfail conclude the treaty without conflict, then you shall have your song.'

Isleen's face began to redden but Lochie placed an arm around her shoulders.

'As you wish it,' he agreed. 'We will work to reinforce the peace in the meantime.'

'Why should we wait?' Isleen snarled.

'We've waited generations,' her companion reasoned. 'A few more days won't make any difference. Come, let us go.' He turned her around to walk her towards the stream. 'We'll return on Samhain Eve,' he promised. 'Let all be made ready for us.'

Then the two of them strode off together into the falling snow and were soon gone from sight.

The night after the battle was hard for everyone. The cold claimed a large number of the wounded on both sides, though Dalan and Sorcha did their best to comfort the suffering.

At dawn the corpse of Goll mac Morna was consigned to the flames of a bonfire. By tradition a traitor's body was treated this way to confound the soul that had recently departed. In the case of mac Morna it was also to ensure the members of his Fian band had no dead hero's grave-mound to venerate as a shrine to the martyr.

Wagons were loaded as soon as it was light. The Sen

Erainn warriors built improvised sleighs to help haul the wounded through the snow to Dun Gur. The Gaedhals' fortress was out of their way but the hosts of the Red Caps had been invited to camp at Dun Gur and celebrate the Samhain feast and the treaty. Eber sent warriors on ahead to scour the country round for food and to bring in everything that could be gathered.

By the time the great army of Eber Finn was ready to leave it was already late morning. They had at least two full days of journeying before them and the certainty that some of the wounded would succumb to their injuries on the way. Sorcha and the Brehon moved between the wagons and all along the line, doing the work of healers as best they could. Before darkness fell Dalan had used every last morsel of the dried herb Beag ní Dé had given him to soothe his weariness. He simply couldn't keep it to himself when he was surrounded by so much suffering.

He and Sorcha were sitting in the forge wagon warming their fingers by the fire, which was always lit there, when the great cart ground to a halt. They were both exhausted from a long night and a seemingly endless day, but they looked to each other and agreed to walk the length of the convoy once more before taking some rest.

Snow covered the road ahead and the horses were slipping their foothold. Warriors were already beginning to clear the snow away. It was intended the convoy would continue through the night, the wagons edging forward whenever a section of road was cleared. Dalan leaned up against the forge wagon, resting while the Druid woman collected what remained of her healing herbs.

As Sorcha climbed down, the Brehon grabbed the sleeve of her tunic. In the far distance a dozen black shapes wheeled through the sky, dipping and weaving. After a short while they began peeling off in threes until only three remained. A hundred paces away two more Ravens broke away, leaving one large bird to soar down to where the two Druids were waiting. With a flourish of her powerful wings the Queen of the Ravens came to rest on the top step of the forge wagon.

'Greetings,' the Raven offered and Sorcha immediately bowed.

Dalan took a few steps back, unable to understand the speech of these creatures but thinking this was the most polite thing to do under the circumstances.

'Where's he going?' the queen demanded.

'He's just giving us some privacy,' the Druid woman replied.

'What for? He can't understand what we're saying unless I wish it.'

Sorcha beckoned the Brehon to come back and stand beside her.

'You've heard what happened to Crínóc and Crínán?' the Morrigán asked.

'Lom told me his part in the terrible affair.'

'I will seek retribution,' the Raven declared. 'And I want Dalan to decide the case.'

'I'll put it to him.'

'He's a Brehon!' the Morrigán spat. 'He will judge the case and I will demand the full honour price be paid for the lives of two of my people.'

'As you wish,' Sorcha bowed.

'Why have my people not been invited to attend the meeting for the Samhain treaty?' she asked. 'Did we not attend the battle?'

'The Ravens arrived on the second morning then flew off and did not return until the very last moments of the fight. King Éremon was already dead by that stage.'

'They would have stayed that morning but for the news that Crínóc and Crínán had been murdered. This was very distressful to my people. The Gaedhals have a reputation as tree-killers. And it was assumed that Eber's people had been involved somehow.'

'It was the two brothers,' Sorcha stated, shaking her head. 'They are Fir-Bolg, not Gaedhals. There was no one else involved in the murders.'

'Are you certain?'

'I have heard Lom's confession. And I believe him.'

'Then the case will be easily concluded,' the Raven retorted. 'Will you speak with the king?'

'I will.'

'Very well.' The Morrigán turned her head sharply towards Dalan. 'That Brehon will have to answer to me for his broken promise.'

'Did Dalan break a promise to you?'

'He vowed to take proper care of the lough around Dun Gur. He promised to find a way of preserving it from the rampaging Gaedhals.'

'I'll speak with him about it,' Sorcha bowed. 'You can rest assured that Dalan and I have the interests of all the forest folk at heart. And we're going to be around for a long time. So you can rely on us to do our part to protect the land from the ravages of the new people.'

The great bird gave a little nod to acknowledge her faith in Sorcha at least. Then she spread her wings in preparation to leave.

'I call the twins Sárán and Lom to be judged before the treaty is agreed on Samhain Eve. And I suggest to the King of the Gaedhals that if he wishes to keep the goodwill of the Raven kind he would be well advised to perform a symbolic act of appeasement.'

'I will present your views,' the Druid woman promised.

As the Morrigán took to the wing Sorcha had an idea about what form that symbolic act should take.

Chapter Twenty-Seven

During the last part of their journey back to Dun Gur
Dalan and Sorcha discussed the matter of the treaty,
the crime the twins had committed and the promise
the Brehon had made to the Morrígan. They both agreed on
the action they should take.

Sorcha took her idea to Eber and he enthusiastically
approved. A proclamation went out through the north and
south that the treaty would be agreed at a crossroads where
the roads from the four quarters of Eirinn converged.

At this crossroads a tree was to be planted as a lasting
symbol of the covenant sworn between the new high-king
and those he was sworn to protect. It wasn't to be just any
old tree. It was to be a Quicken Tree.

Sorcha had a few of the berries and she carefully propagated
one of them until it began to sprout. She kept it warmly
wrapped inside her cloak and tended it with as much attention
as she might have given a little child. And though it was still
snowing, this little seed soon had all the signs of growing into
a fine strong sapling. For Quicken Trees are unlike any others
on the face of the Earth. They will grow in snow or ice. Indeed
they prefer the cold weather to the warm, and some say they
won't grow anywhere but on the island of Innisfail.

Eber was overjoyed because a hardy tree is a good token of

a treaty. A tree has its roots in the deep soil of the land. These roots symbolised the folk who had held the land in times gone by — the Danaans and the Fir-Bolg. The trunk which carried life to the leaves and fruits stood for the Gaedhals. And the branches would in time be strong enough to bear the weight of the Raven kind. Eber declared that this tree would ever after be the black birds' meeting place where they could convene their councils without fear of interruption or attack.

Since the Gaedhals were the trunk of the tree the king further promised to protect the Quicken down the generations. As a sign of this he asked each person who was going to attend the planting to bring a stone from their own country to place in a pit. The tree would be planted over these stones. The northern chieftains were sick of war, and seeing the alliance of different folk Eber had gathered round him, they accepted him as king. Each one brought a stone from the north.

Lom and Sárán were called to account for their actions, and seeing no other way to absolve himself of the sin and get on with his life, Sárán eventually consented. His brother did not even have to think about it.

An ancient circle of stones was located within a short walk of the crossroads. It was here the judgement was to be decided. When Samhain Eve arrived, Sorcha went off to the circle by herself to summon the Queen of the Ravens.

The Druid woman was waiting in the centre of the nine stones when representatives of the Gaedhals, Danaans, Fir-Bolg and Ravens gathered to hear the Morrigán's judgement. Sorcha looked as though she was on the grassy patch in the centre of the ring. But Dalan knew she was not. His instincts told him that somewhere high in the trees a pair of eyes was searching the crowd for him. It was the same uncomfortable tingle that had set his spine to shaking the first time he stayed in Sorcha's turf house in the woods.

The air fairly reeked of the Dark One's presence. Her breath was on the breeze, her malice cut all conversation short. An unusual silence fell upon the assembly as they awaited the appearance of the mystical sovereign of the birds. Morrigán. Queen of the Raven kind. Empress of Crows. Regent over all the feathered creatures of the air, except the geese who traditionally elected their own monarch and would have nothing to do with others of their kind.

Dalan heard the bark of a goose swept up on the wind from over the dry lough. He wondered whether the white birds of the water had sent a representative to this council, but the bird must have flown off for he didn't hear her cry again.

Around the edge of the sacred circle the people stood shivering as the snow began to fall lightly. They wrapped their cloaks about them and wished for their firesides, but they were all determined to wait this out.

There were nine stones along the northern edge of the circle. Here, in pride of place, nine stern Ravens flew in to perch, one on each stone. They each sat with their heads cocked so they could keep one eye on Sorcha at the centre of the circle.

When at last all the interested parties had taken their positions, two of Eber's sentries escorted Lom and Sárán through the crowd. They halted at the perimeter of the circle, leaving the twins to approach Sorcha alone. Both youths had their heads hung low.

The Druid woman softened her anger towards them a little when she realised they were both probably experiencing genuine remorse. Lom came to her first and knelt before her in humility. She touched him on the crown of the head in blessing, whispered to him to rise and then looked directly into Sárán's eyes. The other twin dropped his gaze immediately, unable to accept even the smallest gesture of disapproval.

He too knelt down at Sorcha's feet but she let him stay there a little longer. At last she told him to stand and take his place beside his brother. By neglecting to offer him the same blessing as she had Lom, she left the gathering in no doubt as to who she felt was the guilty party.

Sárán swallowed hard but reminded himself that this ceremony would soon be over. If he showed contrition and admitted his guilt he would be fined and forgiven. By the next Samhain all this would be forgotten.

The Ravens turned their heads to note the reactions of the gathered people. And then just as abruptly they each moved one cold eye back to Sorcha. The Druid woman braced herself, realising the birds had sensed the presence of their queen.

From behind her, high in the trees, Sorcha could discern a rustling sound. Then wings pushed at the air and the breeze they created touched the back of her neck like the stroke of a single black feather.

Sorcha gasped when the Morrigán appeared in front of her on the snow-spattered grass. The great bird slowly drew her broad black wings back to her body. Her eyes were pools of malice and for an instant, for the first time in her life, the Druid woman felt threatened by this creature. Sorcha turned her attention to the gathering. She noticed the frightened faces in the crowd and forgot her own fears.

The great black queen stood to survey Lom and Sárán, her head cocked to the left. Dalan could almost taste the malevolence that filled the air. Sorcha had explained to him that Ravens always watched with their left eye those who'd transgressed the law.

The Raven-queen shifted her attention to the assembly. She passed her right eye over the people, one by one, meeting each person with a glare that could have melted the standing stones. There wasn't anyone present who didn't shudder with the guilt of some ill thought or deed that had been directed against her kindred.

Dalan was surprised when she passed him over as if she couldn't see him. This made him nervous. It singled him out for some special treatment. And he didn't like it at all. His knees turned to jelly, even though he tried to tell himself he had no reason to be so distressed.

When the Dark One had looked into every face she spun around with a little hop and moved to stand beside Sorcha. Then the bird spoke with a guttural caw that brought a collective mumble of awe from the gathering.

'I will speak from the heart of the Lady Morrigán,' the Druid woman declared, translating as the bird spoke. 'She is the three ages of all things. She is the Dark One who brings forth the newborn into the world. She is the Mistress of Transformation and the Keeper of the Sacred Circle.'

The Raven waited until the Druid woman had finished speaking. Then she began cawing again, though now the tones were less formal and the strange sounds flowed more easily.

'I have come to this place seeking justice,' Sorcha continued. 'Murder has been committed. The law has been disregarded. A custom has been breached. And there are two here who, on their own free admission, have accepted responsibility for these crimes.'

The Druid woman took a breath, searched for a word and then continued. 'Who will give me justice?'

This was Dalan's moment. He cleared his throat and brushed the snow out of his beard. Then the Brehon stepped forward into the circle of stones with his head bowed low. He looked up slowly to face the queen. It seemed nothing more than a respectful gesture but it reflected a deep reverence.

'I am Dalan,' he began. 'I am a Brehon judge. I will hear the case and offer you justice.'

The Raven paused for a few breaths before she began her answer but it was apparent she understood him well.

'You've heard the charges and accepted the confessions of the accused. All that is left is for you to approve the judgement.'

'I will accept your word as the injured party. The case is clear and all that is left is to fix an honour price to be paid in recompense,' he stated.

The queen scanned the crowd again quickly before she spoke.

'But your judgements have not been effective in the past,' Sorcha translated. 'And now the Morrigán claims the recompense due under Raven law. The life of a Raven must be paid for with a life.'

Dalan's knees were suddenly weak.

'It's not the first time, I believe, that you've been compelled to make a judgement against these two.'

'It is not the first time,' he confirmed.

'Then you understand the gravity of your duty. These lads were dealt with lightly in the past. I don't believe they learned a lesson from that punishment.'

The Brehon bowed in recognition that the queen might be right. But Dalan also knew that he of all people probably understood these two young men best. He'd watched them since childhood, seen them grow and witnessed their headstrong impulses. He knew they had often acted without regard for others. He could not have found any verdict but guilty against them. Yet he also understood they were not entirely to blame.

'As a judge I wish to call two witnesses to hear their testimony on the lads,' Dalan announced. 'It is my intention to prove that Sárán and Lom were led astray and so cannot be held entirely responsible for their deeds.'

A buzz of excitement passed through the gathering as everyone gave an opinion on who these two witnesses might be.

'I call to this gathering,' the Brehon went on, 'Lochie and Isleen who are known to my people as the Watchers.'

'They are beings of the Otherworld,' the Raven snapped. 'No one here has the authority or the influence to summon them to this place.'

'I could call on them,' Dalan admitted. 'But they might not come. However, if you were to summon them they might take notice.'

'What purpose will it serve?'

Dalan noticed a flash of white among the shadows of the trees. It was a goose spreading her wings in the evening air. The bird had come to listen after all.

'Lochie and Isleen influenced the two lads,' the Brehon contended. 'Indirectly they are also responsible. I can't find that Sárán and Lom were entirely to blame. The Watchers lured them into breaking with custom. And so they must share the penalty.'

The Raven was silent for a few breaths while she considered his words.

'I will not accept their testimony,' translated Sorcha eventually.

'I will not pass judgement until charges are levelled against them also,' Dalan replied with calm defiance.

Many in the crowd hung their heads, ashamed that the renowned Brehon, the personal counsellor to King Eber, could come so close to offending the Morrigán.

The queen grunted but she could see he was determined to press his point. 'I cannot call them,' she informed him.

Dalan knew this but he had another course of action in mind. 'You can call to Danu,' he reminded her. 'And the Goddess of the Flowing Waters may summon them if she chooses.'

The gathering broke out into a chorus of gasps and sighs. The goddess had not been summoned in living memory. The Fir-Bolg shook their heads. The last time she had appeared before their folk it was to curse the reign of Lom. Many among the Gaedhals turned pale or trembled. They'd heard tales of the great mother of the Danaan folk and they feared to look upon her.

'If I call to her, she will surely come,' the Morrigán told

Sorcha who then passed the words on to the assembly. 'But if she comes I insist she pronounce her own punishment on those found guilty.'

Dalan hung his head for a few moments and contemplated her words. Danu was known as a merciful mother. But there was no way of telling what penalty she would levy against Sárán and Lom.

'Call her,' the Brehon decided at last. And he hoped he would be able to argue well for the lads.

'I will. But before I do I want to know your verdict against the twins.'

'You know it already,' Dalan replied sombrely. 'They are guilty.'

'Danu will be here presently,' the queen shot back and there was a certain satisfaction in her cawing.

Before Sorcha had delivered the Raven's words the queen spread her wings wide and emitted a screech that was both high and melodic. There was another great flurry of wings as a huge white shape glided into the circle. It was the goose that had been sitting at the edge of the trees just out of sight.

As the massive bird planted its feet on the soft grass the air glowed with a piercing white light. Folk cowered under their cloaks or behind the standing stones, shutting their eyes against the stinging radiance.

The intense white faded to blue as the form of a woman emerged from the light. A red ball of fire no bigger than a fist soared up to the heavens. It was immediately followed by a beautiful green orb that tinged everything in the immediate area a strange hue.

As these two lights disappeared in the immense carpet of stars all eyes were drawn back to the shape that stepped cautiously forward to stand behind the Morrigán. It took a few breaths for Dalan's eyes to adjust after the bright lights.

But when he could see clearly again he was stunned by what he saw.

After all the stories he'd heard about Danu, he'd expected a gorgeous young woman dressed in the finery of a goddess. The figure who presented herself to the gathering was an old haggard woman. She was dressed in rags and leaned heavily on a stout blackthorn stick.

It was a few moments more before Dalan realised he'd met her before. She was the old woman who had appeared at Lom's king-making. She had put him to sleep when he had questioned her authority.

'Well let's get on with it,' the old woman snapped. 'I've been waiting in the background for most of the evening. I have better things to do with my precious time, you know.'

Her eyes darted this way and that with impatience. 'Come on. Get on with it,' Danu insisted. 'I'm a very busy woman. Someone had better speak up or I'll be off again.'

'With your pardon,' Dalan began nervously, 'I have called two witnesses to this judgement. I seek your help in summoning them and I require your appraisal of their actions. When that is done, I respectfully ask that you set a penalty on the wrongdoers.'

'I'm not a Brehon,' Danu stated. 'That's your talent. Who are these witnesses?'

'Lochie and Isleen. The Watchers.'

The old woman laughed and hobbled over to Dalan. She stood in front of him perfectly still and looked deep into his eyes. Suddenly the Brehon saw a great whirlpool of images swirling all around her.

She raised her right hand and from her fingertips emanated what he would later describe as the very essence of creation. Dalan saw beasts giving birth to their offspring — cows, sheep, serpents, insects and every kind of creature that lived on Earth or in the sea. Men and women appeared lifted up in the passion of their lovemaking.

With a wave of her left hand all these images began to decay into old age, sickness and death. Generations of creatures lived their lives, passed away and were then reduced to skeletons before they disappeared into dust.

So unexpected and profound was this sight that Dalan felt drawn into the tapestry of images. He experienced a strange memory of having passed from one body to another down the generations, taking a different form each time but retaining the same essence.

For a brief instant he saw himself walking down a golden pathway lit by the rising sun. And he knew he had passed this way a thousand times or more. The Brehon was overcome with a strange nostalgia for this place and his heart was filled with longing.

Abruptly these images dissolved into the air and the Brehon was left staring into the deep dark pools that were the eyes of Danu. The old woman smiled, leaned forward and whispered into his ear.

'You are a Watcher now.' She smiled and breathed in deeply. Dalan was surprised that she seemed to be drinking in his scent.

'If Sorcha hadn't seen you first I might have been tempted to take you away to my home and keep you for my amusement.'

The Brehon swallowed hard, confused and overwhelmed.

Danu brushed his cheek with her hand and kissed him lightly on the lips. He closed his eyes, heart racing, and when he opened them again he glimpsed the form of the beautiful woman he'd expected at first. But Danu was only playing with him.

'Do you prefer me in this form?' she asked, her mocking laughter filling the air.

In an instant she'd returned to the haggard shape of an old woman.

'If ever Sorcha changes her mind about you, I'll take you,' the goddess teased.

Suddenly she spun around as the red ball of fire descended from the sky. When it was hovering a hand's breadth above the grass it was joined by the green orb. As the two lights floated there they both began to grow and change until they had taken the rough form of two people.

Slowly the light faded to reveal a woman and a man standing, heads bowed, facing Danu.

'They are here,' the goddess announced as she turned to face the Watchers.

'A claim has been made against you,' the Morrigán cut in, returning swiftly to the business at hand. 'It has been alleged that you've influenced these two lads to the point where they breached both law and custom. Is this true?'

Lochie looked up and his face was pale. 'How did we come to be here?'

'Danu summoned you,' Dalan explained. 'You have nothing to fear if you tell the truth. Sorcha and I will sing the Draoi song for you when you've given your testimony.'

'We shall see,' Danu corrected him. 'I was asked to pronounce judgement and I will.'

'Did you influence these lads?' the Morrigán bellowed, losing her patience.

'We did.'

'But we were only acting in accordance with our nature,' Isleen protested. 'We are seeking freedom from our bond. It is our wish to suffer death so our souls may be released.'

'That is not within my ability to grant you,' Danu told them. 'You made a solemn oath to Balor and you must abide by it. I grant you that your promise might lead you to do wrong. But that in no way excuses your actions.'

'Do you admit to leading these two youths into lawlessness?' the Morrigán pressed.

'Yes,' the Watchers replied in unison.

'Then there is nothing more to discuss, surely,' the Raven shrugged. 'Dalan has heard what he wanted to hear and it is time for a punishment to be meted out to Lom and Sárán, the sons of Brocan.'

'It isn't that simple,' the Brehon cut in. 'The Watchers must surely share the penalty, since they have clearly admitted that without their meddling the two lads would never have committed their crimes.'

He turned to Danu to press his case. 'If there is a fine to be levied against Lom and Sárán, then the payment of it should surely be shared by Lochie and Isleen.'

'The Watchers are above the law,' the Morrigán stated.

'Why?' Dalan shot back.

'Because they are Watchers. What punishment would you give them? I doubt there is anything you can think of that would make them tremble. They're beyond fear. Have you forgotten they're immortal?'

'I know something that would set them to trembling,' he retorted.

'What's that?'

'Set them in stone with their comrades.'

'What did you say?' Danu exclaimed. 'Force them into the eternal prison their seven siblings suffer? That is a very harsh penalty.'

Lochie's eyes widened with a long-forgotten response: terror. This had been the one outcome he had feared. To be unable to steer his own destiny. 'Anything but that,' he begged in a voice that cracked with fear. 'I would submit to any punishment but to be locked away in the stones. I implore you, Danu of the Flowing Waters, do not put this penalty on us.'

'We were doing what any of you would have done in our position,' Isleen reasoned with great desperation in her voice. 'We were already condemned as prisoners generations ago.

What kind of an existence do you think we've led since we fell for Balor's trickery?'

'That has nothing to do with the case at hand,' Dalan noted. 'You have acted deceitfully. That is a fact.'

'You promised to help us find a way to free ourselves,' Lochie spat. 'And now you're pleading for us to suffer a living death. I thought you were an honourable man!'

'Do you really believe you don't deserve the punishment?' the Morrigán inquired.

'He has broken his word to us!' Isleen shrieked, pointing to Dalan. 'I bring a charge of oath-breaking against him. We may have done many wrongs, but we are as entitled to justice as anyone else here.'

'All I'm trying to do is to prove that Lom and Sárán should be judged and punished with consideration of their diminished responsibility,' the Brehon argued. 'And since the means are available to us to free the Watchers from their enchantment, I recommend they be released. But only if they cooperate with this court.'

'What more would you have me say?' Lochie exclaimed. 'If you want me to confess I'll do so. But keep your bargain with us.'

'Answer the Brehon,' Danu demanded. 'I'm tiring of all this.'

'We influenced the lads,' Isleen admitted. 'If it weren't for us the two Ravens would probably be sitting here with us now. But their deaths were an indirect result of our influence.'

'That's enough!' Danu declared. 'I can't sit here all day listening to your petty gripes. I'm the Goddess of the Flowing Waters and it's Samhain Eve. Don't you think I've got other things on my mind?'

'The lads are guilty of murder,' the Morrigán asserted. 'Even Dalan has admitted that. Under the laws of the Raven kind I call for the harshest penalty available. A life for a life.'

'What have you to say in summary, Dalan the Brehon?' Danu asked.

'The young men before you have made many mistakes in the past,' the Brehon admitted. 'They have been punished for their breaches of the law and of custom. And I cannot deny that this crime was a particularly shocking one. But if we were to go over the circumstances of the death I'm sure you'd agree that the entire episode was a terrible coincidence.'

'Life is merely a series of terrible coincidences,' Danu interjected. 'What is your point?'

'These two have taken the Quicken Brew,' Dalan continued. 'They have long lives ahead of them. I ask for a punishment to be meted out to them that will make them consider their actions in the future but will not be too harsh.'

Then he turned to Lochie and Isleen. 'As for these two Watchers, I beg the mercy of the court. It was wrong of me to provoke fear in them as I did earlier by threatening they be set in stone. But it illustrated perfectly how frightened they are of that fate. They have gone to great lengths to avoid it. And in doing so they have been indirectly responsible for the suffering and death of many good folk.'

The Brehon took a breath before he finished his plea. 'No punishment will ever bring the two Ravens back to us. But we can honour their memory by making sure that nothing like this can ever happen again. I call for the Watchers to be set free.'

Everyone gathered around the circle hummed in agreement. Many thought he had presented an impeccable case. Though Lom and Sárán were guilty beyond doubt, there was a general sense that mercy was called for.

Danu must have known this. For her first words were aimed to appeal to this sentiment.

'I have considered both sides of the argument,' she began. 'And I see that clemency could heal the results of this crime.'

She paused to look across at Lom and Sárán.

'I acknowledge that you lads may have been influenced by the Watchers. But you have minds of your own and you know right from wrong. Two Ravens have been killed. The penalty I place upon you is as the Morrigán requested. A life for a life. The sentence will come into effect at midnight.'

'Lady,' Dalan began desperately, 'is this mercy?'

'I haven't finished!' she snapped. 'You will replace the two Ravens whose lives you shattered. Since you are both under the influence of the Quicken Brew, you will remain in Raven form indefinitely. You both have one chance to be released from this bond. You must earn your death.'

Lom dropped his eyes respectfully, accepting the judgement. But his brother's eyes flashed in defiance. And though he said nothing he made a vow to himself that he would not take this penalty lying down like a beaten dog.

The assembled folk were silent. This was a harsh penalty but everyone who knew Sárán shrugged and told themselves he had this coming to him. Those who knew his brother sighed in sympathy for him, but to many the judgement was also a relief. It lifted the curse that had been laid on his kingship, for he would no longer rule as King of the Fir-Bolg.

Danu turned her attention to Lochie and Isleen. 'The Brehon has argued well in your defence,' she began. 'And I believe you should be allowed to throw off the bonds of your enchantment. But you have committed crimes which have not even been touched upon here. This crime was the result of your impatience to find the Draoi song.'

She paused as she noticed the Brehon close his eyes and touch a hand to his forehead in defeat.

'I feel this would be a good opportunity to teach you both patience and forbearance. The Draoi song will be preserved. But you will take up residence in the spring at the source of Lough Gur. This spring will be sealed and only opened during the day for water to be collected.'

Both the Watchers were speechless. Danu, the ancient one, was powerful beyond their understanding. None but she could have inspired such dread in them.

'You will take the form of worms,' Danu went on. 'And in this state you will remain until a new people come to this land. I charge Eber Finn and his descendants to be guardians of the Wellspring of Gur. Your folk will ensure the Watchers do not escape.'

'But what of our freedom?' choked Lochie.

'You will have that. But you will have to earn it. I leave it to the bloodline of King Eber to decide when that time has come. But I forbid it to be within nine generations of this time. The sentence will take effect from midnight tonight.'

Then Danu sighed heavily, stretched and yawned.

'Well I'll be off now,' she announced. 'I've got a few festivities planned for this evening.' She looked up to the sky and frowned. 'I hope the snow holds off for me.'

Dalan looked up but the sky was perfectly clear. The stars were sparkling and the snow seemed to have cleared. But when he turned his attention back to Danu she was gone.

'I'm satisfied,' the Morrigán stated through her interpreter. 'Now it's time to resolve the matter of the treaty.'

Eber Finn stepped forward then and begged everyone to follow him to the crossroads where a pit had been dug for their offerings. It wasn't a long walk but the light snow that had fallen earlier made the ground slippery in places.

So it was quite a while before everyone was assembled. When he thought everyone necessary was present the king called the gathering to silence. Then he spoke about his dream of peace for the land of Eirinn, as the Gaedhals called it.

After he had promised to defend and protect the sovereignty of all the peoples who called the land home, he invited all present to drop an offering into the pit. The Sen Erainn filed past first, each dropping a little stone or a piece of driftwood into the hole. Then came the Fir-Bolg who did the same.

When their king, Lom, approached the pit he did a most unexpected thing. He drew the bronze ceremonial axe from his belt and held it up for all to see.

'This was the symbol of the kingship of my people,' he declared. 'With this weapon I murdered a Raven and so I will be punished this night. I resign the kingship and leave the position unfilled. Let the Fir-Bolg chieftains sit on the Council of the Gaedhals in future. There cannot be two kings of Innisfail.'

With these words he tossed the axe into the pit and walked away to stand with the rest of his people. Mahon followed on after him and gave his small stone from Dun Gur. Then the Gaedhals came. And the northern chieftains, eager for peace, placed their stones as they, one by one, pledged allegiance to Eber Finn. And last of all was Eber Finn. He threw in a rock he'd picked up on the battlefield where his brother had been slain.

Sorcha brought her budding sapling out as the hole was filled by many hands, all willing to help in this historic task. She handed the delicate bud to Eber Finn and he placed it in the earth.

'Let there be peace now in this land between all the peoples as long as this tree shall live,' he intoned.

There was a moment of silence as everyone shared his prayer. Then, with their cloaks wrapped tightly about themselves against the chill evening air, the gathering dispersed to their camp fires to celebrate Samhain Eve.

It was midnight and Lom and Sárán were waiting with Dalan, Sorcha and the Morrigán for the sentence of Danu to be carried out. Few words passed between them. There was little more to be said. At last, though, Lom sensed the time approaching and he reached out to shake Dalan's hand.

'Let yours be the last hand I hold,' he wept. 'Thank you for pleading our case. And thank you for all I have learned from you.'

Then he went to Sorcha and hugged her tightly. 'Let you be the last woman I hold in my arms,' he whispered. 'May your life be blessed.'

'Come and speak with me sometimes,' the Druid woman offered. 'Remember, I understand the speech of the Raven kind.'

'I will.'

The Brehon put a hand on Sárán's shoulder and spoke. 'Do you have nothing to say?'

'You have never had a good word for me,' the young Druid shot back. 'You have misjudged me. You have mocked me. And now, thanks to your testimony, I am condemned to a fate which I can't even begin to understand. I will never forget you, Dalan. Never.'

As he spoke Sárán felt a strange upheaval in his guts. By the time he was throwing up the contents of his stomach he realised his brother was suffering the same affliction. Then he saw something that made him scream in terror.

Lom's face began to contort wildly, becoming long and thin as if someone had stretched his skull beyond all recognition. His brother's arms were suddenly small stubs. And long black quills began to appear all over his skin.

Dalan and Sorcha stepped back in horror. The lads' clothes fell away from them as their bodies shrank. And then at last their feet began to twist and form claws.

A few breaths later the two of them were flapping about on the ground shrieking with their newly acquired Raven voices. In moments they were as indistinguishable as two twins could be. And the Morrigán was screaming at them in her most threatening tone.

'She's telling them to be silent or they'll feel the edge of her talons,' Sorcha explained to the Brehon.

The two bird-brothers took a long while to settle down. And Dalan was broken-hearted to witness their distress. But he knew there was nothing to be done. They had incurred the wrath of the Morrigán and must pay the price.

Still, he couldn't help feeling that one day there would be unforeseen repercussions of this judgement.

'There'll be a bloody war between the Ravens,' he prophesied. 'These two birds will be the start and finish of it.'

'What did he say?' the Morrigán demanded of Sorcha. 'Did I catch something about war between the Ravens?'

'Dalan fears that Lom and Sárán will one day be responsible for some conflict.'

'Nonsense!' the queen snapped. 'I'll watch them as closely as if they were my own fledglings. There'll be no war.'

The Dark One cocked her head to one side and thought for a few breaths. 'Lom and Sárán aren't names for Ravens,' she declared. 'Lom-dubh is a Raven name. And Sciathan-cog, that is a Raven name. This is how you will be known from this night onward.'

Then she forced them to attempt to fly. It took quite some coaching but eventually the three birds took off and flew away to the north. Dalan and Sorcha were left by their little fire as the snow clouds gathered once more.

They huddled down under their cloaks by the fire and held each other close.

'We have one more duty to perform before we can go home to your house in the forest,' Dalan noted.

'*Our* house in the forest,' Sorcha corrected him. 'Once we return from Arainn we will go there and rest.'

'Will it be a long rest?'

'As long as it takes for us to recover. No one will disturb us there. We'll have everything we need.'

'Will you teach me the Ritual of the Sun? And the secrets of the mushroom Frith?'

'I will,' she nodded. 'If you will tell me stories every day.'

Chapter Twenty-Eight

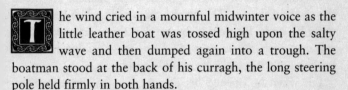he wind cried in a mournful midwinter voice as the little leather boat was tossed high upon the salty wave and then dumped again into a trough. The boatman stood at the back of his curragh, the long steering pole held firmly in both hands.

Five times he tried to bring the boat to the rocky landing place and five times the curragh was picked up on the wind and dragged back out to sea. The boatman was clearly weary from his battle but his determined expression showed he was not about to give in just yet.

Sorcha huddled under the Brehon's Raven-feather cloak to keep dry. But she might as well not have bothered. The sea water soaked everything. Even Dalan's cloak was dripping wet. When she looked out from under her shelter all she could see of the land was a flat grey rocky outcrop which looked as if the waves were likely to crash over it at any moment. The Druid woman was amazed that there were folk who dared to live here and attempt to scrape a living from this place.

It was the boatman's sixth attempt that brought him in close enough for the boathooks to grapple the little craft. Then they were suddenly dragged up the smooth sloping rocks at the shore and quickly helped from the curragh.

The two of them were just starting the climb up the rocky face of the low cliff when a great wave rose up out of the depths like a monster woken from its sleep. The Brehon saw the massive mountain of water coming and his heart must have stopped beating for a moment for he was frozen to the spot in terror.

Sorcha tugged at his arm in panic. He turned around, jolted from his fear, and clambered up the rest of the cliff as fast as he could. Then he flung himself down face first and waited for the wall of wave to strike.

But the expected catastrophe never happened. He heard the crash of the sea. He felt the spray falling like heavy rain upon his body. He even imagined that the great rocky island shivered with the impact. And an image of his torn and broken body came clearly into his mind.

But when he opened his eyes he was still in one piece. Sorcha was sitting beside him, her mouth open in shock.

'You should have seen that!' she gasped. 'I've never witnessed anything like it in my life.'

Suddenly Dalan remembered the boatman and the Red Caps islanders who'd helped them to escape the curragh. He stood up and peered over the cliff, expecting them to have been washed away under the disastrous attack of the sea. But the three men and two women were busily stacking their boats against the cliff wall. The boatman waved cheerily as if it were a bright calm afternoon in summer and nothing was amiss.

'With every day I'm beginning to understand old King Aenghus better and better,' Dalan murmured to himself.

He picked up his shoulder bag, helped Sorcha to her feet and they headed off down the coast towards the great fortification in the distance. There was no snow out here on the island. The wind would have snatched it away in an instant. The rain was incessant, though, and the air colder than anything Dalan had ever experienced in his life. By the time they reached the outer walls of the massive stone fort, the two Druids were shivering from the wet and the cold.

They both wondered aloud how these folk put up with such conditions. At last they struggled over the rough stone path that led to the entrance. Warriors who stood on sentry helped them carry their things up to a roundhouse built entirely from tiny rocks which had been meticulously fitted together.

Once they were inside, their cloaks were taken and they were led to a roaring central fire. Sorcha frowned. She hadn't seen a single tree growing on the island, yet here was plenty of timber being burned for fuel.

They were led to the far end of the roundhouse where a young man sat on a stone chair which had been draped with furs. He stood up as they arrived and put his hands up to silence the gathering of his kinfolk.

'My name is Aenghus mac Ómor,' the youth declared. 'I am King of the Sen Erainn. I am a warrior and a poet. I welcome you travelling Druids to my home.'

'Thank you,' Dalan replied, a little surprised that this young ruler had the same name as the late king.

Then the Brehon realised why the two shared a name. 'We knew your father,' he stated. 'He was a brave warrior, a fine poet and an honourable man.'

The king frowned.

'We farewelled him the morning he rode off to the battle in which he lost his life.'

King Aenghus looked at Dalan as if he were mad. Then he said something in his own language to a crowd of folk sitting in the corner. They immediately burst into uncontrolled laughter.

An old man stood up and threw off his fur cloak. He was thin and frail but his eyes were alive with mirth.

'This is my father,' Aenghus declared. 'This is Ómor.'

Sorcha and the Brehon both looked at one another in astonishment.

'Then who was the man we met?' the Druid woman inquired. 'Was he the leader of the Sen Erainn?'

'That was my elder brother, King Aenghus mac Ómor,' the king explained. 'He was a poet.'

'You have the same name as your brother?'

Aenghus laughed heartily as he explained to his kinfolk what had been said. Once again they burst into uproars of amusement. When young Aenghus had caught his breath he turned his attention back to his guests.

'I have a poem which may clear this misunderstanding up for you,' he told them.

Then he leaned in close so they wouldn't miss a word and began. 'A herring is a fish. A fine fish and very tasty when salted in a barrel. But can you recognise one herring among many? I think not. Let's not try to give each fish a name. It would take all night. Our time is better spent eating them.'

The Brehon gave a strained smile to indicate he understood the point of the poem.

As the king patted Dalan on the back another young man approached them.

'They are a family of worthy fish-poets,' he declared, and Aenghus bowed low at the compliment.

'I am Beag mac Dé,' the young man told them. 'I've been expecting you.'

'Expecting us?' Sorcha exclaimed. 'How is that possible?'

'My teacher told me you would bring her remains with you before midwinter.'

'She foresaw her death?' Sorcha asked.

'Indeed.' The young Druid remembered something his teacher had asked him to deliver. 'This is for you.'

Dalan took the bag Beag mac Dé held out to him and opened it. He was not surprised to find it filled with the healing herb the old woman had made into a tea for him.

'It will be midwinter in two days time,' mac Dé told them. 'We will go to the Crystal House at midnight where there is to be a birth. Then at sunrise we will welcome Beag ní Dé back to our hearth. And I will become her guardian while she continues to instruct me in Druid lore.'

The young Druid suddenly remembered his manners. 'But the king is waiting to share the feast with you and we can discuss these matters later. So sit at the great slate table with us and eat your fill of every breed of fish known to us.'

Sure enough, laid out on the table was an array of fish such as Dalan had never seen in his life before. And all of it was tasty, even the salted herrings. The wondrous food was shared with such goodwill that Sorcha and Dalan still talked fondly of that feast ten generations later.

They slept that night in their own house with a fire stacked high with timber in the centre of the room. There wasn't a hint of the raging icy wind outside. They rested so well, indeed, that neither of them awoke till long after midday. And then it was time for another feast. For midwinter was a sacred time among the Sen Erainn.

In the depths of the hill at the very end of a long dark passage there was an open, high-ceilinged hall no larger than ten paces by ten. In the centre of this womblike chamber there stood a great stone basin.

Within the basin sat a naked pregnant woman up to her neck in warm water. Around her stood Beag mac Dé, Sorcha and the Brehon. The walls around them were covered in many strange and beautiful designs which were lit by the glow of three large candles that reeked of walrus fat.

Dalan tuned the borrowed harp. He hadn't dared bring his own in that little leather boat in such high seas. When the instrument was humming sweetly he began to play.

He was soon interrupted by an old woman who ran down the passage carrying a steaming rock heated in the fireplace outside. She dropped it carefully from her ladle into the water at the feet of the mother-to-be. Steam rose up and the water was warmed a little more.

A few words passed between the old woman and the Sen Erainn Druid in their own language. Then the woman was off hurrying back out into the cold to tend her fire.

'She says the clouds have cleared away,' Beag mac Dé told them. 'That is a very good sign. The baby will soon be with us. My teacher is returning. Play us a merry tune, Brehon.'

The Brehon restrained himself from asking the hundreds of questions that crowded into his mind and set his hands to the harp instead.

The Red Cap Druid dipped into his bag and drew out the skull of Beag ní Dé. It had been stripped of all remaining flesh in readiness for this ritual. He placed it in a small niche in the wall and it looked down with a slightly opened jaw.

Dalan struggled to concentrate on his tune. He didn't want to judge this practice. Yet he knew there were those among his order who would have denounced it as barbaric. He'd seen much more cruel things done to the living. He reminded himself this was an empty, lifeless skull.

The woman in the bath strained and said a few breathless words to the young Sen Erainn Druid.

'Her waters have broken,' he explained to his companions.

Sorcha took the woman's hand to give her comfort. The woman squeezed her fingers hard. The Druid woman had attended countless births, so she knew what to expect. This one would be easy; she could tell that at a glance. The mother was relaxed and the signs were excellent.

The old woman at the mouth of the passage gave a yell which echoed back along the stone corridor to reverberate in the chamber. Immediately Beag mac Dé snuffed the candles out and the room was plunged into a profound darkness.

Dalan had to stop playing for a few moments. He hadn't expected this at all. But when his fingers found their place again he managed to strum a slow gentle melody. Sorcha was surprised that when the candles went out the woman's hand relaxed even though her contractions tensed her body.

'Now I will call upon the spirit of my teacher to return to her people,' Beag mac Dé explained. 'She has not had much time to rest in the Halls of Waiting, but I know she is eager to return home to her kinfolk.'

He stood behind the mother, cradling her head in his arms and whispering into her ear. Then he made his way around to the opposite side of the basin from where Sorcha stood. The Druid woman could hear him breathing deeply and rhythmically and she knew he was inducing a trancelike Frith upon himself.

Long black minutes passed and then without warning Beag mac Dé launched into a song. It was a lulling melody, and though the Brehon and his companion knew none of the Red Cap language, they both understood exactly what he was singing about. Dalan strummed the chords to accompany the song.

Every phrase spoke of homesickness, of a yearning to return to the innocence of youth and the joys of childhood. This was a chant to draw Beag ní Dé back into the world again. It was an invitation to live another life among her kin.

In the world outside the sun was slowly rising. The first rays of its light could be seen at the entrance to the passage. Dalan was awed at the way the door was suddenly bathed in a golden light and he had the sense that something or someone was about to rush down the passage towards them.

If that sight had filled him with awe, the next thing he saw astonished him. With a blinding flash of light the entire corridor was aflame with the brilliance of the sun. The Brehon stopped his playing as a long slender finger of gold extended down the passage until it almost touched the foot of the basin.

Dalan nearly cried out as a strange memory flooded his consciousness. On the way to the battlefield Lochie had granted him a vision. And here was that vision brought to life. The Brehon suddenly understood that he was witnessing another form of immortality.

The woman seated in the water was breathing hard and heavy as her face was illuminated with the mystical gold. At that very instant the child was born into the warm waters of the basin. Sorcha held him there as she had been instructed, waiting for the word from Beag mac Dé.

Dalan dared a glimpse at the child. The lad had the most peaceful expression the Brehon could remember seeing on a child's face. His mother was smiling as she tried to catch her breath and Beag mac Dé had turned to face the back wall of the chamber.

By this time the light had become focused into a stroke of gold as wide as a hand and as tall as a man's thighbone. The light swept up from the floor to illumine the designs cut into the wall. At last it struck a triple spiral and as it passed across the motif the young Druid spoke his teacher's name.

Then he reached down into the basin and lifted the baby straight out of the water. He held the boy in the light so that his shadow was reflected onto the wall. Once again he spoke the name of his former teacher. Then the child opened his eyes, looked at the Druid and smiled.

With Sorcha's help the cord was cut and tied. The child was wrapped in furs. And as the sunlight retreated from the chamber Beag mac Dé carried the baby out into the cold air to show him to his kinfolk.

There were cheers, laughter and many sombre words neither Dalan nor Sorcha could understand. They stayed behind to light the candles and help the mother wrap herself in furs. When that was done she walked out into the cold, took her baby in her arms and, leaning on Sorcha's arm, made her way back to the fortress.

The Brehon followed after them. After a moment he turned to look behind him. The whole mound which had been built over the passage and chamber was faced with small sparkling silvery white stones. Now he understood why Beag ní Dé had called it the Crystal House.

He passed the harp to the Red Cap Druid, who had kindly loaned it to him, and ran ahead to catch up with the mother and baby. The child smiled up at him and grabbed at his finger and he was certain he knew those eyes.

'We have met again in the golden chamber of the silver fortress,' the Brehon said. 'It is good to see you again.'

Then Dalan dropped back to where the Sen Erainn Druid and the young King Aenghus were walking. He fell in with them and in courtesy they spoke in his language. There was a great procession behind them of all the gathered kin of the newborn infant.

'The Sen Erainn are a strong folk,' Dalan remarked, still shocked the new mother was on her feet so soon after giving birth.

'Only the strong survive,' Aenghus replied. 'Only the strongest return to us. That is the way of the Sen Erainn.'

Then the young king added a touch of Red Cap wisdom of the kind Dalan had come to admire.

'A fish may be caught in a net,' he began. 'But a strong wise fish will not find it difficult to break free. These are the tastiest fish of all. That's why we have woven an especially strong net for them.'

The Brehon laughed and Sorcha turned when she heard him.

Their eyes locked for an instant and in that moment he understood the great gift he had been given. He fondly recalled the words of Beag ní Dé who had told him that, even for an immortal, life is too short to waste on petty strife and bother.

The Brehon laughed again.

And the rest of Dalan's days were light-hearted.

Epilogue

n my opinion there's nothing more distasteful or demonstrably unlikely as a blissful ending to a long tale. However, in this case I can attest that Sorcha and her Brehon lived in a state of great contentment for the rest of their days.

That is to say they were contented when I last saw them. And I have no reason to suspect they aren't still just as cheerful. They have a little house in the woods where no one can find them, and every once in a while they take the boat to Arainn to hear fish-poems recited until late into the night.

I like them. They've always had time for me. And I'm told they've frightened the bowel fluids out of more than one wandering woodcutter. So they have their hearts in the right place at least.

As for the rest of them. Well you know what happened to Eber Finn. He married Mughain, fathered a dynasty with her and became a legendary figure in the folklore of your people. And he kept his word about the tree-cutting, even if later generations of you treacherous Gaedhals neglected to heed his promise.

Mahon never tracked Aoife down as far as I know. To this day he's probably trudging the roads from one end of this island to the next, searching for a clue to her whereabouts.

Poor fool. But it keeps his mind active and the outdoor life doesn't seem to have done him any harm.

He paid the price for the death of that guard at Dun Gur. He led the Fian bands and commanded Eber Finn's bodyguard until the old king passed away during his seventieth winter. The Danaan served the king so well they became fast friends and Eber offered him half the kingdom. But Mahon would have none of it. He had a quest to fulfil.

Naithí was wed to Eber's first daughter and founded the Eoghanacht dynasty of the south who built their fortress at Cashel. They were great friends to the Raven kind and they were the protectors of the Quicken Tree.

That is, until the Roman Christians came and the tree was attacked. Then the Ravens fell to fighting amongst themselves. But that's a story for some other tale-teller. You might want to talk to the Wanderers, Mawn and Sianan, if you can find them. They'll give you that story in full and without prejudice.

My brother, Sciathan-cog, is still about and he's a conniving wretch if ever there was one. Vengeful, deceitful, cunning, cruel, conceited. And those are his better qualities. Put him in a smooth pink skin and he'd pass for one of your kind without any questions.

Lochie and Isleen could not evade the judgement of the Goddess Danu. They were transformed into the vilest worms you could imagine. All grey and slithery, each as wide as a horse and seven times as long. The stench that fills the air whenever they pass by would pickle a wagonload of excrement. Thus they are avoided by all intelligent beings with any sense of smell. Every night to this day the steward of the fortress of Dun Gur makes sure the lid is firmly bolted to the wellspring so they don't go roaming in the dark.

It's bad enough they're allowed out to writhe about the dry lough in the daylight hours. I don't know whether Danu has forgotten them or simply wants them to suffer a while longer.

She has no concept of time, that one. She may be the Goddess of the Flowing Waters and all, but she's far from perfect.

And last of all there's me. Lom-dubh. I have a busy social life, as most former monarchs do. The avoidance of my destiny takes up quite a lot of my day. But I still find time for recreational pursuits. Maybe one day soon I'll tire of living and make an effort to earn my passage to the Halls of Waiting. Then again, maybe not. Even for an immortal life is too short. I still like to watch a battle now and then or match wits in a tournament of Brandubh with some ignorant tree-killer. Indeed, I'd teach you how to play but I doubt you'd have what it takes to defeat a renowned champion such as myself.

Some other time we'll play the Raven Game. I'm in no mood for company just now. I've talked too much and brought to mind too many memories that were better laid to rest. I must be off. I have a forest to watch over and a tree-home to protect from the wood-turner's lathe.

May Danu bless you, though she above all knows there isn't a bark-stripper among you that deserves it. And when you finally cross that angry badger's path, as we all must, I hope it is on your own terms.